CARPENTER'S SON

Frank Paul Hill

authorHOUSE

AuthorHouse™
1663 Liberty Drive
Bloomington, IN 47403
www.authorhouse.com
Phone: 833-262-8899

© 2025 Frank Paul Hill. All rights reserved.

No part of this book may be reproduced, stored in a retrieval system, or transmitted by any means without the written permission of the author.

Published by AuthorHouse 04/29/2025

ISBN: 979-8-8230-4568-1 (sc)
ISBN: 979-8-8230-4567-4 (e)

Library of Congress Control Number: 2025905046

Print information available on the last page.

Any people depicted in stock imagery provided by Getty Images are models, and such images are being used for illustrative purposes only. Certain stock imagery © Getty Images.

This book is printed on acid-free paper.

Because of the dynamic nature of the Internet, any web addresses or links contained in this book may have changed since publication and may no longer be valid. The views expressed in this work are solely those of the author and do not necessarily reflect the views of the publisher, and the publisher hereby disclaims any responsibility for them.

DEDICATION

To those who shape us with their hands and their hearts.
To the builders, the dreamers, and the ones who dare to leave a mark.
And to my family, whose love and wisdom
guide me through every chapter of life.

ACKNOWLEDGMENTS

Writing *The Carpenter's Son* has been a journey, and I am deeply grateful to everyone who walked alongside me along the way.

To my editor, Marie Soukup, whose insights and expertise helped me refine this story into its truest form. Your patience and dedication to this project have made all the difference.

To my family, Melba, your unwavering support and love are the foundation upon which this book stands. Your belief in me keeps me grounded and inspired every day.

To the countless mentors, teachers, and writers who have influenced my path, directly or indirectly. Your words, your stories, and your guidance have shaped my own writing in ways I can only hope to repay.

To the readers—thank you for allowing these words to live in your imagination. This book is for you.

And to every carpenter, every artist, and every person who struggles to find their place in the world—may you always build a life worthy of your dreams.

ACT 1

THE BURDEN OF LEGACY AND THE CALL TO FORGIVE

CHAPTER 1

Sawdust and Sorrow

CALEB'S BOOTS CRUNCHED on the sawdust—a sound too loud, too alive in the still breath of his father's workshop. The air hung heavy with the lingering trace of cedar and pine, a presence that seeped into his clothes, his skin, his memories. It wrapped around him like a recollection he couldn't outrun. He hesitated in the doorway, heart pounding with a traitor's rhythm, as if even the walls sensed he no longer belonged.

His fingers brushed over the unfinished slab of wood resting on the old workbench, the grain rough and unforgiving. Like him. Like the conversations never had. Each knot in the wood pulsed with history—lessons etched into the surface like scars. Lessons his father had tried to teach him before everything shattered.

"Damn it, Dad," Caleb muttered, his voice hoarse, as if unused to speaking the truth aloud. It snagged in his throat, rough and aching. The chair in the corner—half-built, spine exposed—watched him. A silent witness to their fracture.

He hadn't stepped into this space since the funeral notice came in the mail with no return address. He'd ignored it then, just like he ignored the rage and sorrow clawing at his insides. But this morning, standing by his mother's bedside as her last breath whispered through cracked lips, something had broken loose. Her hand, frail and warm, had tightened around his.

"Forgive him, Caleb," she'd whispered.

And then she was gone.

He squeezed his eyes shut, but the tears still escaped. Her words weren't just a plea. They were her last wish. And that made them sacred.

The chisel felt heavy in his hand; its handle worn smooth from years of use—years that had shaped other hands. His father's. A man he had loved once. A man he still loved, maybe. But the love was buried under years of silence, of questions never answered, of birthdays missed and pain left to fester.

He used to think unforgiveness was a shield. Now it felt like a prison.

Caleb dropped the chisel back into its cradle, the sound sharp and accusing. His breath caught, shallow. The workshop felt too full, like even the dust remembered. Even the dust judged.

He glanced at the unfinished chair, then the shelves. Ghosts. All of it.

A memory clawed its way in, uninvited.

His father's hands guiding his own, sawdust clinging to their fingers like snow.

"Feel the wood, son. Listen to it. It knows what it wants to be."

He'd wanted that connection to mean something. To be a bridge. But instead, it became a divide. When his father left, he took the language with him.

The silence in the shop thickened. And beneath it, a rumble of guilt.

Caleb took a breath, deep and ragged. He couldn't fix the past, but maybe he could face it. He had to finish the chair. Not for his father, but for his mother. For the memory of who he was before resentment hardened him.

A shaft of golden sunlight cut through the grimy window, slicing across the dust like truth laid bare. Caleb reached for the chisel again. His hand trembled.

"Forgiveness isn't weakness," her voice echoed. "It's strength. It's a choice."

But how could he forgive a man who never looked back? Who never wrote? Never called? His heart tightened. He clenched his jaw, lips trembling as another memory struck.

His mother's quiet prayers at night. Her fingers moving along the wooden beads of her rosary. The way her eyes searched the horizon long after any hope had gone. She never stopped waiting.

And Caleb had never stopped blaming.

He dug the chisel into the wood, the sound biting. A curl peeled away, thin as regret.

His breath steadied.

There was something holy in the act. Creation born from pain. Redemption, maybe.

Tomorrow, they would bury her.

Elena.

The name felt too soft for the woman who had carried a storm of faith through every hardship. She'd worked double shifts. Held him through broken dreams. Kept believing in a God Caleb had all but abandoned.

The church bells would ring tomorrow. The hymns would rise, hollow and trembling. And he would stand there, hands empty, heart gutted, knowing he hadn't said goodbye.

He had to finish the chair.

Not just for the funeral. Not just for her.

For himself.

He moved to the bench, rolled up his sleeves. Sweat broke along his spine. The cedar plank stared back, as if asking him to make a decision.

He picked up the mallet.

The rhythm returned.

Tap. Pause. Tap. Tap.

His father's cadence. The same one Caleb had once matched heartbeat for heartbeat.

Each strike was a word. Each carving, a sentence.

Not yet a story. But maybe the beginning of one.

He worked until dusk swallowed the light. His arms ached. His back screamed. But his soul... something had shifted. The weight of sorrow hadn't left, but it no longer sat alone.

There was room now for something else.

Hope.

He stepped back. The chair was taking shape.

Still rough. Still raw.

Like him.

But real.

And maybe that was enough for now.

He set the chisel down, wiping his hands on his jeans. His gaze landed on a half-carved angel in the corner. His father had started it. Left it unfinished, like so many things.

Caleb walked over, traced the delicate curve of the wing. The wood whispered under his touch.

His fingers stilled.

This wasn't just his father's legacy. It was his.

He could finish it.

And maybe, in doing so, finally understand the man behind the silence

A strangled sob hitched in his throat. His father had walked out, leaving a gaping hole, a void that no carving could ever fill. But he'd also left something else—a legacy, a skill Caleb clung to like a lifeline. Maybe, just maybe, there was redemption in the sawdust and shavings.

Maybe the whispers of the wood were a path back to something resembling peace. One last, lingering touch on the unfinished sculpture. His breath hitched; a prayer caught in his throat. The future was a blur, a terrifying uncertainty. But Tomorrow? Tomorrow, he'd honor his mother, face the mourners in the church, let the hymns wash over him, a wave of grief and remembrance.

He'd let the voices of the living blend with the silence of the dead. He'd remember, and he'd endure. But tonight? Tonight, the chisel was his solace, his sanctuary. The weight of the tool felt strangely comforting in his calloused hand. The rough, unyielding wood pulsed with potential, a silent challenge. And for the first time in a long time, Caleb was ready.

Ready to listen, not to the echoes of the past, but to the whispering voice of the wood, to the rhythm of the carving, to the quiet strength it offered. He started to carve the rhythmic scrape of steel on wood a counterpoint to the turmoil in his soul.

Caleb's fingers caught on the edge of the carving, the wood splintering beneath his touch like a memory breaking open. The *trace* of pine and varnish hung thick in the air—not just the residue of labor, but the ache of someone no longer there. His father's presence haunted the space—not in shadows or whispers, but in every tool left out of place, every project paused mid-breath. Grief didn't shout here; it settled in the quiet, pressed into the walls like dust. And in that silence, Caleb reached for his mother's voice, soft and flickering at the edges of his mind, as if her words could keep him from drowning in everything left unsaid.

"Find it in your heart, Caleb," it whispered, insistent despite its softness. "Forgiveness...it's the solace." He saw her again, frail but resolute, her grip surprisingly firm as she held his hand. She believed in things he couldn't fathom—grace, redemption, this boundless capacity for healing. But he? He'd never possessed her faith, nor the stomach for such immense mercy. He ripped his hand away, clenching it into a fist. His mother's cool and relentless words clung to him like sea mist, lodging in the raw places of his heart. "Forgiveness." The word felt like gravel in his throat, a bitter taste. How could he forgive a man who'd vanished without a backward glance? How could he offer grace to a father who left only questions and a gnawing ache that time couldn't erase?

His gaze swept across the room, lingering on the unfinished Stations of the Cross, a testament to his mother's unwavering faith. Each intricately carved figure spoke of devotion, of hands that had shaped beauty from nothing. His father's hands. The same hands that had built, loved, and ultimately abandoned him. A bitter laugh caught in his throat. He knew forgiveness like wood grain—the theory was sound, the necessity undeniable. But the practice? To actually "feel" it? That was a different beast altogether. Resentment, raw and jagged, resisted smoothing, splintering under the weight of his memories. He slammed his fist onto the workbench, echoing the turmoil within him. "Damn him," he breathed, the words tasting like ash in his mouth. He wasn't just angry; he was broken, and the pieces refused to fit back together.

Father Mike's voice, that steady, measured drone, echoed in Caleb's skull. "Forgiveness ain't some gift you hand out, son. It's a release 'you' gotta grant yourself. Permission to let go, to move the hell on." But moving on felt like tossing his guts into the churning sea. This pain, this gnawing emptiness...it "was" him. How could he just...shed it?

Like a snakeskin? It was woven into the very grain of his being, damn it. Years spent hunched over wood, carving away at stubborn knots… hadn't taught him a thing. Or had it? Suddenly, it hit him like a hammer blow to the chest.

Forgiveness wasn't about erasing the past or pretending it had never happened. It was about moving *through* it, carving space for something new—something better. Something that didn't reek so heavily of regret. He drew in a deep breath, the sharp bite of sawdust and salt spray prickling his nostrils. The workshop—his sanctuary—always anchored him. The aroma of pine and oak clashed with the briny air in a familiar struggle, echoing the unrest within. His fingers brushed across the well-worn handles of his chisels, each one a cold, unyielding promise of change.

He picked up a chisel, the cool steel a comfort against the sweat on his palm. The unfinished carving seemed to stare back, its imperfections mocking him, each a jagged piece of the puzzle he couldn't solve. He saw his father's hands, strong and calloused, shaping similar pieces, the slow, deliberate strokes, the quiet patience. He saw his mother's face, that unwavering faith, how she'd always found the light, even in the darkest corners. And then…" him." His father. Flawed, a runaway, a ghost…but human. Just human.

The first cut was hesitant, a whisper against the wood. But with each stroke, something shifted within him, a tiny, reluctant crack in the dam of his bitterness. He might never understand "why" his father left, might never get the answers he craved, the explanations that could make this pain disappear. But maybe…just maybe…he could carve something new out of the wreckage. Not a forgetting, not an erasure…a "reshaping." As the blade bit into the wood, the first shavings curled away like whispers of the past, and a hesitant hope flickered in Caleb's chest. Forgiveness wasn't a destination; it was a process, a long, arduous climb. Today, he was finally starting the ascent.

The air hung thick with sawdust and regret in his father's workshop. Caleb felt it pressing down on him, a heaviness that clung to his skin and settled in his lungs. It wasn't just the way the sunlight filtered through the air, catching on floating flecks of wood like ash from a dying fire—it was the presence of absence, the echo of dreams left unfinished. Half-carved figures stood like silent sentinels, their gestures interrupted mid-thought, haunted by intentions never realized. Each tool, each curled shaving of pine, murmured of a man Caleb barely knew—a life etched into this space with care, only to be abandoned without warning... and without him.

"Damn it, Dad," he muttered, the words catching in his throat. He wasn't just looking at wood; he was seeing his reflection in every chisel mark, every knot in the grain. He saw the choices he hadn't made, the paths he hadn't dared to tread.

The half-finished carving, a grotesque mockery of a seabird, mirrored his fractured state. It had begun as something else—something grander—before losing its way. Just like him. The silence pressed down. It wasn't the peaceful quiet of solitude but the suffocating weight of unspoken expectations, the echo of a father's disappointment. He imagined his father's calloused hands, the strength he'd possessed, the dreams he'd held so close. Now, only the trace of cedar and the whisper of dust remained.

"Should I finish it?" he whispered to the empty room, the question a desperate plea for guidance. "Or is that just another way to bury myself under his shadows?" He ran a hand over the rough-hewn wood. It felt cold, almost alien, in contrast to the warmth pulsing in his hand. The sea called to him, the promise of escape a siren's song. Port Angeles, a sprawling canvas of opportunity, beckoned with its salty air and the distant, brooding silhouette of the Whispering Cliffs. But the cliffs held their secrets, and Caleb knew he carried his own. The workshop, suffocating as it was, felt more familiar than the vast expanse of ocean, the uncertain future.

He picked up a chisel, the weight of it oddly comforting in the face of his indecision. His father's ghost pressed against him, urging him, judging him. He closed his eyes, the ghost's pressure growing heavier, and then, with a deep breath, he dropped the chisel back into its slot. He knew, with a certainty that chilled him to the bone, that leaving the carving unfinished was his only chance to begin his own life truly. The click of the door as he left was final, irrevocable. It wasn't a whisper; it was a defiant declaration. His father's unfinished symphony wouldn't define him. He would write his own.

The sea air rushed in, a promise of a new beginning, and although fear still gnawed at him, a flicker of hope—small, fragile, but real—ignited within him. The journey would be long, the path unclear, but Caleb felt the weight lift for the first time, a subtle shift away from the shadow of his father's dreams towards the possibility of forging his destiny.

CHAPTER 2

A Priest's Request and an Unfinished Work

THE WIND, A raw, salty claw, ripped at Caleb's dark suit, but he stood rooted, a statue carved from the granite of Saint Peter's by the Sea. His mother's funeral. The town had gathered a sea of black veils and hushed whispers, but Caleb felt utterly alone, adrift in a grief so sharp it felt physical. An invisible wall, he thought, his fists clenched tight at his sides. He'd spent his life shaping wood, smoothing the rough edges, coaxing beauty from raw timber. But this... this jagged, splintered loss defied his skill.

Mourners flowed past, a slow, somber river. Each familiar face, each silent nod, a fresh stab of practiced composure. Their sympathy pressed against him, heavy and suffocating, yet it didn't penetrate the icy core of his despair. He felt a hollowness spreading through him, a void where his mother's laughter used to bloom. The heavy oak doors, his father's legacy, stood open. He'd run his hands over those intricate carvings a thousand times, finding solace in their familiar grooves. Now, the wood felt cold, alien, as if the soul his father had poured into them had leached away with Elena's passing. A bitter twist of irony. His father's faith, his artistry... all felt diminished.

He inhaled the thick, cloying aroma of incense, mingling with the faint, sweet rot of lilies. Stepping inside, the sanctuary's hushed reverence pressed in around him. The vaulted ceiling soared above, its timeworn beams murmuring stories of generations past. Stained glass fractured the afternoon light, casting spectral patterns across the pews. His gaze swept the room—his blue eyes, his mother's eyes—searching the faces she had once touched. Mrs. Anderson, the librarian, dabbed at her eyes. He remembered her library, his mother's voice a gentle comfort as she read to the children. Nearby stood Mr. Gonzalez, the fisherman, his weathered hands clasped in prayer. His wife had been among the first to bring a casserole—a quiet act of grace from a community built on the bedrock his mother had laid, now cracked and crumbling.

A knot of bitterness clenched in his throat. Was this the legacy he'd inherit? A silence so heavy it crushed the air from his lungs. The weight of her absence pressed down, sharper than grief, more suffocating than the guilt gnawing at his insides—that gnawing belief that he should have done more, been more. He wanted to scream at the unfairness of it, to demand an answer from a God he wasn't sure was even listening. But what good would that do? The silence would only answer back.

Caleb had always been the quiet one, a man of few words, a skilled craftsman. But now, the silence roared, vast and endless. He wanted to reach out, to say something, anything, to his father, to the mourners who filled the church like shadows. But if he did—if he cracked open the grief that coiled inside him—would it swallow him whole? Would it destroy him the way it had destroyed his father?

The floorboards groaned beneath his boots, a quiet lament in the hush of the church. Each step forward felt heavier, as if the weight of his mother's absence had settled into his bones. He moved through the receiving line, a ghost in his own life, offering nods, half-muttered acknowledgments, and gripping the hands of strangers who spoke of his mother as though she were merely away on a long journey.

He reached the front. The lilies were stark against the dark wood of the casket—his father's work. A tribute. A prayer carved in walnut and varnished in grief. Caleb's breath hitched as his fingers skimmed the smooth surface, tracing the grain, the effort, the love poured into every joint and curve. His father hadn't spoken much since Elena's death, but this… this was a language all its own.

A fresh wave of pain, visceral and soul-deep, ripped through him. Not physical, but a hollow ache that left him raw. He clenched his jaw, forcing back the tears. Grief had rules, didn't it? Some unspoken expectation that he should hold himself together, be the man his mother believed he was. But the weight of that expectation was suffocating.

A shadow moved beside him. Father Mike. His cassock was worn, the hem frayed, his boots scuffed from years of walking among the broken. He didn't speak right away, just stood there, his presence solid, grounding.

"God's peace, Caleb," the priest murmured, his voice steady, carrying no empty platitudes, no sugar-coated assurances. Just truth.

Caleb swallowed hard. "Father Mike."

"Your mother... she was remarkable." The words weren't forced. They weren't for show. The priest meant them.

Caleb nodded; his throat tight. "Her faith... it was everything," he admitted, though the words came out strangled, barely more than breath. "It should have been everything to me, too."

A pause. The silence stretched between them, thick with unspoken things. Father Mike studied him, his gaze searching, seeing too much.

"Faith isn't a ledger, son. You don't tally up doubts and blessings like debts owed." The priest's voice was quiet but firm, his grip on Caleb's shoulder grounding. "She never expected you to be perfect, only to keep searching."

Caleb let out a hollow laugh, shaking his head. "I stopped searching a long time ago."

Father Mike exhaled; his face unreadable. "Then maybe it's time to start again."

Caleb glanced toward the stained glass, the shifting colors painting his mother's casket in fractured light. Faith. It had been her anchor. And now? Now it felt like a distant shore he couldn't reach.

"Come." Father Mike's voice was gentle but insistent. "Let's walk."

Caleb hesitated, but then his boots scraped against the polished floor as he followed the priest past the mourners, their hushed condolences like whispers in the wind. Each step felt like moving through water, slow, heavy. But somewhere, buried beneath the grief, something stirred—a flicker of warmth in the cold. A fragile hope, barely more than a whisper.

And for the first time in a long while, Caleb didn't turn away from it.

He closed his eyes, the grief a physical weight in his chest, a crushing burden. But beneath it, something else burned—a stubborn ember of hope. Not a resurrected faith yet, but a flicker, a possibility. It wasn't an answer to his pain but an invitation to face it, to begin the long, arduous climb back to the light.

He wouldn't carry this alone, he whispered silently to himself. He wouldn't.

The final "Amen" hung in the air, a fragile thing that slowly dissolved into the silence of Saint Peter's by the Sea. The aroma of aged wood and beeswax mingled with the sharp tang of salt air, a bittersweet reminder of Elena, life, and loss. The stained-glass windows, now dimmed by the setting sun, cast fractured light patterns on the stone walls—a beautiful, heartbreaking testament to faith's fragility and enduring power.

Father Michael Harrington's voice, usually booming with jovial pronouncements, now held a tremor, a fragility that belied the weight of his words.

"Elena Martin," he began, his gaze sweeping over the sea of bowed heads, "didn't just 'live'; she 'radiated' grace. Kindness wasn't a choice for her, it was the air she breathed."

His voice cracked slightly. He cleared his throat, the silence amplifying the unspoken grief. Caleb Martin, rigid in the front pew, felt the polished wood bite into his thighs, a physical manifestation of the unforgiving hardness in his own heart.

"Her faith wasn't just words, people," Father Mike's voice, though still strained, gained strength. He looked directly at Caleb, holding his gaze for a beat that felt like an eternity. "It was the way she lived, the way she loved, even when it hurt. Mercy, not judgment. Redemption, not regret."

The words felt like accusations, an indictment of Caleb's unforgiving heart. Caleb's jaw tightened. Mercy? Redemption? Easy for him to say, sitting up there, untouched by the years of emptiness his father had carved into their lives.

The memories surged—empty chairs at countless family dinners, whispered promises broken like brittle twigs, the unfinished carvings in his workshop, a monument to dreams abandoned. Each unfinished piece was a mirror reflecting his brokenness. He clenched his fists, the wood digging into his palms, a dull ache mirroring the more profound pain. Father Mike continued, weaving a tapestry of Elena's life, each shared memory a small victory against the encroaching darkness of the church. Fleeting and fragile, laughter broke through the solemnity, like sunbeams piercing through storm clouds. Yet, for Caleb, the stories only sharpened the edges of his resentment and highlighted the gaping hole left by his father's absence, a wound that no forgiveness could ever fully heal. The priest's words were a gentle erosion, but Caleb was granite, hardened by years of bitterness. The weight of unforgiveness was his burden, a choice, he realized, that he'd clung to like a life raft. He closed his eyes, fighting back tears, his guilt a bitter companion. Let go? He didn't know how. He didn't "want" to. Not yet.

The hymn *Amazing Grace* swelled and crashed around Caleb like a wave, pulling him under a tide of grief and bitter memories. He sat stone-faced, the words a cruel mockery. His mother's face, etched in the firelight of countless evenings, swam before his eyes—her voice, her touch, the unshakeable faith that had somehow failed to save her. Each note was a gut punch, a relentless reminder of everything he'd lost, everything he'd tried so damn hard to bury. Finally, the music faded, leaving a silence thick enough to choke on. He bolted, escaping the suffocating empathy of the mourners, bursting into the raw, cleansing air. The ocean roared below the cliffs, a symphony of its own, matching the turmoil within him. He gulped the salty wind, but the icy grip of his sorrow remained.

"Beautiful service," Father Mike's low and steady voice cut through the wind's howl. He stood a few paces back, his collar flapping like a distressed bird. There was no judgment in his eyes, only a weary understanding—the quiet patience of a man who'd seen too much despair. "Your mother... she left a hell of a legacy," Mike said, his voice as gentle as a summer rain. "Not just in this church, but in you, son." Caleb grunted; his jaw clenched so tight his teeth ached. "Yeah, she did." The silence hung heavy, charged with unspoken accusations and regrets. Then, like the measured tap of a hammer, Mike said, "Your father's Stations of the Cross... they're unfinished. In your workshop. Waiting. I believe completing them would honor Elena's memory... and maybe, just maybe, bring you the peace she prayed for."

The words hit Caleb like a physical blow. He whirled, disbelief twisting his features. "Those carvings?" His voice cracked. "They're not mine to finish. He abandoned them, just like he abandoned *us*. Left them to rot, just like he left me to rot!" The anger, raw and bitter, tasted like ash in his mouth. Mike studied him, his gaze unwavering. "Forgiveness doesn't erase the past, Caleb. It redeems it. And sometimes, the work left undone isn't a burden, but an invitation. You inherited his skill, maybe even his calling—to create something... something bigger than yourself."

Caleb's fists clenched. He knew those hands. Hands that had shaped wood for years, coaxing beauty from chaos. But his father's Stations of the Cross? That was a monument to a man he'd spent his whole life hating. A testament to the abandonment that still echoed in his bones. Mike's hand settled firmly on his shoulder, a comforting and challenging weight. "Just... think about it, Caleb." The priest's voice held a note of something akin to pleading. "Think about your mother. Think about finishing what he started." The unspoken question hung in the air: *Can you find it in yourself to forgive him, even if just to honor her?*

The salt spray stung Caleb's face, mirroring the bitterness that still gnawed at him. Years. Years he'd spent wrestling with the ghosts of his past, the undertow of resentment pulling him under. He stared out at the churning ocean, the horizon a blurry line between what was and what could be—a reflection of the turmoil inside him. The relentless crash of waves against the cliffs was a soundtrack to his internal war. "I'll... think about it," he mumbled, the words barely audible above the wind's howl. The offer, the chance to finish his father's unfinished Stations of the Cross, felt like a betrayal, a surrender. It was a path back to the pain, a path stained with memories he desperately tried to bury.

Father Mike's smile was gentle, but Caleb saw the understanding in his eyes—a shared understanding of the weight of unspoken grief.

"Your mother believed in forgiveness, Caleb," the priest said, his voice a low rumble that carried surprisingly well over the wind. "Sometimes, we find it in the most unexpected places. Maybe… in the work of our own hands." He watched the priest disappear back towards the church; the figure swallowed by the encroaching twilight. The wind clawed at his jacket, a physical manifestation of the uncertainty tearing at him.

The sea stretched before him, infinite and indifferent, a vast mirror reflecting the bottomless pit of his doubt. This wasn't just about carving wood; it was about carving a path through the wreckage of his life, a path toward—maybe—redemption. His fingers traced the jagged line where sea met sky, a desperate attempt to find purchase in this vast, indifferent expanse. The ocean roared, a brutal reminder of the world's apathy, its relentless waves a mirror to the storm raging inside him.

Unanswerable questions crashed against the shores of his sanity, echoing the relentless waves battering the Whispering Cliffs. The air was heavy with the mingled traces of pine and salt, steeped in memory. His father's workshop—once a haven of creation, filled with warmth and laughter—had become a mausoleum. Dust clung to the half-finished carvings like a shroud, each one a silent accuser of broken promises and an unfinished life. The abandoned Stations of the Cross loomed in quiet condemnation, each incomplete figure a stark monument to his failure.

Father Mike's voice cut through his thoughts, calm yet resonant, laced with the wisdom of a man who'd seen more sorrow than most. "Shared burdens, Caleb. They lighten the load," he said, his voice as comforting as a warm hearth on a freezing night. "Your mother knew that. She carried many crosses, not all of them her own. And she forgave. Can you?" The question hung in the air—a challenge, a plea, and a painful truth that Caleb couldn't ignore. The choice before him felt heavier than the ocean itself.

Elena's words, echoing in Caleb's gut, felt like a punch. His mother, bless her unwavering faith, saw his father, *that* Thomas Martin, not as the ghost of a thousand broken promises but as some saint redeemed by grace. Bullshit. Caleb's throat tightened. He'd never understood her. Never reconciled the gaping hole his father's absence left with the saccharine hope she clung to like a life raft.

Father Mike, his weathered face a roadmap of battles fought and lost, stood beside him, the wind whipping silver strands across his temples. This wasn't some sermon; this man shared hard-won truths etched onto his soul. "Completing the Stations... it's not just about the woodwork, Caleb," the priest said, his voice rough but kind. "It's a testament to your mother's faith—a gift to this community, her family."

Caleb met the priest's gaze, searching for the certainty he desperately lacked. Father Mike's eyes held no judgment, only a weary compassion that spoke volumes. A man who understood loss and spent a lifetime sculpting sorrow into something... meaningful. "Your mother saw beauty in broken things, son," Father Mike said, his voice low. "She believed they could be made whole again. Isn't that what craftsmen do? We take the splintered pieces, the wreckage, and we shape it into something with purpose."

Caleb's hands clenched, the phantom feel of wood grain beneath his fingers, the satisfying resistance of the chisel. His mother always found potential in ruin; could *he* do the same? Could he salvage the wreckage left by the man who'd walked out? The thought tasted like ash.

"Think of it as a conversation, Caleb," Father Mike pressed, a hand resting briefly on his shoulder, a gesture both comforting and insistent. "A joint project between you and your father. A bridge, son, a bridge over the chasm he left behind." The words struck a chord.

A fragile spark of... possibility? A desperate hope that maybe, just maybe, he could build something beautiful from the ruins.

Father Mike clapped a hand on Caleb's shoulder, the gesture more bracing than blessing. "It's your call, son," he said, his voice roughened by years of confessions and whispered prayers. "The same grit that runs in your blood is what's needed. But don't let fear be the leash that holds you back." Mike watched him go, the priest's silhouette stark against the fading light. The wind howled a mournful tune, whipping salt spray and the sharp tang of pine into Caleb's face. Past and future—two jagged cliffs looming over a chasm of uncertainty. The unfinished Stations of the Cross gnawed at his mind, each uncarved panel a silent accusation. His fingers twitched, remembering the weight of the tools and the resistance of the wood.

His father's legacy – a millstone around his neck, a bitter inheritance. But a seed of something else sprouted in the darkness – a flicker of hope, a desperate need for something "more." Maybe finishing the Stations wasn't just about fulfilling a dead man's promise but about carving out a piece of himself he'd lost, a piece his father had taken with him. "Your old man," Mike's voice cut through the turmoil, "had a gift. Precision. He coaxed beauty from the wood, a language only he understood. But you, Caleb, you speak it too."

The words hit hard; a brutal truth disguised as solace. Caleb's throat constricted, his knuckles white as he clenched his fists, the phantom weight of his father's hammer heavy in his hands. Could he fill the void his father left? Could he pick up that chisel and carve a path through this wilderness of grief and doubt? "Those carvings," Mike pressed, his voice low and urgent, "they could be a conversation between you and Thomas. Hell, a scream. There's pain, yeah, but redemption's hiding in there, too. You gotta find it."

Caleb squeezed his eyes shut, the salt spray stinging his face. Years spent running, avoiding his father's ghost, the man who'd walked out. But maybe, just maybe, he could finally find the peace that had eluded him like a phantom in finishing what he'd started. As the first stars pricked the darkening sky, Caleb turned towards the church, his shoulders slumped. The decision? Too heavy for one night. But he wouldn't run. He'd stand before the raw wood, the unforgiving blankness of the panels, and listen to the silence scream. Maybe in that silence, amidst the ghosts of his father and the weight of his doubts, he'd hear his answer. Maybe.

The Pacific wind, raw and salty, whipped Caleb Martin's hair across his face, mirroring the turmoil inside him. He stood on the worn stone steps of Saint Peter's by the Sea, Father Mike's retreating footsteps swallowed by the heavy oak doors. The fiery sunset bled into violet and indigo, a breathtaking spectacle that did nothing to soothe the gut-wrenching grief that clawed at him. "Your father's hands began a work of faith, Caleb," Father Mike's words echoed in his ears, a weight settling on his shoulders heavier than any oak beam in the church. "Perhaps it is time yours finished it."

Finished it? The unfinished Stations of the Cross. His father's legacy, a testament to suffering and grace, left incomplete. A cold fist clenched in his chest. He hadn't understood his father's obsession—that relentless carving, that almost religious devotion to the grain of the wood. It wasn't just artistry; it was worship. He'd seen it, felt it in the rhythmic tap-tap-tap of the chisel against wood, a sound now hauntingly silent. Now, the lingering aroma of cedar and oak only stirred a wave of loss, of a father he'd never truly known—a father whose death left a gaping hole in his soul.

He squeezed his eyes shut, the memory of his father's calloused hands gripping the chisel, the rhythmic whisper of shavings, a sharp contrast to the dull ache in his own chest. This wasn't just about finishing a project; it was about connecting with a man he'd barely known about finding solace in something tangible after a loss so profound it threatened to consume him whole. The town's murmur settled into a hushed quiet, the last mourners gone, leaving behind a silence thick with grief.

His mother—gone. The thought was a physical blow, the wind a cruel hand pressing him against the cold stone. The ocean's call, usually a siren song of escape, was different tonight. No, this wasn't about running. It was about confronting the void left behind, about finding something—anything—to hold onto. A whisper of faith, fragile yet defiant, rose in the face of despair. A chance to honor his father, to find peace within his grief and, maybe, just maybe, finally connect with the man who'd left behind not only an unfinished masterpiece but a legacy of faith and dedication he now had to carry.

Caleb's boots hammered a rhythm against the cobblestones, each step a reluctant beat against the silence of Port Angeles. The town was a stage set, unchanged, but the play within him had rewritten itself. He wasn't just walking; he was marching towards a reckoning. "His father's hands…a work of faith…" the words echoed in his gut, a bittersweet mantra.

The workshop loomed, a black silhouette against the moon's silver wash. His breath caught in his throat. The smooth wood of the door, cool beneath his fingertips, felt both foreign and achingly familiar. The air was heavy with the trace of sawdust and oil—his father's ghost lingering in the atmosphere, dense and stifling. The unfinished cross dominated the space, a silent accusation. He stepped inside, the floorboards groaning beneath him like a warning. His hand trembled as he reached for a chisel, the chill of the steel clashing with the sweat slicking his palms.

Doubt gnawed at him. Could he, *could he* ever match his father's skill? Could his clumsy hands coax hope from the raw wood, carve meaning from the gaping wound of grief? The first cut was pathetic, shallow, a whimper in the face of the task. But the second... deeper. Surer. A sliver of defiance, of resolve, cut through the wood and something within him.

He didn't need to know if he could fill his father's shoes, not really. This wasn't about emulating a master; it was about forging his own path, carving his own truth. The only sound was the rasp of steel on wood, the whisper of wind through the cracks, and the frantic thump of his own heart. This wasn't just about crafting a station of the cross; it was about building a bridge, a lifeline back to himself, a testament not only to the loss he carried but to the stubborn, fragile hope that refused to die.

This wasn't just wood and devotion; it was the desperate, beautiful, terrifying act of rebuilding a life from the wreckage of grief. And Caleb Martin, lost son, grieving craftsman, carved on.

CHAPTER 3

Letters from a Ghost

CALEB MARTIN BRACED himself at the shop's edge, the smell of sawdust hitting like a gut punch of memory. Autumn air scraped at his lungs, but the *air itself*—infused with echoes of laughter and quiet lessons, simmering resentments and words left unsaid—was what truly staggered him. Sunlight slanted through the dusty windows, casting long shadows across the floor. This wasn't just a workshop; it was a mausoleum of a life, a testament to his father's solitude, a cathedral built of silence. He drew in a ragged breath and stepped inside, the weight of memory pressing down like a shroud. Months. Months had passed, and still the place sat untouched, abandoned since the old man had died. Unfinished projects lingered mid-creation, like the unresolved truths between them.

Chisels and planes lay dormant, awaiting hands that would never grip them again. Dust—a fine layer—coated everything, the quiet residue of grief and neglect. His fingers brushed against the unfinished rocking horse, its form half-emerged, a spectral echo caught between life and death. A damn rocking horse. His father's legacy was reduced to an unfinished toy. The irony wasn't lost on him. He'd been too proud, too stubborn to appreciate it while he had the chance. "Damn it," he muttered, the words catching in his throat. The rough grain of the wood felt strangely soothing under his calloused hand. His father had taught him everything: reading the knots, letting the wood guide the blade, and the patience required for perfection. But there'd been a wall between them, an unbridgeable chasm, even as he'd stood here, learning, feeling his father's presence. The regret hit him hard, a tidal wave of what-ifs and should-haves. Years wasted on resentment, years of silent battles fought and lost. He'd hated the man, this ghost in the wood, who'd carved out his legacy in such stubborn silence. But here, amidst the echoes of that dedication, the resentment felt... different. It was blurring, softening at the edges, giving way to something else, something that tasted like ash and sorrow and... maybe, just maybe, understanding.

Caleb's gaze raked over the shop, a whirlwind of half-finished projects, tools arranged with the obsessive precision only his father possessed—even in his absence, the old man's ghost reigned. Each object throbbed with a silent accusation, a reminder of the chasm that had yawned between them. He picked up a mahogany plank, the bevel perfect, a testament to lessons delivered through gritted teeth and barely concealed frustration. A half-carved figure, frozen mid-gesture, mocked him with its unfinished story, a mirror of their fractured relationship. This wasn't just cleanup; it was an autopsy of their past, a brutal excavation of regret. The cedar fragrance, thick and cloying, clung to him like a shroud. The silence was deafening, a stark contrast to the rhythmic clang of mallet on chisel that had once filled the space, a soundtrack to their unspoken resentments.

He felt the weight of it all crushing him: the unspoken words, the missed opportunities, the love that had curdled into bitterness. A chisel, worn smooth by his father's calloused grip, gleamed under the weak sunlight. He hefted it, the familiar weight a bitter comfort. A thousand memories slammed into him—the stubborn silences stretched taut as violin strings, the rhythmic thud of the mallet, the rare, grudging nod of approval that felt more like a tossed bone than genuine affection. Then, frail and pleading, his mother's voice sliced through the memories, a ghost whispering from the other side. "Forgive him, Caleb." The words, spoken in her final days, had been met with his stony silence, a wall of anger he'd built brick by brick. But here, surrounded by the ghosts of his father's life, the words echoed a quiet insistence. Forgiveness.

The word felt alien, a bitter pill, yet it shifted from a demand to a desperate, trembling possibility in this hallowed space of wood and steel. His eyes snagged on an old workbench shoved into the corner, a forgotten sentinel. Something gnawed at him, a prickle of curiosity laced with dread. His fingers brushed its edge as he approached, a silent plea for answers. His hand, almost instinctively, found a small, hidden drawer, concealed like a shameful secret. The lock was simple, almost mocking in its ease. But the intent was clear. Something was meant to stay hidden. Doubt clawed at him. Did he have the right to violate this privacy, to exhume the past? The fear warred with a burning need to know, to understand. The urge to break the lock, to confront the truth, won. He had to know. What secrets lay buried within?

Sweat beaded on Caleb Martin's brow, the workshop's stale air heavy with the musk of sawdust and long-buried resentment. His fingers, calloused and scarred from years of wrestling stubborn wood, fumbled through the chaotic sprawl of his father's workbench. Each tool, each discarded sketch, was a painful echo of the man he'd barely known—a ghost lingering in the place where a father should have stood. This wasn't just a workshop; it was a mausoleum of missed connections, a monument to their fractured bond. "Damn it," he muttered, his voice thick with frustration. He shoved aside a half-finished birdhouse, its delicate craftsmanship a cruel parody of the broken relationship it failed to mend. He needed answers—some damn explanation for the years of silence, the vast emptiness where love should have been.

Then, a glint of brass beneath yellowed blueprints. A key. Small, tarnished, but radiating an almost palpable sense of significance. His heart hammered a frantic rhythm against his ribs. This was the key to whatever secrets his father had guarded so fiercely. He slid the key into the lock of the ancient drawer, the metal cold against his skin. It resisted, a stubborn refusal to yield its secrets, mirroring the resistance Caleb himself had always felt toward his father. A tense moment hung in the air, heavy with anticipation and a desperate hope that was quickly giving way to a familiar dread. Then, a soft click.

The drawer slid open, revealing a worn leather pouch and a single, crisp white envelope. Caleb's breath hitched. His father's handwriting, stark and unforgiving, sprawled across the front: "Caleb." "Jesus Christ," he whispered, his voice barely audible above the pounding of his own blood. He picked up the letter, its weight a physical manifestation of his decades of unspoken questions. Would it be an apology? A pathetic attempt at reconciliation? Or just another cruel reminder of the man who had left him adrift in a sea of silence? Fear warred with a desperate need for closure, a terrifying blend of anticipation and dread. He tore open the envelope, the sound echoing in the suffocating silence of the workshop.

The past, he realized, wasn't some distant shadow; it was alive—palpable and waiting—ready to unleash its fury or, perhaps, offer a long-overdue peace. The paper felt brittle beneath his trembling fingers. His eyes darted over the words, his heart pounding a frantic rhythm, the air heavy with the aroma of aged wood, machine oil, and the faint echo of a father he was still trying to understand. He had to know. He *needed* to know what lay hidden within.

The drawer screeched in protest, metal grinding as Caleb yanked it open with more force than necessary. Decades of stillness stirred. Dust rose like ash from a long-cold fire, drifting into the shafts of pale sunlight that pierced the workshop. The atmosphere—laden with old paper, stale sawdust, and the ghostly whisper of pipe smoke—hit him like a blow to the chest. Nestled in the clutter was a bundle of letters, bound by a ribbon as frayed and fragile as memory itself. Caleb's breath caught. This was it—his father's words. His reckoning. His pulse quickened, drumming out years of silence, abandonment, and aching questions now clawing their way to the surface.

Thomas Martin, the man Caleb had built his life on rejecting, was reaching out from beyond the grave. The weight of it, the sheer audacity of it, almost broke him. He fumbled with the ribbon, his fingers clumsy, trembling. The paper, brittle and yellowed, felt like the skin of a forgotten memory under his touch.

"Dearest Elena," the inscription read, his mother's name a stark, painful reminder of a connection he'd brutally severed. The elegant script, his father's familiar yet unfamiliar hand, felt like a brand searing his soul. "If these words ever find their way to you…" The words hung in the air, heavy with unspoken sorrow. Caleb's vision blurred. His father, a man of few words who'd built walls around himself higher than any fortress, had poured out his soul onto these fragile pages.

The words hit Caleb like a gut punch, shattering years of bitter resentment. He'd built his life on the lie that his father, Thomas, had abandoned them—a selfish coward who'd walked away without a backward glance. But the letters—each one a fragile confession—were chipping away at that carefully constructed wall. Thomas hadn't left out of cruelty. He'd left out of terror, gripped by the chilling fear that the darkness devouring him might one day reach his family. The workshop, once a monument to Thomas's rigid discipline, now felt like a mausoleum of broken things—splintered wood, fractured memories, and Caleb's crumbling resolve. Threads of light filtered through the cracked windows, catching on the letters and gilding them in a soft, fleeting glow, as if the past itself refused to stay buried. His hand trembled as it came to rest on the worn wood of his father's workbench. This was the place Thomas had labored—building furniture and battling shadows. And in the mingled trace of sawdust and sorrow, Caleb could almost feel it: the quiet war his father had waged between faith and fear, hope and helplessness, love and the ache of leaving behind a legacy he never knew how to live.

Caleb folded the letter, his pulse still a frantic drum against his ribs. He'd spent a lifetime trying to understand the man his father was, carrying the weight of unanswered questions like a crippling burden. Now, the answers were raw and unflinching, and they weren't the ones he'd expected. His mother's dying wish had brought him here, to this reckoning. Forgiveness, once a distant, impossible dream, felt suddenly within reach—tangible in the grain of the wood, the ink on the page, the whispered sorrow in his father's words. He leaned back, the breath he exhaled a ragged sigh of relief, of grief, of dawning understanding. The letters wouldn't rewrite history. They wouldn't bring back the lost years. But they could carve a path toward healing, a path toward a peace he'd thought unattainable. A low growl escaped his throat. He wouldn't just "read" them, he'd devour them. He'd absorb every word, every agonizing confession, every desperate plea for forgiveness. He'd piece together the fragments of his father's soul, and in doing so, maybe, just maybe, he could finally mend his own.

His fingers traced the ink-stained script, the bold yet uneven strokes revealing a soul torn between duty and love. The air was thick with the musk of aging paper and sawdust, a suffocating perfume of memory. He cleared his throat, the tightness in his chest squeezing each breath. He reread the words, their raw emotion leaping off the page: *"Each moment away from you carved hollow spaces within me—spaces where whispers of regret nested like sparrows in winter."* These weren't just words—they were a scream, a desperate plea for connection echoing across the years. And Caleb, finally, was ready to listen.

The workshop walls seemed to press inward, trapping him in the stillness. Caleb's gut churned. All his life, he'd painted his father as a coward, a deserter. Thomas Martin—a ghost who'd vanished, leaving behind broken promises and a splintered family. But this... this wasn't abandonment. This was a tragedy—slow, suffocating, the quiet unraveling of a man caught between war and the unrelenting gravity of home. He drew in a shaky breath, the lingering trace of pine and varnish a frail tether to the present. The truth, raw and unflinching, settled into his bones. His father's hands, worn from rifle and chisel, hadn't just built things—they'd fought battles Caleb never saw. And yet, somehow, those same hands had never reached for him. His fingers tightened around the brittle paper, the creases deepening like fault lines. The words wavered on the page; the ink faded to a ghost of what once had weight. *How?* How could a man so hungry for belonging let it unravel so carelessly? How could the same hands that carved such aching beauty also fracture the very thing they were meant to hold together? The question tore at Caleb's chest, insistent and unyielding. A gust of wind shuddered the windowpanes, stirring a thin veil of dust that shimmered in the late sun like memory fragments refusing to settle. His eyes drifted toward the workbench—a shrine of abandonment, cluttered with tools and silence. He let the letter slip from his grip, breath catching in his throat. Then, reaching forward, he lifted a half-carved wooden figurine, its form uncertain, edges raw.

His father's touch had been here, smoothing the grain, shaping the wood into something enduring. Something beautiful. He closed his eyes, a choked sob escaping his lips. For the first time, he wondered if his father had tried to do the same with *him*—to shape something good from the wreckage of his broken past. Another passage jumped out, the ink slightly smeared, as if his father's hand had trembled as he wrote it: "Betrayal is not always a choice made willingly. Sometimes, it is the only path left open to a man at war with himself." The words hit him like a physical blow. The weight of them pressed against his chest, crushing him. His father hadn't deserted them; he'd been lost, battling demons that clung to him more stubbornly than any wood glue.

Caleb let out a slow, ragged breath. The icy grip of resentment, a weapon he'd wielded for years, began to loosen its hold. He'd spent a lifetime carving his father's absence into something he could understand and *control*. But now, the familiar comfort of his anger felt empty. He stared at the unfinished figurine, the wood suddenly feeling impossibly light in his hands. He wasn't sure what to hold onto anymore, but the rage, at least, was gone. A terrifying and strangely liberating void opened inside him.

The amber light, fading fast, cast long shadows across his father's workshop. The air hung thick with the *presence* of sawdust and regret. Caleb traced the worn leather of his father's tool belt, the leather as rough as his memories. Each chisel, lined up with a precision that bordered on obsession, mocked him. Military precision, just like his old man. He'd never known the man, really. Just the ghost of him, haunting the edges of his mother's carefully curated stories.

His mother's voice, soft yet insistent, echoed in his skull: "Forgiveness is the final form of love." *Bullshit.* It felt like a knife twisting in his gut, a surrender he wasn't prepared to make. Forgiveness? It was a luxury he couldn't afford. Not with the anger, the hurt, the years of silence clawing at him. But here, amidst the ghosts of his father's work, something shifted in this sanctuary. It wasn't about erasing the past, he realized, a cold knot loosening in his chest. It was about letting go of the weight.

He picked up the stack of letters, his father's voice trapped in ink, a ghostly conversation across the years. Enough running. He was done with the ghosts. Time to learn from them, damn it. He touched the brittle paper, fragile as a butterfly's wing. He wouldn't discard these remnants, not anymore. They weren't proof of failure but echoes of a fight, a struggle he was only beginning to understand. These weren't just letters; they were a lifeline.

He ran a calloused thumb across the rough workbench, imagining his father's hands, the same hands that had shaped beauty from wood, from nothing. The past was etched in stone, unchangeable. But the future? He could build that. He *would* make that with the same care, precision, and stubborn, defiant hope that had driven his old man, his ghost of a father.

The last rays of sun bled through the dusty windows. He reached for a chisel, the steel cold against his skin. He didn't know what he'd carve but knew he had to start. His thumb traced his father's signature—bold, yet shaky, a tremor beneath the deliberate strokes. *Thomas Martin*. The final word of a man whose silence had been a fortress and a cage. Caleb felt a choked sob rise in his throat. The weight of unspoken words, the years of absence, crashed down on him. He closed his eyes, the image of his father's unsteady hand burned into his memory.

He had to forgive him, not for his father's sake, but for his own. He had to build something beautiful from the wreckage. He had to.

Outside, the Pacific roared—a counterpoint to the quiet scream trapped inside Caleb. He shifted on the stool, the worn wood groaning a protest under his weight. His father's workbench loomed before him, a monument to a life lived in silence. Each tool, each gouge in the aged wood, whispered stories Caleb hadn't known existed.

"Damn it, Thomas," he muttered, the name a raw whisper against the workshop's hushed solemnity. These letters—confessions stained with regret and a desperate yearning for something more—were shattering everything Caleb thought he knew. His father hadn't just been gone; he'd been fighting a war Caleb had never glimpsed. A war fought not with weapons but with a hammer, a chisel, and a heart choked by some unnamed sorrow. He ran a hand over the smooth wood of a half-finished rocking horse, a familiar pang of grief hitting him. It was beautiful, a testament to his father's skill, but now it felt like a cruel mockery—a symbol of the life Caleb never really had. The letters revealed a man ravaged by self-doubt who poured his pain into these beautiful, cursed objects. The weight of it was crushing.

Years of carefully constructed peace crumbled, replaced by a chaotic storm of guilt, anger, and a desperate need for truth. He'd spent so long trying to fill the echoing silence left by his father's absence, to banish the lingering trace of cedar and regret that seemed woven into the very walls, but now that silence came roaring back—amplified by the revelation of his father's hidden pain. Elena, his mother—her belief in redemption had always felt like something delicate, a prayer cast into the wind and hoping to land. He remembered her voice, etched into his memory: *"There's always a second chance, Caleb. Always a way to find grace in the hardship."* But could grace bridge this chasm? Could it mend a wound this deep and long ignored?

He slammed the drawer shut, the lock clicking like a final judgment. It wasn't a barrier anymore, but a promise. A promise to himself. He wouldn't let this knowledge consume him. He wouldn't let his father's unfinished story become his own damnation. He would finish it. He would understand it. He would finally honor the man, flaws and all, buried beneath the layers of silence and cedar. He picked up his father's worn pen, the weight of the untold story settling heavily in his hand. The fight, he realized, had just begun.

Caleb pushed himself up, the rough wood of the workbench familiar beneath his calloused fingertips. Years of his father's work, etched into the grain – not just relics, but a lifeline. This workshop, once a refuge, now felt like a pressure cooker, brewing something dangerous, something vital. His gut churned; the solitude had been a shield, but the shield was gone. He faced the doorway, the dying sun painting the threshold gold. Port Angeles sprawled beyond, the ocean's breath a salty whisper on the wind. The town held his past, his father's ghost, but the journey ahead... that was a different beast entirely. Unanswered questions clawed at him; unspoken prayers choked his throat. He felt the pull, relentless as the tide, a force he couldn't ignore, even if he wanted to.

A shudder ran through him. Leaving this sanctuary meant facing something far greater than himself – a reckoning, a desperate attempt at reconciliation, a maybe-too-late redemption. His father's letters hadn't brought peace; they'd sparked a fire. They'd handed him a map to a place he wasn't sure he wanted to go but knew he must. Caleb Martin, carpenter and reluctant adventurer, was ready or not. The door clicked shut behind him, a final, quiet thud. The past remained locked inside, but its weight – his father's words and regrets – settled deep in his bones. The road ahead was uncertain, a terrifying stretch of the unknown. But Caleb, despite the tremor in his hands, wasn't a man to back down from a challenge. The sawdust clinging to his palms felt like an anchor, a reminder of the tangible world he was about to leave behind. The ache in his chest, the burden of his father's legacy, pushed him forward. He stepped into the twilight, the promise – or the threat – of tomorrow hanging thick in the air. The tang of the sea mingled with the woody aroma that still clung to his sleeves, forming a strange cocktail of grief and anticipation. He was walking toward something. He just didn't know what. And that unknowing was as real, as biting, as the salt spray on his face.

CHAPTER 4

Sarah's Escape and a Town's Watchful Eyes

RAIN SLICKED THE cobblestones, mirroring the sheen of sweat on Sarah's palms. The bus lurched to a halt, spitting her onto the Port Angeles pavement. Her suitcase thumped—a dull rhythm against the frantic drum of her heart. The ocean's salty tang, sharp as a memory, clawed at her throat. "Home." The word burned like ash. This town, once a canvas of childhood wonder, now loomed as a dark, familiar landscape of escape and regret. Seattle's chaos still clung to her like a shroud, the shattered remnants of her life forming a jagged mosaic of bad choices and worse luck. She'd run, but from what? And to what? The question gnawed at her, a relentless tide eroding her fragile hope.

She shifted the weight of her bag, the cheap fabric digging into her shoulder. A single streetlight flickered, casting long, skeletal shadows that mimicked the doubts twisting in her gut. St. Anne's rectory. Uncle Mike. Her last lifeline. The letter had been terse, a desperate plea veiled in polite requests. "Needed space. A fresh start." Lies, really. She'd needed him. His simple yet profound reply echoed in her mind: "The door is always open." But would he still open his arms? Reaching the rectory gates, she hesitated, fingers tracing the cold iron. The house stood sentinel against the darkening cliffs, weathered but resolute. It wasn't just bricks and mortar but a fortress of memories, whispered prayers, and quiet solace. A place where she'd felt safe once upon a time. But could it still be? A sob caught in her throat. She swallowed the lump, the lump a bitter taste of fear and longing.

Pushing through the groaning gates, she paused before the heavy oak door, its grain coarse beneath her trembling hand. This was it. No turning back. She knocked—three short raps that cracked the evening stillness like breaking glass. The door creaked open to reveal Uncle Mike. His salt-and-pepper hair was neatly combed, but his eyes carried a weight that went beyond his usual gentle warmth. He studied her, something unreadable flickering in his gaze before he spoke, his voice a low, gravelly murmur. "Sarah? Is that really you?" The unspoken question hovered in the space between them. Sarah couldn't find her voice. Instead, she stepped into his arms, the familiar trace of beeswax and old books in the air grounding her like a whispered memory in the storm she carried inside.

"Oh, Mike," she whispered, tears filling her cheeks. "I... I don't know what to do." He held her tight, his arms strong and comforting. "Come in, child. Come in. We'll talk." Though steady, his voice had a tremor of concern that mirrored the turmoil in her heart. The sanctuary she sought might not be as simple as she remembered.

"Thank you, Uncle Mike," Sarah whispered, her voice trembling. The words felt inadequate, a pathetically small offering for the colossal weight crushing her chest. She hadn't realized how much she'd been holding in until now, until the sanctuary of his rectory offered a fragile crack in her defenses. He pulled back, his gaze intense, a flicker of something unreadable – worry? Understanding? – in his kind eyes. He nodded, a silent acknowledgment of the storm raging within her. "Come in, Sarah. There's tea, and I suspect you need something warm to soothe that soul of yours."

The rectory's sitting room was a haven, familiar and comforting. Stained glass cast shifting hues across the walls, and the warm aroma of baking bread offered a soothing contrast to the damp chill outside. A fire roared in the hearth, a defiant blaze against the darkness she carried within. This was a place of peace, a place where, perhaps, she could begin to heal. She sank into the worn armchair, its embrace both familiar and forgiving. Mike settled opposite, placing two steaming mugs on the table between them. The silence stretched—thick, palpable, and heavy with unspoken anxieties.

"Troubled waters, Sarah," he began, his voice a low rumble, the same measured tone she recalled from his sermons, yet softer now, infused with a gentler compassion. "They're part of the journey. But even the fiercest storm eventually passes, always leaving a harbor in its wake." She swirled the tea, the steam mirroring the turmoil inside. "Leaving Seattle felt like jumping off a cliff, Uncle Mike," she confessed, her voice tight. "I know it was the right decision, logically. But the fall… it never ends." The words caught in her throat, a raw, bitter truth. Leaving behind her life, her career, the only home she'd known… it was a self-inflicted wound that bled relentlessly.

Mike leaned forward, his elbows resting on his knees. "Sometimes, we have to step back from the storm to see the path," he said, his voice low and steady. "Healing isn't about running away, Sarah. It's about finding the courage to begin again. To rebuild, brick by painful brick." His gaze held hers, unwavering. He knew her well enough to understand the depth of her despair.

Her fingers tightened around the mug. "And what if I don't know how?" The question was a desperate cry, a testament to the fear gnawing at her. "You don't have to. That's the grace of it, Sarah. It meets you where you are, right in the midst of the chaos." She stared into the fire, its dancing flames reflecting the questions burning within her. Could she truly believe in this grace? This second chance? The doubt was a cold weight in her stomach.

A long silence fell, heavy but not suffocating. It was a silence filled with unspoken prayers, hesitant hope, a fragile promise of peace she wasn't sure she deserved. "Tomorrow," Mike said, his voice firm yet laced with gentleness, "we'll walk by the shore. The sea… it reminds us that it always returns even when the tide retreats. There's always renewal, Sarah. Always a second chance." She looked up, searching his eyes for the unwavering faith he possessed. She didn't feel it in herself, not yet. The belief felt like a distant star, obscured by a heavy cloud of self-doubt. But she was here. And for tonight, that was a start.

Setting down her mug, she leaned back, a sigh escaping her lips. For the first time in what felt like forever, she could breathe. Though still thick with sorrow, the air held a hint of hope. A tiny spark flickering in the darkness.

Port Angeles. Home. Or at least, the place where maybe—just maybe—she could piece herself back together. The lie tasted like ash in her mouth, but she swallowed it down. The bell above the door—*jingle*—shattered the afternoon's quiet. Sarah stepped into Wheeler's Hardware and Workshop, the air thick with sawdust and oil, hitting her like a punch to the gut. A good punch, though. Familiar. The aroma of a life she'd tried to bury—a life that felt both impossibly distant and achingly close. Her fingers traced the cold steel of a hammer head, the rough bristles of a paintbrush, the smooth heft of a screwdriver. Everything was exactly as she remembered it. The same comforting chaos. The same stubborn refusal to modernize. A sanctuary, standing in stark contrast to the frantic, soulless city she'd fled. But was it escape… or a cage of her own making?

And then she saw him. Caleb Martin. Hunched over a set of chisels, his broad shoulders tight with a tension Sarah recognized instantly. Years hadn't softened the sharp angles of his face, only deepened the lines etched by hard work and, she suspected, a whole lot of unspoken regrets. His dark hair, always a little too long, fell across his forehead as he meticulously examined each tool, his calloused thumb tracing the edge with the practiced ease of a master craftsman. The sight of him, so completely absorbed in his work, stirred something deep within her – a ghost of a terrifying and strangely comforting feeling.

Doubt gnawed at her. Was she doing the right thing, coming back? Was she strong enough to face him, to face "herself"? She took a shaky breath. This was it. No more running.

"Looking for something specific?" she asked, her voice lighter than she felt, a carefully constructed mask over the tremor of anxiety in her chest. He turned, his striking blue eyes widening in recognition. The silence that followed was thick, heavy with unspoken words and the ghost of a love she'd buried. A love that, despite everything, still held the power to both exhilarate and terrify her.

A slow smile touched his lips, softening the harsh lines of his face but not erasing the worry etched beneath. "Sarah?" he breathed, the question hanging between them. "I... I didn't know you were back." His voice was rough, laced with a guarded hope that mirrored her own. The years melted away, leaving only their past's raw, volatile energy. And the terrifying uncertainty of their future.

Neither did I, until recently," Sarah admitted, a hesitant smile playing on her lips. It felt brittle, and this smile, a fragile thing, quickly shattered. The years had etched lines around her eyes, a map of unspoken anxieties. They stood there, a chasm of time yawning between them. Caleb, the boy who'd once charmed his way out of trouble with a grin and a witty quip, held himself with a quiet strength now, a stillness that spoke of battles fought and won. A raw ache of longing, a memory of shared laughter, tightened in Sarah's chest. He hadn't changed as much as she'd expected, but then again, some things, she realized, never truly leave you.

He shifted the chisel in his calloused hands, the tool a familiar extension of himself. "Still working on those incredible pieces of yours?" His voice, rough around the edges, was a welcome sound. Sarah chuckled, a low, throaty sound. "It's been a while. Life... it gets in the way, you know?" The words hung heavy, hinting at a life less than fulfilling. A life she wasn't ready to unpack, not just yet. "And you? Still shaping wood into something beautiful?" she asked, her voice barely a whisper. She'd always admired his skill, the quiet dedication he poured into his craft.

He nodded, a thoughtful crease etching itself across his forehead. "Yeah, there's always something. Wood has a way of talking to you, if you listen. It's...honest." His gaze held hers for a moment longer than polite conversation demanded. "Patience was never my strong suit," she confessed, a self-deprecating laugh escaping her lips. The truth stung, a reminder of her impulsive nature, the choices she regretted. "Maybe not," he said, a ghost of a smile playing on his lips. "But I remember someone who could spend hours perfecting a lesson plan. Someone meticulous, someone... dedicated." He watched her, his gaze searching. The warmth of his teasing, the effortless ease of their conversation, was a lifeline in the turbulent sea of her uncertainty.

The years melted away, the familiar rhythm of their banter a soothing comfort to her frayed nerves. They walked down the aisle, their steps falling into an unspoken synchronicity. The silent history between them hung heavy in the air, a tangible connection transcending time. "Things have changed since you left," Caleb said, his voice low, the unspoken weight of his words a palpable thing. "Change is the only constant, isn't it?" Sarah replied, her green eyes flickering, a hidden fear beneath her composure. The unspoken question hung between them: how much had she changed? How much had he? He studied her, a storm of emotions churning in his eyes. "Seems so," he finally said, with unspoken regret and longing.

Reaching the checkout, Sarah hesitated. The air crackled with unspoken possibilities, a bridge waiting to be crossed. A dangerous bridge, one that might lead her to places she wasn't sure she was ready to go. "Maybe we could…" she began, her voice trembling slightly, her heart pounding a frantic rhythm against her ribs. The words caught in her throat. The past loomed, heavy and menacing. "Grab a coffee? Catch up?" Caleb finished for her, his voice steady, a quiet strength underlining his invitation. The unspoken invitation held a hint of desperation, mirroring her own need.

Relief washed over her, a fragile wave pushing back the tide of her apprehension. "Yeah," she whispered, "I'd like that." The bell above the door jingled as they stepped into the crisp autumn air. The aroma of woodsmoke and damp leaves, rich with memory, filled her lungs. Caleb led the way, his stride steady and sure, and as they entered the cozy embrace of the coffee shop, Sarah felt a flicker of hope—delicate yet stubborn—spark to life within her. The heat inside, mingled with the familiar fragrance of freshly brewed coffee, felt like a quiet promise. But what if that promise broke, as brittle as the smile she'd offered him earlier? The thought crept through her, a chill against the café's warmth.

The worn wooden table groaned a silent protest under their elbows, a testament to countless conversations spilled over coffee and time. Sarah's fingers, bone-white against the dark mug, tightened around the warm ceramic. It was a flimsy anchor in the storm brewing inside her. Caleb watched her, a familiar ache tightening in his chest. He'd known her since they were kids, building rickety tree houses and dreaming impossible dreams. "Remember that disaster we called a treehouse?" he asked, a ghost of a smile playing on his lips.

Sarah chuckled, a brittle sound that belied the tremor in her voice. "How could I forget? We were so sure we'd conquer gravity that afternoon."

"Your optimism was legendary," he teased, though the words felt thick with unspoken things. "We barely got the platform nailed before the whole thing came crashing down."

"Turns out," Sarah said, shaking her head, "good intentions are about as useful as toothpicks in a hurricane." The laugh died in her throat, replaced by a chilling silence.

"True," Caleb said, the grin fading. His gaze was sharp, assessing. "But I learned something that day—measure twice, cut once. Always have a plan." He paused; the unspoken hanging heavy between them. "Speaking of plans… what are yours now that you're back?" The question hung in the air, a lead weight. It wasn't about logistics; it was a lifeline, an invitation to share the burdens she'd been shouldering alone.

The unspoken was a fist in her gut. Sarah's gaze dropped to the swirling coffee. The dark liquid mirrored the turmoil within. "Still figuring it out," she whispered, the words barely audible above the café's low hum. Caleb nodded, a silent understanding passing between them.

"Take your time," he said softly. "Sometimes you gotta sit with the wood for a while before you know what it wants to become. Maybe life's the same."

Fragile as a butterfly's wing, a sliver of hope fluttered in her chest. Maybe he was right. Perhaps she didn't have to have all the answers. His hand reached across the table, his fingers brushing hers—a fleeting touch, yet grounding.

"You don't have to do this alone, Sarah."

She looked up, meeting his eyes. The boy she'd once known was gone, replaced by a man etched with strength, patience, and a kindness that cut through her carefully constructed defenses. A choked sob threatened. She fought it back, her eyes stinging. For the first time since her return, a crack appeared in the wall she'd built around her pain. Maybe, just maybe, she didn't have to carry it all.

The warmth of the mug did little to chase away the chill buried deep in Sarah's bones. The aroma of coffee drifted through the air, rich and familiar, yet powerless against the bitterness of memory clawing its way to the surface. She tightened her grip on the ceramic, using its solidity to anchor herself. Across from her, Caleb watched in that quiet way of his—a steady presence amid the storm still raging within her.

"It's strange being back," she said, her voice barely louder than the murmur of the café. "Port Angeles feels... like a place I dreamt up. Familiar, but distant. Like I don't belong here anymore."

Caleb didn't rush to fill the silence. He never did. He just *was* an anchor in the shifting tide of her thoughts. His eyes—steady, patient—never wavered from her face.

Sarah exhaled sharply, a breath that felt too thin for the weight pressing on her chest. "Jake... he was a hurricane." The words scraped her throat raw. "At first, it felt like flying. The intensity, the way he could make me feel like the only person in the world." She shook her head. "But then the winds changed. And suddenly, I was just... holding on. Trying not to be torn apart."

A single tear slipped down her cheek, hot against her cold skin. She let it fall.

"Leaving him—" Her voice broke. She swallowed, forced herself to push through. "It was like clawing my way out of a pit, one handful of dirt at a time. Every inch forward felt impossible. And some days... I still feel like I'm slipping."

Caleb's jaw tightened, but he didn't interrupt. When he finally spoke, his voice was low, steady. "You're not just climbing, Sarah. You're rebuilding. Taking back what was stolen. That takes more strength than most people ever find."

His words seeped into the cracks of her, filling places she hadn't realized were hollow. But doubt coiled in her gut, a quiet whisper of *what if?*

She looked at him then, really looked, and for a moment, she wasn't drowning. She was here, sitting across from a man who had always been solid ground beneath her feet.

"Thank you, Caleb," she said, barely more than a whisper. "For listening. For—just being here."

His fingers brushed hers, rough and calloused, yet impossibly gentle. The weight of the moment settled between them, heavy and unspoken. He searched her face, seeing more than she wanted to reveal. And then he spoke, his voice almost a confession.

"I've spent my life working with broken things," he said. "Wood that others would toss aside, too warped, too damaged. But sometimes, those pieces… they turn into something stronger than before. More beautiful because of what they've endured."

The words hit harder than they should have. Sarah sucked in a breath, something raw and painful tightening in her chest. Could she be remade? Did she even want to be?

The past clung to her, whispering its cruel certainty: *People don't change. They just break in different ways.*

She pushed back her chair, the legs scraping against the floor, sharp against the hush that had fallen between them. She traced her fingers over the table's surface, feeling the worn grooves of its history beneath her touch. A grounding act, a moment of hesitation.

"Caleb." Her voice was steadier now, a thread of something unyielding woven through the fear. "Thank you. For listening. For being here."

The words were small, but they felt like the first bricks in something new, something fragile but real.

Caleb held her gaze. There was something in his eyes—understanding, patience, something deeper than promises. When he finally spoke, his voice was quiet but firm, as sure as the earth beneath them.

"Always."

A simple word. A vow, unspoken but understood.

Sarah nodded, but deep inside, the doubt lingered.

Could he always be there?

Could she let him?

The answer, for now, remained just out of reach.

They stepped out, and the coffee shop bell gave a small, hesitant chime as if uncertain whether to mark their exit. Outside, the Port Angeles sunset raged across the sky, a breathtaking riot of crimson and violet. The light spilled over the town, coloring the buildings in hues of absolution. Sarah inhaled deeply. The salt-laced air burned a little, a sharp contrast to the lingering bitterness of memory. The ocean murmured, rhythmic, unbroken—an echo of time moving forward, of change.

For so long, she had curled inward, retreating like a hermit crab into the safety of its shell. But now, something stirred. An ache, a pull, a whisper of a life she had nearly lost. She wasn't sure if it was courage or desperation.

Caleb shifted beside her; his hands buried deep in the pockets of his flannel. The evening air had a bite, but he didn't notice. He watched her with that quiet, steady presence that made it hard to look away.

"See you at the workshop?" His voice was casual, but underneath it lay something else. A thread of hope. A plea he didn't dare voice.

The workshop wasn't just a place to shape wood; it was where he made sense of the world, carving order from chaos. The aroma of pine, the scrape of the chisel against the grain—it was the language he understood best, the only way he knew how to heal. And maybe, just maybe, it could do the same for her.

Sarah hesitated. Not out of reluctance but out of fear. A familiar, well-worn fear that told her she didn't belong anywhere, not anymore. The weight of the past nearly yanked her back. But Caleb was still looking at her, waiting. Solid, unwavering.

"Yes," she said finally. A single word, but it felt like crossing a chasm. Her smile, hesitant yet real, warmed something deep inside him. "I'd like that."

At the corner, they parted ways. The streetlamp buzzed to life, casting long, shifting shadows over the pavement. Caleb turned once, his silhouette sharp against the smoldering horizon. For a second, she wanted to call him back. But she didn't.

She walked on; each step deliberate. The fear, the gnawing self-doubt, the ghosts of yesterday—they weren't gone. They would never be gone. But they had shrunk from boulders pressing against her chest to pebbles in her shoes. Manageable. Bearable. And something else, something small but defiant, had taken root inside her: hope.

Not the delicate, fleeting kind, but the raw, stubborn variety that clings to life even in the most barren soil.

The last sliver of the sun melted away, leaving behind a sky bruised in deep purples and angry oranges. Sarah didn't look back. She had spent too many years staring over her shoulder, trapped by the weight of what she had lost. But the past had no power over her unless she let it. And she wouldn't. Not anymore.

The wind kicked up, sharp and sudden, curling around her like a warning. A shiver traced her spine. It wasn't just the cold.

A twig snapped.

She froze, her pulse slamming against her ribs. Slowly, she turned. The street behind her lay empty, but the shadows stretched long and uncertain—too uncertain.

Her fingers curled into fists. "Show yourself."

The words barely scraped past her lips. The silence swallowed them whole.

Sarah's breath came faster, shallower. Maybe it was nothing. Perhaps it was paranoia, the echoes of old terror playing tricks on her. But she knew better. Knew what it was to be hunted. Knew what it was to be seen by something she couldn't see in return.

Her grip tightened around the strap of her bag. She forced her feet to move. Forward. Always forward.

But she wasn't alone.

She never was.

CHAPTER 5

The Stranger in the Workshop

CALEB'S FINGERS TRACED the unfinished wood, the grain alive beneath his touch. The Stations of the Cross, a testament to his father's faith and skill, mocked him with their silent incompleteness. The aroma of pine and cedar, once a source of comfort, now hung in the air like a shroud, a suffocating reminder of his father's legacy—a legacy he felt woefully inadequate to uphold. Doubt gnawed at him, a relentless worm boring into the core of his self-belief. Could he, a novice in the face of his father's mastery, dare to finish this? The weight of it pressed down, a physical burden.

A sharp crunch shattered his reverie—gravel beneath boots. He whirled around as sunlight slashed through the open workshop door, casting long beams that caught the suspended shimmer of sawdust in the air. A tall, imposing figure stood framed in the doorway, carved into the brightness like some solemn prophet stepping out of scripture.

"Good afternoon," the voice boomed, rich and steady, yet surprisingly gentle. "Joshua Shepherd."

The name resonated, striking a deep, unexpected chord within Caleb. He felt a prickle of unease, something ancient and unknown stirring within him.

Shepherd stepped inside, carrying the tang of salt and pine, the very essence of the sea clinging to his worn clothes. Caleb, his blue eyes narrowed, remained silent. Strangers didn't just wander into this isolated corner of Port Angeles. Shepherd's gaze swept over the carvings, lingering respectfully on the unfinished Stations.

"Remarkable work," he murmured.

Caleb's breath hitched. "Not mine," he rasped, the words thick with a lifetime of unspoken doubts. "My father's."

Shepherd nodded, moving closer. His eyes focused on the half-carved hands of Christ; the sorrow etched yet still latent within the untouched wood.

"Then I see a father who knew his craft, and a son who carries the same gift, whether he admits it or not."

Caleb's jaw tightened. The man's insight and uncanny accuracy felt invasive and strangely validating. A crippling self-doubt had overshadowed years of watching his father transform wood into devotion.

"What if I fail? What if I desecrate something sacred?" The thought sent a chill down his spine.

Shepherd's calloused fingers gently touched a carved figure, a silent prayer in his touch. "I'd like to help, if you'll allow it."

The offer hung in the air, simple yet weighty. Caleb studied him—this Shepherd, with his steady gaze and the quiet confidence of a man who'd faced life's storms head-on. He wasn't just a passerby; there was a depth to him, a familiarity tinged with something... otherworldly. He seemed to radiate both toil and transcendence.

"Help?" Caleb echoed; his voice laced with skepticism. "Why?" His gaze challenged Shepherd, demanding an answer, a justification for this unexpected intrusion into his grief and his private struggle.

Joshua's smile was a crooked thing, knowing, hinting at battles fought and won. "Ever seen a tree on a windswept hill, Caleb? Battered, stripped bare, almost broken? But it's still there, isn't it? Roots deeper, stronger than before."

Caleb's jaw tightened, the metaphor a punch to the gut. He'd felt like that tree. Years of bending, of storms he'd weathered alone since his father just disappeared. The silence of the workshop once filled with his father's laughter and the rhythmic rasp of his tools, now screamed emptiness. He hadn't admitted it to anyone, not even himself, but the loneliness was a physical weight crushing him.

Joshua's voice, quiet but steady, cut through the silence. "Resilience ain't about never falling, son. It's about getting back up. Every damn time."

The air hung heavy, thick with the aroma of sawdust and cedar, dense with unspoken questions. Caleb swallowed the war inside him—a raging inferno. Could he trust this man? More importantly, could he trust himself to take this leap of faith? His fingers tightened around the worn handle of a chisel, the familiar weight offering a flicker of comfort. His father used to say the wood whispered secrets to those who listened. Maybe it was more than just the wood speaking now. Perhaps something else was whispering... something greater.

He exhaled, the breath shaky, and looked up at Joshua. There was no pressure in the man's eyes, only a stark, raw offer. A choice. Fear coiled in his stomach, a cold knot of doubt. But beneath it, something else stirred—a flicker of hope, a desperate need for something... more.

"Alright," Caleb finally rasped, his voice barely a breath. "Let's see what you can do."

Joshua moved deeper into the workshop, the light shifting, painting the floor with long, dancing shadows. For the first time in months, Caleb felt a shift in the atmosphere, more than just a stranger's presence. It was something older, something... holy. A story waiting to be carved from the raw materials of his faith, his doubts, and his desperate need for redemption.

This was just the beginning, he knew. But the beginning of what?

He paused at the workshop door, the familiar trace of cedar and pine stirring a bittersweet ache in his chest. This was where he'd grown up—where wood shavings danced at his feet, and the rhythm of his father's tools became a lullaby. But now, a hollow stillness lingered in the place where his father once stood. His father was gone. The workshop had become a mausoleum of memories, a stark reminder of loss and the heavy uncertainty that had settled in its wake.

His heart hammered a frantic rhythm against his ribs. Could he face what awaited him inside? The air was thick with the essence of sawdust and old faith, a presence Joshua drew in with familiar comfort. His gaze, dark and sharp as a hawk's, swept over the unfinished Stations of the Cross. These weren't just carvings—they were cries of devotion; prayers etched into wood. He ran a calloused thumb across the grain of a tormented Christ, a silent conversation with the ghost of the artist.

Caleb stood rigid, arms clamped across his chest, his skepticism coiled tight beneath his skin. Threads of golden light sliced through the workshop, catching on the floating remnants of sawdust like the unsettled thoughts churning in his gut. "Your hands know wood," he muttered, the words sharp-edged with reluctant respect, barely masking the resentment smoldering just beneath.

Joshua met his gaze, a ghost of a smile playing on his lips. "Many years," he replied, his voice low and resonant. "Each piece whispers its story, waiting to be released."

They stood before the third station—Christ's first fall. The figure was brutal, raw, and unfinished. The chisel lay abandoned, its edge dull, reflecting Caleb's weariness and fall from grace. A lifetime of unspoken expectations weighed him down, a legacy he hadn't wanted.

"May I?" Joshua's request was a plea laced with respect and a hint of something deeper, something Caleb couldn't quite name.

Caleb nodded curtly, his throat tight. He watched, mesmerized, as Joshua picked up the chisel, his movements fluid, effortless, almost mystical. The rasp of the blade on wood was a heartbeat in the heavy silence. Shavings curled like dying leaves, a silent testament to the years of skill, the patience honed by grief. Caleb couldn't tear his gaze away. It wasn't just skill; it was a communion, a revelation.

He saw his frustrated anger reflected in the unfinished lines of the carving, the very wood itself seemingly yearning for completion. "I never understood," Caleb breathed, his voice barely audible above the rhythmic scraping, "how my father poured so much of himself into these... these things. It's like he left pieces of his soul behind."

The words tumbled out, raw and unexpected, dredged from a place he'd long buried. A sudden, sharp grief clawed at him. The unspoken weight of his father's expectations and his failure to live up to them choked him.

Joshua paused, the chisel hovering. The silence stretched thick with unspoken emotions. He understood. He knew the burden of legacy.

He knew the price of devotion. "Perhaps that is the gift," Joshua said softly, his voice full of a quiet understanding that resonated deep within Caleb's soul, "to leave something that echoes long after you're gone. Something that offers solace, even in suffering."

The words were a hammer blow, shattering the walls Caleb had built around his heart. He saw his father's worn hands, the quiet devotion in his eyes, not as a burden but as a testament to faith, love, and a life of fierce, quiet intensity. The doubt that had choked him began to loosen, replaced by a dawning understanding, a fragile hope, and the stirrings of a long-dormant connection to his father's legacy. The chisel continued its work, shaping wood, grief, and Caleb himself.

Sweat beaded on Caleb's brow, the tang of sawdust heavy in the air, clashing with the faint, reverent aroma of the aged wood. He slammed his chisel down, the sharp clang ricocheting through the cramped workshop. The half-finished carving lay forsaken—a raw emblem of his rising frustration. Perfection, that unreachable ideal, gnawed at him once more.

Joshua, his weathered face etched with the wisdom of countless sunrises, picked up fine-grit sandpaper, his movements slow and deliberate as if handling a sacred relic. He worked on a piece depicting Simon of Cyrene, the weight of the cross heavy on his shoulders, mirroring the weight Caleb felt crushing his spirit.

"Every piece has its story," Joshua murmured, his voice a low rumble, more a statement to himself than to Caleb. "Like that old master, the one who chased perfection like a phantom."

Caleb grunted; his gaze fixed on the discarded wood. "Did he ever catch it?" he asked, the words sharp, laced with a bitterness he couldn't quite mask. He knew the answer and understood the futility of the chase. He'd spent years chasing that same phantom, a ghost of his father's legacy, leaving only hollowness in its wake.

Joshua chuckled—a warm, earthy sound that cut through the tension. "Hell no. He found a knothole, a damn ugly knothole, tried to fix it, sand it down, but the wood fought back. He was ready to toss the whole thing." He ran a finger over the Simon of Cyrene carving, the gesture gentle, almost reverent. "But his daughter… she saw something else. She saw the way the light danced in that imperfection, how it made the whole piece sing. That 'flawed' piece? Became his masterpiece."

The parable hit Caleb like a punch to the gut, the unspoken words echoing his self-doubt. He stared at his calloused hands, the years of relentless work etched into his very being. He'd thrown away so much, convinced his work was unworthy, a failure marred by imperfections he couldn't erase. The shame burned, hot and sharp.

"Sometimes," Caleb rasped, his voice tight with emotion, "the truth... it hides in the cracks we try to fill."

Joshua's dark eyes met his, unwavering and filled with a quiet understanding. "That craftsman learned something, son. The imperfections? They tell the truest story. They're not flaws; they're the proof it was lived."

Caleb swallowed, the lump in his throat tightening. He picked up his chisel, its weight suddenly different and lighter. He ran a finger over the rough edges of his unfinished work. It wasn't a failure but a story waiting to be told. With its dips and hesitations, the unfinished wood suddenly felt alive, reflecting his struggle. A quiet peace settled over him, a fragile thing but real. He felt it, finally, a break in the suffocating grief that had clung to him since his father's death.

This workshop wasn't just a place of burden; it was a legacy, a link to his father, and a place where he, too, could shape something—not just wood, but something deeper. Something real. Something true. Caleb's smile, genuine for the first time since Joshua's arrival, felt brittle, a thin crack in a wall of grief.

"Thank you," he rasped, the words catching in his throat. "For... reminding me." The unspoken hung heavy: *reminding me that there's still beauty, even in the wreckage.*

Joshua's smile was a slow burn, ancient wisdom in his eyes that made Caleb's stomach clench. He saw it then, the understanding that transcended words, a shared burden of unfinished business etched into their souls. Joshua's nod was a silent acknowledgment of the brutal climb ahead.

Turning back to the wood, Caleb's hands—usually trembling with doubt—were steady. His heart, however, pounded a frantic rhythm against his ribs. The sharp tang of pine and cedar filled the air, almost suffocating in its intensity. The afternoon light, a cruel mockery of warmth, sliced through the haze of fine particles suspended like memories too stubborn to settle. Outside, the wind howled—not a gentle whisper, but a mournful cry that echoed the emptiness tearing at him.

Silly, silhouetted against the dying sun, Joshua seemed to absorb the workshop's chaos, a still point in a swirling vortex. Caleb had seen countless craftsmen, but Joshua… Joshua was different. It wasn't just skill but reverence, a fierce devotion bordering on the religious. The way he moved, a prayer carved into flesh and bone.

"Who… who are you, really?" Caleb blurted, the question a desperate plea choked out in a breathy whisper.

Joshua's gaze remained fixed on the wood in his hands. "Someone who answers the call of the wood… and the Maker." His voice was calm, devoid of theatrics, a simple statement of undeniable fact.

Caleb let out a harsh laugh, the sound brittle and hollow. "Vague much?" he scoffed, but the curiosity gnawed at him, a persistent ache. He knew some questions couldn't be answered with words; they demanded a lifetime of living.

The silence that followed wasn't empty. It pulsed with unspoken truths, heavy and thick as the musk of aged oak. Caleb's attention snapped back to the half-finished carving—his father's legacy, a weight that settled on his shoulders like a mantle too large to bear. He could almost feel his father's calloused hands guiding his own, the ghost of his touch lingering on the worn tools. This wasn't just wood; it was an unfinished symphony, a story suspended in time, waiting for his flawed, grief-stained hands to either complete it—or destroy it. The pressure was immense. He had to finish it. For his father. For himself.

Caleb's hand trembled as he picked up the brittle parchment. His father's faded script felt like a ghost's touch, each looping letter a painful echo of a life cut short. A bitter taste rose in his throat. "These carvings… they ain't all he left," Caleb rasped, his voice cracking. "He wrote letters. To Ma, to me. Never sent 'em."

He ran a finger over the script, the ink barely clinging to the paper. "Why? If he wanted to say it, why the hell didn't he just say it?" The unspoken words hung heavy in the air, thick as the sawdust swirling around them.

Joshua, his face etched with a quiet understanding that mirrored Caleb's turmoil, finally met his gaze. "Sometimes, son," he said, his voice low and gravelly, "the things we keep bottled up... they're the heaviest burdens we carry."

A choked sob hit Caleb. "So that's why you're here? To help me carry what he couldn't?" The question felt desperate and fragile; a prayer whispered into the silence of the workshop. Hope sparked within him, a flicker he hadn't dared to acknowledge.

Joshua's calloused fingers brushed against the nearly finished carving. "Maybe," he said, his tone gentle but firm, "or maybe I'm here to help you carve your own damn path. Through the wood, through the memories. Every cut, every stroke... it's part of letting go."

Caleb exhaled, the pent-up air whooshing from his lungs like a sigh of relief. The rhythmic scrape of chisels resumed, a shared rhythm, a silent conversation between grief and healing. They worked in tandem, their movements falling into a shared harmony, shaping not just wood but Caleb's soul's raw, jagged edges.

The chisel froze in Caleb's hand. He watched Joshua, the setting sun painting the workshop in hues of amber and shadow. Joshua's face, though, remained an island of calm amidst the swirling dust motes, his gaze fixed on something beyond the physical world.

"This work," Joshua murmured, his voice a low rumble, "it ain't just art, Caleb. It's a testament. To faith. To the struggle of it all." He looked at Caleb, his eyes sharp, knowing. "Your old man left you something, not just in those words, but in this unfinished piece. That burden of unspoken things... it ain't yours alone to carry."

A deep ache, long dormant, stirred within Caleb. A tiny seed of hope pushing its way through the cracked earth of his sorrow. He remembered Father Mike's sermons—shared burdens, forgiveness, faith bridging the chasm between past pain and future healing. He'd heard those words countless times, but in the quiet sanctuary of the workshop, with Joshua at his side, they finally took root. They burrowed deep, anchoring themselves to the very core of his being.

Forgiveness," Joshua said, his voice rough-edged like the wood they worked, "ain't some polished sermon. It's like this carving – raw, messy, and a fight." His calloused hands moved over the rough-hewn wood, tracing the grain. "Takes patience, chip by chip, to get at the heart of it. To find something...pure amidst the wreckage." Caleb's grip on the chisel tightened, then loosened, the wood resisting him as much as his bitter memories. He'd been a fool to let the anger fester, to bury himself in self-recrimination. This wasn't just about his father but about "him," about escaping the shadow that had haunted him for years. The wood seemed to yield a little with each hesitant cut, mirroring the thawing of his own frozen grief. He was shaping the stations, but more than that, he was shaping himself, chipping away at the hardened shell of resentment.

Twilight bled into the workshop, painting long shadows across the walls. Their chisels' rhythmic "tap-tap-tap" became a heartbeat, a shared rhythm pulsing through the silence. Caleb worked alongside Joshua, their movements mirroring each other, a silent communion in the face of grief. The sanctuary of the workshop felt less like a refuge and more like a crucible, forging something new from the old.

"Joshua," Caleb finally said, slightly shaky but with newfound strength, "I... I don't know why you're here. But I need this." The words were raw, admitting the vulnerability he'd been fighting against for so long. Joshua paused, wiping his hands on a stained rag, a ghost of a smile playing on his lips. "Healing ain't a straight path, Caleb. It's a maze. But gratitude? That's your compass." He paused, his gaze settling on Caleb. "Sometimes, the biggest steps forward come from the smallest acts of letting go." Caleb nodded, the weight of the past settling not as an anchor dragging him down, but as a foundation, a testament to the battles fought. He would finish the stations. He would face the grief and not be defined by it. The wood reflected that, yielding only to persistent effort.

Joshua hung the tools with deliberate care, the quiet movements full of a strange reverence. Caleb watched, a slow understanding dawning. This man, this stranger, hadn't just taught him to carve. He'd helped him carve out a path through his soul. "Thank you," Caleb repeated, the words finally fully realized, filled with a depth he hadn't known he possessed. The simple words hung in the air, heavy with unspoken emotion. Joshua's smile was gentle, a quiet affirmation in the gathering dusk. They had carved more than just wood. They'd carved a pathway to hope into the fabric of the workshop, a testament to the promise of redemption found not in what was left undone but, in the willingness, to finish the story, no matter how hard it got.

The last sliver of sun bled through the workshop's grimy windows, igniting the suspended haze in the air with a fiery gold. Joshua Shepherd, outlined in the fading light, looked more like a ghost than a man. This wasn't goodbye—not truly. It felt more like the hush before a storm's return, a breath held too long. A promise lingered in the space between them, fragile as a threadbare hymn. "I'll be back," Joshua said, his voice a low rumble, each word weighted like stone. His eyes locked with Caleb's, a silent conversation crackling between them—a desperate plea met by reluctant acceptance.

With a curt nod, he was gone, swallowed by the encroaching darkness. The crunch of his boots on the gravel was a fading echo, lost to the sigh of the wind whispering through the eaves. Caleb stood rooted; the silence heavy, thick as treacle. It wasn't emptiness; it was a suffocating weight of unspoken things, a grief that gnawed at him, a fear that clawed at his insides. His gaze drifted to the Stations of the Cross, their sorrowful figures seeming to writhe in the gloom. Each meticulously carved detail screamed of agony, sacrifice, and love that defied comprehension. They weren't just wood and shadow; they were witnesses to his soul's turmoil.

A ragged breath hitched in Caleb's chest. He moved, his fingers gliding over the worn wood of his father's workbench—every groove etched with memory. The air carried the trace of sawdust, pine, and cedar—a potent blend of earth and spirit, like a whisper of his father lingering in the grain. The tools weren't just tools; they were extensions of the man himself, fragments of a legacy Caleb felt both unworthy of and bound to carry. A legacy shadowed by the same darkness that plagued Joshua. His father's chisel lay untouched, yet warm—as if memory alone had kept it alive. He picked it up, its weight settling in his palm like a familiar, solemn truth.

It wasn't just a tool; it was a weapon, a means of creation, redemption, or maybe just a way to silence the screams in his head. He found the mallet, its smooth surface whispering tales of countless hours spent in this very workshop, hours now stretching into a void of absence and sorrow. He gripped it tight, knuckles white. The hollow ache in his chest was a cavernous void he desperately hoped to fill. He turned to the unfinished panel, the eleventh station – Jesus nailed to the cross. The scene was a brutal sketch, the outlines crude, unfinished, mirroring the state of his spirit.

Caleb placed the chisel against the wood, his breath hitching in his throat. Doubt, a cold serpent, coiled in his gut. Could he truly honor his father's legacy? Could he bear the weight of this unfinished masterpiece, this unfinished life? With a fierce breath, he swung the mallet. The first chips of wood fell like tears, a silent promise of creation and a desperate bid to confront the past and build a future from the wreckage of his grief.

The rasp of steel on cedar shrieked a counterpoint to the frantic hammering of Caleb's heart. Each mallet blow was a desperate prayer, a frantic plea carved into the wood grain. But doubt, a rabid rat gnawing at his guts, whispered insidious lies, echoing Joshua's chilling words: "Imperfection. Grace." Lies! He needed perfection, a flawless Christ to wash away the stain of his life, a life-stained crimson with choices he couldn't undo. The crushing weight of guilt eased only with each precise cut, each meticulously shaped contour of the outstretched hand. This wasn't craftsmanship; it was a brutal, self-inflicted penance.

"Lead me," he breathed, the words raw, a confession choked out in the suffocating silence of his workshop. "Show me, God. Show me the beauty... in the "unfinished"." The lie tasted like ash in his mouth. Unfinished meant failure. He glanced at the space where Joshua had stood, the memory of the stranger's unsettling calm a bitter pill. Resilience? Grace? Joshua hadn't carried "his" burden. He hadn't lived with "his" ghosts.

Outside, the indifferent stars pricked the velvet night. Indifference was a luxury Caleb couldn't afford. He needed answers, not platitudes. The past wasn't just scars; it was a brand seared onto his soul that burned with the heat of a thousand regrets. He slammed the chisel down, the sound shattering the silence. He'd poured his grief and guilt into this carving, but it wasn't enough. The Christ figure remained a hollow shell, a mocking testament to his inadequacy.

Fear, a razor-sharp shard of ice, pierced the quiet sanctuary. "Damn it all," he snarled, the words a raw, guttural whisper. "What if I "can't" carve my way to redemption? What if this is all… pointless?" The doubt was a tide, threatening to drag him under, to drown him in the black depths of despair.

But then, a flicker of defiance ignited within him, a stubborn ember refusing to be extinguished. He wouldn't let it win. He wouldn't let the past dictate his future nor let Joshua's cryptic pronouncements be his epitaph. He picked up the mallet, the cedar surprisingly solid beneath his calloused hands—a grounding force in the maelstrom of his soul.

The rhythmic thud of the mallet, a frantic heartbeat against the stillness of Port Angeles, became a testament not to surrender but to stubborn, desperate defiance. He would carve out of the darkness, even if it killed him. He had to. He had to prove Joshua wrong. He had to prove "himself" right.

ACT 2

CARVING THROUGH PAIN AND UNEARTHING TRUTH

CHAPTER 6

Shadows That Follow

SARAH MARTIN'S VOICE, a low hum of authority laced with quiet warmth, resonated through the classroom. She wasn't just lecturing; she was weaving a spell, each carefully chosen word a thread in the tapestry of history. Her students, a kaleidoscope of bright, curious eyes, hung on every syllable. This wasn't just a job but a lifeline, a desperate attempt to outrun the ghosts that still haunted her. The stories of past battles – the triumphs and heart-wrenching losses – were a solace, a way to connect with something larger than her fractured self.

"History isn't just dusty old facts," she said, her voice catching slightly, betraying the tremor of emotion beneath the surface. "It's a mirror reflecting our choices, a compass guiding us toward... or away from... disaster." She looked at each student, searching their faces for understanding. This wasn't just about dates and names. It was about survival, about learning from the mistakes of others so she wouldn't repeat them. A pregnant silence filled the room, heavier than the afternoon sun pouring through the dusty windows. Then, a collective nod rippled through the students, a shared understanding transcending the dry facts.

Sarah felt a pang of something akin to hope. Maybe, just maybe, she could escape the shadows clinging to her. Perhaps she could build something good here, in Port Angeles—something real. She moved among the desks, the familiar trace of old paper and youthful energy wrapping around her like a well-worn quilt. A glance at a girl's essay—a hesitant hand, but a promising voice—prompted a quiet word of encouragement. A boy's eager question about the Peloponnesian War—a question that mirrored her lifelong struggle with the unseen battles—spurred a lengthy discussion, a shared exploration of the devastating consequences of unchecked ambition. She thrived in these moments, these fleeting connections, these small victories that kept the darkness at bay.

The bell, a harsh clang that shattered the fragile peace, jolted her back to the present. The rush of students, a chaotic symphony of backpacks and hurried goodbyes, momentarily washed away the fragile hope. She smiled, offering encouragement, each a tiny shield against the looming threat that lurked just beyond the doorway.

The last student vanished into the hallway, and Sarah let out a shaky breath. The momentary calm was a deceptive illusion, a brief reprieve before the storm. Then she saw him. Jake Macall. Standing at the edge of the schoolyard, silhouetted against the fading light, he was a specter from her past, a palpable weight pressing down on her chest. The cheerful chatter of the children faded, replaced by the frantic drumming of her heart. The golden light of the afternoon seemed to dim, swallowed by the chilling shadow he cast.

"Dammit," she whispered, her voice barely audible above the rising tide of dread. The quiet contentment was gone, replaced by a cold, hard knot of fear. He was here. And this time, she didn't know if she could escape.

He always had this effect on her. Even now, years later. Sarah's grip tightened on the papers, her breath catching in her throat. The memories slammed into her – the whispered fights that bled into the dead of night, the icy silence that stretched between them for months, the slammed doors echoing in her memory, the bruises she'd hidden under long sleeves and forced smiles. The ghosts of those nights clawed at her, threatening to drag her under.

Jake stood rigid; a tremor barely contained in his hands. Thinner, yes, but still imposing, a coiled spring of suppressed energy. His shoulders were as tight as a drum, his stance military-sharp – every inch of him screamed of a war fought and lost within. His dark eyes, intense, searched hers, unwilling to let go.

Sarah swallowed, a lump of bitter resentment choking her. Nothing he could say mattered. Nothing he could offer hadn't already been left behind in the dust of their shattered past. And yet, here he was, a ghost from a life she'd buried, standing at the edge of the sanctuary she'd painstakingly built. A dozen accusations, a hundred questions, raged inside her, but she held them captive.

She squared her shoulders, her fingers white around the strap of her satchel, clinging to it like a lifeline. He had no business here. Not in this quiet coastal town, not in this school brimming with innocent laughter, not in "her" life, a life she'd finally begun to reclaim. But his presence, a toxic shadow, threatened to shatter the fragile peace she'd fought so hard to build.

She stepped outside, the cold ocean wind a physical blow against her skin. The cries of the gulls were a cruel counterpoint to the heavy silence between them, thick with unspoken accusations and simmering resentment. Jake remained motionless, a statue carved from regret and hidden intentions. She couldn't read him, and the uncertainty gnawed at her.

"What do you want, Jake?" Her voice was steady, a carefully constructed mask hiding the turmoil within.

He hesitated, a flicker of something – remorse? Doubt? – crossing his face before vanishing. "I just…" He stopped, breathing hard, the words a struggle to force out. "I needed to see you."

A chill deeper than the ocean wind settled in her bones. She'd spent years waiting for those words, longing for them, and now? Now, they were hollow, meaningless.

"You don't get to do this," she said, the quietness of her tone belying the steel in her voice. "Not here. Not now."

The years of hurt and betrayal welled up, a bitter tide threatening to drown her carefully constructed peace. This wasn't just about seeing him; this was about him shattering everything she'd fought to rebuild. The future she'd carved out for herself, one painstaking day at a time, hung in the balance.

His jaw tightened. "Sarah, please," he rasped, the words catching in his throat. The plea was raw, desperate, starkly contrasting to the controlled anger simmering beneath the surface.

She shook her head, her chin lifting in defiance. "No." The single word was a stone wall, a finality that echoed the years of silent battles fought within her. Gone was the woman who would melt at the sound of his voice, the woman who had once believed his every word. That Sarah was buried deep, a casualty of heartbreak and a relentless fight for survival.

Jake took a step closer, and the air around him carried a familiar blend of woodsmoke and something else—something uniquely his that stirred old memories. A wave of nausea surged within her. She stepped back, each movement tearing at her resolve. This wasn't just about him; it was about who she had become and who she refused to be again. It wasn't about love or forgiveness anymore; it was about survival.

"Whatever ghosts brought you here," she breathed, her voice tight with the effort of maintaining control, "they won't win."

The weight of his gaze pressed down, heavy and suffocating, as if he were trying to wish her back into the past, to the woman she'd left behind. One step forward, and she'd be lost in the undertow of their history; one step back, and all her hard-won gains would crumble.

The wind clawed at Sarah's hair, whipping salt into her eyes, stinging her skin. A shudder rippled through her—not from the cold, but from the weight of everything pressing down at once. The past, sharp and merciless, surged through her like a tide she couldn't fight.

Eggshell nights. Bruises that took too long to fade. Words that cut deeper than fists.

She thought she had escaped. Thought she was free. But here he was. Again.

Jake stood too close, his presence a tether she had spent years trying to sever.

His smirk was a ghost from another life, the same one he wore when he would apologize—when he would swear it was the last time. When she was naïve enough to believe him.

No.

She would never be that woman again.

Sarah forced air into her lungs, squared her shoulders. She could do this. She had to.

But before she could speak, a voice sliced through the tension.

"Mrs. Rayburn-Macall?"

Sarah's head snapped up, her heart lurching at the unexpected intrusion.

Helen Thompson.

The woman stood with the quiet poise of someone who had seen things, who understood the weight of unsaid words. Her sharp, assessing gaze flicked from Sarah to Jake, missing nothing.

Sarah swallowed hard, a sudden wave of shame curling at the edges of her thoughts. She hated this. Hated how easily fear could unravel her resolve.

"Everything alright?" Helen's voice was careful, but there was something beneath it. Something dangerous.

Jake shifted beside her, his casual stance a lie. Sarah recognized the tension in his jaw, the flicker of calculation in his eyes. He was waiting. Measuring.

Sarah forced herself to nod, even as her pulse drummed an erratic rhythm. *Lie. Lie. Lie.*

"Just... unexpected." The words scraped her throat like broken glass.

Helen didn't move. Didn't blink.

"Jake," she said flatly. *"Is he bothering you?"*

A simple question. A lifeline.

Sarah's breath caught, pride warring with panic. If she admitted the truth, what then? What did it change?

Jake's low chuckle made her stomach lurch. *"That's cute,"* he muttered, his smirk widening. *"You running to someone else to fight your battles now, Sarah?"*

The words hit their mark, but this time, they didn't burrow deep. This time, they burned away something else—something small and tired and *done*.

Sarah lifted her chin. *"Get out of my way."*

Jake's smile faltered, just a flicker, but she saw it.

Helen did, too.

Without hesitation, she pulled out her phone, her movements crisp, decisive. The glow of the screen cast sharp shadows on her face.

"Caleb, it's Helen. I'm at the school with Sarah. She needs you. It's urgent."

Sarah barely registered the rest.

Caleb.

The name landed like an anchor in storm-tossed waters.

For the first time since she had laid eyes on Jake again, Sarah felt something other than fear.

She felt the promise of *safety*.

Helen tucked the phone away, her expression unreadable. But her voice was firm.

"He's on his way."

And for the first time in a long time, Sarah let herself believe that she wasn't alone.

The rumble of an engine shattered the stillness, a distant growl that morphed into the familiar roar of Caleb's truck. The sound was a promise, a tangible manifestation of her hope, and a painful reminder of her weakness. Caleb: her rock, her steady hand in the storm.

The truck screeched to a halt, the silence that followed thick and heavy. The door creaked open, and Caleb emerged, his presence a solid wall against the encroaching darkness. He was a sculpted oak, every inch of him radiating strength and quiet power. Years spent wrestling with wood, shaping it into something beautiful and strong, had forged him into something unshakeable. Something Sarah desperately needed.

The long shadows of the setting sun stretched across the schoolyard, a fragile truce between Sarah and the ghosts that relentlessly pursued her. The air crackled with unspoken fear and anticipation.

Caleb's eyes, the blue so familiar it ached, met hers. The unspoken question hung between them, thick as the humid air clinging to the Louisiana night: *Are you safe?* She didn't need words. He knew her better than she knew herself. The tremor in her hand, the way her breath hitched – he saw it all.

Then his gaze shifted, the change as brutal as a slammed door.

Jake.

Jake straightened, a sneer twisting his lips. The air crackled. "Well, well, Martin. What brings you to this little…rendezvous?" His voice dripped with a venomous sarcasm Sarah knew all too well. The memories, sharp and bitter, clawed at her.

Caleb's voice, low and steady, cut through the tension. "Making sure everything's alright. And you need to leave." The words were simple, yet the iron in his tone was unmistakable. This wasn't a request.

Jake scoffed, taking a step closer, the **reek of stale beer and simmering rage** washing over Sarah. "Like hell I will. This is between me and Sarah." His voice, a dangerous growl, echoed the storm brewing inside him. "This is my woman." The unspoken words hung heavy.

Caleb didn't flinch. He moved, a silent predator, placing himself between them. His body was a solid wall, a shield against the fury radiating from Jake. "Right now," Caleb said, his voice unwavering, "it's between you and me. And I'm telling you, she doesn't want you here."

Jake's eyes darted to Sarah, searching for a crack in her resolve, a flicker of doubt to exploit. He found nothing but the cold, hard stare of a woman who'd finally had enough. *Since she asked for my help*, the unspoken words hung between them, a silent declaration of war.

Rage contorted Jake's face, but beneath the fury, something else flickered—a ghost of regret, a splinter of the man he used to be. His fists clenched so tight his knuckles blanched, and his breath came in ragged gasps. Silent and still under the dimming sky, the schoolyard seemed to mock him with its placid normalcy, starkly contrasting the war raging inside him.

Caleb stood firm, an unshakable force against the storm before him. "Go home, Jake," his voice was quiet but heavy with meaning, each syllable deliberate. "Sort yourself out."

It wasn't just a command. It was a plea. A bridge stretched across the widening chasm between them.

Sarah held her breath. Would he fight? Would the dam break, and the torrent of old wounds and fresh rage consume them all?

For a fleeting moment, something cracked in Jake's eyes—recognition, guilt, the weight of a thousand wrong turns. Then, just as quickly, the moment passed. He stiffened, his body coiling like a retreating viper, and turned. Each step away felt like an unspoken scream, unraveling something raw and fragile.

Silence settled over them, dense and unyielding. But in its weight, there was relief. A reprieve.

Caleb exhaled slowly before turning to Sarah. His eyes were softer now yet still searching. "Are you okay?"

Her breath hitched, a jagged sigh breaking free. The fear still lingered, curling around her ribs like smoke. The weight of Jake's presence had lifted, but it left behind bruises she wasn't sure would ever fade.

But Caleb was here. And for now, that was enough. It had to be.

He offered his arm, the gesture simple yet profound—a vow spoken in silence. She hesitated—a beat, a lifetime—before reaching out. His warmth steadied her, something solid amid uncertainty.

The setting sun painted the pavement in gold, a deceptive glow against the long, stretching shadows. They walked forward, but the question lingered—could they truly outrun the darkness?

* * *

Jake's breath came fast and shallow. He stopped at the edge of the lot, hands flexing, fists clenching. He could still feel the weight of Caleb's gaze, steady and unyielding. It burned, not with anger, but with something worse understanding. He wanted to lash out at it, at him, at everything.

Instead, he turned back.

"Can't you see?" His voice cracked, splintering into the cold air. "I'm drowning, man. I need… I don't even know what I need."

Caleb remained still, an oak against the wind, his voice measured, unwavering. "I see a man lost in the shadows, Jake. Light waits for you. But you have to turn toward it."

Sarah stood motionless, her pulse drumming a frantic rhythm. The space between them was an abyss. How often had she tried to bridge it, only to fall short? The words Caleb spoke weren't just for Jake. They were for all of them.

Jake laughed, but it was a hollow, bitter sound. "Back? There is no back, Caleb. Just this... this emptiness. It swallows you whole."

Sarah flinched. She knew that void, that nothingness. The way it clawed at your bones, whispering that you were too far gone.

Caleb took a step forward, his hands rough with years of work, scarred from coaxing beauty from broken things. "Nothing is beyond repair, Jake. Wood can be reshaped. Re-formed. Even the most splintered pieces can be made whole again."

The words hung in the air, heavy and potent.

Jake's breath hitched. His gaze fell to Caleb's hands, calloused and sure, hands that had built, restored, and healed. Hands that offered something more than pity. The words "re-shaped, re-formed" clung to him, foreign yet familiar. Hope was a dangerous thing. It demanded things of you. Things he wasn't sure he had left to give.

"Reshaped..." he murmured, tasting the word like it was fragile.

Caleb extended his hand—no pressure, no force. Just an offering.

"Come on," he said, his voice low. "Let's find a path that leads somewhere good."

Sarah held her breath. This was the moment. The line between falling and climbing back up. Jake stood on the precipice, and for a heartbeat, she thought he might reach out.

Then, something in him recoiled. His body stiffened, his jaw locked, and he stumbled back, retreating into the comfort of the darkness he knew.

Caleb didn't move, his hand still outstretched, unwavering.

Jake turned and walked away. The tension ebbed, but in its place, a dull ache settled in Sarah's chest—a hollowness mirrored Jake's own. The storm hadn't passed; it only shifted, and its force momentarily lessened. And in that slight easing, Sarah found the tiniest flicker of hope. Fragile, yes. But real.

She turned to Caleb, her throat tight, a silent thank you forming on her lips. But the words felt inadequate, unable to capture the weight of the moment—the agonizing near-miss, the brutal reality of Jake's continued struggle. The fight was far from over.

Caleb's gaze lingered on Jake's retreating figure, a knot tightening in his gut. No triumph swelled in his chest, only a bone-deep weariness. This wasn't a victory. It was a reprieve, and he'd bet his life on Jake's return—a faith forged not from naive optimism but from shared scars, from knowing what it meant to fall and get back up.

They turned, their steps slow, each footfall a deliberate act of grounding themselves. The whispering giants of the forest stood silent, the ocean breeze threading through the trees, a salty caress against their skin—a reminder that healing was possible but never easy.

"Sarah?" Caleb's voice cut through the hush, low and steady.

She flinched, a barely perceptible tremor running through her. "I'm... better," she said, though the words caught in her throat. A long pause. Then, almost inaudible, "Seeing him... it brought it all back." The raw, visceral fear hung between them, thick as smoke.

Caleb's eyes softened. "Old wood splinters, Sarah," he murmured, his voice like the grain of something worn but strong. "But the rings tell a story—of growth, of weathering storms. It can be reshaped. Made stronger." He hesitated, then added, "Just like us."

She looked at him then, really, and something within her shifted. It is not a clean break but a realignment. A glimmer of hope, as delicate as a bird's fragile bones, settled in her chest.

They reached the edge of the schoolyard and paused, unspoken words hanging heavy between them. The late afternoon sun cast a golden glow over the Beacon of Learning, gilding its windows in stubborn defiance of the encroaching shadows. Even in darkness, light persisted. A truth she wanted to believe in.

Side by side, they walked toward home, toward the whispering cliffs and the familiar trace of sawdust and salt in the air. Caleb had shown her something today—without uttering a word, he'd reminded her of the endurance of hope.

"Even from the deepest wounds, the Master Craftsman can carve beauty," Sarah thought. Caleb's quiet strength was a lifeline in the storm, his belief in her a steadying force. Her fingers brushed his sleeve, a fleeting touch as light as a summer breeze yet charged with unspoken emotion. The silence between them wasn't empty; it thrummed with understanding.

"Thank you, Caleb," she whispered, her voice trembling slightly. More words would have shattered the fragile peace between them, and she clung to the moment as if it were all that kept her afloat.

The shadows in Sarah's green eyes weren't just fear; they were the deep etchings of trauma, barely masked by practiced composure. But beneath the weight of it all, there was something else—a flicker of defiance, a stubborn spring bloom pushing through the frost. Caleb saw it, and it gave him a sliver of hope. He'd seen that kind of resilience in the grain of wood he shaped. Each scar is a testament to its strength.

His chest ached—a familiar companion. Sarah's suffering mirrored his own, their pain interwoven in a landscape neither had chosen. "Always," he said, throwing her a lifeline in the storm. The salt-laced wind, usually a comfort, felt heavy tonight, laden with words left unsaid.

Port Angeles, their sanctuary, felt different now—suffocating, almost. The rhythm of the waves, once a soothing lullaby, now echoed the erratic beat of Caleb's heart. He saw Sarah's fingers fidgeting with a loose strand of auburn hair. A tell. She was barely holding it together. And he saw every subtle shift, a barely perceptible crack in her armor.

"Let's get you home," he said, his voice carefully steady, a mask against the turmoil ripping through him.

Home. The word felt like a cruel joke. It wasn't a refuge. It was a battlefield where ghosts still waged war. The man who had haunted her, who had stolen pieces of her, still cast a long shadow over everything.

They walked in silence, the rhythm of their steps a fragile echo of what they used to be. The streetlights flickered on, their glow casting long, accusing fingers across the pavement. As they neared her uncle's house, Caleb hesitated. His protective instincts screamed at him, a primal urge to shield her from the darkness, but he knew he couldn't.

Sarah, gripping the strap of her book bag like a lifeline, turned to him. Her eyes pleading. "I'll be okay," she whispered, barely audible above the wind's mournful sigh.

Caleb exhaled slowly; tension still coiled tight in his chest. He nodded; the movement stiff, unconvincing even to himself.

"If you need anything—"

"I know," she cut him off, soft but sure. "You'll be here."

The unspoken promise hung between them, a fragile bridge over a chasm of fear and uncertainty. He had to be there for her. No matter what.

A hesitant smile, delicate as a butterfly's wing, touched her lips. It wasn't much but a lifeline in the churning sea of their fear. That trust—however fragile—hit him harder than any blow. He understood the weight of it, the terrifying vulnerability it represented. And more than she knew, it meant everything.

She turned; her form swallowed by the deepening shadows. Caleb clenched his fists at his sides, his gut twisting. He could coax life from dead wood and shape beauty from rough-hewn timber—but he couldn't carve away the terror in her eyes. He ached to be her shelter, to build her a fortress against the storm raging inside her. Something stronger than fading memories and desperate prayers.

"Damn it," he muttered, the words lost to the wind. This wasn't a battle of swords and shields. This was a war fought in the hidden chambers of the heart. And he had no armor for that.

The last light bled from the sky, painting the Olympic Mountains in bruised purples and fading golds. Caleb's prayer was a ragged breath, a desperate plea whispered into the gathering dusk. He prayed to the same force that had sculpted those peaks, the same force that had given him the strength to build, create, and love—that it would mend the shattered pieces of Sarah's soul.

He turned toward home, the weight of his promise settling heavily on his shoulders. Come hell or high water, he wouldn't abandon her in this fight. He'd stand beside her, even if all he could offer was his presence, his stubborn carpenter's heart refusing to break. He'd be her anchor in the storm.

No matter what.

CHAPTER 7

Whispers of the Sea, Whispers of Healing

THE CAR DOOR slammed shut, a sharp counterpoint to the whisper of the wind whipping off Whispering Cliffs. Salt spray stung Caleb's face, a familiar bite he usually found comforting. Not today. Today, the ocean's usual consolation felt like a mocking mirror. Sarah stood beside him, the setting sun painting her hair the color of a fading sunset. Years etched lines around her green eyes, but beneath the calm surface, Caleb saw the tremor. He knew that look. He knew the silence. He didn't push. Some wounds needed time, a slow, agonizing healing.

"Damn it all to hell," he muttered, his voice snatched by the wind, but Sarah flinched like she'd heard every syllable. He didn't apologize. The storm inside him didn't leave room for polite remorse. He stared at the horizon, where the sea swallowed the sky in a smudge of bruised gold and steel. The letters in his coat pocket seemed to weigh more than his hammer ever had—each one a memory not his own, each one a confession from a man who had never spoken enough in life.

They walked in silence. Gravel crunched beneath their boots like bones. Sarah's pace was uneven. Caleb noticed but didn't say anything. She held her arms tight across her body like she could squeeze herself smaller, invisible. He'd seen her do that before—back when she'd first come back to Whispering Cliffs. Back when Jake Macall was just a name from a closed chapter.

But now that chapter had cracked open, bleeding back into the present.

"Jake's back in town," she said.

Caleb stopped cold. His boot slid on loose gravel, sending a pebble skittering over the edge. The wind was louder now, howling like a warning. His pulse spiked; his jaw clenched.

"He's got nothing left to lose," he said, and the bitterness in his voice startled even him.

A gust whipped Sarah's coat against her legs. She didn't look at him. "I saw his truck outside the old diner. Same dent on the tailgate. Same bumper sticker." Her voice was thin, worn. "It felt like I was thirteen again."

Caleb's hand flexed, aching for something to break, to fight, to control. But there was nothing here but stone and wind and the memory of every moment he'd failed to protect someone he cared about.

"He shouldn't be here," Caleb growled.

Sarah's silence agreed.

"These changes everything," she said. Her voice trembled, but she held it steady, like a tightrope walker over a pit of fire.

Caleb took her hand. Hers was cold, the kind of cold that came from the inside out. He squeezed, not to warm her, but to remind her she wasn't alone.

"We'll face it together," he said, and this time the wind didn't steal the words.

She looked at him, truly looked, and something in her shoulders softened, though her eyes remained shadowed. "I don't want to run anymore, Caleb. But I can't go back to who I was then. I won't survive it."

"You won't have to," he said, though the promise tasted like salt and ash on his tongue.

Sarah hugged herself again, shivering. "It's like walking into a room and finding the walls have closed in while you weren't looking. Only it's not a room, Caleb. It's the whole damn town."

His heart ached at that. Sarah was made of fire and tenderness—he knew how hard she fought to walk through life without armor. But now the past was crashing down like a wave against the cliffs, dragging her back into the undertow.

"I found letters from my father," Caleb said, his voice breaking the silence like a hammer on glass.

Sarah turned sharply. "Letters?"

"In the workshop. Tucked away in an old cedar box I never noticed before. He wrote them to me, Sarah. All those years he was silent—he was writing."

She stared at him, disbelief flickering into understanding. "What do they say?"

Caleb hesitated. The truth was tangled. He pulled the letters from his coat, the edges curled and faded like old scars. He handed them over.

"That he wished he'd been a better father. That he regretted letting his anger consume everything. That he prayed for me every night, even when I thought he'd stopped believing in anything."

Sarah took the pages like they might crumble in her hands. Her lips moved silently as she read. When she looked up, her eyes were glassy, reflecting both pain and wonder.

"I never would've guessed," she whispered. "He was always so hard. So—"

"Distant," Caleb finished.

He sat on a stone, elbows resting on his knees, his breath coming in slow, uneven waves. "I thought his silence was his judgment. That maybe I reminded him too much of the man he hated becoming."

Sarah sat beside him. "Maybe silence was all he had left after all he lost."

He blinked hard. "He carved hope into every splinter. Said he thought if he made enough beauty, it'd drown the broken parts."

Sarah traced a finger over the grain of the letter in her lap. "That's what you do too."

Caleb didn't respond. His eyes followed a bird soaring far above the cliffs, free, untouched by the weight of memory. How did he tell her that sometimes the act of creating was the only way he knew how to beg for grace?

"Jake being back... it makes these letters feel like a cruel joke," he said. "Like I'm being handed peace with one hand and thrown into war with the other."

Sarah nodded slowly. "I know the feeling. He used to say no one would believe me. That I was a liar. That I needed him." Her voice cracked. "And for a while, I believed him."

Caleb's fist clenched. "I wish I could kill that version of him."

Her eyes found his. "So, do I. But we don't fight hate with more hate, Caleb."

"You still believe that? Even after everything?"

Sarah stared out at the horizon. "I have to. Otherwise, I'm just another version of what he made me into."

The wind calmed briefly, like the world had paused to listen. Caleb watched her, the way her chin lifted despite the tremble in her lips. She wasn't fearless—she was choosing to walk forward with the fear, and that made her stronger than anyone he'd ever known.

"Sarah," he said quietly, "if I ever seem like I'm slipping—into anger, into darkness—I need you to pull me back."

She looked at him, startled. "Caleb—"

"I'm serious. My father spent his whole life trying to carve a better version of himself. I don't want to spend mine running from the parts of me that look like him."

Sarah reached up and brushed her fingers against his temple, the touch soft, grounding. "You are not your father. And you're not Jake. You're the man who stops to pray before he picks up his tools. The one who listened to my silence and never tried to fill it with noise."

The letters fluttered in her lap as the wind picked up again.

"Maybe that's the grace of it, Caleb," she said. "Maybe you're finally getting a chance to truly know him."

He looked at her—and really saw her. The wind whipped strands of auburn hair across her face, but she didn't push them away. Her green eyes held a quiet strength, the kind carved out of surviving, out of learning to live with ghosts. She understood the weight of regret, the way the past could sink its teeth into you and refuse to let go.

Caleb turned back to the water, watching the tide roll in. Maybe Sarah was right. Maybe grace wasn't about fixing what was broken but learning to live with the jagged edges. The tide would ebb and flow. Life would continue. But the weight of his father's unspoken words, the fear in Sarah's eyes—those would stay with him. A reminder of the battles still to be fought. The wounds still needing to heal.

His hands trembled, rough and calloused from years of coaxing stories from wood. The letters felt brittle beneath his touch, whispering secrets of a man lost to time yet still present in the lingering trace of sawdust clinging to Caleb's skin. Each word was a fresh cut, reopening wounds he thought had long since scarred over.

"He fought his demons in every sunrise," Caleb rasped, his voice cracking. "Said he sought forgiveness in the breath of pine, in the feel of cedar beneath his tools. Thought if he carved enough, shaped enough, he could whittle away the darkness inside him."

Sarah's fingers brushed his hand, warm against the cold air. She didn't try to fill the silence with meaningless reassurances. She just stood there, solid, unmoving. An anchor.

"He loved you, Caleb," she said at last, steady despite the wind whipping around them. "Even in the silence. Even in the guilt. He loved you."

The letters rustled in his grip, thin and fragile, a shield against the storm inside him. The cliffs loomed overhead, ancient and unyielding, silent witnesses to every storm that had battered this shore. He felt like them—eroded, shaped by forces beyond his control, trying to hold his ground against the relentless pull of memory.

"It's like carving through a damn forest of ghosts," he said, voice raw. "Trying to find the man he was before... before he became a stranger."

He turned to Sarah then, searching her face, his eyes dark with something vulnerable, something unspoken. "Do you think... do you think I'll ever truly know him?"

Sarah didn't answer right away. She held his gaze, steady, unwavering. Then she reached up, pushing a wind-tossed strand of hair from his face with a touch so light it could have been the wind itself.

"I think," she said carefully, "the only way to know him now is to stop searching for who he was... and start seeing the man he *wanted* to be."

Caleb swallowed hard, the taste of salt and sorrow thick in his throat. He turned the words over in his mind, testing their weight.

Maybe she was right.

Maybe that was the only way forward.

Caleb's words hung in the air, thin and brittle, like splinters of a shattered dream. Sarah's hand, calloused but gentle, found his arm, anchoring him to the raw, present moment. He felt the familiar comfort of her touch, a silent testament to their shared history, their mutual capacity for both breaking and mending.

"Remember the first time you tried to carve?" Sarah's voice was soft, a low hum against the wind's howl. The memory, sharp and painful, hit him. "You nearly took your thumb off! I laughed, but you never gave up. You said, 'Every piece of wood has a story, Caleb. It's just waiting to be told.'" A ghost of a smile touched Caleb's lips. He saw it again – the clumsy fourteen-year-old him, fumbling with the knife. He'd been terrified of failing his father, of not living up to the legacy of his family's craft.

"Yeah," he managed, his voice rough, "and you? You sanded that stupid dove for two hours. Thought you'd erase every flaw."

Sarah's gaze met his, a flicker of vulnerability in her eyes. "I wanted it perfect. Like everything else." She looked out at the turbulent sea, mirroring the storm inside her. "But you taught me... the imperfections are part of the story, right? The knots, the cracks... they all have a place." Her voice hitched. "Just like us."

A brutal gust of wind whipped salt spray into their faces. Sarah's eyes, suddenly distant, were fixed on the horizon's fiery sunset. "Healing isn't about fixing things perfectly," she continued, her voice barely a whisper above the wind. "It's about finding the beauty in the broken pieces. Rediscovering the joy, you thought was lost forever."

The unspoken hung heavy between them. Caleb remembers his father just walked away – the raw, gaping hole it left – threatened to consume him. But, like gentle tools, Sarah's words chipped away at the suffocating grief, carving a space for something else. Something... hopeful. He let out a shaky breath, the sound lost in the wind's roar. The pain remained, a dull ache in his chest, but it felt different now, somehow manageable. Like he could carry it, but he wouldn't be crushed by it.

They fell into a rhythm of shared memories, desperately clinging to simpler times. Sun-drenched afternoons at the shore, their laughter echoing against the cliffs, the unspoken pact woven between them under a sky full of stars. Laughter mixed with tears, a raw and beautiful blend that washed over them, painting the cliffs with the hues of their shared past.

Caleb laughed, a harsh, ragged sound. "Remember old man Harper's oak? You dared me to climb the highest branch. I nearly crapped myself."

Sarah grinned, wiping a tear away with the back of her hand. "And you did it, you crazy fool! You always reach higher than you think you can, Caleb. That's what makes you such a damn good craftsman. And a better friend than you know." Her voice cracked. The unspoken question hung between them: could they salvage what remained? Could their friendship withstand this new storm? The answer, like the unpredictable tide, remained to be seen.

Caleb finally saw her—truly saw Sarah—not as the girl he once knew, but as a woman tempered by trial, standing unyielding in her truth. "Thank you, Sarah," he murmured, the words rough-edged and trembling. His gratitude wasn't polite; it was primal, aching. The cliffs, ageless and unmoved, devoured his voice. They bore silent witness to the gulf between who he had been and the fragile, emerging thread of what might yet be.

The last light bled into twilight. Caleb folded the letters, his touch reverent. His father's words weren't anchors anymore, dragging him down. They were a compass, faint whispers in the wood, guiding him forward. But a deep-seated fear still gnawed at him – what if he failed to live up to his father's legacy? What if this newfound path was just another dead end?

At Whispering Cliffs, under the vast, indifferent sky, Caleb and Sarah found solace in the ghosts of the past and the trembling promise of a future they were carving together. But the promise felt fragile, a delicate thing quickly shattered by the cruel winds of fate.

The sunset blazed—a final, defiant gasp of color. Amber, rose, and violet bled into the restless ocean, reflecting the storm churning inside Caleb. The sea's rhythm beat against the jagged rocks with a relentless pulse, echoing the chaos of a world beyond control. Caleb perched on the cliff's edge, the weight of it all pressing against his chest like a tide refusing to ebb. The wind, salty and sharp with the tang of cedar, lashed around him—a fierce, swirling mirror of the turmoil within.

Sarah sat beside him, her breathing slow and controlled, starkly contrasting to his agitated state. Their silence wasn't empty; it hummed with unspoken fears and hopes. A shared understanding that ran deeper than words. His gaze locked onto the horizon, where sky and sea met in an endless, ambiguous embrace. The feeling was overwhelming – a profound sense of both profound loss and unexpected discovery.

Years of wandering, self-doubt, and searching for something he couldn't name had led him here. But tonight, in this sacred stillness, the fear still lingered. He felt the pulse of something eternal, something larger than himself, but the weight of his responsibility felt crushing. He'd found his rhythm, but could he maintain it? The question hung heavy in the air, as heavy as the salt spray on his face.

A gull screamed, its shriek tearing through Caleb's fragile peace. Muscle ache gnawed at him after that endless vigil on the cold earth. He exhaled, the air thin and tight in his chest, and looked at Sarah. The dying sun kissed her face, highlighting the stubborn strength in her eyes – a strength that mirrored, yet somehow challenged, his own.

He offered his hand, the gesture both simple and profound. Her fingers laced through his, the familiar pressure a grounding force. They rose, their movements deliberate, neither hurried nor hesitant. The winding path beckoned, leading them back to a world with unanswered questions, looming burdens, and a thin faith. But tonight, the ocean had held their secret, the cliffs had witnessed the silent shift in their hearts.

Gravel crunched under their boots – a muted counterpoint to the ocean's vast hush. Port Angeles shimmered beyond the hills, promising warm lights and quiet streets. Caleb slid behind the wheel of his truck, the engine's rumble a comforting roar. He stole a glance at Sarah. She stared out at the familiar landscape – fields, houses, the comforting ordinariness of home – but her expression held a new intensity.

This resolute calm mirrored the unsettling quiet in his soul. The weight of their shared revelation lingered in the air, heavy with the unspoken understanding of a chasm crossed. The town enveloped them with the familiar fragrance of pine and salt, the soft glow of porch lights casting warmth into the night, and a distant melody spilling from a shop down the street, weaving its way through the stillness.

Home. It had always been here, a constant, unwavering presence. Though words remained unspoken, Sarah's presence beside him felt like an anchor, a tangible tether to something genuine. But the quiet didn't ease the tremor in his hands.

Caleb hesitated at the doorway, his pulse thrumming in his ears. The workshop was unchanged—wood, dust, and the memory of his father's steady hands shaping the grain into something whole. The air was thick with sawdust, but it clung to his throat instead of its usual warmth, making it hard to breathe. His fingers curled around the doorframe as if anchoring himself.

Sarah's touch on his arm was grounding. "Caleb?" Her voice was gentle but searching, probing past the silence. "Are you alright?"

He forced himself to swallow, though his throat felt lined with sandpaper. "It's just... different now." His gaze dropped to the worn floorboards, where he once sat at his father's feet, eager to learn. "Like everything's shifted beneath me."

Sarah squeezed his arm, a quiet promise in her touch. "It has. But we're here. Together." Her voice carried a conviction she might not entirely believe, but she needed him to.

Inside, the rhythmic tap of a chisel against wood filled the silence. Joshua Shepherd's frame was hunched over the workbench, his hands steady despite the tremor of years. He didn't look up, but Caleb knew—he felt—his father's awareness of him. The lantern's glow cast jagged shadows along the walls, stretching and twisting like unspoken words between them.

Caleb stepped forward, his boots scuffing softly against the sawdust-laced floor. The lingering trace of pine, once a source of solace, now stirred a tightness in his chest. His gaze fell on the half-finished carving—a block of oak destined to become the fourth station of the Cross: Jesus meeting His mother.

A weight settled in Caleb's gut. He knew what his father asked of him before the words were even spoken. He reached for the chisel he'd once used as a boy. The handle was smooth, shaped by years of use, but it felt foreign in his grip.

Joshua's voice came low, the rasp of it cutting through the silence. "The oak's been waiting." He finally met Caleb's gaze, his brown eyes worn with sorrow and something else—something that made Caleb's throat tighten.

Regret.

"I don't know if I can, Joshua." Caleb's voice barely carried over the workshop's hush.

Joshua's hand, calloused and firm, rested on his shoulder. It wasn't a command or an expectation. It was something else entirely.

"You're stronger than you think, son. We all are."

The chisel trembled in Caleb's grip. This wasn't just about shaping wood. It was about shaping himself, about carving a path back to something he wasn't sure he deserved.

His friend's eyes held steady, waiting. Not pressuring. Not demanding. Just waiting.

Caleb exhaled, the breath shaky, and positioned the chisel against the grain.

Maybe this was how redemption started—not in grand gestures, but in the quiet, steady work of making something whole again.

Caleb closed his eyes, drawing in the earthy aroma of cedar, letting it fill the emptiness within him. He exhaled slowly, his breath wavering, before setting the chisel against the grain. The first stroke was tentative, uncertain, as though the wood might resist him, just as his past had. But then came another stroke, and another—each shaving that curled away felt like peeling back another layer of himself, exposing the vulnerable, unguarded part beneath.

Joshua worked beside him; their movements synchronized in the hush of the workshop. Joshua's mallet tapped in a slow, steady rhythm, each strike measured, each movement precise. Something in the way he worked, a quiet reverence, made Caleb's chest tighten.

"Damn it," Caleb muttered under his breath. The chisel slipped, leaving a jagged scar on the surface. His grip tightened, frustration burning in his veins. "It's like the wood's fighting back."

Joshua let out a low chuckle, deep and familiar. "It always does." His voice was steady, carrying the weight of lessons learned the hard way. "Just like life, son."

Caleb pressed his lips together, the words stirring something bitter in him. He wanted this to be perfect. He needed it to be. His hands trembled as he ran his fingers over the rough spot as if he could smooth it away with sheer will. "It's not supposed to be this hard," he said, voice tight. "I just… I want it to be right."

Joshua finally looked up, his gaze steady but soft. "Right doesn't mean perfect." He set his chisel down and wiped his hands on his apron, studying Caleb. "Perfect's a lie we tell ourselves, so we don't have to face the truth. Your mother… she wasn't perfect. Neither was I. But love—it ain't about perfection. It's about what you do in spite of the mess."

Caleb swallowed hard. The letters burned in his mind—the ones he'd found hidden in the old chest, the confessions his father had never spoken aloud. The weight of them had settled in his bones, pressing down until he could barely breathe. "Those letters," he started, his voice barely above a whisper. "They changed everything."

Joshua exhaled, slow and measured. He nodded. "Some truths shape us in ways we never expect. Sometimes they carve pieces out of us." His fingers traced the curve of the nearly finished Christ figure on his workbench. "But it's what we do with the pieces that matters."

Caleb's chest tightened. He stared down at his carving—the Mary figure, her sorrow etched deep, mirroring his own. He swallowed against the lump rising in his throat. "I don't want to be shaped by pain," he admitted, his voice thick. "I want to—" He hesitated, searching for the words. "I want to choose what I become."

Joshua's hand landed on his shoulder, warm, grounding. "You already are son."

Silence settled between them, not empty but heavy with unspoken understanding. The rhythmic tap of Joshua's mallet resumed, steady and sure. Caleb let out a breath, picked up his chisel, and carved again.

The last rays of sunlight slanted through the grimy windows, painting the workshop in gold and shadow. The air smelled of sawdust and sweat, of labor and time. Caleb's hands moved with new certainty, shaping the wood and himself. He carved not for perfection but for truth.

As twilight deepened, he stepped back, breath catching in his throat. The Mary he had carved wasn't perfect—her lines were uneven, the grain rough in places. But she was real. Whole. Like him. Or maybe, almost.

Joshua wiped his hands and studied the figure, his expression unreadable for a long moment. Then he nodded. "The masterpiece ain't in the wood, Caleb," he said, voice rough but sure. "It's in the hands that shape it."

Caleb stared down at his work, the chisel marks, the imperfections that made it uniquely his. He traced the contours of Mary's sorrow and felt the tremor in his own fingers. The weight inside him shifted, something raw and uncertain but real—maybe even grace.

His voice cracked as he spoke, but he didn't look away. "It's not about perfection, is it?"

Joshua met his gaze, steady as the earth beneath them. "Nope." He gave a small, knowing smile. "It's about the fight. The shaping. Finding grace in the mess."

Caleb nodded in a slow, deliberate motion. He wasn't whole yet. Maybe he never would be. But he was carving something from the wreckage. He was shaping himself, one imperfect stroke at a time. And maybe, just maybe, that was enough.

CHAPTER 8

A Father's Battle, A Son's Awakening

A VISE SQUEEZED CALEB Martin's chest as he approached Saint Peter's by the Sea. The Whispering Letters, brittle as autumn leaves, felt heavier than any book in his hands—his father's legacy, a testament to unspoken pain, to battles fought in the silent trenches of his mind. Each footfall echoed in the quiet streets of Port Angeles, a drumbeat against the cobblestones, mirroring the frantic rhythm of his heart. The wind screamed off the cliffs, a mournful cry mimicking the gull's overhead, carrying the sharp tang of salt and the weight of his dread. The church bell, a somber toll, felt like a summons he couldn't ignore, a final reckoning. The rectory door, ancient oak groaning under the strain of its iron hinges, seemed to resist him. He shoved it open, the chill wind contrasting with the sudden warmth that enveloped him.

The familiar scent of beeswax and aged wood fought with the lingering salt spray, a testament to the church's long vigil over the town. The silence was thick, heavy with unspoken prayers, a suffocating blanket of anticipation. "Caleb." Father Michael Harrington's deep and resonant voice cut through the hush. He stood in his office doorway, his salt-and-pepper hair a map of years spent comforting the broken. Kindness shone in his eyes, but Caleb saw something more beneath it—a grim understanding that mirrored his growing terror. It was the same look he'd seen years ago when his mother had stood here, her pleas for a husband lost to the war's unseen wounds echoing in the hallowed halls. "Come in, my boy," Father Mike said, his voice a lifeline in the storm raging inside Caleb. The gesture was kind, but his eyes held a gravity that chilled Caleb. He knew. He had to know. Caleb hesitated, a flicker of defiance against the overwhelming weight of it all, but he couldn't stay out there in the wind any longer. He stepped inside.

Lined with books worn smooth by time and countless hands, the room felt comforting and suffocating. The Stations of the Cross, solemn sentinels above the shelves, watched him. And then he saw them—his father's unfinished wood carvings, a silent testament to a faith that couldn't quite conquer the darkness. His fingers trembled as he touched one—Simon helping Jesus carry the cross. The detail was exquisite, a testament to his father's skill, but the incompletion was agonizingly clear. A mirror of his own fractured life. A mirror of his own unfinished business. "Father," Caleb began, his voice cracking, "I… I need your help." The words spilled out, a torrent of pent-up fear and desperate hope. "It's about the letters… about everything."

Caleb slumped into the chair opposite Father Mike, the aged letters clutched in his trembling hands. He slapped them down on the polished wood between them, the yellowed pages brittle and curling like autumn leaves caught in a sudden gust. The weight wasn't just in the paper; it was a physical ache in his bones, a deep-seated dread that had festered long before he'd touched these fragile confessions. Father Mike watched him, his gaze steady and kind, but Caleb felt the weight of his unspoken judgment. "You don't have to carry this alone, son," the priest said, his voice a low rumble.

Caleb's breath hitched. He slammed his fists on the table, echoing the turmoil inside him. "I don't know where to begin, Father. It's… it's all too much."

"Start with your heart, Caleb. Let it guide you."

The simplicity of the words and the quiet confidence in Father Mike's voice offered a sliver of solace. Caleb nodded, his throat tight, and picked up the top letter. The paper felt thin beneath his fingertips, worn smooth by years of handling, the ink faded and smeared, a testament to his father's struggle to articulate his pain. He swallowed hard, his Adam's apple bobbing nervously. He began to read, his voice a ragged whisper.

"Dear Son," the words seemed to claw their way out of the past. "I've spent years fighting a war that never ended. It followed me home, burrowed into my soul, and I didn't know how to keep it from poisoning the people I loved."

The room held its breath. Caleb's breath hitched. He'd always sensed the darkness clinging to his father, a long, menacing shadow. But reading his father's raw confession, the weight of his unspoken torment—it felt like a physical blow. The man who'd built cradles and carved wooden toys with those same hands that had held a rifle... his father had been fighting a silent battle all along. A battle he'd lost.

Father Mike remained silent, offering only the quiet support of his presence. The priest's silence was different this time; it wasn't judging but understanding.

"I regret..." Caleb's voice cracked, the words catching in his throat. He wrestled for control, his knuckles white as he clenched his fists. "I regret the wall my silence built between us. I regret that you saw only the shadow of a man when all I wanted was to protect you from the truth. Every day was a war I couldn't leave, and every night... I fought demons you should never have seen."

The words blurred before his eyes. Tears stung, blurring the ink on the page. The silence hung heavy, punctuated only by a church bell's distant, mournful toll. The bell's toll felt almost mocking in its unwavering rhythm.

Father Mike leaned closer; his voice soft. "He carried a heavy burden, Caleb. A crushing weight."

Caleb nodded, a shuddering breath escaping his lips. "And he carried it alone." The words were a bitter accusation, a self-reproach.

Father Mike's hand rested lightly on Caleb's. "But he left you these," he said, gently tapping the letters. "He left you, his truth. He wanted you to understand. To see him, not just the shadow, but the man he truly was." The priest's eyes held a deep compassion that soothed and spurred Caleb on. The weight remained, but now it felt lighter, less like a crushing burden and more like a shared responsibility to understand.

Caleb's knuckles whitened around the worn, brittle pages. "What if I don't 'want' to know? What if the truth just... breaks me?" His voice cracked, the question a raw, desperate plea. He wasn't just afraid of the truth; he was terrified of what it might do to the fragile peace he'd painstakingly built.

Father Mike, his gaze steady, saw the tremor in Caleb's hands, the fear clinging to him like a shroud. "Caleb," he said, his voice low and gravelly, carrying the weight of years spent witnessing human suffering. "Truth isn't a comfortable blanket. It's a jagged stone you gotta pick up, whether you like it or not. You can let it crush you, bury you under the weight of it… or you can use its sharp edges to carve something beautiful, something meaningful from the wreckage."

The invitation hung heavy in the air, less a suggestion and more a stark challenge. Caleb's eyes flickered to the unfinished woodcarvings on the wall—his father's legacy, a testament to a man who'd wrestled demons into the shape of art. The image struck him hard: his father's calloused hands, strong and sure, transforming splintered wood into something enduring. Could he do the same with his own shattered life?

He flipped a page, the whisper of paper a fragile counterpoint to the racing thoughts in his head. The past wouldn't change, but maybe, just maybe, he could forge a different future. A future worthy of his father's sacrifice.

The sanctuary of Saint Peter's by the Sea held its breath, the dying sunlight painting the stone floor in hues of crimson and gold, a silent, solemn witness to his inner turmoil. Father Mike sat opposite, his weathered Bible open on the heavy desk, a flickering candle casting shadows that danced with the turmoil in Caleb's heart. The priest's silver hair seemed to glow, but the sorrow etched deeply into his face was brutally honest.

"Your father wasn't just a parishioner to me, Caleb," Father Mike said, his voice breaking slightly. The raw emotion in the air hit Caleb like a punch to the gut. "He was my brother. We fought in Nam together. We saw things… things that'll haunt you till your dying day." He paused, his gaze drifting to some distant, painful memory. "Vietnam… it changed us. It 'broke' us."

The words landed with the force of a revelation. Caleb had known fragments, hazy snapshots of his father's past, but now the brutal truth slammed into him. He understood, finally, the depth of his father's struggle—a battle that raged not just on foreign soil but within his soul, long after the guns fell silent. The weight of it settled heavily in Caleb's chest; the profound, enduring impact of war on a man he had only ever seen as strong.

Damn it, Caleb," Father Mike rasped, his voice scraping against the weight of regret. His knuckles, pale as bone against the cracked leather of his Bible, trembled ever so slightly. "I should've been there. When we got back... the war didn't end on some piece of paper. It lived inside us. Thomas... he fought his battles alone. And I... I failed him."

The words hit Caleb like a sledgehammer, knocking the breath clean from his lungs. His father—his distant, storm-swept father—had been drowning all this time, and Caleb hadn't seen it. No, he had seen it. He just hadn't understood. The restless nights. The furious carving. His father would flinch at a sudden sound or lock himself in the workshop for hours, emerging with eyes that looked but did not see. A sickening understanding curdled in his stomach.

Father Mike snapped his Bible shut. The sound cracked through the still air like a gunshot. "PTSD, son," he said, voice clipped and hard-edged. "It ain't just remembering. It's living it. Every goddamn day. Waking up with the war still raging in your head."

Caleb swallowed hard; his throat raw with unspoken years. The puzzle pieces he'd never been able to fit together suddenly locked into place. The cold, empty stares. The walls were built from silence. The way his father's hand had hovered, just for a second, before clapping his shoulder—a gesture that should've been instinct but always felt like an effort.

He looked down at the faded letters, his father's confessions scrawled in somehow heavier ink than stone. "He hid it well," Caleb whispered, his voice ragged.

Father Mike's gaze softened, but the years of weight in his eyes didn't lift. "He loved you, Caleb. The only way he knew how." He set a firm, steadying hand on Caleb's shoulder. "And love, son, doesn't end with death. It just... it asks to be understood."

Caleb exhaled, shuddering, the air heavy in his lungs. The weight of his father's pain wasn't a burden anymore. It was a legacy. Truth to be honored.

Father Mike hesitated before speaking again. "There's someone who might help you understand all this." His voice was quiet but firm. "Robert Blakely. He's been through the same hell. Maybe he can shine some light on these shadows you're wrestling with."

The name was foreign, an anchor tossed into unfamiliar waters. Caleb's stomach churned. Another man with war behind his eyes. Another story etched in scars and silence. He didn't know if he was ready. But ready or not, he needed this.

"I'll talk to him," he said, the words tasting like iron on his tongue. A promise. To himself. To his father's ghost. The road ahead was uncertain, but for the first time in a long time, it wasn't a dead end.

Father Mike gave a tight, knowing nod and led him down the hushed rectory corridor. Once comforting, the scent of aged paper and incense now pressed against Caleb like an unwanted hand on his back. He felt like a man walking to his execution. Not to death—but to truth. A different kind of finality.

The sun burned low in the sky, casting the room where Robert Blakely waited in molten gold. The man wasn't just big—he was carved from something unshakable, radiating a quiet strength that made the air feel heavier. His handshake was firm, not crushing but steady, a silent promise of shared burden.

"Caleb," Blakely said, his voice low, deliberate. "Come in."

This wasn't a church. In this room, ghosts lingered in the corners, where pain had been named and spoken aloud. A room that understood.

Caleb sat, his fingers gripping his knees, his knuckles white. He had faced storms before, but this one was inside him. And there was no running from that.

Blakely's gaze was sharp, cutting through the silence. "Father Mike says you're carrying a heavy load."

Caleb exhaled slowly; his chest tight. "Yeah," he rasped. "More than I can bear."

Blakely leaned forward, forearms resting on the table, his presence grounding. "Your father, Caleb. Let's talk about him. Let's peel back the layers, one by one. Together."

The breath caught in Caleb's throat; a strangled sob barely caged. The air felt thick and heavy, with everything unspoken. Maybe, just maybe, this was the first step toward understanding. Toward something that wasn't just grief and silence. Toward something whole.

But a cold dread curled in his stomach. What if understanding only brought more pain? What if the truth shattered him instead of setting him free?

Caleb's calloused thumb traced the grain of the oak table, the worn wood beneath his fingertips an anchor to the past. The scent of sawdust, familiar and sharp, filled his lungs. He had watched his father carve for hours, shaping rough wood into something beautiful. Maybe—just maybe—this was his chance to do the same.

To carve truth from the silence. To build something from the ruins.

"My old man…Thomas…war carved him, silence shaped him," Caleb finally said, the words rough-hewn, a confession hammered out on the anvil of his grief. "I grew up in the shadow of his pain, never understanding the depth of what he carried."

Robert's face remained impassive, a mask of controlled emotion, but his eyes, deep and knowing, held a flicker of understanding, the empathy born of shared suffering. A subtle nod, a craftsman coaxing shape from raw material.

"Did that past ever…manifest? In unexpected ways?" Robert asked, his voice a low rumble, gentle but insistent. He wasn't filling the silence; he was creating a space, carving a path through Caleb's tangled emotions.

Caleb let out a ragged breath, the memories flooding back, raw and visceral. He rubbed a hand over his knee, the rough fabric scratching against his skin, a physical manifestation of the inner turmoil.

"Yeah," he rasped, his voice tight with barely suppressed emotion. "His silences were… bottomless. And when they broke… it was like a dam bursting. Only, the flood was full of ghosts, Robert. Ghosts that still haunt me." His voice cracked, the unspoken fear hanging heavy in the air. He clenched his jaw, fighting back the tears threatening to spill.

"I…I don't know if I can face them." The confession hung between them, a raw, vulnerable thing.

Robert leaned in, his silence comforting, not the suffocating kind. He knew the drill; some wounds needed airing before they could even begin to scab over. Caleb let the memories claw their way to the surface—his father's disappearances, those lonely nights bathed only in the flickering blue light of the TV, the sudden, terrifying explosions of rage. But worse than the anger and the fear was the emptiness, the vast, echoing silence that had carved a cavern in Caleb's soul.

"War," Robert said, his voice low and gravelly, the wisdom of a thousand confessions etched into its timbre, "War leaves scars deeper than any battlefield. Your father's time in Vietnam, Dai Do… it wasn't just something he survived. It became him." Caleb's throat tightened. He'd spent his life trying to solve the riddle of his father, to piece together the man from fractured whispers and averted gazes. The fragments were snapping into place, a horrifying, heartbreaking mosaic. His father hadn't been distant because he didn't care. He'd been distant because some of him had stayed lost on that distant battlefield.

"Those scars," Robert continued, his gaze steady, unwavering, "They change you. They warp how you see the world, how you love. The anger, the distance… those weren't failures. They were the weight of memories he couldn't bear." The truth hit him like a physical blow, a chisel finding its mark. He'd always viewed his father's pain as something alien, something he couldn't comprehend. Now, he saw it—the unending battle, the burden that had crippled not only his father, but him too.

"Understanding doesn't excuse it," Caleb rasped, his voice barely a whisper. "But maybe… maybe it's a start." Robert's gaze never wavered. "Forgiveness isn't about excusing, Caleb. It's about acknowledging the wound and letting the healing begin." In the hushed sanctity of the rectory, the scent of old wood and beeswax heavy in the air, something shifted within Caleb. Not a sudden epiphany, but the fragile, tentative bloom of hope. His eyes drifted to the stained-glass window. Sunlight sliced through, painting vibrant mosaics on the stone floor—a silent testament to the interplay of light and shadow.

His thoughts flew to Sarah, her strawberry-blonde hair starkly contrasting the church's somber tones. The image felt like a stab of guilt. "Sarah," he breathed, the name heavy with unspoken pain. "She came back from teaching… changed. Withdrawn. Like… like a ghost." He swallowed hard, a tremor in his voice. "I don't know how to reach her." The unspoken question hung in the air— "how can I save her?" The fear was a cold knot in his stomach. He had to try. He had to. For her. And for himself.

Robert's gaze sharpened, a flicker of recognition in his eyes. "Sarah Rayburn-Macall," he murmured, the name a weight on his tongue. "Some scars run deeper than others, don't they?" His voice held a weariness Caleb hadn't expected, a hint of shared experience lurking beneath the calm exterior. Caleb nodded grimly. "The nightmares… the way she flinched, the haunted look in her eyes. It was like a piece of that hellhole clung to her, a shadow she couldn't shake." He felt a familiar tightness in his chest, the echo of his buried pain.

Robert leaned closer, his presence a solid anchor in the quiet church. "War leaves its mark, Caleb. Different battlefields, same damn wounds." His voice was low, almost a whisper, but the words resonated with a raw honesty that cut through the hushed reverence of the place. The scent of old wood and incense did little to mask the underlying sorrow. Caleb traced the grain of the pew, the wood cool and smooth beneath his fingers. His father's agony, Sarah's suffering… two separate tragedies etched in the same cruel script of loss and resilience.

A slow, dawning understanding unfurled in Caleb's chest— unsteady, like the first cautious blossom after a long winter. It didn't come in a rush of epiphany or a thunderclap of divine clarity. It came as a whisper, threaded into the silence that had haunted him for years. Empathy, stubborn and tender, wove its way through the barbed wire of his past, its roots curling around pain and memory, refusing to let go.

"See those parallels, Caleb," Robert said softly, voice thick with something older than wisdom—something hard-earned. "It's in the seeing, in the understanding, that healing begins."

His words settled on the air like dust after a storm. Caleb nodded slowly. It felt like lifting a mountain.

The past still clung to him like a second skin. The memories wouldn't vanish. The guilt. The accusations he'd rehearsed for years. But something in him shifted. Not release. Not absolution. Just…a recalibration, like finding a new center after being off-balance for too long. Like discovering the weight he'd carried wasn't disappearing—but maybe, finally, he could carry it without breaking.

He closed his eyes and inhaled, the scent of aged wood and warm beeswax grounding him. His father's workshop flashed behind his eyelids—the air thick with sawdust, the walls lined with tools worn by time and care. He could still see the old man at the workbench, fingers curved around the chisel like they were meant to fit, steady hands creating beauty from what others would call broken.

Then Sarah's face rose in his mind. Not smiling—no, that wasn't the image that came. It was her silence. The tight way she held herself together, like she was stitched from glass and afraid of shattering. She had always spoken more in what she didn't say. And in those silences, Caleb had begun to hear the echoes of his own.

He saw the fractures—Sarah's, Robert's, his father's, his own. But the cracks didn't just reveal the damage. They let the light in.

The Whispering Letters trembled slightly in his hands. He ran a thumb across the worn edges, the fibers soft and frayed. Each smudge, each faded line of ink was a mark left by time, by pain, by desperate hands reaching through silence. His father's battles—once buried, once denied—were here, captured in words that trembled with both shame and love.

They no longer felt like anchors. They felt like keys.

The rectory held still, like it was listening.

He wasn't sure what scared him more: what the letters revealed about his father…or what they revealed about himself.

"Caleb," Robert said again, gentler this time, "you know this won't fix everything."

"I know," Caleb whispered, voice rasping against the dry walls of his throat. "But it has to start somewhere, right?"

Robert gave a slow nod. His face looked carved from stone, weathered from too many late nights, too many prayers that felt unanswered. "It starts here."

Caleb exhaled sharply, a breath he hadn't realized he'd been holding. His boots tapped the wooden floor, the rhythm sharp and deliberate. Each step forward felt like cutting into new wood, rough but full of promise. He was a carpenter, after all. But this—this was different. This wasn't about shaping cedar or maple. This was about shaping what had been broken in the people he loved. Including himself.

His heartbeat thundered in his chest.

"What if I screw it up?" he asked suddenly, voice tight, the question tearing from somewhere deep.

Robert's brow furrowed. "You will," he said plainly. "We all do. But grace isn't earned through perfection. It's found in the trying."

Caleb nodded again, but his throat burned. This wasn't a noble march toward peace. It was a plunge into the unknown, blind and terrifying. Every instinct told him to turn back, to retreat to the quiet comfort of resentment and avoidance. But something deeper—something he hadn't trusted in a long time—urged him forward.

Faith? Maybe. Or just the fragile hope that things could be different.

Father Mike stood at the open door, robes ruffling in the coastal wind. He didn't smile, didn't speak at first. His presence was still, but his eyes shimmered with something fierce. Expectation. Hope. Maybe a little fear.

"You carry a fire with you, Caleb," he finally said, voice rough with age and prayer. "Don't let the world snuff it out."

And then, from Robert—just a glance. A nod. As if to say: You know what to do. Go.

"Don't forget who you are," he added quietly. "And don't lose yourself trying to save someone else."

The words hit harder than Caleb expected. Because they weren't just a warning. They were a lifeline.

He gripped the letters tighter. "Thank you," he said, barely louder than the wind.

Caleb stepped outside. The heavy wooden door groaned shut behind him. The click echoed down the empty street, final and undeniable.

Port Angeles had never felt so strange. The town he'd known forever—summers spent diving off the docks, winters wrapped in quilts beside a dying fire—now looked different. It felt...distant. The buildings leaned in like silent witnesses. The cobblestones whispered doubt under his boots.

He stared out across the horizon, where the gray sea kissed the sky, endless and uncertain. The brine in the air burned his lungs. Or maybe that was just fear.

The letters rested against his chest like embers, still smoldering. They didn't just speak of his father's mistakes. They spoke of guilt, yes—but also of longing. Of a man who wanted to be more than the sum of his failures.

Caleb had spent years defining his father by his silence. Now, those silences had voices. And those voices were pleading for something more than blame.

His chest ached. Forgiveness, he realized, wasn't something you just gave. It was something you fought for. Over and over. With trembling hands and a bleeding heart.

He walked.

The town didn't welcome him. But it didn't push him away either.

As he passed the familiar streets—the bakery his mom used to take him to, the old church bell that hadn't rung since Easter—he felt both older and younger than he was. Like time folded in on itself here. Like he was walking not just forward but backward too.

The scent of pine and salt caught him mid-stride. It pulled at something raw inside. A memory: His father wiping sweat from his brow, the sun caught in his graying hair, wood shavings clinging to his shirt.

"Patience, Caleb," he used to say, tapping the table gently. "Even the hardest wood yields if you understand the grain."

But Caleb had misunderstood. He thought the grain was failure. A stubbornness that couldn't be shaped. He thought his father's silence meant he didn't care.

Now he wasn't so sure.

The letters weren't perfect. They were fractured, painful. But within the jagged lines, Caleb found glimpses of a man trying to speak. Maybe too late. But trying.

He stopped outside the old workshop.

The windows were dusty. The paint had chipped. But the foundation held.

His hand trembled as he reached for the latch.

This wasn't about crafting something beautiful.

It was about stepping into the truth—even if it left splinters.

He looked up at the sky, gray and wide and wild, and whispered, "I'm here, Dad."

Then he stepped inside.

The door creaked behind him.

The air smelled of cedar, varnish, and something older—something sacred.

And in that sacred silence, Caleb made a choice.

He wouldn't be ruled by anger.

He wouldn't pretend the past hadn't hurt.

But he would face it.

And with each heartbeat, each breath, he would carve something new from what remained.

Something strong.

Something honest.

Something that might, one day, be called healing.

CHAPTER 9

Carving a Future, One Stroke at a Time

CALEB'S KNUCKLES WERE white, gripping the chisel so hard his joints ached. The Stations of the Cross weren't just some pious projects; they were a tombstone, a monument to his father's life cut short. Each meticulous carve was a prayer, a desperate attempt to understand a loss that gnawed at him, a hollowness that no wood could ever fill. The wood screamed under his relentless assault, a mirror of his inner turmoil. He wasn't just carving; he was wrestling with grief, trying to sculpt something beautiful from the raw agony of the past.

"Damn it," he muttered, the chisel slipping slightly, a thin line of sweat tracing a path down his temple. He'd inherited his father's workshop, a cluttered sanctuary smelling of sawdust and regret. It was a tangible link to the man he barely remembered, whose unfinished masterpiece rested heavily on Caleb's shoulders. Finishing it felt like a betrayal, a hollow act that couldn't bring back the vibrant, flawed artist he'd been. But leaving it unfinished felt worse—like abandoning a fallen comrade.

A breath of salty air, the ocean's mournful sigh, cut through the workshop's silence. The door creaked open—Joshua. Caleb didn't need to turn to know it was him. He could feel the shift in the air, a subtle change in pressure, like the arrival of a phantom. Joshua's presence was an unwelcome interruption, a jarring dissonance in Caleb's carefully constructed world of grief and wood. He'd always been the enigma, the silent observer, a man who seemed to move through life with an almost supernatural grace.

He crossed the room, his movements fluid and catlike, and picked up a piece of lignum vitae, its dark heartwood shimmering with an almost unnatural luminescence. "This," Joshua said, his voice a low murmur, a counterpoint to the rhythmic tap-tap-tap of Caleb's hammer, "deserves something more... something bolder."

Caleb didn't respond. He couldn't. The words caught in his throat; a lump of raw emotion too heavy to swallow. He watched Joshua's hands work, long, elegant fingers coaxing the wood into submission. It was effortless, almost magical, a display of skill that fascinated and infuriated him. Joshua's mastery was a constant reminder of Caleb's limitations. His father's, too. Joshua looked up; his gaze meeting Caleb's across the small workshop.

"You're fighting it, Caleb. Letting the grief... dictate the shape."

Caleb slammed his hammer down, the sound echoing in the cramped space. "It's not just wood, Joshua. It's... everything." The words were choked with a grief too profound to articulate.

Joshua held up the smoothly shaped wood. "It can hold everything, Caleb. The good, the bad... the unfinished." He paused, his eyes softening slightly. "Your father would have wanted you to finish it, but he would have wanted you to finish it your way." The unspoken challenge hung heavy between them, a silent duel of wills and shared grief. The air crackled with unspoken emotions.

The ocean's roar, the rhythmic fall of the chisel, the silence between them—it was all a testament to the weight of their shared past and the uncertain future that stretched before them.

Caleb's chisel bit into the cedar, a frantic rhythm against his heart's slow, deliberate thump-thump-thump. Christ's agony took shape under his hands—a ravaged face, thorns a cruel crown. But as the figure emerged, so did Caleb's torment. His father's letters, cryptic scrawls spilling ink like blood, lay scattered—a damn puzzle he couldn't solve. Each word screamed, "You'll never understand, but keep carving!" The weight of it, the unshakeable pressure of his father's legacy, threatened to crack him open.

The doorway sighed open, and Sarah Rayburn-Macall filled the space. She was a paradox, calming yet unsettling, like a ghost who knew your deepest secrets. Her eyes, sharp as a hawk's, drilled into him, the wood, the unfolding scene. It wasn't just the carving that captivated her; it was Caleb himself—the boy scattered like autumn leaves, now forged into something more complex, more mysterious. Yet, the hesitation remained—those micro-pauses between breaths that whispered, "Lost, but searching."

"Caleb," Sarah's voice was soft but cut through the workshop's quiet intensity. "You're pushing yourself too hard."

He didn't look up, his jaw tight. "It has to be perfect."

"Perfect for whom?" A challenge, laced with understanding.

Joshua, working nearby, moved with a fluid grace that made Caleb's frantic efforts seem clumsy. His movements were a dance, not a struggle. Sarah knew this wasn't a competition; both men wrestled with their demons, shaping destinies from wood and sweat.

"He's… different now," Joshua said, his voice low, almost a murmur, as he watched Caleb. "The grief… it's still there, but it's… sharper."

A tense silence hung in the air, thick with unspoken words, the aroma of pine and cedar lingering heavily around them. This wasn't just grief, redemption, or forgiveness—it was something beyond, a fragile hope nestled between their breaths, the faint possibility of healing.

The sunlight streamed through the dusty windows, painting long shadows that seemed to hold their shared burden. Sarah wondered if this stubborn act of creation, this slow, agonizing birth of art, was faith itself.

"It's not just about the wood, is it?" Sarah said softly, breaking the silence.

The question hung in the air, unspoken but deeply felt by all three.

Caleb finally looked up, his eyes haunted, the reflection of the Christ-like figure in his eyes.

"No," he breathed, his voice thick with emotion. "It's about… finding my way back."

The sea roared outside, a relentless rhythm against the quiet intensity of their work. Wood shavings fell like silent tears, each chip a piece of their past, a step toward an uncertain future. They carved not just wood but their lives, one agonizing, hopeful cut at a time.

CARPENTER'S SON

Sweat beaded on Caleb's brow, clinging to the dust that coated his skin. The chisel, a familiar weight in his calloused hand, felt suddenly alien, heavy with the unspoken. This wasn't just wood; it was a confession carved in oak; a desperate plea hammered into the grain. Get it right, Caleb, his frantic heart hammered. Get it right.

Sarah's arrival wasn't a gentle entrance; it was a seismic shift in the air, a change in the very atmosphere of the workshop. Caleb didn't need to see her to feel the tremor of her presence, the unspoken weight between them pressing down like a physical force. He knew, with a sickening certainty, that this wasn't just about carving wood. This was about facing the ghosts that haunted them both.

"Those hands," Sarah breathed, her voice raw, cutting through the silence like a shard of glass. "They remember, don't they? Everything."

Caleb's gaze locked on hers. The wood, a lifeline, felt suddenly fragile under his touch.

"Even when the mind forgets," he replied, his voice a strained whisper, a tightrope walk over a chasm of guilt and regret.

He swallowed hard, the lump in his throat a bitter testament to all the unsaid words between them. And God, there were so many.

Joshua, the ever-patient observer, looked up from his meticulous work, the sunlight filtering through the window and catching the fine particles suspended in the air, like memories hanging just out of reach. The light traced the gentle curve of his smile—a smile tinged with a quiet weariness that felt older than his years. He was a witness, yes, but also a silent accomplice to the weight of their shared past.

"Each stroke, Caleb," Joshua said, his voice soft but carrying the weight of years of unspoken wisdom. "It's not just the carving. It's… it's about finding your way back. Redemption, they call it. Or at least, that's what all those dusty old books I've read seem to suggest."

Sarah moved closer, her eyes fixated on the Stations of the Cross emerging from the wood, the detail excruciatingly precise. Her fingers traced the lines, her touch hesitant, almost reverent.

"It's like the Master Craftsman," she murmured, her voice catching. "The one who shapes us, molds us… and judges us."

Joshua nodded slowly, his gaze unwavering. "Aye. The Master Craftsman never wastes a shaving, Caleb, not a single moment. Efficient, wouldn't you say? Terribly efficient."

His words hung in the air, a chilling echo of the unspoken consequences of their actions.

This wasn't just about carving wood; it was about carving a path towards atonement. And the question wasn't whether he would succeed but whether he deserved to.

The scent of cedar hung heavy in the air, thick and sweet, mirroring the bittersweet ache in Caleb's chest. He ran a calloused thumb over the smooth curve of the wood, the grain yielding slightly beneath his touch. "This..." he murmured, his voice rough, like bark scraping against stone, "this is... different. These letters... my father's words... they're... a confession I never heard." He looked up at Sarah, his eyes, usually calm pools, now stirred with a tempest of unspoken emotions. "Regrets. Hopes... things I didn't know I needed to hear. Apologies..." The final word hung in the air, a fragile thing.

Sarah, her face etched with a concern beyond empathy, took a tentative step closer. Her voice, usually a bright melody, was hushed, fragile. "He was trying to reach you, Caleb. Even from beyond." Caleb scoffed, a short, bitter sound. "Maybe. But it's more than just words on paper, Sarah. It feels like... like he's guiding my chisel, showing me... showing me how to carve out forgiveness... for both of us." A silence stretched, thick and uncomfortable, punctuated only by the rhythmic tick of a clock in the corner. Sarah hugged herself, and the quiet workshop suddenly felt cold and vast. The memories, sharp and cruel, clawed at her. "I'm terrified, Caleb," she whispered, the words barely audible, chased by a tremor in her voice. "That night at Jazz Alley... it haunts me. The past... it won't let go."

Caleb set down his tools with a deliberate thud, the sound sharp and final in the stillness. His gaze, steady and unwavering, met hers. "You're not alone in this, Sarah," he said, his voice a low rumble, a quiet strength that belied his turmoil. The words were simple, yet they held the weight of a promise. "These fears... they don't define you. They're just... rough edges. Time... time will smooth them out." Sarah's smile was a ghost, a flicker of something lost. "Time," she repeated, her voice laced with a weary despair. "Sometimes it feels like an endless ocean, Caleb. Unpredictable. Vast." He nodded, understanding flooding his gaze. A quiet resolve hardened his features. "Even the wildest seas can be navigated, Sarah. And you've always had a damn good compass." Their eyes locked, a silent exchange of understanding passing between them, a silent contract forged in shared pain and unspoken hope.

Joshua stood silently beside them, a silent observer to their unspoken reconciliation, a testament to the resilience of the human spirit. The afternoon sun slanted through the workshop window, casting long shadows that stretched and twisted like the memories they both carried. But a fragile peace began to take shape in the shared act of carving, in the rhythmic scrape of chisel against wood. Because sometimes, when the world feels too heavy, when the past weighs you down, the only way forward is to carve out your peace, one careful stroke at a time.

The joke would come later, a flimsy bandage over a wound already festering. Right now, the air in the workshop hung thick, a suffocating blend of cedar and unspoken dread. It had been one of those afternoons where the world held its breath, a fragile truce with the chaos brewing inside Caleb. The rhythmic scrape of his chisel, usually a soothing mantra, felt frantic, a desperate attempt to drown out the rising tide of something he couldn't name. Joshua's voice, that honeyed whisper, sliced through the forced calm. Caleb knew that voice, carefully chosen words, the deliberate pauses – a prelude to something that would unravel him.

Sarah stood in the doorway, a ghost in the periphery, her stillness more unsettling than any storm. He could feel her there, a silent witness to the impending earthquake. "Once there was a tree," Joshua began, his voice low, almost conspiratorial. "Not just any tree, mind you. Battered, scarred…alone at the edge of the Whispering Cliffs. A hell of a view, but you wouldn't know it, would you?" He chuckled, a brittle sound that didn't quite reach his eyes. The casual dismissal was a mask, a thin veneer over a deep well of something Caleb couldn't fathom.

Caleb's chisel froze, the cedar unwavering beneath it. He glanced at Joshua, a flicker of something akin to pleading in his eyes. This wasn't a story; it was a mirror, reflecting the cracks in Caleb's soul. He needed this story to not be about him, but it was already creeping into his bones. "Most folks saw just an old relic," Joshua continued, his gaze sweeping over them both. "Ready to fall. Ugly, right?" He gestured dismissively, but the movement lacked its usual grace. "But some...they saw something else. Strength. Roots hidden deep, the kind you don't see, the kind you need when the ground gives way beneath you."

The dramatic pause was heavy with unspoken meaning, hanging in the air like the scent of woodsmoke. "It didn't ask for anything... but it offered everything. Shelter. Solace..." His voice trailed off; the final word swallowed by the sudden, suffocating silence. Sarah shifted, a barely perceptible movement, the tremor revealing the weight of what they all knew. The story, the tree—it wasn't about a tree at all. It was about them, their fragile hold on everything they thought they had. The weight of it sat on them all, and Caleb felt the chill wind of fear cutting right through his carefully constructed defenses. He needed to say something, but the words wouldn't come. The joke felt miles away. Far, far too distant for such a moment.

A silence hung heavy, thick as a wool blanket. Caleb's chisel danced across the wood, a restless energy fueling the strokes. He wasn't sure what he was carving – a bird? A woman's face? – but the wood felt right, somehow mirroring the turbulent landscape of his soul. Joshua's words, raw and honest, had cracked open something within him, a stubborn lock of grief finally yielding.

"Funny," Caleb muttered, the words a breath against the rasp of the chisel. "How a tree can teach a man about forgiveness. Or maybe it's just showing me how to hide it better." The self-deprecation bit him, sour and sharp. He hadn't forgiven himself, not really. Not yet. But the wood, at least, was a willing accomplice, offering its grain as a canvas for his unspoken remorse. Each shaving felt like a confession, a shedding of burden.

Joshua's voice, gravelly and calm, cut through the quiet. "The wood speaks, Caleb. It really does. Every cut reveals a bit more of the story, doesn't it? Like life. Full of unexpected twists, knots you gotta work around. You just gotta keep carving." He gestured with his chisel, a practiced hand shaping a graceful curve. He was maddeningly at ease, a whirlwind of philosophical pronouncements amid the fragrant wood shavings. It felt unfair, Caleb thought, this effortless grace in the face of such shared pain.

Sarah watched from the doorway, a silent observer in the scene. She saw the men and their wood and the unspoken threads binding them together. Hope? Maybe. Or just a shared weariness that transcended words. The sound of Caleb's chisel accelerated, a frantic rhythm mirroring her heart's urgency.

"Beautiful," Sarah breathed, the word a soft crack in the silence. "It's... it's truly beautiful, Caleb." Caleb looked up, his gaze meeting hers. A fleeting moment of connection, raw and electric. Something hung between them, unspoken, yet thick with the weight of shared history and unspoken desires. He nodded, then returned to the wood, but his touch, he realized, had altered. It held a lightness he hadn't felt in years, a growing assurance that perhaps, just perhaps, healing was possible.

Seemingly oblivious to the emotional currents swirling around him, Joshua resumed his carving. Then, as if a distant memory had surfaced, he spoke again. "The wood doesn't lie, Caleb. Every knot, every crack, it's all part of the story. You find it, and, well... you shape not just the wood, but yourself in the process." His voice held a weariness that belied his earlier nonchalance. The shared experience touched him, too, Caleb realized. Even the unflappable Joshua carried burdens. Their burdens, though different, intertwined.

And as Caleb carved on, he felt a quiet resolve take root – not just to shape the wood but to shape his own life, too, finally.

Sarah felt the words sink in, a quiet relief soothing her frayed nerves. Caleb's rhythmic carving filled the workshop, the fading light painting long shadows across the rough-hewn wood. A chill touched the air, but the warmth inside—a fragile peace—held her fast. She realized it wasn't just the wood that needed shelter, a sudden, sharp understanding piercing the quiet. They all did. And maybe, just maybe, they'd stumbled upon it, here in this sanctuary, this refuge. But a knot of anxiety tightened in her chest. This peace felt too fragile, too quickly shattered. The memory of Joshua's desperate plea, the fear in his eyes, clawed at her. Was this enough? Could this carved haven truly withstand the storm brewing outside?

Caleb's chisel hung frozen; a sliver of steel poised above the whispering pine. The silence in the workshop pressed down, thick and suffocating, a weight heavier than any timber. He glanced at Sarah, her face etched with the same bone-deep weariness that gnawed at him. He hadn't seen her this drained since… since the fire.

"This wood," he rasped, his voice a dry scratch against the smooth grain, "it remembers. Everything. The good, the bad… the unbearable." The words felt like confessions ripped from his throat.

Sarah's breath hitched. "And us, Caleb? What do *we* remember? What do we hold onto?" Her question hung in the air, raw and desperate, a plea disguised as an accusation.

He slammed his fist onto the workbench, echoing the turmoil inside him. "Hope, Sarah. Stubborn hope. We cling to it, even when it feels like dust in our hands." He ran a calloused thumb across the wood, tracing the grain, the ghost of his father's touch in his own. "This isn't just wood, it's… it's a fight. A testament to us refusing to let go."

"But what if we *do* let go?" Sarah's voice cracked, the fear palpable. The tightrope image, the chasm below, was a stark reality in her eyes. The memory of her own father's loss burned fresh.

Caleb met her gaze, his own eyes dark pools reflecting her terror. "Then we start again," he said, his voice steadier now, the sculptor's resolve hardening his features. "We rebuild. We find strength in the wreckage, in the shared weight of… of everything."

He raised the chisel, the steel glinting like a fragile promise. The chisel bit into the wood, a decisive *thunk* sliced through the silence, a defiance thrown into the face of their shared grief.

The late sun, a bruised plum in the sky, cast long shadows across the shop floor. Fine pine dust curled lazily through the golden light, shifting like restless memories unwilling to settle. The aroma—sharp, clean, unyielding—filled his lungs, a cruel reminder that his father's ghost lingered, not just in the grain of the wood, but in every pause between Caleb's breaths.

Sarah's arrival had been a sudden, icy gust of wind. There were no pleasantries; she was a hurricane in a quiet dress. She didn't just look at his work; she saw the grief bleeding into the grain, the shadows mimicking the fragmented memories that haunted them both. His father's hidden letters, the cryptic carvings, the unspoken words—a legacy that clawed at his soul.

"Look," she whispered, her voice barely audible above his chisel's rhythmic *thunk-thunk-thunk*. "The shadows… they're like memories, flickering."

Her green eyes, usually so alive, held a haunted depth that mirrored his own. Caleb stopped, the chisel trembling in his hand. He saw it, too – the shapes dancing on the wood echoes of his father's absence and secrets. The unspoken words were more than just carvings; they were a scream trapped within the wood, and it was a scream he recognized.

He felt his grief rise like a bitter tide, threatening to drown him. He had to finish this, for himself, for her, for the memory of his father. He had to carve a new path through the darkness.

"Memories are a shroud, a sanctuary," Caleb finally rasped, the words tasting like ash. It wasn't just the wood but his father's unfinished symphony, a melody he felt compelled – terrified – to complete. The weight of it pressed down, a physical thing.

Sarah's nod was slow, a silent acknowledgment of the shared burden. The green in her eyes deepened, mirroring the shadows clinging to the workshop walls. "Your father would be proud," she said, her voice low, a firm anchor in the swirling anxieties. It wasn't platitude; it was truth, a lifeline thrown across the chasm of their unspoken grief. But the unspoken question clawed at them: how long until the weight crushed them?

Caleb didn't crave praise, not really. But his father's imagined nod, that ghost of approval in the dust-motes, hit him like a punch. A fragile connection forged in sawdust and sweat. A future, maybe. But a cold fear slithered into his elation. *Had he earned it? Or was it pity?* The doubt gnawed.

Joshua, ever Joshua, lurked at the periphery, a watchful gargoyle. He felt the workshop's rhythm, creation hum, and unspoken anxieties swirling as thick as sawdust. This wasn't just a workshop but a forge shaping wood and souls. Caleb felt the transformation – sweat slicking his palms, muscles screaming – a desperate need to prove himself worthy.

"He's good, isn't he?" Sarah's voice, soft as a sigh, pierced his concentration. He didn't meet her gaze, the chisel a frantic extension of his own racing heart, each stroke a desperate plea for validation.

Joshua grunted, calloused fingers tracing his wood's smooth, untouched surface. "Patience, Sarah. Some things… take root slowly." His voice, rough with years and quiet wisdom tinged with melancholy, held the weight of a thousand silent battles. He saw the fight raging in Caleb's eyes, mirrored in the wood grain itself.

Caleb's tap-tap-tap chisel became a frantic heartbeat, a desperate counterpoint to the silence. Sarah watched her expression, a heartbreaking blend of hope and empathy. She saw beyond the carving, Caleb wrestling with his demons, each hesitant stroke a step toward a reconciliation he wasn't sure he could achieve. He wasn't shaping wood; he was shaping his relationship with his father and his self-worth. He was carving his future from the very core of his doubts.

The air hung thick with unspoken dread, heavier than the lingering sawdust suspended in the slanting light of the crimson sunset. His gaze settled on the half-finished carving, and Joshua felt that familiar ache of helplessness stir in his chest. This wasn't just woodwork—it was Caleb's soul, raw and exposed, etched into every imperfect groove. He'd seen too many souls come undone in this very room, witnessed the fragile balance between resilience and surrender. He ached to step in, to shield Caleb from the storm gathering inside him, but Caleb's fierce independence—so noble, so maddening—held him at bay. This was a battle Caleb had to fight on his own terms. Still, Joshua would remain close, a steady presence just beyond reach, ready to gather the pieces when they fell.

Sarah's hand sought Caleb's, her grip surprisingly firm, a silent vow of resistance against the encroaching darkness. The tremor in her voice was undeniable, but her resolve burned fiercely. "We face him together," she declared, the words a fragile shield against the impending storm.

The last rays of the sun bled out, plunging the workshop into a twilight heavy with foreboding. The silence was no longer tense; it was pregnant with the threat of violence. The battle wasn't a mere possibility; it was imminent.

Caleb's heart hammered against his ribs, a desperate drumbeat against the approaching darkness. With a chilling certainty, he knew this fight would define them – break them or forge them into something more substantial, unyielding.

CHAPTER 10

The Gathering Storm

THE CHILL WIND bit at Sarah Rayburn-Macall's cheeks, a counterpoint to the autumn sun painting Port Angeles in fiery hues. She ignored the beauty; her gut clenched tighter than the worn leather strap of her satchel. Each breath was a ragged gasp, her senses screaming warnings even before she saw him.

Across the street, a silhouette against the dying light. Jake Macall. Leaning casually against a lamppost, he was all deceptive ease, a predator disguised as a man waiting for a bus. But his gaze, that icy, unwavering stare, hit her like a physical blow. The accusation in his eyes was a tangible thing, a rope around her throat, choking the air from her lungs. He was a specter, a constant reminder of the life she'd desperately tried to outrun.

"He's still here," she thought, a cold dread blossoming in her chest. "He hasn't let go."

"Damn it," she muttered, her voice swallowed by the wind. She had to move. She had to. This was her town, her life, and she wouldn't let him—couldn't let him—steal it back. Her steps were brisk and resolute, a defiant rhythm against the tremble in her hands. Laughter drifted from a nearby café, the crisp tang of salt and cedar in the air offering a fragile thread of comfort against the rising tide of fear. This was the life she had fought to reclaim, one free of his shadow. Yet the past moved like an undertow, always waiting to drag her beneath the surface.

The familiar trace of sawdust and varnish, once a source of calm, now barely dulled the ache. Wheeler's Hardware felt less like a safe haven and more like a bandage slapped over a wound still bleeding.

The hinges groaned as she entered, echoing the tight, unsteady beat of her heart.

Peggy Wheeler, a woman carved from the same stubborn oak she worked, stood over a piece of cedar, her silver hair pulled back tight, a carving knife poised like a question mark. "Sarah," Peggy said, her voice the steady tap-tap-tap of her chisel, a rhythm that belied the storm in her eyes. "You look like you wrestled a grizzly and lost."

Sarah's voice cracked, the carefully constructed wall around her emotions crumbling. "It's Jake, Peggy. He was across from the school. Watching."

The words felt small, insufficient to contain the terror that clawed at her throat. Peggy's hand froze, the knife hovering inches from the cedar, the silence stretching taut, heavy with unspoken fear. Slivers of light slanted through the workshop window, catching on the still air like whispers left hanging—quiet, cruel reminders of how fragile everything had become.

"Again?" Peggy's voice was low, a rumble of weary anger. "Damn him, he won't stop, will he?" The calm in her eyes had vanished, replaced by a dangerous glint, a predator's awareness. "What does he *want*, Sarah? What the hell does he want?"

Sarah swallowed, the lump in her throat tightening. "He wasn't close enough to speak, but... I *felt* him, Peggy. I knew he was there." A raw and primal shiver ran down her spine, a cold finger tracing the fear etched into her bones. The wind howled outside a mournful counterpoint to the frantic beat of her heart.

Peggy's calloused thumb brushed away a smear of sawdust from Sarah's cheek, the motion softer than the words that soon followed. "Come here, kiddo," she rasped, her voice a low rumble that betrayed the tremor in her hands. The sharp odor of varnish and aged timber barely concealed the heavy atmosphere, thick with the unease that seemed to cling to the air like an oppressive fog. It was a fear that mirrored the cold, tightening grip around Sarah's heart, suffocating and relentless.

Jake. His shadow stretched long and menacing in her mind, a chilling reminder of the power he wielded, the control he craved.

Hesitantly, Sarah moved, drawn to the warmth from Peggy, a haven in the storm brewing inside her. She buried her face in Peggy's worn apron, the familiar scent of wood and sweat a grounding presence. Peggy's embrace was a rock, solid and unwavering, a stark contrast to the shaky ground beneath her feet.

"He... he was at the school," Sarah whispered, her voice choked with unshed tears. The words were a confession, a stripping bare of her vulnerability. The fear wasn't just for herself; it was the suffocating weight of responsibility for others.

Peggy tightened her hold. "I know, sweetheart," she murmured, her voice thick with empathy. "But he won't touch you here. Not while I'm breathing." The words were a fierce vow, a testament to the intense loyalty burning in her heart. It wasn't just protection but a promise from a deep, unspoken understanding.

Sarah pulled away, her eyes glistening. "Thank you," she choked out, ragged and raw. "I... I don't know what I'd do without you, Peggy."

Peggy's gaze softened. "This ain't just a workshop, Sarah. It's home. And you'll always have a place here."

The storm inside Sarah raged on, but Peggy's unwavering presence carved a small pocket of calm. A fragile peace, a precarious truce. But peace was a fleeting luxury. Jake was still out there.

* * *

Across town, Caleb Martin's chisel sang a frantic rhythm against the pine. Each precise cut was a controlled explosion of rage, a desperate attempt to channel the fury that threatened to consume him. The scent of pine and sweat filled the air, thick with the unspoken tension.

He'd heard the whispers, the chilling accounts of Jake's menacing presence near the school. His gut twisted; Sarah's vulnerability was a raw nerve. He'd watched from the shadows, a silent guardian consumed by his inaction. No more.

The wood groaned, a sound mimicking the protest in Caleb's gut as his chisel bit too deep, splintering the already fragile figure of Christ. These Stations of the Cross weren't just a religious exercise anymore;

they were a desperate plea, a frantic attempt to carve out a future where Sarah survived.

Caleb stood at his workbench, the chisel trembling in his grip. The sharp aroma of cedar lingered in the air, but it did nothing to soothe the storm within him. His workshop, once a sanctuary, now felt stifling—the walls pressing in, mirroring the weight of his helplessness. His hands, once precise in their craft, betrayed him now—fingers aching from the strain, movements faltering with frustration.

Each meticulously etched detail in the wood was a plea, a desperate prayer carved into something tangible. He needed something to hold on to that wouldn't slip through his fingers like everything else. But faith felt fragile tonight, distant and hollow. He slammed the chisel down, its sharp clang against the workbench, echoing the rage roiling beneath his skin.

Sarah was in danger. And he was failing her.

The thought nearly knocked the wind from his chest. He clenched his jaw, muscles taut as if bracing for a blow. He had spent his life-solving problems with his hands, shaping raw, unyielding wood into something with purpose. But this—this fight, this looming threat—was something he couldn't carve into submission. He had no blueprint for this, no measured strokes to follow.

A deep voice cut through his turmoil. "Rough day?"

Caleb didn't turn. He didn't need to. Joshua Shepherd's presence was as steady as the carved Stations of the Cross lining the far wall, a quiet counterbalance to Caleb's unrest. The older man stepped inside, his movements fluid and precise. He picked up a block of maple, running a calloused thumb along its grain, a small gesture of respect. Caleb envied the ease with which Joshua moved, the control in his hands, the certainty that radiated from him like a steady flame.

"Sarah's in danger," Joshua continued, his voice even edged with something deeper, unspoken.

Caleb exhaled sharply. "Understatement of the century. And I... I'm failing her."

Joshua's gaze was unwavering, unreadable. "You sure about that?"

Caleb let out a bitter laugh, shaking his head. "I should be doing something. Anything. But instead, I'm here. Whittling away at a hopeless prayer."

Joshua's fingers drummed against the wood, a quiet rhythm that seemed to measure Caleb's turmoil. "Ever hear the parable of the oak and the reed?"

Caleb shot him a look, weary and sharp. "You gonna start laying fables on me? Think I'm some stubborn mule that needs a good lesson?"

A small, knowing smile played at the corner of Joshua's mouth. "Would I be far off?"

Caleb didn't answer, jaw tightening as he looked back at the ruined piece of wood before him. His father's voice echoed in his memory—steady, instructive, always patient. Caleb had spent his childhood watching those strong hands work, shaping wood with purpose, each stroke deliberate. But his father was gone now, his wisdom nothing more than a ghost in the grain of unfinished work.

Joshua leaned against the workbench; arms folded. "There was this oak," he began, voice low and measured. "Mighty, stubborn, refusing to bend in any storm. Next to it, a reed—slender, flexible, swaying with every gust. When the big one hit—the kind that tears the earth apart—the oak fought. It fought until it broke."

Caleb swallowed hard. "And the reed?"

Joshua's gaze softened. "The reed bent. And lived."

Silence stretched between them, thick with unspoken fears. The storm outside raged against the workshop walls, and the wind howled through the cracks, but inside, there was only the weight of Joshua's question.

"So, Caleb... are you the oak?"

Caleb exhaled shakily, his grip loosening on the chisel. He had spent his whole life standing firm, refusing to yield. But this wasn't about pride. This wasn't about being unshakable. This was about surviving and protecting what mattered most.

His gaze drifted to his father's unfinished masterpiece—"Agony in the Garden." The carved lines of Christ's suffering mirrored his own turmoil, the weight of an unbearable burden pressed into the wood. He traced a finger over the unfinished edges, the rawness of it a reflection of himself.

He didn't want to break.

"I don't know how to bend, Joshua," he admitted, voice barely above a whisper. "I don't know how to let go."

Joshua nodded as if he understood something Caleb couldn't yet put into words. "Then maybe it's time you learn."

"Damn it, Joshua," Caleb breathed, his voice raw. "You think I haven't seen that?" The confession hung between them, thick with unspoken years. Joshua's gaze held a flicker of something akin to pain, a shared understanding etched deep within his lines. "I'm saying... sometimes resilience isn't about a damn fight, Caleb. It's about knowing when to bend. When to... let go."

The rhythmic whisper of the plane, the creak of the ancient wood—the sounds of their shared sanctuary—faded beneath the weight of their fear. Outside, a dove's mournful coo mocked the storm raging inside Caleb. He stared at the half-finished panel, the carved agony mirroring his own. He'd fought this project tooth and nail, a desperate attempt to wrestle control from the grief that clawed at him. Now, Joshua's simple yet profound words shattered his carefully constructed walls of self-reliance.

Surrender. Was it wisdom or weakness disguised? The thought choked him. He closed his eyes, a shuddering breath escaping his lips, years of stubborn resistance finally giving way.

"Flexibility," he whispered, the word tasting alien, foreign to the rigidity of his soul.

"Over brute force..." Joshua's smile was small, but it held a deep understanding that reached Caleb's core. "Strength has many faces, Caleb. Sometimes, the strongest thing you can do is admit you can't do it alone."

As Joshua resumed his work, a quiet shift occurred in Caleb. He picked up his chisel, the familiar weight feeling different, lighter somehow. It wasn't a weapon now but a tool for healing, a conduit for his grief. Each stroke became a prayer, a weaving together of wood, sorrow, and reluctant acceptance.

* * *

Across town, in Sarah Macall's cramped workshop, the aroma of wood and varnish did little to mask the icy dread that clung to her. Her fingers trembled as she traced the grain of the old workbench, the familiar comfort offering no solace.

"Jake... he's not just going to... disappear, is he?" Her voice, a mere breath, cracked with fear so raw it ached. The question hung in the air, thick and suffocating, mirroring the terror that clawed at her insides.

Peggy's sandpaper stilled. Her gaze, sharp as shattered glass yet softened by a lifetime of hard-won wisdom, met Sarah's. "Storms don't just vanish, honey," Peggy said, her voice rough but laced with a deep empathy born of experience. "They leave scars. You gotta stand your ground, Sarah. Be the lighthouse on those cliffs—shine your light, but don't let the waves drag you down."

Sarah's breath hitched. The unspoken question—" how?"—clawed at her throat, a physical thing. Panic, raw and visceral, choked her. How could she possibly shine, a flickering candle against this suffocating darkness? The fear wasn't just a feeling but a lead weight crushing her chest.

Peggy's hand, rough as bark, squeezed Sarah's. The worn leather notebook felt strangely solid in her palm. "Write it all down," Peggy's voice rasped, urgency lacing her words. "Every shiver, every whisper, every damn message. Then you go to Father Mike. The police, if you have to. But you don't fight this alone, you hear me? You're not alone."

The words weren't calming but a spark. A tiny, defiant ember against the creeping cold. Sarah clutched the notebook, its texture a lifeline in the swirling chaos of her fear.

"Not alone." The words tasted like ash and hope.

* * *

Night swallowed the Sanctuary of Wood and Memory, the shadows deepening. The silence hummed with untold stories, a symphony of whispered fears and forgotten faith. His face etched with a weariness that mirrored her own, Caleb met her gaze. He hadn't spoken much, but the shared weight of their private terrors seemed to bridge the chasm between them. His eyes, usually bright with mischievousness, held a haunted depth.

He knew. He understood the battle raging within her, mirrored in his heart.

"It's not a ghost, Sarah," Caleb finally said, his voice low, a counterpoint to the rustling leaves. "It's something... else. Something that feeds on fear."

He flinched, a tremor betraying the fear he tried to mask. His demons weren't just whispering in the dark anymore. They were snarling beasts nipping at his heels. The weight of family secrets, the gnawing guilt of past mistakes, was a constant companion.

Sarah nodded; her fear momentarily eclipsed by recognizing a shared struggle. "I know," she whispered back, her voice trembling. "And I'm terrified."

The admission felt strangely liberating. They were both terrified, yet in that shared vulnerability, a fragile understanding bloomed. Perhaps, just perhaps, facing the darkness together was the only way to find the light.

The battle was far from won, but for the first time that night, neither of them felt completely lost in the suffocating shadows.

* * *

Caleb's rough fingers, calloused from years of battling both wood and demons, traced the unfinished panel. The cedar grain, stubborn and intricate, mirrored the knots in his soul. The chisel felt heavy, a lead weight in his hand, a physical manifestation of the unresolved grief that clung to him like a shroud. Like his life, this carving was a fractured thing, its meaning buried deep within the heartwood, demanding skill and an act of courage he wasn't sure he possessed.

A low hum vibrated from the workshop—the comforting rhythm of saws and planers—a counterpoint to the frantic beat of his own heart. The sea's sigh, a familiar lament, whispered through the open window, starkly contrasting the tempest still raging within him.

"Think you'll ever finish it, Caleb?" Joshua's voice, low and steady, broke through Caleb's turmoil. He didn't need to turn to know Joshua was there, a steadfast presence.

Caleb swallowed, the lump thick with unshed tears and unspoken words. "I... I don't know, Josh. Sometimes I feel like I'm just hacking away at the darkness, not carving anything real."

Joshua's hand landed on his shoulder, a comforting weight. "It's not about hacking, Caleb. It's about letting the story reveal itself. You're letting it out, bit by bit."

Their shared silence was more potent than words, a testament to their years navigating life's treacherous currents. Caleb saw the concern etched onto Joshua's face, which understood the depths of Caleb's pain, not pity, but with the hard-earned empathy of a true friend. He picked up the mallet, the polished wood warm against his calloused palm. Each blow, once fueled by rage, was now deliberate, a prayer hammered into the cedar's heart. With every precise cut, a sliver of anger, regret, and suffocating fear loosened its grip. He wasn't carving peace; he was coaxing it out, allowing the story within the wood—and within himself—to unfold.

* * *

The late sun, a bruised apricot in the western sky, cast long shadows across Port Angeles' cobblestones as Sarah stumbled out of Peggy Wheeler's workshop. The sharp, clean air felt like a reprieve after the stifling claustrophobia of the cluttered space. The past few months had been a relentless assault, a brutal cycle of fleeting peace and gnawing dread. But something felt... different. Lighter. Maybe.

Peggy's words, raw and unflinching, echoed in Sarah's ears, a powerful counterpoint to the suffocating silence she'd endured for so long. Someone had listened. Listened. The difference was staggering. Each step away from the workshop felt like shedding a layer of lead. The weight on her shoulders hadn't completely vanished, but it was more manageable now, like carrying a heavy backpack instead of a condemned man's scaffold. The fear hadn't completely dissipated, but a fragile ember of hope flickered in its place, a tiny spark in the encroaching darkness. It was a delicate thing; this hope was quickly extinguished, but for now, it was enough.

Saint Peter's Church, its spire a defiant finger against the bruised sky, loomed. Hope, stubborn and desperate, clawed at Sarah. The closer she got, the stronger the pull, a humming in the stones, a silent plea for salvation. This town hadn't entirely rejected her; a flicker of kindness, maybe even hope, remained.

The heavy church door groaned open, drawing her into a hush of sacred stillness. Stained glass fractured the dying light into a shifting kaleidoscope. The familiar aroma—beeswax, aged wood, incense—wrapped around her like memory. Caleb stood near the altar, a dark silhouette framed by flickering votives, looking almost... at peace.

Doubt, a cold sliver, pierced Sarah. This wasn't impulsive; it was something more profound, a pull she couldn't name. Caleb worked with quiet intensity, his hands moving with a surgeon's grace. She saw the flex of his forearms, the controlled power—years of honed skill. This wasn't just craftsmanship but a prayer, a silent offering.

"Caleb," she whispered, her voice barely audible. "Your work... it's breathtaking."

He looked up, startled, but fleeting yet genuine relief warmed his blue eyes. Their depth held the unwavering intensity of the sea. "It's... almost done," he murmured, rubbing his neck, a nervous tic. "Each piece... it's part of a story. The town's, mine... ours."

His voice was hesitant, yet a raw vulnerability choked Sarah. The unspoken question hung heavy: would their stories finally intertwine, or would fear tear them apart?

Sarah's gaze landed on the half-finished panel. Christ slumped beneath the cross, hands clawing at the earth—a raw, visceral depiction. Her throat tightened.

"Which station is this?" she asked, her voice rougher than intended.

His chisel was still in hand, and Caleb stepped back, a muscle twitching in his jaw. "The third. Accepting help when you fall."

He avoided her eyes, the silence thick with unspoken things. He knew the bitter irony, the agonizing struggle of accepting help, especially after the abyss he'd stared into.

Their eyes finally met. Sarah saw it—the same weary battle she fought, the ghost of a man buried under grief. He'd lost more than she knew, the burden on his face. This shared understanding wasn't comfort, but a brutal bond forged in suffering. A bond that both terrified and strangely, fiercely comforted her.

The weight of his sorrow mirrored her own, a silent understanding transcending word. She felt a desperate need to reach out, to offer the fragile hope she still clung to, but the fear of rejection, of pushing him further into his despair, held her back.

Heavy and potent, the unspoken question hung between them: Could they genuinely find solace in each other's pain, or would it consume them both?

We'll get through this," Sarah whispered, the words catching in her throat, brittle and fragile. Not blind optimism—faith. A desperate clinging to something real against the crushing weight of grief. The words felt paper-thin, but they were all she had.

Caleb nodded once, sharp, almost mechanical. But his hands betrayed him, trembling where they rested at his sides. "Together," he said, the word like splintered glass in his mouth.

Silence stretched between them, thick and suffocating, threaded with everything unspoken. The weight of shared loss pressed down like an iron shroud. Healing wasn't a miracle—it was a fight, a brutal climb up a cliffside of jagged grief.

Inside Saint Peter's, the old wooden pews groaned beneath their weight, and the fragrance of incense curled through the air—warm, familiar, like a memory half-forgotten. The church offered no grand revelations, no burning-bush epiphanies. Just stillness. The quiet dignity of a place where pain had been carried before, where faith had been tested and found either wanting or unbreakable.

Later, in the workshop, the last slanting rays of light turned floating dust into flecks of gold. Caleb stood before the unfinished Stations of the Cross, his breath uneven. The swirling patterns in the oak grain mirrored the storm inside him. The aroma of pine tar and sawdust clung to his skin—his father's legacy, both a comfort and a chain.

This place was his inheritance. And his prison.

His fingers brushed the unfinished wood, calloused skin against smooth grain. The contrast felt cruel. Could he finish his father's work? Could he even start without drowning under the weight of expectation?

The chisel lay abandoned on the bench, its steel blade catching the last light. An accusation.

His gaze settled on the third station—Christ accepting help.

A raw ache bloomed in his chest, sharp and deep. The truth coiled around his ribs, suffocating: he wasn't meant to do this alone. But solitude had always been his armor, a shield against disappointment, against failure. Against the quiet, gnawing fear that if he reached out— if he trusted—he'd only be left behind. Again.

He exhaled sharply; the sound harsh in the quiet.

Sarah's touch lingered on his sleeve, a warmth he wanted to shake off. Needed to. But the weight in her eyes, the quiet understanding, made something in him crack. She saw it. Saw him.

The grief. The fear. The crushing exhaustion of pretending he could bear it alone.

His throat burned.

"Endurance," he whispered, the word rough, jagged. "Isn't a damn solo act."

The image of Simon of Cyrene flickered in his mind—the shared weight, the communal lift. He needed that. Needed them. The bitter creed his father had drilled into him—*bend, don't break*—fought to take root, but he shoved it down. Survival wasn't the victory. Strength wasn't in enduring alone. It was in letting himself be *carried* when his knees buckled.

The cold night air crept through the open window, sharp against his skin. Above the cliffs, the first star broke through the bruised sky.

He let out a slow breath.

The day was over. But this—this was just the beginning.

His fingers curled around the chisel, the steel grounding him, steadying him. The weight of it was familiar. A promise.

The wood held its secrets, its stories, waiting to be coaxed free. And he would carve them out. One stroke at a time. Not alone. Not this time.

Tomorrow, he would carve.

Tomorrow, he would trust.

And maybe—just maybe—tomorrow, he wouldn't carry the weight alone.

ACT 3

FORGIVENESS AT THE EDGE OF GRACE

CHAPTER 11

A Prodigal Father Found

SUNLIGHT SLANTED THROUGH the high windows of Caleb's workshop, painting long golden streaks across the wooden floor. Particles hovered in the still air, suspended like fragments of memory caught in a hush. The scent of pine and varnish hung thick around him, comforting in its familiarity. His chisel, warm from his grip, carved delicate lines into the sorrowful face of Christ. Each careful cut felt like a prayer, each fine curl of wood a whispered plea for something he couldn't quite name.

The weight of the past week pressed against his ribs. Sleep had been elusive, his thoughts gnawed at by worry and regret, by memories he hadn't meant to unearth. But here, in the hush of his workshop, the chaos quieted. The rhythmic scrape of his chisel was the only voice he could bear to listen to.

Then, the phone rang.

The shrill, insistent tone knifed through the stillness, shattering the fragile peace he'd woven around himself. Caleb flinched. The chisel slipped. A harsh gash marred the delicate curve of Christ's cheek, a wound that had not been meant for Him. A curse rose to his lips, swallowed before it could take shape.

He set the chisel down, exhaling through his nose, jaw tight. The carving had taken him weeks, hours of labor poured into every groove and ridge. It was meant for Saint Peter's by the Sea—a piece of himself offered to something greater. Now, the flaw seemed irreparable. A scar across divinity.

The phone rang again, each shrill note tightening the coil of unease in his stomach. Caleb wiped his hands on his apron, the motion slow, deliberate. He didn't want to answer. Calls at this hour never carried good news. His fingers hovered over the receiver, a hesitation thick with something nameless, something close to fear.

Finally, he forced himself to lift the phone to his ear.

"Father Mike?" His voice came out rough, sandpaper against stone. A throat dry from sawdust—but also from something deeper, something raw.

A pause. Then, Father Mike's voice, steady but threaded with urgency.

"Caleb, my boy... I have news. News I pray you're ready for."

The room seemed to shrink, the warmth of sunlight turning cold against his skin. Caleb gripped the phone tighter, bracing himself for the words that would change everything.

The priest's words carried weight, an unsteady gravity that settled deep in Caleb's chest. His fingers tightened around the receiver, the old wood smooth beneath his grip.

"What is it?" He swallowed, but his pulse was already surging, thudding against his ribs.

The silence stretched too long. Then, finally, the words came, and they landed like a hammer strike.

"It's Thomas... your father," Father Mike's voice wavered, a tremor barely contained. "He's been found. Alive."

Alive.

The word hit Caleb with the force of a gut-punch, knocking the breath from his lungs. The room seemed to tilt, the walls pressing in. His free hand found the edge of the workbench, steadying himself as something sharp and cold sliced through him. Disbelief. Anger. A tangle of emotions that clawed their way to the surface.

Alive?

His father—who had vanished like a ghost, leaving nothing but an aching absence. The man he had spent years trying not to hate. The man he had grieved, resented, and, eventually, forced himself to forget.

The receiver slipped from his fingers and clattered against the wooden table, but Caleb barely heard it. His breath came shallow, uneven.

Twenty years. Twenty years of silence. Of walls-built brick by brick, of carving away the hollow parts of himself until he could stand in the world without them. And now, with two words, those walls threatened to crumble.

He dragged a hand through his hair, fingers shaking. "Alive?" The word escaped him, half a whisper, half a plea.

He stared at the carving in front of him—the unfinished shape of a figure, its details blurred in the dim light. His hands had been steady only moments ago, but now, they trembled.

The aroma of pine hung thick in the air, mingling with the salt of the sea breeze drifting through the open window. The carvings around him, his silent companions in solitude, seemed to lean in, listening. Waiting.

Caleb forced himself to breathe, to claw back some semblance of control. His voice came low, tight. "Are you sure?" He needed it to be a mistake. A misunderstanding. Something—anything—that would let him push it all back into the past, where it belonged.

Father Mike's answer came swift, unyielding. "Very sure." A beat. Then, softer, the weight of compassion thick in his tone. "It's a long story, Caleb. But your father—he's asking for you. He needs you."

The line went dead.

Caleb stood there, phone still in his hand, the dial tone droning in his ear.

He hadn't seen Thomas in two decades. Hadn't spoken his name in years. Had trained himself not to wonder, not to feel.

And now, against all reason, the past had come knocking.

His father was alive.

And he wanted Caleb to come.

But could he?

Would he?

The weight of twenty years pressed against his ribs, and for the first time in a long time, Caleb wasn't sure if he could bear it.

"Damn it," he breathed, the words unraveling beneath the sudden roar swelling in his ears. He stared at the scattered wood shavings, their once-comforting aroma of cedar now acrid and biting, clinging to his throat like smoke. Sunlight slashed through the workshop window, illuminating fine particles suspended in the air—tiny fragments of wood and memory drifting like ash from a fire long extinguished. He dragged a trembling hand through his hair, the motion jagged, mirroring the erratic drumbeat of his heart. "Why now?" The question burst from him, raw and unfiltered, like something wounded. After all this time—after locking Thomas away in the attic of his memory, sealed behind years of silence and carefully kept distance—why had the past chosen this moment to break free?

A bitter laugh escaped him. Hope? The word felt like a betrayal, a cruel joke. "Hope?" he spat, the word tasting like ash in his mouth. "How the hell could I... after everything he did?" He was trapped, frozen in the heart of his chaos, and suddenly, the sanctuary of his workshop was a cage. Once his solace, the tools felt alien, cold, and menacing.

That's when he heard the quiet sigh of the door opening. He didn't need to turn. He knew that steady, peaceful presence. Joshua. A consolation on the storm raging inside him. "Joshua," Caleb whispered, his voice barely audible, cracking under the strain of his turmoil. Joshua didn't speak, just stood there, a silent pillar of strength. His eyes held a deep understanding beyond words, a quiet acknowledgment of the war raging within Caleb. He didn't push. He never did.

"Father Mike called," Caleb confessed, the words tasting like sawdust and salt, thick and painful. "It's about my... my father." The admission was a physical blow, leaving him breathless and reeling. The silence that followed stretched, taut and heavy, the unspoken questions hanging between them, a suffocating blanket. The weight of twenty years of abandonment and unanswered questions pressed down on him, threatening to crush him.

Joshua's gaze, soft yet unwavering, held Caleb's. "Sometimes," he said, his voice a low rumble, "life leaves us with half-finished carvings, Caleb. But we get the tools, see? Even if we don't know how to use them." Caleb sucked in a ragged breath, the air tasting stale in his lungs. The tension, a vise around his chest for years, eased fractionally. Joshua's words weren't a magic cure for the anger and confusion that gnawed at him, but they cracked open a sliver of space, a place to just... exist. He understood, finally. He wouldn't face whatever came next alone. Not this time.

His fingers, trembling slightly, hovered over the rough-hewn wood, the chisel poised like a frozen question mark. The half-carved figure, a silent testament to broken dreams, seemed to stare back at him, a blurred echo of a life he'd barely known. His eyes, dark and stormy, locked onto Joshua's. Years of suppressed fury, of unanswered questions, threatened to burst forth.

The floodgates had already started to crack, hitting him with a sickening jolt. "Thomas is alive," he breathed, the words bitter as ash. The truth struck like a jagged chisel, tearing through the walls he had built around his heart. "They found him... at the VA hospital in Port Orchard." His voice, stripped bare, carried the weight of years spent fortifying himself. Speaking the words felt like ripping away scar tissue, exposing the raw wound beneath.

Joshua remained motionless, a granite statue against the storm raging within Caleb. His eyes held a calm that bordered on unsettling, a quiet refuge in the chaos. "That's... unexpected," he said, his voice a steady anchor.

"Unexpected?" Caleb's laugh was a bitter, brittle thing, laced with disbelief. "A man vanishes, leaves a gaping hole in your life, and now... now he's back? Is this some cruel joke?" His voice cracked, the dam holding back his emotions finally crumbling. Tears stung his eyes, blurring the image of the half-carved figure.

Joshua moved closer, his warmth a tangible counterpoint to Caleb's chilling isolation. "Your father's been on a long, hard road, Caleb," he said gently, his voice soothing. "But it's not just the miles. It's what he carried... all those years."

Caleb's gaze drifted to the window, the endless expanse of the ocean stretching before him. It should have been peaceful, but he only saw a blurry expanse of memories, a vast, unforgiving horizon. "What he carried..." he whispered, the question too heavy to bear aloud. The weight of it pressed down on him, suffocating him.

Joshua's eyes held a depth of understanding. "Everyone carries their cross, Caleb," he said, his voice a steady pulse. "Some crosses... you can't even see. But they weigh just as heavy. Maybe his return... it's not just a reunion. Maybe it's the unfinished carving, waiting for the artist to come back and finish it."

He paused, letting the weight of those words settle between them, heavy with unspoken implications and the promise of a painful, uncertain future.

The silence hung thick, pine-scented, and heavy with unspoken things. Strands of light pierced the air, catching in the fine mist of sawdust that hovered like breath held too long. Caleb remained still, as if the room itself waited for him to move. Joshua's words—unexpected and piercing—had struck deep, like a chisel to stubborn grain. Something long buried shifted inside him, a slow unraveling of the knot he'd carried for years. His muscles loosened, trembling under the weight of hope he hadn't dared to name. Maybe his father wasn't lost forever.

"Redemption," Caleb breathed, the word barely more than a whisper, a fragile thread unraveling from somewhere deep inside him. It felt foreign on his tongue, like something he had no right to claim, yet something in him clung to it anyway. His voice wavered, raw, exposed. "I... I thought I was past that."

The lie sat heavy in his mouth, bitter as ash. He wasn't past it—he'd only buried it, packed it away beneath layers of self-reliance and quiet resignation. Redemption wasn't for people like him. It belonged to the saints, the ones who never faltered, never failed. Not to a man who had spent years running from the wreckage of his own choices.

Joshua's gaze didn't waver. He had a way of looking at Caleb that made it impossible to hide. It wasn't pity—Caleb would have bristled at that—but something steadier, more relentless. Like Joshua could see the weight Caleb carried and refused to let him pretend it wasn't there.

"Redemption doesn't demand perfection, Caleb." Joshua's voice was low, even, but it carried through the cramped workshop like an unshakable truth. "Sometimes, it finds you in the cracks you thought were beyond repair."

Caleb exhaled, a slow, uneven breath, and leaned back in the creaking chair. The wood groaned beneath him; the sound almost mocking. He stared at his hands—calloused, stained with varnish and time—and flexed his fingers. The Stations of the Cross loomed before him; their unfinished forms carved in rough, uncertain lines. He should have completed them by now. But every time he picked up his tools, something inside him resisted.

The past clung to him like dust in the air, settling in the spaces he thought he'd cleaned. He had tried to carve his way out of it, shaping wood into something sacred, something worthy. But was that enough? Could penance be measured in hours at a workbench? In the smooth planes of a hand-carved Christ, arms outstretched in suffering and grace?

Joshua leaned against the worktable, arms crossed, waiting. He never rushed Caleb, never filled silences just to ease the weight of them. It made it impossible to ignore the ache in his own chest.

Caleb ran a hand through his hair, fingers gripping tighter than necessary. The weight in his chest pressed down harder, suffocating. "It's not that simple," he muttered, the words scraping against the raw edges of his doubt. "I don't know if I believe it's even possible."

Joshua stood still, hands in his pockets, watching him. Not judging. Just watching. He let the silence settle between them, like a pause before a crucial note in a song. Then, finally, he spoke. "Belief doesn't have to come all at once. Sometimes, it starts with showing up."

Caleb let out a dry, hollow laugh, shaking his head. "And if I can't even do that?"

Joshua shifted, his voice softer now, but firm. "Then maybe you let someone stand with you until you can."

The words landed heavy, an anchor to steady him or drag him under. Caleb didn't know which yet. But something inside him shifted. The weight of his guilt didn't disappear—nothing ever erased it—but for the first time in years, it wavered.

His gaze dropped to the figures on the workbench, carved from the same wood, yet each distinct. Some smooth, others rough, their faces locked in expressions of agony or serenity. He'd poured himself into them, every chisel stroke cutting deeper than the wood itself. But no matter how much he shaped them, they never felt whole. Like him, they were unfinished.

The raw edges of regret remained, splintering beneath his fingertips. His father's absence had carved something jagged into him, something he never learned to sand down. Now, the thought of seeing Thomas again felt like pressing an open wound against salt. He had spent a lifetime learning to live in the silence, shaping his world around the space where his father used to be. Shattering that fragile peace—stepping into the unknown of what Thomas had become—felt insurmountable.

What if there was nothing left to salvage? What if forgiveness was just another empty promise, another carving left half-finished on the bench?

His mother's voice, steady and familiar, curled around the dark corners of his mind. *Forgive, as you have been forgiven.*

Elena had never held her pain like a weapon. Even when the world had cut her down, she had spoken of grace as if it were breath itself, something freely given, even to those who had stolen from her. Even to Thomas.

Caleb closed his eyes. The aroma of pine drifted into his nostrils, grounding him for a moment, but it did little to ease the tightness in his chest. He had a choice—a terrifying, life-altering choice. And the clock was ticking.

His fingers traced the rough-hewn wood of the figure before him, a Christ bent beneath an impossible burden. The carving mirrored his own weight, his own wounds. Forgiveness. The word stuck in his throat like gravel. Could he let go of the bitterness he had carried for years, the anger that had anchored him in place for so long?

He didn't know. He wasn't sure he wanted to.

"Everyone carries their cross." Joshua's voice cut through the thick silence, the truth of it sinking deep.

Redemption wasn't a single moment. It wasn't a clean, easy resolution. It was a climb, a battle waged in the deepest part of himself. And some days, he wasn't sure he had the strength for it.

He shoved back from the bench, chair legs scraping against the worn wooden floor. The sound was sharp, jarring, a reflection of the storm inside him. The workshop, once a sanctuary, felt suffocating, the walls pressing in too close.

He took a step toward the door.

A test. A risk. A wager on his own capacity for change.

The weight in his chest didn't disappear, but for the first time, he wondered if he had to carry it alone.

Frozen mid-agony, the unfinished *Stations of the Cross* were silent judges of his struggle. As he crossed the threshold, the weight of his decision pressed down, heavy and unforgiving. The long shadows stretched like accusing fingers across the room, painting the unfinished carvings in a somber light. Caleb's breath hitched. *"Could I forgive myself?"* The question hammered against his ribs, a relentless pulse in the silence. The answer remained elusive, a ghost dancing just beyond his grasp.

The choice hung in the air, thick and suffocating, like sawdust clinging to his lungs. The carved figures seemed to watch him, their silent vigil a constant reminder of his unresolved pain. He slammed the last window shut, the sharp click echoing the finality of his decision—or lack thereof. Once a refuge of quiet solitude, the workshop now reeked of unspoken regrets, of choices deferred. He moved with a forced calm, his steps deliberate, but his mind was a runaway train, careening towards a future he couldn't imagine. His gaze lingered on the *Stations*, their wooden forms warped by the fading light, seeming to stretch into the encroaching darkness. They were frozen in time, just like him.

He pushed the door shut with a final, resounding thud, a sound that mirrored the grim, gnawing ache in his gut. The unresolved question remained, a heavy, unspoken weight pressing down on him as he stepped out into the twilight. The journey had begun, but the destination remained maddeningly unclear.

The old Ford coughed to life, its engine a familiar growl that vibrated through Caleb's bones. Port Angeles, his hometown, spread before him—a postcard of memories, each street a stab of nostalgia and guilt. The storm inside him raged louder than the wind whipping through the town. He saw it all: the blurry shops on Main Street and ghosts of happier times before *it* happened. Before the truth shattered everything.

Saint Peter's by the Sea, its steeple a skeletal finger against the bruised sky—a monument to faith he wasn't sure he deserved anymore. The church stood silent, a cold judge. He needed answers, damn it, but the only response was the relentless rhythm of the tide; a constant reminder of life's indifference, of the fragility of everything he held dear.

The road twisted toward the ocean, the grey waves a mirror to his tormented soul. A lone gull screamed overhead, a harsh counterpoint to the quiet despair gnawing at him. *Freedom. Forgiveness.* Both felt miles away, unattainable luxuries. His knuckles, white as bone, gripped the worn steering wheel. His mother's soft yet unwavering voice echoed in the wind: *"Forgiveness."* The words, once a comfort, now felt like a cruel taunt.

Could *he* forgive him? The bitterness, a thorny vine, choked the life out of his heart. Next to him, the chisel gleamed, catching the dying light. A tool of creation, a symbol of transformation. Could he carve a new path? Could he sculpt something beautiful from the wreckage of his life? His heart, a battlefield, raged with doubt and a desperate flicker of hope.

He hit the outskirts of town, the familiar comfort dissolving into the chilling unknown. Joshua's words, a seed of defiance planted deep within him, began to sprout: *"Dare to face what you fear."* He wasn't sure he was ready. Hell, he was terrified. But the possibility of change, a faint glimmer on the horizon, beckoned him forward, a dangerous promise beyond his grasp.

The truck lurched, tires spitting gravel. He slammed on the brakes, a shudder running through him. *"Damn it, damn it all,"* he muttered, his voice tight with frustrated rage. He snatched the chisel, the cold steel comforting in his trembling hand. The ocean wind whipped through the open window, carrying the salty tang of the sea and the raw scent of his fear.

He stared at his hands, rough and calloused from years of hard work, years he'd spent trying to outrun his past. Now, it was catching up, and he wasn't sure he had the strength to fight it any longer. A low growl escaped his lips. *"This ends today,"* he whispered, a fierce determination hardening his gaze.

The road ahead was uncertain and unforgiving, but he would face it. He had to. For himself. For his mother. For everything he'd lost.

Gravel crunched under Caleb Martin's boots, a harsh counterpoint to the silence clinging to the Port Orchard VA. The hospital loomed ahead, a monolith of cold concrete, a stark contrast to the warmth of his woodshop. He killed the engine, and the sudden silence settled over him like a held breath. The truck's cab smelled of sawdust and oil, familiar, grounding—yet the antiseptic sting in the air beyond the windshield cut through it, sharp and invasive. A gut punch. A reminder of everything he'd spent years trying to bury.

His fingers tightened around the wheel, knuckles white. He could still turn back. No one knew he was here. No one would ask why he hadn't come. His workshop waited cedar clinging to his clothes like an old friend, the feel of smooth wood beneath his hands a quiet solace. But unfinished projects lingered there too—carvings paused mid-motion, stories left untold, much like this chapter of his life. The Stations of the Cross, abandoned at the third station. The rough-hewn face of Christ stared back at him with silent understanding, still waiting.

With a slow, shuddering breath, Caleb pushed the door open. The air was colder than he expected, biting through his jacket. The automatic doors hissed as he stepped forward, the fluorescent glare inside casting an unforgiving light over the sterile world beyond. The acrid tang of bleach and illness curled in his nostrils, awakening a sick sense of déjà vu. It had been years since he'd stepped foot in a place like this. Years since he'd allowed himself to feel the weight of helplessness.

His boots echoed against the tile, an unnatural sound in a place designed to suppress noise, to hush suffering into quiet corners. He felt like an intruder. Like an imposter in his own story.

A receptionist glanced up as he approached.

"I'm looking for Thomas Martin," he said, voice tight, betraying nothing of the war inside him. He passed over his ID, his fingers betraying a faint tremor as they brushed the counter.

The woman smiled, but it was the weary kind—polite, practiced. "Room 217, down the hall, second left."

The paper she handed him crinkled in his grip. Directions. A path. No excuses now.

The hallway stretched ahead, impossibly long, each step dragging him closer to something he wasn't sure he was ready to face. He stopped outside the door, staring at the metal plate: Thomas Martin.

The name felt foreign and familiar all at once. A ghost he had spent years running from. His mother's voice whispered in his mind: *Mercy heals the deepest cuts, son.*

But what if some wounds weren't meant to heal?

His fingers hovered over the handle, a breath away from crossing a threshold he could never uncross. A lifetime of anger, of absence, of silence pressed against him. What if his father didn't care? What if he regretted coming? What if he walked in, only to walk out unchanged?

A carpenter knew how to mend broken things. He had spent his life shaping wood into something whole, something worthy. But some breaks ran too deep. Some wood splintered beyond repair.

He swallowed hard, the taste of sawdust and regret thick on his tongue. His calloused hand tightened into a fist, then slowly—achingly—relaxed.

He pressed the door open. The hinges creaked like an old floorboard, like a memory coming back to life.

And there he was.

A frail man lay propped against sterile white sheets, skin sallow, eyes sunken. His father. Or what was left of him. The broad-shouldered, iron-willed man from Caleb's childhood was a shadow now.

Caleb felt something twist inside him, something sharp and unrelenting.

His father stirred, eyes flickering open, blinking against the light. He frowned, confusion flickering across his features before recognition dawned—slow, uncertain.

"Caleb?" The voice was rough, paper-thin. A voice he had once feared. A voice that had once commanded respect or at least demanded it. Now, it wavered, cracked at the edges.

Caleb's throat tightened. He had imagined this moment a hundred times, a thousand, rehearsed the words he would say, the accusations he would hurl. But standing here, looking at the man before him, all of those words turned to dust.

His father blinked, as if trying to confirm this wasn't some fevered dream. "You came."

The simplest of statements. And yet, Caleb felt it cut deeper than any chisel, deeper than any wound he had ever tried to carve away.

"I—" The words stuck, tangled in the weight of years unspoken.

His father exhaled, long and slow. "I didn't think you would."

Caleb let out a breath that felt like it had been caged for a decade. He stepped forward, the weight in his chest pressing heavier with each inch between them closing.

"I didn't think I would either."

Silence stretched between them, filled with too much history to ever be empty.

His father shifted, grimacing slightly. Caleb's instinct kicked in before he could stop it—his hand shot forward, steadying the old man's arm. It was thin beneath his fingers, fragile in a way that didn't seem real.

A lifetime of silence between them, and now this. A hesitant touch. A gesture neither of them could put words to.

His father looked down at their hands, then back up at him. "You always were good with your hands."

Caleb swallowed. He wanted to pull away, to retreat back into the safety of anger, of resentment. But something in him—something raw and aching—refused to let go.

He nodded once. "Yeah," he said. "I am."

And for the first time, he wasn't sure if he was talking about wood anymore.

CHAPTER 12

A Reckoning in the House of God

THE HUSHED WHISPERS in Saint Peter's felt less like a tide and more like a suffocating blanket. Sarah Rayburn-Macall clenched her hands in her lap, fingers digging into the worn fabric of her skirt. The sermon was supposed to bring solace, but it only served as a cruel reminder of how tenuous her peace was. The stained-glass windows, usually a sanctuary of light and color, felt garish, almost mocking. Every hue seemed to sneer at her, a gaudy reminder that tranquility was an illusion.

She'd come to church this morning hoping for stillness, something sacred. Not answers—she'd stopped praying for those—but a moment of quiet where the ghosts in her mind might fall asleep. But they never did, not really. Her mind raced through old memories like a needle skipping across a damaged record. Jake's voice yelling. The slam of a door. The crack of glass beneath her trembling hands. The blood on the floor that wasn't hers but could've been.

Father Mike's words drifted in and out of focus. She caught snippets: *forgiveness, redemption, light*. Each word stung. Like salt in a wound, she pretended had healed.

But nothing—nothing—prepared her for the creak of the church doors.

Her breath left her like she'd been punched. The air itself seemed to shift, to narrow into a single corridor of panic.

She didn't need to turn around. She knew. Her body remembered the way a soldier remembers the snap of a tripwire.

Jake Macall.

Her fingers closed tighter around the rosary in her lap, each bead a desperate anchor. The pew beneath her, once solid oak, now felt like splinters pressed against the backs of her knees. Caleb, sitting beside her, tensed—a small, imperceptible shift. But Sarah felt it. He had always known when danger walked into a room. Maybe it was his time on the streets. Maybe it was instinct.

Jake stepped into the sanctuary like a ghost with unfinished business, his silhouette backlit by pale morning light. He looked like he hadn't slept in days. The beard was new—patchy, unkempt. His eyes, once the mischievous blue that had charmed her in their youth, now resembled storm clouds—heavy, swollen with unshed pain.

"Sarah," he said, and that single word shattered everything.

Not Mrs. Macall. Not "hey." Not even "I'm sorry." Just her name. A whisper from a time she thought she'd buried.

She blinked. Her heart pounded so loud she wondered if anyone else could hear it. "What do you want?" she asked. The words came out more brittle than she intended, but she didn't care.

He flinched. That tiny recoil—it gave her something. Power? Maybe. Proof that he hadn't expected her to fight back. Definitely.

Then Caleb rose beside her. Slowly. Not a threat. A barrier.

"Jake," Caleb said, his voice low, calm, but with an edge of steel. "This isn't the time. Or the place."

Jake's gaze flicked toward him. Something flickered in his expression—recognition, maybe even respect. But his fists stayed clenched at his sides.

"I'm not here to cause trouble," he murmured. His voice cracked. "I just... I didn't know where else to go."

Sarah stood. Her knees wobbled beneath her skirt, but she kept her chin lifted. Ten years ago, she might've folded. Not now.

"You don't get to say that" she said, her voice shaking with fury and something else grief, maybe. "Not after everything."

Jake looked down, ashamed. "I know," he said. "I just thought... maybe I could talk to you. Just for a minute."

"You lost that privilege the day you raised your hand against me," she snapped, louder than she meant to. Several heads turned. The pews stiffened like a field of deer sensing a predator. And yet no one moved. They were watching. Waiting.

Then Jake whispered, "You didn't tell me."

That stopped her cold.

"What?" Her voice faltered.

"You didn't tell me," he said again, louder this time. "About the baby."

A gasp caught in her throat. The sound was so sharp, she didn't even realize it came from her.

Caleb stiffened. His gaze flicked to her, and in that instant, she saw the questions burning behind his eyes.

Sarah's hands trembled. The beads slipped from her fingers and clattered to the floor, each one a ricochet of a memory she'd tried to erase. Jake had no right. Not here. Not now.

"You don't get to use that," she whispered, her voice hollow. "You gave up every right to that child when you…" Her voice broke. "When you chose rage over love."

Jake stepped forward. Caleb immediately blocked him with a quiet, unspoken promise of protection.

"I didn't know," Jake said, his voice cracking. "I swear on everything, Sarah. If I had known—"

"But you didn't!" she shouted. "Because you didn't stay. You never stayed, Jake!"

The sanctuary fell deathly silent.

From the front row, a child whimpered. Somewhere near the back, an elderly woman muttered a prayer. Sarah's chest heaved. Her hands curled into fists. She didn't even realize Caleb had placed a gentle hand on her shoulder until her breathing started to steady.

Jake looked at the floor, ashamed. Then up again, eyes wet.

"I know I was poison," he said. "I know I scorched everything I touched. But I've changed. I went to rehab. I go to meetings. I work construction now. I haven't raised a hand in four years, not even in a fight. And I swear—swear to God—I didn't come to rip your life apart."

Caleb's eyes narrowed. "Then why now?"

Jake looked up. "Because I'm dying."

The words landed like a sledgehammer.

Sarah's mouth opened, but no sound came out.

Jake gave a sad, bitter laugh. "You don't believe me. Why would you? But it's true. My liver's done. Doctors gave me a year, maybe less."

Silence stretched, brittle and vast.

"I don't want your pity," Jake added. "I just... I wanted to say I'm sorry. I needed you to know I wasn't always a monster. That I loved you. That I loved that baby, even if I never knew them. I wanted to be better. But I waited too long."

Sarah's eyes stung. She wanted to scream. To throw something. But the rage she'd carried for so long had frayed, worn down by time and grace.

Behind her, someone whispered again: *Grant us peace.*

Another voice followed: *Grant us understanding.*

The prayer rippled through the pews, quiet but steady.

Sarah turned to Caleb. His jaw was tight, his expression unreadable. "I didn't know you didn't know," she whispered.

He gave the smallest nod. Then said gently, "You don't owe him anything, Sarah. But maybe... maybe you owe yourself closure."

She turned back to Jake. He looked like a man already half-buried.

"What are you asking?" she said, exhausted.

"Just... to talk. Five minutes. Outside. Then I'll go."

Before she could answer, another presence moved down the aisle—Joshua. Older than both men, his steps slow but purposeful. He walked like someone who had made peace with many things and still carried the scars of it.

He placed a steady hand on Jake's shoulder. "A heart ain't meant to carry this alone," he said. "That weight—it wasn't meant for your shoulders."

Jake closed his eyes. A tear slid down his cheek. Sarah didn't move.

"You don't have to forgive me," Jake whispered. "But I needed to tell you. I'm sorry."

Sarah didn't speak. Couldn't. But her hand found Caleb's again, and this time, it didn't shake.

She made a choice.

Sarah felt a cold dread seeping into her bones, freezing her to the spot. Caleb, thank God, stood beside her, his hand a solid weight on her arm, a silent promise of protection against the storm that Jake had unleashed. She squeezed her eyes shut, the familiar comfort of the rosary beads in her hand suddenly cold and slick with sweat.

Jake choked out a breath, the word tangled somewhere between a plea and a sob. "Please. I... I just need a moment. With you."

His voice, ragged and raw, carved through the heavy silence of Saint Peter's like a dull knife. His eyes—bloodshot, desperate—locked onto Sarah's, pleading, not for forgiveness, but for understanding, for the smallest thread of mercy. This wasn't a request. It was a last gasp before drowning.

Sarah swallowed hard, her pulse hammering in her ears. The weight of unspoken words between them was unbearable, pressing against her ribs like a vice. She knew what had brought him here, what had driven him to this breaking point. The secret. The one they had both buried so deep it had become part of them. She had told herself she was protecting him, protecting them both. But now, standing here in the flickering candlelight, surrounded by whispers of faith and the weary prayers of strangers, she wondered if she had only been delaying the inevitable.

Behind her, the congregation remained motionless, their silence more suffocating than any outcry. Fear flickered in their eyes, their fingers gripping rosaries like lifelines. She could hear their whispered prayers, a fragile chorus against the storm of Jake's despair. Even the stained-glass saints lining the sanctuary seemed to bear silent witness, their sorrowful eyes illuminated by the dying light. In the fragmented glow of crimson and violet, Sarah felt the weight of her choices reflected back at her.

A voice—soft, fragile—broke through the hush. "Grant us peace."

Sarah turned, startled by the gentle command. An elderly woman, her face lined with years of both suffering and wisdom, clasped her hands before her, her gaze unwavering. Another voice joined, firmer but equally worn, "Grant us understanding."

The words were not just a plea but an indictment, a quiet demand that Sarah act. The congregation, the saints, the very walls of this place—they all waited. But what was she supposed to do? If she reached for Jake now, if she gave in, would she be offering him salvation or merely prolonging his suffering? If she turned away, would it be an act of mercy or betrayal?

The air grew thick with waiting.

Then, a voice cut through the tension, grounding and steady. "Jake."

Caleb's tone was low, firm, the voice of a man who had fought his demons and survived. He stepped forward, his posture unshaken, his presence filling the space between Jake and Sarah. "This place... it's sanctuary. Not just from the world, but from the wars we carry inside us."

There was no judgment in his words, no empty platitudes. Just truth. A soldier speaking to another soldier, both knowing what it meant to battle ghosts long after the war was over.

Jake's breath hitched; his body taut as a bowstring. The last of the afternoon sun slanted through the stained glass, casting the sanctuary in shades of blood and dusk. For a fleeting moment, the storm inside him seemed to still. The scent of old wood and incense clung to the air, a tangible memory of something sacred, something untouched by pain. Hope. Fragile as spun glass, but there.

From the back of the church, a shadow moved. Joshua stepped forward; his presence quiet but undeniable. His stride, measured and deliberate, held the calm of a man who had long since made peace with the burdens others still carried. He did not rush, did not push—just arrived. A lighthouse against the tide.

"Jake," he said, his voice low but steady. "A heart ain't meant to carry this alone. That weight—it wasn't meant for your shoulders."

The words weren't pity. They weren't even comfort. They were a challenge. A dare to let go.

Something shifted. A hairline crack in the steel Jake had forged around himself. His jaw clenched; his breath shallow. His eyes, granite-hard for so long, flickered with something different. Something he didn't know how to name.

The silence stretched, taut as a wire. Sarah could feel it unraveling, thread by thread. Could see it in the way Jake's shoulders slumped, the way his fists loosened at his sides. It was like watching a dam begin to break, water seeping through the fractures, unstoppable now that the first breach had formed.

Joshua didn't waver. He met Jake's stare head-on, patient, relentless. "Remember the first Station. Christ condemned. Innocent. Forced to bear a burden He never deserved."

The words rippled through the sanctuary like a quiet revelation. Eyes turned toward the carved images lining the walls, each one telling the same ancient story. The road to suffering. The road to redemption.

"Your service, Jake," Joshua continued, his voice unwavering. "That was your burden. A Via Dolorosa you walked alone. You carried it, just as He did. But you don't have to anymore."

Jake exhaled, a sound that was half sigh, half surrender. He turned, slowly, his gaze drawn to the Stations of the Cross. The images, the suffering etched into wood and stone, weren't just sacred relics. They were a mirror. A reflection of the torment he had lived, the choices he had made, the ghosts he had refused to lay down.

Sarah held her breath as he took a step forward. Just one. Small, but monumental.

Joshua's voice was softer now, but no less resolute. "Every step is a chance, Jake. A chance to let go. A chance to heal."

The air in the sanctuary seemed to shift, the heavy weight of expectation lifting ever so slightly. Outside, the sea whispered against the cliffs, the sound barely audible through the thick stone walls. But inside, in the quiet hush of faith and desperation, a new sound emerged. A heartbeat. Unsteady, hesitant. But real.

The first pulse of something that might, just might, be hope.

Caleb felt the shift before he saw it. The glacial grip of Jake's pain began to loosen, to unravel. The Stations, Christ's agony, were a reflection, yes, but also a roadmap. They weren't just a reminder of pain but a promise of hope, a path leading out of the darkness, into the uncertain, terrifying light of forgiveness. A chance at peace.

The silence stretched, thick with unspoken emotions, before Jake finally spoke. His voice, raw and rough, barely a whisper, broke the stillness. "It's hard, isn't it?" he asked, his voice betraying the decades-long battle raging within. "Letting go."

Caleb nodded, understanding dawning in his eyes. He knew what that fight felt like. He knew the weight of unseen burdens, the agony of carrying an unbearable load. "It is," Caleb agreed, his voice rough with sympathy. "But you're not alone in this fight, Jake. We're here for you."

The church air hung heavy, thick with the trace of beeswax and lingering fear, a miasma clinging to the ancient timbers. But something shifted. A crack formed in the suffocating dread. Caleb felt a breath of possibility for the first time in what seemed like forever. Hope, fragile as a newborn bird, dared to flutter.

Joshua's words, quiet but resonant, punched through the suffocating silence. "Let us help you carry it, Jake," he said, his voice a low rumble that held the weight of a thousand shared burdens and unspoken prayers. "Let us help you lay it down."

Caleb felt the tension leach from his bones. The anger, the years of carefully constructed walls—they crumbled like dry earth giving way to a spring thaw. He stole a glance at Sarah. Her eyes, shining with unshed tears, mirrored his relief. Their unspoken bond, forged in the crucible of shared trauma, held them fast in this fragile moment of grace.

"This," he thought, "is what it means to be part of something bigger."

They stood there, three figures bathed in the dim light of Saint Peter's – protectors, healers, witnesses to the slow, agonizing unraveling of a man shattered by war. Jake, the invincible warrior, was now a tremor of vulnerability. His dark hair, a tangled mess, framed eyes that held the haunted echoes of a thousand nightmares. The warrior's armor, meticulously forged over years, was cracking. Each drop of sweat that beaded his forehead seemed to chip away at the stone facade.

Caleb watched, his gut twisting with sorrow and a hesitant hope. This wasn't just about Jake. This was about the brutal toll of war, the insidious creep of PTSD, and the terrifying isolation that gnawed at the soul.

Jake's voice, a ragged whisper, shattered the silence. "I can't…I can't carry this alone anymore," he choked out, the words tearing through him, raw and exposed.

The confession hung in the air, thick and heavy, settling on the hearts of everyone present. It was the sound of a dam breaking, releasing the pent-up torrent of his pain. Each syllable was a brick pulled from the fortress of his self-imposed exile, revealing the broken man beneath. A man, Caleb, despite his demons, wanted to reach out and help.

A wave of empathy washed over him, starkly contrasting the icy detachment he usually maintained. Sarah squeezed Caleb's hand, her unspoken question hanging between them: "Can we fix this?"

The weight of that question pressed down on him, heavier than Jake's burden. He couldn't promise anything, but in that moment, surrounded by the quiet strength of faith, he found the strength to try.

Caleb felt a crack in the ice, a tremor in the earth. The rigid steel of Jake's demeanor, that impenetrable wall of soldierly stoicism, softened. He wasn't just a soldier anymore, a ghost haunted by the battlefield. He was a man. A man finally letting himself breathe. A man Caleb could almost touch with his hands, calloused from years of shaping wood. The fear that had coiled tight in Caleb's gut, turning his muscles to stone, began to unravel. He exhaled, the tension draining from his shoulders like water from a worn-out sponge. The storm, the monstrous tempest threatening to tear them apart, retreated, leaving behind only a bruised sky and the promise of dawn. The congregation felt it, too. A collective hush, thick with unspoken understanding.

Saint Peter's, usually a cold, echoing shell of stone, thrummed with a life force Caleb hadn't known it possessed. It wasn't just forgiveness hanging in the air; it was redemption, tangible as the rough-hewn pews beneath their bottoms. Each whispered prayer felt like a hammer blow, chipping away at the walls separating them, carving out a space for healing and shared humanity. "Jake..." Caleb's voice, rough but low, broke the silence. He saw the tears welling in Jake's eyes – a dam finally breaking after years of holding back. "It ain't over, you know," Caleb continued, his voice thick with emotion, "but... it's a start."

Jake swallowed hard, his Adam's apple bobbing visibly. "I... I never thought..." he stammered, his voice cracking. "I thought I'd carry this... this weight... forever." His gaze dropped to the worn floorboards, his hands clenching into fists. "I thought I deserved to carry it." Caleb stepped closer, placing a hand on Jake's shoulder, the gesture as simple and powerful as a prayer. "Damn right you didn't deserve it," Caleb said, his voice firm but gentle. "No one does. But letting go... that ain't weakness, Jake. That's the strongest thing a man can do." A woman in the front row sobbed softly, her sound a counterpoint to the quiet strength filling the church. The battle hadn't been won with brute force or with the cold logic of war. It had been won with grace, with a brutal, beautiful act of surrender. Caleb knew, deep down, in the marrow of his bones: True strength wasn't about holding onto the past, clinging to the pain, to the pride. It was about letting go – finding peace in the hope of a new dawn, here in this sacred space, this testament to the enduring power of forgiveness.

Sarah cut through the silence, her steps deliberate, a warrior queen striding into a battlefield. Strawberry blonde hair, catching the candlelight, haloed her face – a deceptive fragility masking the steel in her spine. She stopped before Jake, the space between them crackling with unspoken sorrow. Green eyes, usually bright with mischief, now held a deep understanding that chilled Caleb to the bone. He knew this wasn't just about Jake but about Sarah confronting her ghosts. "Jake," she said, her voice a low thrum that resonated in the hushed church. "You're not alone." The words weren't just platitudes; they were a battle cry, a defiant roar against the despair that threatened to consume them all. "We all carry our burdens. But it's the love – the damn love – of others that keeps us from drowning. And right now, we're all throwing you a lifeline."

The weight of their unspoken pain pressed in like the heavy air before a storm. Caleb could feel it in the stiffened shoulders of the congregation, in the way their breath hitched collectively at Sarah's outstretched hand. Not an invitation. A plea. A bridge built over years of wreckage, stretching toward Jake, who stood at the edge of that chasm, teetering between past and possibility.

Caleb's fingers curled into his palms, the pressure grounding him. He had once been the hammer driving the nails into this fractured reality, the weight of his own guilt an iron brand against his ribs. Could he now be the hands that mended?

Jake's jaw clenched, his breath coming short and shallow. The fight in his eyes flickered, a candle struggling against an unseen wind. He wanted to reach for her, Caleb could see it. The raw desire to believe, to grasp the lifeline offered—but old wounds screamed louder than hope.

From the corner of his vision, Caleb caught Joshua's nod. Subtle, measured. Not approval, but recognition. This wasn't about absolution or erasing the past. This was war—the slow, grueling kind that left scars in its wake.

Jake's fingers twitched. A tremor of hesitation, of yearning. And then, finally, he reached. Not gracefully, not without resistance, but he reached. And as their hands met, the silence in the church deepened, the very walls seeming to lean in, bearing witness to a battle fought in breath and trembling fingers.

Caleb's pulse pounded. The battle wasn't over. It had only just begun.

Father Michael's voice cut through the thick air, steady but firm, a lighthouse against the storm of Caleb's thoughts. His words wove through the congregation, but they did little to soothe the unrest churning in Caleb's chest. He knew these words. Knew them in the marrow of his bones, had heard them whispered in the dark when forgiveness felt like a myth. But knowing was not the same as believing.

Beside him, Sarah's hands were folded so tightly that her knuckles had paled. He could feel the tension radiating from her, the same desperate hope that clawed at his own insides. When she finally exhaled, it was like watching a dam break, her body releasing a burden too heavy for one person to carry.

She turned to Caleb then, her green eyes holding something he didn't know how to name. Something raw and quiet and terrifying.

"This isn't just about Jake," she murmured. "This is about all of us."

The words settled in his stomach like stones. He swallowed hard, his gaze drifting to the stained glass above them, the fractured light bleeding across the worn wooden pews. The colors blurred, a swirling storm of uncertainty. Could he believe in this? In healing? In a future untainted by past mistakes?

Joshua's quiet presence beside him felt like an anchor. He'd seen them all at their worst. He knew the fight ahead better than anyone. And still, he nodded. A silent affirmation that this—this impossible, fragile thing—was worth it.

The organ swelled, the music a tidal wave that swallowed the air, vibrating through Caleb's bones. The notes were not gentle. They were sharp, unrelenting, a mirror to the storm inside him. A melody of endings and beginnings, of regret and redemption.

As the final Amen echoed, the silence that followed felt heavier than the words themselves. The rustle of hymnals, the creak of pews as the congregation rose—mundane sounds that grated against Caleb's nerves. This wasn't an end. It was the eye of the storm.

Outside, the salt air bit against his skin, the sharp tang of pine filling his lungs. It was grounding, real—but it did nothing to silence the doubts clawing at his ribs.

"Grace," he muttered, the word tasting like rust on his tongue. "That's a luxury we can't afford."

"Caleb." Sarah's voice was low, urgent. A warning. "Don't start this again. We agreed—"

"To what?" Joshua cut in; his voice tight with frustration. "To pretend everything's fine? To bury it all under a layer of pious platitudes?" His eyes burned with something raw, something that twisted in Caleb's gut. "Because it's not fine, is it? It never will be."

The words hit like a gut punch. Caleb flinched, swallowing against the sharp sting of truth. He saw the fear in Joshua's gaze, the same fear that had lived inside him for too long.

Sarah stepped closer, her voice trembling. "We have to try."

The weight of everything pressed in, thick and suffocating. The road ahead wasn't paved with easy forgiveness or neatly tied endings. It was jagged, uncertain, a battlefield littered with the ghosts of who they had been. But standing here, in the crisp evening air, he felt something shift.

Not peace. Not yet.

But the distant echo of possibility.

CHAPTER 13

A Son's Journey, A Father's Truth

CALEB'S KNUCKLES TIGHTENED around the chilled metal of the car door; his grip so fierce it sent a dull ache up his arm. He yanked it open, the rasp of his boots scraping against the pavement, the sound jarring in the heavy silence. Sarah and Joshua stood beside him, their breaths visible in the crisp air, their fragile truce forged in shared dread.

This wasn't just a visit; it was an act of penance, a march toward something neither of them were ready to face. The VA hospital loomed ahead, its cold, unfeeling walls a mausoleum for lost battles—some fought on foreign soil, others in the minds of men who had never truly come home.

Caleb's pulse pounded, erratic and sharp against his ribs. He wasn't sure if it was fear or guilt tightening in his chest, but both had taken root. His father, Thomas Martin—the man who had once seemed unshakable, a granite force standing against the tides of Whispering Cliffs—was now a ghost, hollowed out by war, by regret, by time. The man who had taught him to carve, to shape something beautiful from something lifeless, had been reduced to someone unrecognizable. And Caleb knew, deep down, that it was partly his fault.

"This place..." Sarah's voice was barely more than a whisper, the sound fragile, like glass on the verge of shattering. Her strawberry-blonde hair caught in the fluorescent glow of the streetlights, making her seem even paler, the tremor in her hand betraying the strength she was trying so hard to hold onto.

Joshua shifted beside them; his usual quiet demeanor hardened by the grim reality ahead. "Yeah," he murmured, his voice rough, as if dragged over gravel. He placed a steady hand on Caleb's shoulder, a silent promise of support. Caleb appreciated it, but it did nothing to ease the tight knot coiled in his stomach. It wasn't just his father on the line—it was himself. If he failed here, if he let his father slip further into the shadows, what would stop him from following?

The automatic doors hissed open, expelling sterile air thick with antiseptic and something more intangible—a kind of sorrow that clung to the walls. The white linoleum floors stretched ahead like an empty canvas, but instead of possibility, they reeked of resignation.

Each step Caleb took felt heavier, as if the weight of the past was pressing down, dragging him back to the moments he wished he could undo. He swallowed against the metallic tang of fear coating his tongue.

Seagulls. He could almost hear them, their raucous cries carrying over the cliffs of Port Angeles, their world vibrant and alive, so unlike the hushed silence of the hospital. He used to love those mornings, standing with his father, watching the ocean churn against the rocks, their bond unspoken but understood. But now, that bond felt frayed, a relic of a time that no longer existed.

A voice dragged him back.

Sarah looked at him, her expression softening. "He's your father, Caleb. And he's hurting. We need to be here."

He wanted to believe that, but the fractures ran deep—not just in his father, but in himself. The last time they had spoken had been a decade ago, a mess of anger and slammed doors. He still carried that fight with him, the words carved into his memory deeper than any scar.

The aroma of pine and tobacco lingered in his mind, conjuring images of calloused hands guiding his own over unfinished wood, shaping saints and crosses with a devotion that once felt unshakable. Those same hands had once lifted him, held him when he was small, made him feel safe.

But those moments had become splinters, embedded too deep to remove without pain.

Sarah squeezed his arm, grounding him. "We don't get to rewrite the past," she said, her voice steady despite the emotions that thickened it. "But we can decide what happens next."

Caleb swallowed hard, nodding, but the hallway ahead still felt too long, too stark, too filled with ghosts he wasn't sure he was ready to face.

One foot in front of the other. That was all he could do.

"Almost there," she whispered, her voice a low hum against the roar in his ears.

The memory of their carefree laughter, a ghost of their past, flickered—a cruel taunt in the face of this grimness. He nodded, the movement stiff, his gaze fixed on the number etched into the metal door.

"Almost there," he repeated silently, the words tasting like ash.

But the storm raging inside him was far from over. He saw the reflection of it in Sarah's worried eyes—the man who once found solace in the smooth grain of wood was now grappling with the splintered wreckage of his soul. The father he'd idolized, the man who'd taught him everything he knew, had become a stranger, a ghost of the man he remembered.

The resentment, a bitter poison, gnawed at him. He wanted to scream, to lash out, but all he could manage was a strained nod. Joshua's presence loomed, a silent sentinel. No words were needed; the man's steady gaze offered a grim understanding. Caleb saw it in those eyes, a lifetime of burdens borne silently, a wisdom earned through hardship. Joshua's almost imperceptible nod was a lifeline, a silent acknowledgment of the brutal, agonizing work of healing.

It wasn't quick or easy, and the foundation was shattered. But they would rebuild.

"We will," Caleb thought, his resolve flickering, then strengthening. His hand, typically so deft, trembled as it closed over the cold metal handle.

The click of the latch echoed a stark punctuation in the oppressive silence. Caleb stood on the precipice, uncertainty clawing at him. This wasn't just a visit to his father's prison cell; this was a confrontation with his fractured past, a reckoning with the broken pieces of his faith. He swallowed, the lump in his throat physically manifesting his fear and self-doubt.

He thought of his father's face, hardened with years of confinement. He imagined the bitter words, the unspoken accusations, the festering wounds that had driven a wedge between them. Could he face it? Could he forgive? Could he even find the words to bridge the chasm that had opened between them?

Taking a shaky breath, Caleb pushed the door open, the sound a sharp crack in the suffocating stillness.

He stepped into his father's prison, into the heart of the storm, and into his soul's unknown depths. The work of mending, restoration, and forging something new from the wreckage had begun. The Master Craftsman—that was him now, and the task before him was the most demanding he had ever faced.

Sunlight sliced through the window, painting harsh stripes across the sterile floor. Caleb felt the cold slap him in the face, starkly contrasting to the comforting, sawdust-scented embrace of his father's woodshop—a place that now felt a lifetime away. The antiseptic smell choked him, a brutal reminder of the reality he couldn't escape. His father, Thomas, sat hunched against the weak light, a ghost of the man Caleb remembered. The vibrant energy that had once crackled around him was gone, replaced by a stillness that felt heavier than any grief. The familiar lines etched into his face weren't just wrinkles; they were canyons carved by years of unspoken burdens. Once bright with the fire of a thousand sunsets, those eyes were now clouded with something Caleb couldn't name—confusion? Resignation? Fear?

A flicker. A ghost of recognition in Thomas's eyes as he finally turned. For a heart-stopping second, Caleb saw it—a connection, a bridge across the chasm of years and unspoken resentments. The years of anger, the bitter words left unsaid—they all fractured, momentarily dissolving under the weight of that fleeting contact. He could almost breathe again. "Dad," Caleb rasped, the word a choked sob tearing through the dam he'd built around his emotions. It wasn't just a greeting but a desperate plea, an attempt to reach a man slipping away. But the light died in his father's eyes as quickly as a snuffed candle. The connection vanished, leaving Caleb drowning in the icy grip of reality. The anger, that bitter, familiar companion, clawed its way back, a tidal wave threatening to consume him. His fists clenched, knuckles white. The sorrow, the rage, the crushing weight of what he hadn't done, hadn't said—it all crashed over him.

"Son?" Thomas's voice was a whisper, brittle as dried leaves. The unraveling was audible, a stark testament to years of silence, missed opportunities, and a love left to wither. Each step felt like dragging an anchor through quicksand. Every movement was weighed down by regret, guilt, and the crushing knowledge of a bond fraying beyond repair. He stared at his father's face—the strong features dulled; the once-unwavering confidence replaced by a haunting vulnerability. His father's hands, once capable of crafting beauty from raw wood, lay still and trembling on the blanket, a silent testament to time's relentless march. Caleb's throat tightened. He fought back tears, but they threatened to spill over. "Dad," he choked out again, his voice cracking. "I... I didn't mean..." The words failed him. The unspoken accusations, the simmering resentments, now felt monstrous, suffocating him. He wanted to say so much, but the words caught in his throat, leaving only the raw, agonizing silence.

Caleb's hand hovered, a hesitant bird about to land. The silence in the room pressed down, thick and suffocating, a chasm yawning between him and his father. Doubt gnawed at him—was this even possible? Could he bridge the years of unspoken resentment, the festering wounds of a fractured past? Then, gently, his hand settled on his father's shoulder. The weight of it, the sheer physicality of the contact, hit him harder than he had anticipated. It wasn't just a touch but a desperate plea, a silent confession of a son's failures, a desperate hope for reconciliation. Thomas's voice, a dry rasp, cut through the tension. "Still got your strength," he mumbled, more to himself than Caleb. The words hung in the air, heavy with the weight of shared history—the good times, the brutal fights, the unspoken regrets. Caleb felt the echoes of those battles, phantom pains in his gut, the ghosts of accusations and silences that had poisoned their relationship for decades. This wasn't just about physical strength but the strength to face the truth and forgive, a strength Caleb wasn't sure he possessed.

A tremor ran through his father's frail body, a mirror image of the earthquake shaking Caleb's soul. His father's pride, once a towering oak, was now a withering sapling. But it was still there, a stubborn ember glowing faintly beneath the ash. It was a connection, a fragile bridge of shared pain and a desperate yearning for repair. A thin, almost invisible thread connecting their broken past to a possible, tentative future. "Dad…," Caleb began, his voice cracking, the words catching in his throat. He wanted to say so much, to apologize for the years of distance, for the stupid pride that had kept them apart. But the words failed him. He swallowed hard, the lump in his throat a physical manifestation of his internal struggle.

Sarah's hand found his, a silent reassurance. He squeezed it, grateful for the unspoken support. Joshua's steady gaze held a quiet strength that calmed Caleb's turbulent emotions. He didn't need words; their presence was a lifeline in the storm raging within him. The antiseptic smell of the hospital faded, replaced by the phantom scent of pine, a vivid memory of the woodshop, their sanctuary, their battleground. Time seemed to warp, the outside world a distant hum. All that mattered was the steady rhythm of two hearts beating in the suffocating silence, a fragile symphony of father and son, a desperate hope for redemption woven into the fabric of the moment. The question remained: was it enough? Would the embers ignite into a flame, or would they simply fade, forever separated by the ashes of their past?

Caleb's hand tightened on his father's shoulder, and the tremor beneath the surface was a silent scream. It wasn't just a tremor; it was an earthquake rumbling through the man who'd once been his rock. This fragile contact was all he had left—a promise, maybe, a pathetically hopeful one. Years of swallowed words, unspoken grief, a chasm carved by silence… could they bridge it? He had to believe they could. He had to. He settled into the creaking chair, the sound a mournful counterpoint to the heavy silence in the sterile room. The air felt thick with regret, a palpable weight pressing down on him. His father lay there, a ghost of the man who'd once ruled the waves, his eyes closed, his breath shallow. The years, the years, had ravaged him. But Caleb wouldn't let them win. Not today.

"Hey, Dad," Caleb said, his voice a low rumble. The words felt clumsy and inadequate, like trying to sculpt a masterpiece with a rusty spoon. He'd spent a lifetime shaping wood, finding solace in the grain, but this… this was harder than anything he'd ever faced. "I've almost finished the Stations… the carvings you started."

Thomas's eyelids fluttered. A slow blink, like a shutter struggling to open. His gaze drifted, unfocused, lost somewhere beyond the sterile walls. A battlefield? A jungle? Hell, Caleb couldn't tell. "The wood… speaks, doesn't it?" Thomas's voice was a whisper, frayed and thin as a spider's thread. "You listen, boy?" His voice was full of pain, regret, of memories he desperately wanted to hold onto. Caleb nodded, a lump forming in his throat. His father's eyes never met his, lost in a past that Caleb couldn't penetrate. A past filled with ghosts; with choices he didn't understand.

"Yeah, Dad. I listen. Just like you taught me."

"Good," Thomas breathed, the words almost swallowed by the silence that filled the room. "Marine… duty…" His voice trailed off, lost in the fog of memory, his words hanging like a prayer. The ache in Caleb's chest tightened, a vise around his heart. The years stretched out before him, a wasteland of missed opportunities, of unspoken love, of a father he couldn't reach. This man, this broken soldier, was adrift in a sea of memories, and Caleb was desperate to pull him back.

"Your duty… you did what you thought was right," Caleb said, his voice steady, a lifeline in the swirling storm. He needed to make his father see, needed to make him understand, that he wasn't judging him. Thomas's eyes flickered open, a spark of recognition or confusion. The uncertainty stabbed at Caleb.

"Right?" Thomas whispered, his voice laced with self-doubt. "Right is… hard to know."

The doubt in his father's voice was the most painful thing Caleb had ever heard. He had to help him. He had to. The guilt, the regret he carried, was a heavy weight. If he could just make his father see his worth, perhaps his pain might be healed. The clock was ticking. He had to do something, anything.

Caleb leaned forward, the rough-hewn calluses on his hands a roadmap of years spent wrestling with wood, a silent testament to his stubborn resilience. His father, Thomas, lay in the hospital bed, a frail ghost of the man who'd taught him everything. "I'm learning, Dad," Caleb said, his voice tight, the words catching in his throat. "Sometimes, the right thing… is just being here." It felt like a pathetically small victory, a flimsy bandage on a gaping wound. Years of silence, of unspoken resentments, loomed between them, a chasm wider than any canyon he'd ever carved. But maybe, just maybe, this was a crack of light in the suffocating darkness.

Outside, Sarah, and Joshua, kept vigil, their silent presence a tangible comfort, a whispered promise against the encroaching despair. Their love was a lifeline, keeping him anchored in this suffocating moment. His gaze fell on his father's hands, those once masterful hands that had coaxed beauty from rough timber, now trembling, lost in the folds of the hospital blanket. They looked alien, uncertain, as though they'd forgotten their purpose. The man who had shaped wood into art and taught him the language of creation was lost in a fog of fading memories. A familiar rage, a hot, bitter resentment, clawed at him. "Why now? Why couldn't he have held on just a little longer?" He swallowed, the lump in his throat a physical manifestation of his grief and guilt.

"Remember the oak at Whispering Cliffs, Dad?" he asked, his voice breaking the heavy silence. "The one we thought was too stubborn to yield?" A flicker. Just a flicker, but Caleb saw it – a spark of recognition in his father's clouded eyes. For a fleeting moment, the past had reached out and touched him. "Yes…" Thomas rasped, his voice a fragile whisper. "It… it stood firm." Brittle and delicate as spun glass, a small smile touched Caleb's lips. "Sturdy as our faith," he whispered back, the words a revelation, a truth born of years of struggle and self-doubt. The strength of the oak and their family's strength resided not in the visible branches but in the unseen roots, deep within the earth, hidden and tenacious.

Joshua moved closer, his quiet presence a solid anchor in the swirling storm of emotions. "There's a parable about an olive tree, Thomas," he said, his voice calm, steady, a comforting solace. "Grew on rocky soil, yet it bore fruit because its roots reached deep, drawing strength from hidden places." Thomas's gaze shifted to Joshua, and again, that fleeting spark of understanding ignited in his eyes. A single, precious moment of connection. "Roots are like… like memories," Thomas whispered, his voice barely audible, each word heavy with the weight of a lifetime, a lifetime of unspoken regrets and missed opportunities. Caleb felt a tear trace a path down his cheek, a silent acknowledgment of the shared pain, the shared burden of their fractured past. He wasn't just a son here; he was a man struggling to make peace with his legacy, his roots buried deep in the same troubled soil. He squeezed his father's hand, a silent promise. They would find their way back together.

"Exactly," Caleb breathed, the words catching in his throat. His heart hammered a frantic rhythm against his ribs – a desperate drumbeat against the suffocating silence that had choked their relationship for years. This wasn't just about some abstract strength; it was about his strength, the strength he'd needed to find to face his father, the man who'd been more ghost than parent for so long. It was a lifeline in the churning sea of doubt and resentment that threatened to drown him. The fading light painted the room in lengthening shadows, each a stark reminder of the chasm between them. Years bled into decades in Caleb's mind – lost birthdays, missed opportunities, a lifetime of unspoken hurts. But something had shifted. He saw it in the flicker of his father's eyes, a ghost of the man he remembered, ravaged by illness but not entirely extinguished.

The change was subtle, almost imperceptible, but it was there, a fragile ember glowing in the ashes of their broken past. And Caleb clung to it like a drowning man to a raft, desperate for connection. His hand trembled, hovering above his father's worn shirt. Inches separated them, but it felt like a lightyear. Years of silence, a vast, unforgiving ocean of unspoken words, of festering wounds, pulsed between them. But as his fingers finally brushed the coarse fabric, something cracked within him – a dam of pent-up emotion threatening to break. The touch was light, almost tentative, but it carried the world's weight. The weight of his father's failings, his regrets, the crushing burden of a relationship built on absence. Yet, even amidst the pain, a sliver of hope pierced through.

In the sterile, antiseptic chill of the hospital room, the hum of machines a constant, intrusive drone, Caleb felt his father's fragility beneath his hand. Thomas's body, once a monument of strength, was now frail, a driftwood carcass tossed about by the relentless tide of time and regret. Caleb's hand wasn't just resting there; it was a plea, a lifeline thrown into the turbulent waters of their fractured relationship. It wasn't forgiveness, not yet. Not for the wasted years, the missed chances, the mountains of unspoken words piled up between them like toxic dust. But it was something. It was an acknowledgment. A silent pact, forged in the hushed intimacy of the moment, a promise that they would navigate this storm, together, if they possibly could.

The antiseptic smell and the cold, unforgiving linoleum faded into the background as Caleb focused on the essential truth. This wasn't just about time or disease—it was about something deeper, something far more enduring. A bond that had been strained, battered, almost broken, yet stubbornly refused to die. A connection as fragile as a whispered prayer, yet as resilient as the human spirit. And in that quiet moment, Caleb felt the impossible: a delicate, tentative bloom of peace.

"Hey, Dad." Caleb's voice was rough, raw with emotion, yet imbued with a surprising strength, bearing the weight of years, unspoken longing, and a son's desperate need for connection. His voice was steady, a promise. "I'm here."

The words were simple, stripped bare, yet they resonated with a power transcending their simplicity. They were a hammer blow shattering the silence, a declaration of presence, a desperate hope for reconciliation. Thomas didn't speak, but the shift was palpable. His father's shoulders slumped a fraction, a feather-light surrender into the warmth of Caleb's hand. Years of that rigid stance, that damn-the-torpedoes posture, finally cracking. Not a surrender, no, but a chasm opening up, revealing something raw and vulnerable. Caleb felt it, a jolt in his chest, a choked sob threatening to escape.

This wasn't just some sappy reconciliation scene. This was a damn earthquake. He glanced at Sarah. Her green eyes, usually bright, were shadowed, but there was understanding there, a depth that mirrored his turmoil. She hadn't judged him, not even during those blackest nights. She'd been the sea itself, constant, patient, battering him with waves of her concern but never pulling away. The gratitude hit him like a freight train. It wasn't just this moment; it was every day she'd spent unflinching, unyielding at his side.

"Thank you," he rasped, the words thick with the weight of it all, their shared history, her sacrifice.

A simple nod from Sarah, nothing more needed. She understood. God, she understood. His gaze landed on Joshua, an oak of a man, silent as ever, but his gaze held the wisdom of centuries, the strength of mountains. This carpenter, this unexpected bolt of lightning in their lives, had quietly shaped everything. His presence, his simple, unwavering support, had been an anchor in Caleb's storm-tossed soul. With a nod—sharp, determined—Caleb gestured to the door.

"Let's go home," he said, his voice stronger now, not a command, but a declaration, a punch to the gut of this sterile, soul-crushing place. "They can't hold us anymore."

The afternoon sun bled across the parking lot as they walked, the weight of the day clinging to them, a shared burden, a testament to their resilience. The memory of his father's rough skin, still warm under his hand, burned in his mind. It was a reminder, a brutal reminder, of everything leading to this moment, and the terrifying, hopeful expanse of what lay ahead. Home. It was a word heavy with uncertainty, yet filled with the promise of something new, something hard-won. Something they'd face together.

The salt spray kissed Caleb's face, sharply contrasting the thick pine air. Port Angeles hung in the distance, a shimmering mirage of sawdust-filled workshops, stained-glass churches, a town perpetually wrestling with hope and despair—a city that mirrored the turmoil in his soul. He inhaled deeply, the cool air an ointment against the lingering burn of the hospital. Sarah and Joshua stood beside him, their presence a quiet anchor in the storm of his emotions. Peace, fragile but real, settled in his chest. This wasn't the end, not by a long shot. But together, they'd navigate whatever came next.

"Thank you," he breathed, the words barely audible, yet carrying the weight of a lifetime.

They didn't need grand pronouncements; their bond was forged in these quiet moments of shared understanding. Sarah's smile was a flicker of warmth in the fading light. "Always," she whispered back, her voice husky with unspoken anxieties. Joshua, ever the pragmatist, cut through the charged silence.

"Where to now, Caleb?" His simple question held the weight of the unspoken—the uncertainty, the fear, the sheer daunting enormity of what lay ahead.

Caleb's gaze drifted to the rugged cliffs, his childhood playground, then to the school where he'd wrestled not only with algebra but the demons of his past. He saw the church, a sanctuary and a battleground, where faith had been tested and reaffirmed. Each place and step was a scar, a lesson, a piece of the fractured puzzle he was slowly trying to assemble.

"Home," he finally said, thick with a bittersweet emotion. "Home."

The walk to the car was measured, with each step deliberate and each footfall as precise as the strokes of his chisel shaping a piece of wood. The road ahead was a jagged path, he knew. The shadows of his past—the loss, the guilt, the crippling self-doubt—would stalk him, threaten to crush him beneath their weight. But today, a single step had been taken. And that, more than anything, felt like the fragile dawn of something new, something worth fighting for. A flicker of defiance, fierce and quiet, ignited within him. He wouldn't let them win. Not this time.

Caleb's smile, a fragile thing, barely touched his lips as they walked. The sun was gone, swallowed by the horizon, but a stubborn ember glowed in his chest. Hope. A pathetic, flickering thing, as frail as a newborn's breath, yet it burned. It whispered promises of masterpieces born from the wreckage, from the splintered fragments of this brutal, broken day. He clenched his jaw, the taste of ash thick on his tongue. This hope… it was a lie, he knew it. A desperate gamble. But what choice did he have?

"Caleb," Sarah's voice, sharp as shattered glass, cut through his thoughts. Her hand, icy and trembling, tightened on his arm. "We're almost there, but… I don't know if I can…" Her voice cracked, betraying the carefully constructed facade of bravery. Fear, raw and visceral, clung to her like a shroud.

He stopped, turning to face her. He saw the fear and exhaustion etched deep into her face, mirroring his own. Their shared desperation pressed down on him, heavy as a tombstone. He hadn't truly allowed himself to feel it until now.

"We have to, Sarah," his voice was rough, gravelly. "For everything we've lost. For what we still might save." He swallowed, the words tasting like bitter bile. This wasn't just about some abstract ideal but survival and redemption. About proving to himself, above all else, that he wasn't a failure.

"But what if we fail?" she whispered, her breath hitching. "What if it's already too late?"

He looked back toward the looming silhouette of the city, a jagged scar against the bruised purple sky. The answer hung heavy in the air, unspoken yet palpable. Failure wasn't an option. Not today. Not ever.

He squeezed her hand, his grip firm, conveying a silent vow. They would keep walking. They would keep fighting. Even if the dawn never came.

CHAPTER 14

Lost Between Then and Now

SUNLIGHT SLASHED THROUGH the workshop's grimy windows, painting the floor in shifting bands of gold and dust. The aroma of pine and oak, once a balm to Caleb Martin's restless mind, now clung to him like a phantom—thick, lingering, and suffocating. Before him, the unfinished Stations of the Cross loomed in silent judgment. Each figure, carved in painstaking detail, bore a frozen expression of suffering that echoed the turmoil knotted in his chest.

He exhaled sharply, his shoulders sinking under the weight of things unsaid. The past. The present. A future he couldn't quite bring himself to imagine. His tools—chisels, gouges, mallet—lay scattered across the worktable in a chaotic reflection of his thoughts. He reached for a chisel, his fingers closing around the familiar metal, but the weight felt foreign. Alien. This tool, once an extension of himself, now felt like a relic of another life, a bridge to a father who had left too many unanswered questions in his wake.

After his visit to the VA, the old letters had been all he could think about. The parchment, worn and faded with time, carried the desperate scrawl of a man trying to reach out from the depths of his own suffering. Caleb had read them over and over, the words cutting deep, their meaning only now unraveling in painful clarity.

Thomas Martin, the man who had taught Caleb how to carve, how to find beauty hidden within the roughest grain of wood, had left behind more than just skill. He'd left scars. Absences. Ghosts that had never truly settled.

Caleb swallowed against the tightness in his throat, his gaze locked on the unfinished carving of Christ. The agony in the wood was almost too much to bear. A sob clawed at his chest.

"Damn it, Dad," he breathed, his voice raw, breaking into the silence. "Why didn't you just tell me?"

Silence answered him, vast and deafening.

For years, this workshop had been a refuge. He could still hear the quiet hum of his father working, the rhythmic tap of chisel against wood. But now, it was a battlefield, the weight of what had been left unsaid pressing down on him. He traced a calloused hand over the carved lines of Christ's suffering, his fingers shaking.

"It's like you're talking to me," he whispered, his voice barely above a breath. "Telling me things I need to hear. But I'm too damned scared to listen."

The chisel in his grip felt heavier than before. How could he finish this? Every stroke, every cut, felt like peeling back the layers of a past he had tried so hard to bury. His father—brilliant, shadowed, lost in the depths of his own pain. Caleb could still picture his hands, once steady and sure, now stilled forever by demons he could never defeat. The guilt gnawed at him.

This unfinished work held more than just religious significance. It was a reckoning. A burden. A brutal, self-imposed penance.

The salty tang of the Pacific filtered through the workshop, grounding him in the present, tethering him to the ache in his chest. He had a choice. He could let the past swallow him whole, or he could carve his way through the darkness, one stroke at a time.

A groan from the workshop door snapped him from his thoughts. Caleb stiffened, the chisel a rigid extension of his taut arm.

Sarah.

Her silhouette stood framed in the doorway, her green eyes scanning the room before landing on him. The weight of her gaze pressed into his spine, steady and knowing. She took a cautious step inside, her presence filling the space with something warm, something grounding.

"Caleb," she murmured, her voice soft but firm, a contrast to the storm raging inside him.

He didn't turn, but his shoulders eased slightly.

She moved closer, her fingers trailing along the edge of the worktable, pausing at the carvings. She studied them, her brow furrowing.

"Uncle Mike showed me these once," she said, her voice carrying a quiet reverence. "He told me that art heals. That even when it's unfinished, it still speaks."

Her words settled in the space between them, threading through the heavy air like light filtering through stained glass.

Caleb let out a breath, slow and shaky.

Sarah reached out, touching the wood lightly, as if she could feel the sorrow carved into its surface. "Sometimes," she continued, "teaching those kids feels like this. Messy. Incomplete. Like I'm not getting through to them." She traced a finger over a jagged line, her expression a mix of exhaustion and fierce determination.

"But maybe," she whispered, "that's where the real work happens. In the gaps. In the unfinished."

Her voice, raw and unguarded, tightened something deep in Caleb's chest, a knot of unspoken grief and relentless self-doubt. He swallowed hard, staring at the carvings but seeing something else entirely. Himself. The void his father had left behind. The questions he had been too afraid to ask.

He gripped the chisel tighter, his knuckles paling under the pressure. Maybe Sarah was right.

Maybe the unfinished wasn't failure.

Maybe it was an invitation to keep going.

"Maybe," he finally whispered, his voice barely carrying in the cavernous silence of the workshop. But Sarah heard him. He saw it in her eyes—a reflection of his own private hell. The weight of expectation. The crushing fear of failing a legacy too great to bear. A shared understanding that went deeper than words.

Sarah's gaze softened, a flicker of something almost like hope lighting its depths. "Your dad… he understood that too, Caleb. He started something beautiful. Something unfinished." Her voice cracked, the emotion slipping through the cracks of her carefully controlled exterior. "And you… you're the one to finish it."

The words hit like a blow. A cold, brutal truth that sent a tremor through him. The workshop, once a place of warmth and creation, now felt suffocating, haunted by the ghosts of what could have been. The air was thick with sawdust and memory. His father's absence loomed heavy in the space between them, pressing against his ribs, his breath, his will.

"I don't know if I can," Caleb muttered. The chisel in his hand felt foreign, an imposter's tool. Heavy with doubt. His gaze dropped to the unfinished carving, the Stations of the Cross his father had begun but never completed. A project meant to honor faith, sacrifice, redemption. His father's faith had been unshakable.

Caleb's? It had fractured long ago.

"I've been pretending like I don't care," Caleb said, barely above a whisper. "Like I'm fine just... walking away. But every time I pass by this door, it's like I hear him breathing behind it."

Sarah stepped forward slowly, as if afraid to break something fragile between them. "Because he's still here. Not in a ghost-story kind of way, but in the way that love stays after someone's gone. In the things they shaped. In the people they believed in."

His knuckles tightened around the chisel. His heart beat an uneven rhythm. "He believed in his God, Sarah. And in this craft. I used to think... maybe he didn't have room to believe in me too."

Sarah reached for him, her touch warm against his arm, grounding him. "You're stronger than you think," she said, her voice a quiet force of its own. "Your father saw that in you. He always did."

He wanted to believe that. Wanted to let the warmth of her voice break through the layers he'd built up—the resentment, the shame, the ache that whispered he'd never measure up.

His chest ached at the words. He tried to picture his father's hands—rough, calloused from years of carving, moving over the wood with an ease Caleb had never mastered. A sharp pang of loss twisted inside him. He had watched his father work a thousand times, but it had never felt like enough. Like he had been waiting for a tomorrow that never came.

He thought of the days he had lingered in the doorway, too afraid to speak, too proud to ask. How often had he wanted to learn—not just the strokes, the pressure, the depth of cut—but the meaning behind them? And now... the silence where instruction used to be unbearable.

Now, the chisel felt like both a lifeline and a curse.

"Adversity," Sarah murmured, breaking the silence, "it's like the grain in the wood. It resists; it fights back. It hurts like hell, but... it shapes the beauty. It makes the beauty." She exhaled slowly. "It takes patience. But most of all... it takes faith in yourself."

"But what if I don't have that kind of faith?" Caleb snapped, his voice rising, sudden and raw. "What if all I've got left is a mess of doubt and guilt and things I should've said when he was still here?"

Sarah didn't flinch. "Then start with that. With the mess. You don't have to come to God all polished. He meets us right in the chaos. Right in the silence. Isn't that what the Stations are about? A God who stumbled under the weight of everything... and still got up?"

The chisel still felt heavy. But Sarah's words chipped away at the walls he had built around himself. He wasn't just working with wood. He was working with his grief, his past, his future. He had to believe in the possibility of beauty rising from the wreckage. The possibility of finishing his father's work—and forging his own.

His eyes met Sarah's. Stormy green, filled with a quiet strength, a resilience honed by her own battles. He saw it now—the depth of her belief, not just in his father's work, but in him.

"Your father," she said, voice steady, "left these carvings for you to finish. Not despite your fears, but because of them."

A flicker of something new, something dangerous, stirred inside him. Hope. It felt like standing at the edge of a cliff, wind roaring past his ears, the ground both too far and too close.

"Sarah," he exhaled, the confession slipping out before he could stop it. "I'm terrified. My hands'll shake. I'll ruin everything he started. What if I can't finish it? What if I fail him—fail myself?"

The workshop held its breath. The weight of the past and the future pressed against him from both sides, threatening to crush the fragile middle ground where he stood. The silence thickened, wrapping around him like smoke, suffocating, oppressive.

Sarah moved closer; her voice unwavering. "Failure isn't the end of the story, Caleb. It's just another chapter. Your journey—our journey—doesn't stop with a chipped chisel. It's in picking it up again that we find our way."

Caleb flinched at the word "our." He hadn't realized until now how much he needed it—not just someone believing in him, but someone choosing to walk beside him. His mom had left faith behind when his dad died. His own heart had followed not long after.

The storm inside him wavered. Her words weren't just words. They were a lifeline. A quiet challenge. Not to be fearless. But to move forward despite the fear.

The chisel in his grip no longer felt quite so foreign. His breath steadied, though the fear still coiled tight in his gut. It didn't strangle him this time. It didn't own him.

Across the room, Joshua stilled. The half-finished carving rested in his hands, momentarily forgotten. Yet his presence was unwavering, an unspoken reassurance that Caleb wasn't alone in this.

Joshua's eyes met his—dark, knowing. A silent message passed between them.

You've got this.

Caleb exhaled, a breath that felt too shallow, too fragile. His fingers curled around the chisel's worn handle, its grooves fitting against his palm like an old memory. A familiar weight, yet somehow heavier.

The workshop air was thick—sawdust and pine mingling with something older, something sacred. This wasn't just a space filled with tools and unfinished projects. It was a sanctuary, steeped in prayers whispered through wood shavings and calloused hands. Here, redemption wasn't spoken in grand gestures but in the quiet scrape of a chisel against timber. Each cut, a prayer. Each stroke, a confession.

Joshua shifted beside him, his voice low, steady. "Ready?"

It wasn't really a question. It was a challenge. A shared burden.

Caleb swallowed, his throat tight with unspoken doubts. "Yeah," he murmured, though his voice lacked conviction. Still, he forced himself to believe it. To trust in the hands that had shaped this craft. To trust in the hands that had once belonged to his father.

The weight of it all pressed down—the unfinished legacy, the ghosts of his past, the crushing expectations. His pulse thrummed against his ribs as he traced a rough outline on the wood, his father's voice echoing in his mind, a mixture of pride and relentless demand.

A craftsman's work is his soul made visible.

But what if his soul wasn't worthy? What if everything he carved crumbled under the weight of his failures?

His fingers tensed around the chisel. The steel felt cold, grounding. The uncarved wood before him was more than just a project; it was a reckoning. A promise. A plea for something he couldn't name.

Joshua nodded, a quiet push forward.

Caleb tightened his grip. The first strike landed with a crisp, clean sound, sharp against the silence. A heartbeat. A beginning.

The chisel bit deep. The scent of fresh pine curled in the air, mingling with the sweat on his brow. Each careful stroke manifested his turmoil—hesitation giving way to determination. He wasn't just shaping wood. He was carving a space for himself, chipping away at the weight of a legacy that had nearly broken him.

This wasn't surrender. This was reclamation.

But the ghosts still lingered. His father's expectations. His own self-doubt. The memories clawed at the edges of his mind—the sharp reprimands, the endless pursuit of perfection. The Stations of the Cross, carved by his father's hands, had once been shackles. Now, beneath Caleb's grip, they were transforming into something else. A testament to endurance. A defiant act of self-forgiveness.

The chisel struck again, and his heart pounded a frantic rhythm—each impact a battle between past wounds and present resolve.

Then, a voice.

Sarah.

She stood at the threshold of the workshop, her presence a quiet anchor. Her gaze held something more than admiration—understanding. She saw the war waging beneath his skin.

"Remarkable, Caleb." Her voice was soft, but it carried weight. It reached into the hollow places he tried to ignore.

His breath shuddered. He looked up, meeting her gaze. A flicker of something sharp pierced his chest—gratitude, fear, something in between.

"Thank you," he rasped. "For believing in me. Even when I didn't."

Sarah's smile was fragile but unyielding. "Always," she whispered. "We face this together. No matter what."

Caleb turned back to the wood, his pulse steadying. The chisel, an extension of himself once more. The tools, his voice. And with renewed ferocity, he carved—not just into the wood, but into the uncertainty that had kept him frozen for so long. Each strike was a step forward, away from his father's shadow and toward the man he was meant to be. The work wasn't just about finishing the Stations—it was about finishing the fight within himself.

Joshua continued carving beside him, his strokes steady and deliberate. The rhythmic scrape of steel against wood filled the small workshop, the sound both grounding and relentless. It tethered Caleb to the present, kept him from spiraling into the dark corners of his mind where doubt and guilt thrived.

The chisel in his hand no longer felt foreign, no longer an extension of his father's expectations but something that belonged to him. And yet, the weight of unfinished work pressed heavy against his chest. He needed to finish this. He had to.

Sarah's voice, gentle yet unwavering, broke through his mounting tension. "Caleb, breathe. You're doing fine."

Her words were a lifeline, but his grip tightened around the mallet, his knuckles turning white. He couldn't meet her eyes. If he did, she'd see the truth—see how close he was to unraveling beneath the burden of his father's legacy. This wasn't just wood and steel. It was atonement, an offering, a desperate plea for absolution.

"Fine?" he rasped, the word barely escaping his throat. His voice cracked under the weight of his fear. "Sarah, I... I can't."

The confession hung in the air, thick as the sawdust that clung to his sweat-dampened skin. His gaze locked onto the half-finished figure of Christ. The weight of the cross on its shoulders mirrored the weight of his own grief. His father's voice, distant but unrelenting, whispered in the back of his mind: Finish what you start, Caleb.

Without pausing in his work, Joshua spoke, his voice a steady undercurrent of strength. "Your father wouldn't want you to quit." The certainty in his tone was unshaken, a quiet assurance that cut through Caleb's spiraling doubt. "He'd want you to finish what you started."

Caleb swallowed hard. The lump in his throat felt immovable. He risked a glance at Sarah. Her eyes held no judgment, only quiet belief—a belief he couldn't quite muster for himself. In their depths, he saw not just concern but an unwavering conviction that he could do this. That he was more than his failures.

He had to believe. He had to finish this. Not just for his father. Not just for Sarah or Joshua. But for himself.

Taking a steadying breath, he picked up the mallet once more. His hands trembled, but he forced them to move, to strike, to shape. Each swing was an unspoken prayer, a desperate promise. The chisel bit into the wood, carving not just form but meaning, stripping away doubt as it revealed something truer beneath. The sound of his labor filled the space, steady and unyielding, a counterpoint to the racing of his pulse.

The wood yielded beneath his hands, exposing the contours of Christ's suffering face. Caleb's movements grew surer, his strokes more certain. With every chip of pine, he carved away years of guilt, of self-doubt, of exile. This wasn't just about redemption. This was survival.

He worked with an urgency that bordered on desperation, a frantic need to reach the end, to see the piece finished. The Stations of the Cross lined the walls behind him, silent witnesses to his struggle. Their shadows flickered in the dim workshop light, a reminder of the path he walked—the path he had yet to complete.

The air in the workshop felt dense with unspoken words, the lingering aroma of sawdust weaving through the silence like a memory that refused to fade. Tension hung in every breath, every creak of the wooden floor beneath their feet. And then, at last, the final stroke was made—decisive, deliberate—cutting through the stillness like a quiet exhale after holding back too long.

Caleb stepped back, his breath ragged, sweat trickling down his temples. The figure of Christ stood before him, bowed beneath an unseen weight, yet undeniably whole. The late afternoon sunlight slanted through the dusty window, catching on the grains of wood, turning them golden.

He wiped a hand across his brow, leaving a streak of sawdust in its wake. The carving was finished, but the ache in his chest remained. Doubt gnawed at the edges of his triumph. Was it enough? Was he enough?

Sarah's voice cut through his thoughts, strong and steady. "Looking good, Caleb."

There was more in her words than just approval—there was understanding. There was history. The weight of everything they had both lost and carried in silence pressed against them, unspoken but deeply felt.

Caleb let out a shaky breath, offering a ghost of a smile. "Getting there." The words felt like an admission, a reluctant surrender to hope.

Across the room, Sarah and Joshua exchanged a glance—an entire conversation passing between them in silence. Years of grief, of standing by while he broke apart and withdrew, had forged a bond between them stronger than words. Joshua nodded, barely perceptible, but Caleb caught it. It was the same nod his father used to give him—a quiet approval, a sign that he was on the right path.

Sarah's smile didn't waver. "We'll be going now." Her voice was softer now, laced with something unspoken but understood. Joshua nodded in agreement. They had given him what they could. The rest, he had to face alone.

As the door creaked shut behind them, silence settled over Caleb like a shroud. He turned back to the figure before him, the unfinished sculpture staring back like a reflection of the man he saw in the mirror—unfinished, uncertain, struggling beneath the weight of his own cross.

Through the workshop's small window, Sarah lingered, her gaze tracing the lines of his hunched shoulders, the tension in his jaw. She saw more than his doubt, more than his past. She saw the man she knew he could be the one buried beneath guilt and regret. He wasn't just carving wood. He was carving out a space for something else forgiveness. For himself. But until he saw it too, until he let himself believe, it would remain just that: unfinished.

Inside, the silence wasn't peaceful; it pressed in on him, dense with unspoken memories and the weight of unfinished words. The workshop still held the lingering traces of pine and sawdust, woven into the very grain of the walls. But tonight, it held something deeper—an essence of the past, a breath of memory that clung to the air like invisible thread. Caleb could almost feel his father's presence in it, a quiet echo in the shadows, a phantom warmth near his shoulder. His throat tightened, the ache of grief catching him off guard. Slowly, his fingers curled around the chisel—familiar, worn—but he paused. The tool felt heavier than usual, as if it, too, remembered. His grip faltered.

Doubt gnawed at him, sharp and relentless. This wasn't just about shaping Christ's face; it was about carving something out of himself, out of his past. A man who could finish this piece would be one with faith, one with purpose. But did he still believe? Did he still have a place in the world his father had once imagined for him?

A sharp memory stabbed at him—his father, brow furrowed in disappointment, words clipped and cool: *You don't start what you can't finish, son.* Caleb flinched as if the words had been spoken aloud. He ran a thumb over the rough-hewn wood, its grain cool beneath his calloused skin. Every chip, every stroke of the chisel, should have been a prayer. But all he felt was the bitter taste of failure clinging to the back of his throat.

The chisel slipped. A jagged crack splintered through the smooth curve of Christ's shoulder. Caleb swore under his breath, dropping the tool with a sharp *clang* against the workbench. A tremor ran through his hands. *This was a mistake.*

He turned away, pacing the length of the workshop, dragging both hands through his hair. His chest ached with frustration, with longing, with something he didn't know how to name. Maybe Sarah was wrong. Maybe this wasn't about redemption. Maybe it was just another thing he'd fail at; another promise he couldn't keep.

His eyes landed on the wooden frame of the doorway, where his mother had once stood, watching him with quiet faith. *You are more than your mistakes, Caleb,* she had told him, her voice steady, unshaken. *God isn't asking for perfection. He's asking for your heart.*

His breath shuddered out of him. He turned back to the carving, his fingers itching to fix what he had broken. His hands were steadier now. Not because the doubt had disappeared, but because something in him whispered that maybe, just maybe, his mother had been right.

He picked up the chisel again. This wasn't just about carving wood. It was about cutting a new path, one paved with hope, if he dared to believe it could exist.

CHAPTER 15

The Carpenter's Son and the Lesson of Wood

THE WIND, A raw fist, ripped at Caleb's coat as he stood at the edge of Whispering Cliffs. Dusk bled into night, painting the sky in bruised purples and angry oranges. He was a silhouette, rigid against that fiery canvas, the turmoil inside him mirroring the chaotic dance of the waves below. Each crash was a hammer blow against the ancient rocks, a relentless rhythm that echoed the frantic beat of his own heart. His father's legacy—a cursed inheritance of skill and expectation—felt like a millstone, grinding him down. "Damn it all," he thought, the words a bitter taste on his tongue. He smelled salt, sharp and clean, a counterpoint to the faint sweetness of wildflowers the wind tossed his way. The vast and indifferent sea whispered of cycles, endings and beginnings, and forces far beyond his control. It urged surrender, a release from the crushing weight of his father's expectations, but the path to that release remained shrouded in a fog of doubt, thick and suffocating.

Caleb closed his eyes, drawing a shuddering breath. The cliff face, solid beneath his feet, offered a fragile comfort. He clung to it, the unwavering earth a stark contrast to the turbulent sea that mirrored his soul. "Find peace," he urged himself, but the words felt hollow, swallowed by the roar in his ears. A sudden, sharp sound—the crunch of gravel. Joshua. Caleb didn't turn. He let Joshua's approach weave into the symphony of the wind and waves, a counterpoint to his internal chaos. Joshua's voice, low and steady, cut through the noise. "Beautiful, isn't it?" His gaze wasn't on the ocean but on Caleb, sharp and knowing, as if he could see right through the carefully constructed walls Caleb had built around his pain. "The way the sky… it cradles the sea. Reminds us of some things… some connections… are eternal."

Caleb finally turned; his face etched with a weariness that belied his years. "Eternal?" he rasped, his voice thick with skepticism. "My father's legacy feels anything but. It's a damn anchor, dragging me under." Joshua placed a hand on Caleb's shoulder, his touch surprisingly firm. "Your father's skill… it's a part of you, Caleb. But it's not all of you. He pushed you, I know that. But he also… he loved you. In his own way." Caleb scoffed, the sound brittle. "His way involved expectations that could crush a mountain. I'll never measure up."

"Don't say that" Joshua said, quiet but firm. "You're already surpassing him. You're finding your own voice, your own way. The way you shape wood… it's different, more… fluid. It's 'you.'" Caleb looked back at the churning ocean, a battleground of light and shadow. He saw his father's face in the waves, stern and demanding. But then, beneath that image, a flicker of something else… pride? A ghost of a smile? He turned back to Joshua, his expression unreadable. "I don't know, Josh. I feel so… lost." Joshua squeezed his shoulder gently. "Lost, maybe. But not alone. We'll find your way, together." His eyes held a quiet strength, a promise whispered against the roar of the unforgiving sea. The weight, for the first time, felt a little lighter.

Caleb's head snapped up, a ghost of a smile playing on his lips. Joshua's words landed not with the gentle ease of dawn but with the force of a wave crashing against a cliff. It wasn't some picturesque vista that held Caleb, but the raw, brutal honesty in Joshua's voice. Connection wasn't some prize to be won; it was a damn lifeline, frayed but unbreakable, humming beneath the surface of everything. Joshua leaned on the railing; his gaze fixed on some distant point only he could see. He was a statue carved from granite, drawing strength from the wind, a silent communion Caleb couldn't fathom.

"There was another carpenter's son," Joshua murmured, his voice a low rumble in Caleb's chest. "He inherited a legacy, all right. Not of two-by-fours and hammers, but something… bigger. Something he never saw coming." A prickle of anticipation crackled between them.

Caleb shifted, his own heart echoing the restless rhythm of the ocean. Joshua's voice deepened, thick with the gravity of a life lived hard, a tapestry woven from triumph and despair. "This carpenter's son," Joshua continued, his words precise, deliberate, "his hands were made for shaping wood, for building. But life... life had other plans. His burdens weren't planks and nails, but the damn weight of a world falling apart. And yet... he carried it. With grace, they say. His pain became his purpose. His trials... his triumphs."

Joshua's words weren't just words; they were blows, chipping away at Caleb's carefully constructed walls, revealing the raw, bleeding heart beneath. The carpenter's son, a figure Caleb had always known as myth, suddenly felt like a mirror reflecting his agonizing struggle. The doubts, the crippling self-doubt, the crushing weight of his father's legacy—they were all there, mirrored in the other man's journey. This wasn't some ancient legend; it was Caleb's damn life.

Joshua paused, his gaze sweeping the horizon. The dying sun gilded his hair, turning it to molten gold. "Through every storm, every damn trial, that carpenter's son never broke. His work... his craft... it became a testament. Not just to endurance, but something more. It came from surrender, Caleb. From trusting the damn process, trusting the shape of his own soul." Caleb choked back a sob. This wasn't a parable; it was his confession. The doubts, the paralyzing fear, the crushing uncertainty about living up to his father's name all clawed at him. But Joshua's words, rough as they were, offered a glimmer of something more. Redemption wasn't a reward; it was forged in the fires of the struggle. Purpose, Caleb realized, was born from the heart of the pain. He looked at Joshua, a question hanging in the air between them, unspoken but palpable: Could he, do it? Could he find that strength?

The wind roared, a banshee wail against the cliffs, mirroring the tempest in Caleb's gut. He stared out at the churning sea, the spray stinging his face. Joshua's silence hung heavier than the sea mist, a palpable tension that stretched between them like a taut rope. Doubt, a familiar, gnawing beast, clawed at Caleb's insides. He'd always thought escape was the answer—running from the shadow of his family's legacy, the weight of expectations crushing him like a tidal wave.

Finally, Caleb broke the silence, his voice barely a whisper above the wind's howl. "Was it... was it always this hard for him?" Joshua's gaze held his, unwavering, a storm of his brewing in his deep-set eyes. "Aye, lad. But the sea, she tests a man, doesn't she? She breaks some, but she strengthens others." He paused; his voice gruff but laced with a weariness that spoke of years spent battling the unforgiving ocean. "The carpenter's son... he was tested beyond measure."

Caleb swallowed, a lump forming in his throat. The revelation that Joshua, this grizzled old fisherman, knew his family's story felt like a betrayal and a comfort. "He... he found peace?" The question was desperate, a lifeline tossed into the churning waters of his uncertainty.

Joshua chuckled, a dry, rasping sound. "Peace? Nay, lad. He found something better. He found understanding. He found... redemption." Joshua's tale unfolded; a raw, visceral narrative etched in the very rhythm of the crashing waves. He spoke of the carpenter's son, a man consumed by grief, haunted by failures, wrestling with a legacy he couldn't escape. But with each carefully crafted word, Caleb saw a reflection of himself—the same struggle, pain, and desperate longing for escape.

"Each day," Joshua's voice boomed, almost swallowed by the wind, yet still cutting through Caleb like a sharp chisel, "he picked up his tools. Not because he 'had' to, but because... because it was 'him.' His hands, calloused and scarred, shaped the wood, and the wood, in turn, shaped his soul. He found solace in the rhythm, the repetition. A rhythm that mirrored his own internal struggle."

Caleb felt a shift within him, a profound understanding dawning like sunrise over a stormy sea. The path ahead wasn't clear, far from it. But it wasn't a path of running anymore. It was a path of facing the storm within, of carving his redemption, one painstaking stroke at a time. The sea roared its approval, a symphony of acceptance. The journey home, he realized, wasn't about avoiding the waves; it was about learning to navigate them.

Caleb," Joshua said, his voice low, a gravelly whisper against the wind's howl. His eyes, the color of weathered oak, bored into Caleb's. "The wood doesn't fight the carver, you understand. It yields. It reveals its truest self in the shaping." The unspoken hung between them – the weight of generations, of a legacy Caleb hadn't asked for. Caleb's gut clenched. He'd spent years wrestling with the anger, the bitter resentment towards his father's infamous legacy, the Stations of the Cross. It wasn't just wood he carved; it was the ghosts of his family's history, the suffocating pressure of expectation. He'd felt trapped, bound to a path paved with the pain of his father's mistakes. But now, a crack of doubt formed in the hardened shell of his defenses. Joshua's words... they resonated somewhere deep, stirring something ancient.

"It's...different this time," Caleb finally managed, his voice raspy, betraying the turmoil within. He felt the familiar knot of anxiety in his chest, a suffocating pressure he'd grown accustomed to. "I...I feel it." Joshua's gaze softened, though the intensity didn't waver. He saw the fight still flickering in Caleb's eyes, the ghost of the rebellious son he'd been. But there was something new, too: a flicker of hope, a desperate yearning for release. "The fear won't vanish overnight, son," Joshua said, his voice gruff but laced with understanding. "But you can learn to carve around it. To use it to shape something beautiful."

The ocean roared its approval, a symphony of crashing waves that mirrored the storm within Caleb. He looked out at the relentless horizon, the vast expanse a mirror to his uncertain future. The Sanctuary, his father's creation, loomed in his mind – a tomb or a testament? A prison or a pathway? "It's not just about the wood anymore, is it?" Caleb breathed, the words catching in his throat. He felt the years of pent-up grief threatening to spill over. "It's about...forgiveness. For myself. For him." Joshua nodded, a rare smile gracing his weathered face. "Your father's mistakes... they're not yours to carry alone. You can choose to honor his memory, not by repeating his sins, but by forging your own path. A path carved with your own hands, guided by your own heart."

Caleb took a deep breath, the salty air stinging his lungs, a physical manifestation of the cleansing he desperately craved. He felt the weight of the Stations of the Cross ease, not disappear entirely, but shift. They were no longer shackles but signposts, markers on a journey toward redemption, a journey he was finally ready to begin. The Sanctuary of Wood and Memory would not be a mausoleum but a rebirth. A place where the past found peace, not through passive acceptance, but through active transformation. Once clenched in frustrated anger, his hands now felt the familiar weight of his carving tools, poised to create something new, something powerful, something truly his own. This wasn't just about carving wood; it was about carving out his soul.

Caleb Martin, Thomas's son, stood at the precipice, the weight of his father's legacy a physical thing in his hand – a worn chisel, its edge dulled but not broken, mirroring the state of his soul. The road ahead felt less like a path and more like a sheer cliff face, each jagged outcrop a fresh wound from the past. But it was his road. Every cut of the chisel, every grain of wood he shaped, would be a prayer, a desperate plea for forgiveness, not just for his sins but for the unforgivable sins of his father. This wasn't just about carving wood; it was about carving out a new Caleb, a man free from the shadow of his past. He was ready, or at least, he told himself he was. The truth was a cold knot in his stomach.

Though rough and strong, Joshua's hand landed on his shoulder, a silent blessing against the wind's howl. It wasn't just comfort; it was a shared history etched in the very lines of their palms. "Ready, Caleb?" Joshua's voice was low, roughened by years and the salty air, but laced with a quiet strength that Caleb desperately needed. Caleb swallowed; his throat tight. "I… I think so," he managed, the words catching on the tremor in his voice. He hadn't felt this vulnerable… since before it all fell apart. Joshua squeezed his shoulder, the gesture contrasting the storm raging around them. "Doubt's a liar, boy. It whispers of things that aren't true. You've faced worse." He let his hand fall away, but the warmth lingered, a ghost of their shared trials.

Their eyes met, and Caleb saw a flicker of understanding, of shared pain, reflected in the depths of Joshua's gaze. It wasn't pity he saw, but something more substantial – a brotherhood forged in the fires of grief and resilience. A small, almost imperceptible smile touched Caleb's lips, momentarily banishing the grim set of his jaw. Even the relentless gulls seemed to hush, the wind momentarily still, as if nature acknowledged this silent exchange's gravity. Turning from the edge, Caleb walked away from the abyss, the ocean a vast, unknowable expanse below. With each deliberate step, he shed a layer of self-doubt, the churning waters mirroring the turmoil he'd wrestled within himself. He wasn't running from the cliffs, but towards something – redemption, peace, maybe even forgiveness.

The workshop, his sanctuary, loomed ahead, no longer a prison of painful memories, but a crucible, a place where he would forge his destiny, a place where he would finally, truly become a master craftsman, not just in wood, but in the art of living. He was ready to claim it, make it his own, and finally, build something beautiful from the wreckage of his past. This wasn't a journey of escape but a climb towards self-acceptance. Caleb's hands, raw and scarred from years of wrestling stubborn wood, ached for the familiar bite of chisel against grain. Each knot, each whorl in the unfinished Stations of the Cross – his father's legacy, a half-finished testament to a broken man – whispered a story, a promise of redemption that clawed at him. He'd once seen it as a millstone, a weight anchoring him to the past's bitter failures. Now, it felt different: a key, not a chain. A damn key to his freedom.

The wind, sharp and salty, whipped at his back as he walked away from the cliffs, each step a rejection of the suicidal despair that had gnawed at him. The scent of pine battled the ocean's spray, a strangely comforting mix. The restlessness that had poisoned him, the urge to simply end it all, began to loosen its grip. Not entirely gone, but less of a suffocating vise. This path, uncertain as it was, felt like his own carving, his damn creation. And Joshua, walking beside him, wasn't a preacher, just a quiet, unwavering presence, a testament to the fragile hope that dared to flicker.

"Think you'll ever forgive yourself, Caleb?" Joshua's voice, low and steady as the rhythm of their steps, broke through Caleb's internal battle. Caleb swallowed, the lump in his throat thick and bitter. "Don't know, Josh. Some days, forgiveness feels like a luxury I can't afford." They fell into a rhythm, a silent pact against the ghosts of the past. The cliffs, with their ceaseless mournful song, receded, but their echo remained – a brutal, insistent reminder of the truths they'd stared into the face of. Truths etched into his soul like scars that refused to fade.

As the workshop emerged from the pines, a familiar haven nestled amongst the trees, Caleb's heart hammered a frantic rhythm against his ribs. It wasn't a place of pain anymore, but of possibility. His father's sanctuary, once a tomb of unfinished business, now stood as a defiant monument to what he could achieve. The Stations, incomplete, beckoned with a fierce urgency. He could almost hear his father's voice, a ghostly whisper urging him onward. "Finish it, son. Finish what we started."

Reaching the threshold, the sharp tang of sawdust and the lingering trace of aged oak filled his nostrils, striking him with the force of memory—a visceral jolt that both unsettled and strangely soothed him. It wasn't the finished piece that haunted him, but the grueling ritual of shaping it—the splinters, the sweat, the hours lost in silent struggle. Each stroke of the chisel had been an act of penance, each grain of wood a confession. Joshua stood motionless in the doorway; his figure cast in shadow against the twilight seeping through the windows. He said nothing, yet the weight of his presence bore down like judgment, heavy and unspoken.

Caleb," Joshua finally said, his voice low, a rumble of stones tumbling down a hillside. The unspoken hung between them, thick and suffocating. "It's…a lot to bear, isn't it?" Caleb swallowed, the lump in his throat the size of a fist. "Yeah," he rasped, his voice cracking. "It's… everything." He couldn't meet Joshua's steady gaze, the weight of his failings a crushing burden. "I…" He trailed off, the words refusing to come. Joshua didn't press. He simply stepped aside, allowing Caleb to enter the sanctuary of his father's workshop – a place that held both the comfort of memories and the sharp sting of regret.

The air was thick with the past, a phantom presence threading through the shadows like smoke that refused to clear. The scent of fresh sawdust stung his senses—familiar, but taunting—like a perfume worn by a memory that never left. He felt his father's spirit woven into the cedar and pine, drifting in the slanted beams of light that pierced through the grime-streaked window, not dancing, but hovering—weighty and unmoved, like judgment waiting to speak. His heart pounded a frantic rhythm against his ribs, a relentless drumbeat echoing the guilt he couldn't carve away. The tools lay scattered across the workbench, silent sentinels to all he had left undone. He reached for the chisel, its worn grip grounding him for a moment in a world that otherwise felt foreign. The smooth wood beneath his hand was too perfect, too still, jarring against the turbulence inside him. He let his fingers drift along the grain, as if the curves and ridges could reveal some buried truth—some hidden absolution—that only sweat, and time could carve free.

The chisel felt like an extension of his soul, cold and hard, mirroring the unforgiving nature of his regret. His hands, weathered and scarred, moved with the precision of a seasoned craftsman, but beneath the practiced movements lurked the frantic tremors of a man desperately seeking peace. The rhythmic tap-tap-tap of the chisel echoed the unsteady beat of his heart, a lonely rhythm in the cavernous workshop, a frantic plea carved into the very wood he shaped. Tonight, he wouldn't just be shaping wood; he would be shaping himself, or perhaps, trying to.

Sweat beaded on Caleb's brow, the scent of pine and sawdust thick in the air. His chisel, a familiar weight in his calloused hand, bit into the dark wood. The grain pulsed under his touch – a mocking heartbeat, a reminder of the life that had ended too soon. This wasn't just carving; it was a damn exorcism. He'd promised himself this. It was a way to honor his father and wrestle the ghost of his legacy from the suffocating grip it held on to him. But the wood felt resistant, stubborn, mirroring the turmoil in his gut. Each shaving that fell was a tiny shard of his doubt, a whisper of failure echoing in the silence of the workshop.

"Damn it," he muttered, the words catching in his throat. Fear, cold and sharp, pricked at him. He wasn't just carving wood; he was carving his soul. What if he failed? What if this wasn't enough? What if the grief, the crushing weight of responsibility, swallowed him whole? The rhythmic rasp of the chisel was a frantic counterpoint to the hammering in his chest. He saw his father in the grain – his father's stooped shoulders, the lines etched by years of hardship, the quiet strength that had always been there, buried beneath the weight of their shared struggles. This wasn't about escape; it was about facing the demons, understanding the man he'd lost, and, more importantly, understanding himself.

"Redemption," he whispered, the stranger's words a ghostly echo in the cavernous workshop. It wasn't a gift; blood, sweat, and tears poured into this piece of wood, a testament to his struggle and will to survive. Each stroke was a prayer, a battle fought and won, inch by agonizing inch. The workbench, once a symbol of loss, became an altar. His father's tools, extensions of his own heart, pulsed with a new purpose. They weren't just instruments of creation but weapons against his despair. With each chip of wood that fell, a piece of the past died – the guilt, the anger, the crippling fear that had paralyzed him for so long. The weight of his father's legacy remained, but it felt different now—a guiding star instead of a crushing burden, pulling him toward the light. He was finally carving his path, creating something beautiful and brutally honest. And that, he realized, was freedom.

Sweat beaded on Caleb's brow, stinging his eyes. The Stations weren't just stone anymore; they were scars, mirroring the ones etched onto his soul. Each chipped detail, each painstakingly carved figure, was a raw confession, a testament to the unforgiving weight of his past. He'd hated these Stations once, seen them as monuments to his father's suffocating piety. Now, the chisel felt like an extension of his own battered heart, each blow a desperate plea for release. The peace wasn't some ethereal calm; it was a hard-won truce, fragile as the wood beneath his tools.

The expectations, the ghost of his father's disappointed gaze, still clawed at him. But this time, the weight felt different. It wasn't crushing him; it fueled him. He was chipping away at the stone, but more importantly, he was chipping away at the stone wall he'd built around his broken heart.

"Damn it," he muttered, the words a ragged whisper in the hushed sanctuary. The rhythmic "thwack-thwack-thwack" of the chisel was his mantra, his desperate attempt to drown out the incessant whispers of doubt. He wasn't sure if it was God he felt or simply the raw, exhausted relief of finally facing his demons. Maybe it was both.

The stranger's words echoed in his memory – "redemption isn't a gift; it's a damn fight." He'd scoffed at the time, but the sentiment now resonated with a brutal honesty that left him breathless. This wasn't a stroll through a sun-drenched meadow but a bloody, brutal climb up a jagged mountain. Each stroke was a victory, a testament to his stubborn refusal to succumb to the shadows that had haunted him for so long.

He paused, hand trembling, the weight of the chisel feeling unbearable. He wanted to stop, run, and bury himself in the comforting darkness of denial. But he wouldn't. Not this time. He wouldn't let the ghost's win. He wouldn't let his father's legacy define him or crush him. This was *his* path, his damn redemption, and he would walk it, one agonizing, hopeful stroke at a time.

He slammed the chisel into the wood, the sound a defiant roar in the quiet sanctuary. The work continued.

ACT 4

REDEMPTION AND THE MASTER CRAFTSMAN'S PLAN

CHAPTER 16

A Reckoning with the Past

CALEB GRIPPED THE cold, pitted metal of the Port Orchard VA door, his knuckles white and slick with sweat. He couldn't decide what unsettled him more—the sterile sting of antiseptic hanging in the air like a silent accusation, or the invisible weight of the promises he'd made to Sarah, heavy as lead in his chest. The grooves in the handle, worn smooth by countless desperate hands, scraped against his palm like old wounds reopening. This place, this so-called "institution," throbbed with a sorrow so dense it seemed to seep into his marrow, echoing every unspoken fear he carried with him.

Sarah's hand, small and strong in his, squeezed. Her silence was a rock, anchoring him in the churning sea of his anxiety. He glanced at her, catching the flicker of fear in her usually unwavering eyes – a fear he mirrored, a fear that ate at the edges of their shared hope. He knew this wasn't just about Jake; it was about them, about their fragile future, built on the shaky ground of past traumas.

"Ready?" he rasped, his voice barely audible above the frantic drumming of his heart. Sarah nodded, her throat tight. "Let's get this over with." The steel in her voice, a carefully constructed dam against her well of fear, surprised him. The shared glance, brief and loaded, spoke volumes. This wasn't just about-facing Jake's demons but confronting their own.

Their footsteps echoed through the corridor, each one landing like a hammer strike against the oppressive hush that filled the building. The hallway stretched before them, seemingly endless, a tunnel carved from cold sterility. The sharp, almost acrid odor of disinfectant clung to the air, scraping at his throat and tightening around his chest like an invisible fist. Every instinct screamed at him to turn back, to flee to the parking lot where at least the air felt real. But Sarah walked beside him—calm, unwavering—a tether to something solid. Her presence, quiet but unyielding, anchored him. When they reached the door, Caleb paused only a moment before pushing it open, his hand trembling. It wasn't courage that moved him—it was defiance. A refusal to let fear decide for him.

Inside, Jake sat hunched over a scarred table, a monument to his inner turmoil. His broad shoulders, once symbols of strength, now drooped under the weight of unseen battles. His eyes, usually bright with mischief, were dull, lost in the grain of the wood. He didn't look up as they entered. The silence was a physical presence, thick enough to choke on.

Caleb cleared his throat, the sound brittle and unnatural. "Jake?" Jake's head snapped up, his eyes widening slightly. He looked older, weathered beyond his years. A flicker of recognition sparked in his gaze, then died quickly, replaced by a guarded mask of indifference.

"Caleb," he finally mumbled, his voice a low, gravelly whisper, "Didn't expect to see you here." The words were devoid of warmth, a stark contrast to the brotherly bond they once shared. The unspoken question hung in the air, heavier than the silence itself: *What kind of hell had he been living through?*

Jake's eyes, haunted and weary, snagged on theirs. The intensity hit Caleb like a gut punch – a raw, exposed nerve. It wasn't just pain in those eyes; it was a desperate search, a grasping for something solid in the wreckage of his life. A flicker of something... more. Recognition? Hope? For a heart-stopping second, Caleb thought he could almost touch this fragile thread of redemption buried under years of silence and self-inflicted wounds.

Caleb's throat was a vise. He wrestled for words, the dam finally breaking with a ragged, "Jake..." The word felt ancient, like a stone he'd carried too long.

"It takes guts to admit you're drowning," he rasped, his voice raw with something akin to desperate hope. "Facing yourself? That's a tougher fight than any battlefield." His blue eyes, the color of the Port

Angeles sky on a clear day, locked onto Jake's with a fierce compassion. His hands, gnarled and calloused from a lifetime of shaping wood and a life even more challenging to shape, clenched the chair arms until his knuckles shone white. Anger, hurt, the gnawing need to heal – it was all a tangled mess inside him.

Sarah slipped beside him, a quiet anchor. Her green eyes, wise and knowing from a life spent mending broken people, met Caleb's, a silent understanding passing between them before settling on Jake. Her gaze was gentle but firm, like a seasoned teacher guiding a lost student. "We can't rewrite the past," she said, her voice a low, soothing relief against Caleb's harsh words, "but it doesn't own us."

Each word was measured, an invitation, a lifeline. She stood tall, as unwavering as the cliffs guarding Port Angeles, firm against the relentless tide. "The past is a teacher," Sarah's voice hardened with conviction, "not a jailer." Her words resonated with a depth born of her battles, her hard-won healing. This wasn't abstract wisdom; this was lived experience. Her strength wasn't the absence of pain, but her defiance. Her steady voice wove a tapestry of compassion and hope, a lifeline reaching out to Jake and the tormented Caleb.

The Kitsap Veterans' Haven's sterile chill bit Sarah and Caleb, but their shared warmth defied the cold. They were islands of resilience in a sea of despair, a testament to the stubborn power of hope. They'd seen it all – the shattered men, the broken promises, the slow, agonizing climb back to life. But Jake… Jake was different.

Jake's fingers drummed a frantic rhythm on the worn table. The sound echoed the turmoil inside him. He looked at Caleb, his eyes—a stormy grey—holding a lifetime of regret. "I can't… I can't fix it, Caleb," he rasped, his voice barely a whisper. The words hung heavy, thick with self-loathing. "The damage… it's too much. I'm trying, God knows I'm trying, but I'm drowning in the wreckage." His voice cracked, the raw emotion threatening to overwhelm him.

Caleb, his face etched with the map of his battles won and lost, met Jake's gaze steadily. "Jake," he said, his voice a low rumble, laced with empathy born from shared experience. "Words are cheap. It's the doing. The *next* step. Forget the apologies. What are you *going* to do? That's what defines you now. That's what carves the path ahead." He leaned forward, his eyes conveying the hard-won wisdom of a man who'd wrestled with his demons and emerged, scarred but alive.

Sarah, observing their exchange with a quiet intensity, finally spoke. Her voice, though soft, held an unshakeable conviction. "Actions, Jake. They're the consolation. We're not here to judge, but to witness. To see you climb. And we'll be right there, walking with you, if you let us." A tremor of compassion ran through her tone. She knew what it meant to be broken. She'd been there.

Jake stared at them; disbelief etched onto his face. He swallowed hard, the simple act a monumental effort. "Walk with me?" he asked, the words a question both of himself and of them. The weight of his actions pressed down on him; the guilt was a physical burden. "After what I've done… after *everything*…" His voice trailed off, lost in the abyss of his remorse.

Sarah's gaze softened. "Even the Whispering Cliffs, those stubborn giants, they crumble," she said, her voice unwavering. "They erode, reshape, become something new. Nothing's static, Jake. Not even us. We're all works in progress. And we're all capable of change." The words hung in the air, a promise, a lifeline thrown into the turbulent waters of his guilt. The silence that followed was not empty but pregnant with healing potential.

Jake's gaze darted between Caleb and Sarah, the steady calm in their eyes starkly contrasted with the hurricane raging inside him. *Operation Rhino*. The precision, the purpose… it felt like a lifetime ago. This civilian world? A damn minefield. He'd traded the predictable roar of choppers for a silence that amplified every ghost.

"Sometimes," Jake rasped, the words catching in his throat, "I hear those choppers. The noise… the chaos… it made *sense*. Here? The quiet's deafening. The past screams louder than anything."

Caleb nodded; a grim understanding etched on his face. He knew the silence's bite. The gnawing emptiness that followed the explosion of action. His own father's unfinished wood carvings were a testament to that.

"Let the past be your chisel, Jake, not your chain," Caleb said, his voice low and sharp, like the crack of a well-aimed shot. "You don't *have* to let it define you. You choose your future."

A flicker. A spark. Jake looked up, hope, fragile as a newborn bird, fluttering in his eyes. Beneath the scars, the weariness, something stirred. Something… "more." He sat up straighter, the crushing weight of his past momentarily lightened. His hands, once weapons, trembled. Its raw vulnerability hit him hard. He clenched his fists, trying to dam the flood of emotion, but it was like holding back the tide.

"Take your time, Jake," Caleb said, his voice gentle but firm. "There's strength in vulnerability. In letting go. We all carry knots in our hearts. But those knots… they can unravel. We can reshape our lives."

Sarah's green eyes, filled with a quiet understanding that went beyond words, held his gaze. Her hand, hesitant at first, gently covered his clenched fist. A silent promise. A lifeline. The room shifted. The tension eased. A fragile light pierced the gloom. Jake's shoulders slumped, his grip loosening, the knot in his chest starting to unravel. The fight wasn't over, but for the first time in a long time, he felt a sliver of hope—and the strength to keep fighting.

Jake swallowed hard; his throat dry as sandpaper. "Thank you," he rasped, the words tasting foreign, unfamiliar, as if they belonged to someone else. The weight of them settled in his chest like a stone, pressing against old wounds that had never quite healed. He glanced at Caleb, then at the other man in the room, searching their faces for something he couldn't name. Maybe forgiveness. Maybe understanding. Maybe just proof that he wasn't completely alone.

The silence that followed wasn't peaceful. It was taut, charged with an energy neither comforting nor condemning. This wasn't the hushed reverence of a church sanctuary, nor the eerie stillness of a battlefield after the final shot had been fired. It was something in between—a truce born not of peace, but of exhaustion.

Caleb exhaled slowly, the tightness in his chest familiar yet no less suffocating. The phantom pain of old injuries lingered, a dull ache that never quite went away. He thought of his father's unfinished carvings back in the shop, their edges rough and jagged, waiting for a skilled hand to smooth them into something whole. The thought gnawed at him. He understood wounds that refused to close.

Jake shifted in his seat, as if the very air pressed down on him, suffocating. The sterile walls of the rehab center felt oppressive, too clean, too cold—nothing like the burning dust and deafening chaos of the past. He could still hear it, still see it, even when he closed his eyes.

"Afghanistan," Jake murmured, the name itself a wound. The word left his lips like a confession, hushed and hoarse. "There was this kid… just a local boy. He looked like my little brother, Timmy. Same smart-ass grin. Same way of tilting his head when he was thinking really hard." He swallowed, his Adam's apple bobbing. The memory slammed into him like a wave, knocking the air from his lungs. "He didn't make it."

The room was too small to contain the silence that followed.

Jake rubbed a hand over his face, as if trying to wipe the past away. "I should've been the one," he whispered, his voice raw. "It should've been me."

Caleb's hands curled into fists. He knew that feeling—the relentless guilt, the echo of every 'what if' screaming in his head at night. He met Jake's gaze, the storm behind his eyes familiar.

"You don't carry that alone anymore," Caleb said, his voice steady, a quiet anchor in the storm. "We're here."

Jake's breath hitched, his gaze flickering between Caleb and the older man beside him. There was no pity in their expressions, only understanding—something Jake hadn't realized he was desperate for until now. The other man, whose name Jake still didn't know, reached out and placed a calloused hand on his arm. A simple gesture, yet it carried the weight of unspoken solidarity. A lifeline in the darkness.

Jake let out a shaky breath. "Thanks." The word felt small, inadequate, but it was all he had.

Sarah shifted beside them, the soft rustle of fabric drawing their attention. The dim light from the overhead lamp cast a warm glow on her hair, turning it into a halo against the gloom. Outside, the thick Port Angeles fog swallowed the world beyond the windows, leaving only the uncertainty of what lay ahead.

"Jake," she said gently, her voice a steadying hand on a trembling shoulder. "I know what it's like to ask why. Why them, not me? Why am I the one left behind? That question… it doesn't go away overnight." Her gaze was steady, holding the weight of her own ghosts. "But I do know this—survival isn't a punishment. And it's not a mistake."

Jake stared at her, his breath shallow. Sarah's voice held no judgment, only truth, and something deeper understanding, perhaps. A knowing that came from carrying her own wounds, unseen but no less real.

"The pain," she continued, softer now, "it doesn't just vanish. It carves you open. But those hollow spaces? They're where strength grows."

Jake swallowed, his throat tight. He wanted to believe her. God, he wanted to. But the darkness was familiar, and stepping out of it felt impossible.

Sarah leaned forward, her hands resting lightly on the table, an offering of presence rather than platitudes. "Hope doesn't erase what happened. It doesn't make the past hurt any less. But it does something better—it builds bridges. It helps us move forward, even when we're certain we can't." She exhaled, a small, almost sad smile touching her lips. "Healing isn't about pretending we're not broken. It's about finding the pieces that still fit together and making something new. Something stronger. Something beautiful."

For the first time in what felt like years, Jake allowed himself to imagine that possibility. The weight of grief didn't disappear, but the suffocating pressure eased, if only by a fraction. And in that moment, it was enough.

Caleb felt it too—the shift, the quiet unraveling of something that had held them all captive for too long. The air in the room was thick, heavy with the weight of words left unspoken and wounds too deep for mere apologies. He looked at Jake, and for the first time, he didn't just see the wreckage of a man drowning in his own torment. He saw something else—something fragile, uncertain, but undeniably there.

Hope.

"So, that's it then?" Jake's voice was hoarse, frayed at the edges, as if speaking at all costs him something he wasn't sure he could afford.

He shifted in his chair, the metal legs scraping against the tile, the sound a jagged rip through the silence. His fingers twitched against the armrests, restless, uncertain.

Sarah nodded; her gaze unwavering. "It's a start, Jake. A damn hard one, but a start."

Her voice carried the weight of conviction, but underneath it, a tremor betrayed just how much this moment cost her too. This wasn't just about Caleb. This was about Jake and the years of damage they had all endured. The fractures in their lives didn't disappear overnight. They weren't whole, weren't even close, but for the first time, they weren't just standing amid the wreckage. They were moving.

Caleb swallowed hard; his throat thick with emotions he didn't know how to name. He had carried his anger like armor, like a second skin that had grown so tight he didn't know how to shed it without losing himself in the process. But now, here, in the quiet of the rehab center, he felt it peeling away, layer by painful layer, leaving behind something raw and exposed.

Letting go to wasn't easy. It never was. But maybe, just maybe, it was time.

Jake exhaled sharply, running a hand over his face as if trying to wipe away the exhaustion clinging to his bones. "I don't know how to do this," he admitted, his voice quieter, stripped of the bravado he so often wore like a shield.

Sarah's expression softened. "Neither do we. But we're here. And we're not giving up."

A heavy silence followed, filled with all the things none of them could say just yet. The scrape of chairs against the floor felt like the closing of one chapter and the hesitant beginning of another. Their goodbyes were quiet, sparse, each glance holding more meaning than words ever could.

Caleb reached out, clapping Jake on the shoulder, a simple gesture, but one that carried the weight of everything unsaid. Years of resentment, of bitterness, of waiting for a moment like this—one where maybe, just maybe, they could start again. Jake tensed beneath his touch, but he didn't pull away. That was something.

Sarah lingered for a beat longer, her gaze steady, warm. "One step at a time, Jake."

Jake nodded, just once, but it was enough.

Outside, the sterile trace of antiseptic dissolved into the atmosphere, giving way to the brisk tang of salt carried in on the coastal breeze. Overhead, the sky unfurled in sweeping hues of amber and lavender, the final threads of sunlight melting into the horizon's edge. Caleb drew in a deep breath, the briny essence of the ocean air flooding his lungs. It didn't erase the bitterness lodged inside him, but it softened its grip—if only for a moment—reminding him there was still beauty beyond the walls he'd just left behind.

Sarah walked beside him, quiet, but present. He glanced at her, a small smile tugging at the corner of his lips. "Feels like we've been holding our breath since... forever."

She let out a breath, shaking her head. "Yeah. And we're still here."

Caleb nodded, the weight of the evening pressing down on him, but it no longer felt like it would crush him. There was uncertainty, still, an unease that whispered of setbacks and relapses, of battles not yet won. But for the first time, the future didn't feel like something to fear. It felt open, waiting.

"We took the first step," Sarah murmured. "And he took his."

Caleb didn't answer, but he felt the truth of her words settle inside him. Hope was a fragile thing, delicate as a butterfly's wing, but maybe—just maybe—it was strong enough to carry them forward.

They walked in silence, steps in sync, the familiar streets stretching out before them. Shadows pooled in the alleyways, stretching long under the glow of streetlights. The ghosts of the past still lingered, but they didn't feel as suffocating as they once had.

"Remember when we thought growing up was the hardest thing?" Caleb asked, his voice rough around the edges, a bitter smile playing at his lips.

Sarah chuckled, low and dry. "Lives got a twisted sense of humor, doesn't it?" Her gaze flickered toward him, something wistful in the way her eyes softened. "Those two kids, playing on Saint Peter's steps, dreaming about the future... We thought we had it all figured out."

She swallowed hard, the weight of their past pressing between them. "And look at us now."

Caleb met her gaze, a silent understanding passing between them. They had lost so much, stumbled, broken, rebuilt. But they were still here.

"Two friends," he murmured, "standing by another who's lost his way."

His voice carried something else, something unspoken but felt. The fear that Jake might never truly find his way back. The knowledge that sometimes, no matter how much you tried, some people stayed lost.

Sarah reached for his hand, squeezing it briefly before letting go. "Funny, huh? How the weakest bonds sometimes burn the brightest."

Caleb exhaled, watching the sky darken. "Yeah. Funny."

They kept walking, the night settling around them, the road stretching forward, uncertain and vast. But for the first time in a long while, it didn't feel impossible.

It felt like a beginning.

Sarah's fingers brushed the silver cross hanging around her neck, a habitual gesture, a silent prayer. The cold comfort of the metal was a familiar weight, a tangible link to the faith that had carried them through the darkness. "Stronger and more precious," she whispered, her voice barely audible. "But what if this is too much, even for us?" The question hung unanswered, a silent testament to the fear that gnawed at the edges of their hard-won hope.

The wind lashed against them, howling through the trees, carrying the scent of pine and the bitter bite of the coming night. Caleb halted, his breath uneven, his heartbeat thrumming against his ribs like a war drum. The Whispering Cliffs stood in the distance, their jagged silhouette a stark contrast against the bruised sky, yet they felt impossibly far away. His fingers curled into fists at his sides. He couldn't let himself believe in the illusion of peace. Not yet.

Sarah stood beside him, arms wrapped around herself, but not from the cold. Her gaze flickered toward him, searching. She knew him too well to be fooled by the front he put up. His jaw tightened as he forced himself to meet her eyes. The tension between them was palpable, as if the air itself carried the weight of everything unsaid.

"Jake's still got a long, hard road ahead," Caleb muttered, his voice raw, the words scraping against his throat like gravel. "And so do we." He exhaled, slow and measured, trying to rein in the storm inside him. "But today... today, we started something. Maybe it's nothing. Maybe it won't hold. But maybe—just maybe—it's the first real step forward."

The uncertainty hung thick between them, a ghost neither could ignore. Sarah's eyes, usually lit with defiance, dimmed with unspoken fears. She pressed her lips together, but when she reached for his hand, her grip was solid, her touch grounding.

"We'll be there for him, Caleb. For each other," she said, her voice low but steady, a quiet promise against the rising wind.

He wanted to believe her. Wanted to let the warmth of her words seep into the cracks forming inside him. But doubt was a patient, insidious thing. It slithered through his mind, whispering that nothing built in the wreckage of what they had lost could ever hold.

His fingers tightened around hers. "You really think we can pull this off?" The question was barely a whisper, as if saying it out loud might shatter the fragile hope he was clinging to.

Sarah's fingers squeezed his. "I think we don't have a choice."

He let out a rough chuckle, the sound bitter. "That's not exactly reassuring."

She tilted her head, her gaze unwavering. "Reassurance doesn't change reality, Caleb. We fight, or we let it all crumble. And we're not letting it crumble."

Her conviction should have steadied him. Instead, it made the weight on his shoulders press down harder. He wasn't afraid of the work, the fight, the sheer exhaustion of pushing forward. He was afraid that after all of it, they'd still lose. That nothing they built would survive the next storm.

"Let's go home," he finally said, voice rough with exhaustion. He needed to move, needed to put one foot in front of the other, needed to believe that motion meant progress.

Home. The word tasted strange on his tongue. It wasn't a sanctuary anymore. It was just another battlefield, littered with memories of what they were trying to rebuild.

They walked side by side, their hands still locked together. The silence between them was not empty but filled with the weight of everything they had yet to say. The crunch of gravel under their boots was the only sound, a metronome marking the uneasy rhythm of their steps.

Above them, the first stars blinked into existence, cold and indifferent. The road ahead stretched dark and uncertain, and the gnawing fear of failure curled in his gut. But then he glanced at Sarah, saw the unshaken determination in her eyes, and something inside him shifted. Maybe fear would always be there. Maybe doubt would never fully leave. But neither would she.

For now, that was enough.

But how long could they hold on before the storm swallowed them whole?

CHAPTER 17

The Final Chisel Stroke

THE PALE LIGHT slanted through the workshop's grimy windows, catching on the fine shavings curled across the floor like remnants of breath held too long. Caleb's knuckles blanched as he gripped the chisel, the steel biting cold into his skin. He stared at the unfinished Station of the Cross—his father's last piece. A jagged, incomplete wound, echoing the one that festered in his own chest. The acrid scent of pine, sharp and relentless, scraped at his throat, a constant reminder of the silence that had settled like rust between them. He'd avoided this moment, delayed it like a man dodging a funeral. That cross wasn't just a carving—it was a gravestone. A monument to everything unsaid, to faith left half-built, to a relationship buried beneath years of silence and shadow. His father had once carved devotion into wood with reverent hands—and now he was gone, leaving Caleb only questions, and a hollow ache only the thud of his chisel against oak could hope to answer.

"Damn it, Dad," he muttered, his voice rough, the words a choked prayer. "Why leave me with this?" The oak, stubborn and unforgiving, resisted his touch. Each painstaking cut was a battle against the wood, reflecting his internal war. Doubt gnawed at him. Was he worthy? Could he possibly honor the memory of a man who seemed as distant now as the saints he depicted? He remembered his father's calloused hands, how he'd held the chisel, the precision in his movements. A flash of anger, sharp and sudden, cut through the grief. Anger at the unanswered questions, the unspoken words, the life unlived between them. He'd been too young, too stubborn, to bridge the chasm that had always existed between them.

"He never said… he never said he was proud," Caleb whispered, the words catching in his throat. A tear traced a path through the dust on his cheek. He slammed the mallet down, the sharp sound echoing through the quiet space. The wood splintered. Damn it all. He'd failed again. This wasn't just about finishing the carving; it was about completing the reconciliation that had never begun. But then, a different kind of strength – stubborn, defiant – took root within him. He wouldn't let the anger win. His father's legacy, flawed as it was, wasn't a burden. It was a challenge, a chance to connect with the man he had lost finally. The chisel felt lighter now, and his movements had a purpose. Each swing became an act of defiance, of atonement. He had to finish this. Not only to honor his father but to carve out a place for himself in a world that suddenly felt profoundly lonely and uncertain. He would finish this, and in doing so, maybe, just maybe, he would finally forgive himself.

He inhaled the scent of oak—earthy, bitter, grounding—and blinked against the sting of sweat and sawdust. His fingers trembled with the weight of every memory, every accusation he'd hurled at God in the quiet nights since his father's death. The silence between them had been as thick as mortar. His father had spoken in wood, not words—every carving a sermon, every sculpture a hymn. Caleb had spoken in anger, in slammed doors, in running away.

And now, here he was, back where it all started, trying to chisel his way out of shame.

The rhythmic tapping of the mallet was not just the beat of his heart; it was the steady pulse of his redemption. The rasp of the chisel, a rhythmic counterpoint to the frantic hammering of his heart, was Caleb's prayer. Each sliver of wood, each carefully sculpted curve, was a confession, a desperate attempt to carve away the guilt that gnawed at him. This wasn't just a statue; it was a penance, a testament to a father's dying wish and a son's crippling failure. The wood, stubborn and yielding in equal measure, mirrored his inner turmoil. The ocean's relentless assault on the cliffs outside his workshop – a constant, unforgiving reminder of his self-destruction – echoed the storm inside him. He'd been shaped by those waves, battered and bruised, a wreckage clinging to the shore.

His wrist ached. But he kept going, ignoring the pain. He couldn't stop—not now. Not when the image of Christ was beginning to emerge from the raw timber, not when the face—His face—looked so much like the peace Caleb had never dared believe in.

"Dad, why couldn't you just tell me?" he muttered, forehead pressed to the cool wood. "Why'd you have to leave everything unsaid?"

A creak from the floor behind him drew him back. He didn't need to turn. The presence was familiar—weighty, yet calm. Joshua.

"Still got the magic touch, I see," Joshua said, his voice low, a comforting rumble against the sudden silence. It wasn't just a compliment; it was a lifeline. Caleb offered a ghost of a smile, a rare, fragile bloom in the desolate landscape of his soul. The unspoken words hung heavy between them – a shared history etched deeper than any carving. Joshua's presence wasn't just friendship; it was a silent testament to the bond they forged in the crucible of their shared past, a past Caleb desperately hoped to leave behind. The air crackled with unspoken anxieties; the unspoken fear in Caleb's eyes was palpable. He needed this; he needed Joshua. More than he was willing to admit, even to himself.

Joshua stepped closer, gaze settling on the unfinished figure. "He looks like He's listening," he said quietly. "Like He's waiting on you."

Caleb swallowed hard. "I…I don't know if I can finish it," he said, barely louder than a breath.

Joshua didn't react right away. He walked slowly around the table, his gaze steady. "Why not?"

Caleb's hands curled into fists, the mallet clattering to the ground. "Because I don't think I believe what I'm carving."

Joshua raised an eyebrow. "You mean in Christ?"

"No." Caleb's voice cracked. "In myself."

He backed away from the carving, like it might accuse him of being a fraud. "This… this was his vision, not mine. He saw redemption in every line of the wood. I see the cracks. The flaws. I see what's missing."

Joshua leaned against the workbench. "And maybe that's what makes it real."

Caleb turned to him, eyes dark and hollow. "What do you mean?"

"I mean maybe God doesn't want perfect carvings," Joshua said, his voice steady but kind. "Maybe He wants the ones shaped by broken hands. Hands that know what it's like to lose. To doubt. To fall."

Caleb looked away; jaw clenched. "I've fallen a long way, Josh."

"I know," Joshua said. "I watched you climb back every time. I saw the nights you didn't sleep, the days you drank too much and still showed up the next morning. I know what you're made of."

"But it wasn't enough," Caleb said. "Not for him. Not for me. And definitely not for God."

Joshua's silence felt like a door opening, not closing. He didn't argue, didn't soothe with empty words. Instead, he stepped closer and looked directly at the carving. "You're wrong, you know. He did say he was proud."

Caleb stared at him.

"I was there. That last hospital visit. You were on a job site out of town. He held your old carving knife the whole time. Kept running his thumb over the worn grip like it was the most precious thing in the world. When the nurse asked why he wouldn't let it go, he said, 'Because it's my boy's. He's got the gift. He's got my hands and his mother's heart. He just doesn't know it yet.'"

Caleb's breath caught. Something in him broke wide open.

"I didn't know that" he said hoarsely. "Why didn't you tell me?"

Joshua shrugged, eyes glinting. "Because you weren't ready. But you are now."

The silence that followed wasn't heavy. It was sacred.

Caleb turned back to the carving. His fingers brushed Christ's face, tracing the curve of sorrow carved into the wood. It looked different now. Not less painful, but less alone.

"You think He forgives people like me?" he asked. "The ones who mess up everything they touch?"

"I think," Joshua said, "He came for people like you."

A long pause passed between them.

"I used to think faith was for the weak," Caleb admitted. "But maybe... maybe faith is what happens when there's nothing else left."

"That sounds about right."

Caleb picked up the chisel. His grip was firm, steady.

"I still don't know if I can finish it," he said.

"Then just take the next cut," Joshua replied. "Just one."

The twisting grain of the wood mirrored the twisted path of his life – a life he'd thought irrevocably broken, stained by a past he couldn't outrun. The spiraling wood shavings – sawdust ghosts of his guilt, his shame, the crushing weight of his father's legacy – piled at his feet. He'd hoped the carving would bring him peace; instead, it was dredging up the muck he'd tried so hard to bury. He wrestled with the image taking shape before him, Christ's serene face starkly contrasted to the tempest raging inside him. Could he ever truly be worthy of such serenity?

Joshua's voice, quiet and steady, broke through his turmoil. "Each cut... a step," he said, his gaze perceptive. The words weren't just an observation; they were a challenge. Caleb's chisel stilled. The air hung thick with unspoken things. "A journey I thought was only for him," Caleb rasped, his father's name a bitter taste on his tongue. "The penance, the... atonement. I thought I was beyond redemption." Joshua's smile was gentle, but his eyes held a steeliness that Caleb had come to trust.

"And yet," Joshua said, his voice low, "this isn't a solitary pilgrimage, Caleb. You're not alone." A sob caught in Caleb's throat. The dam finally broke. Years of suppressed grief, of self-recrimination, threatened to drown him. Joshua's words weren't just comfort; they were a lifeline. He wasn't alone. The crushing weight, the agonizing burden of his father's sins, suddenly felt... lighter.

"Thank you," Caleb choked out, the words raw with emotion. He wasn't just thanking Joshua; he was thanking God for sending him this unlikely companion. This unwavering anchor in the storm of his soul. Joshua placed a hand on Caleb's shoulder, the touch surprisingly strong. "Your hands are the tools, Caleb," he said, his voice warm and firm. "But it's your heart that breathes life into the wood. And into yourself."

The implication hung between them, heavy and unspoken: forgiveness, both given and received, was the actual carving.

Sweat beaded on Caleb's brow, the air thick with the scent of pine and the ghosts of his past. This wasn't just wood; it was his penance, his prayer. Each chisel stroke felt like a confession; a desperate plea hammered into the grain. The carving—Christ's descent into the tomb—mirrored his damnation, the years of self-loathing he'd buried deep. He'd carved this before, countless times in his mind, the image a constant companion to his insomnia. This time, though, felt different. This time, it had to be different. He glanced at the half-finished piece, the smooth curves of the wood mocking his rough edges. "Peace, forgiveness, grace"—hollow and desperate words echoed in his head. He'd promised himself a clean slate forged from the heart of the storm. But the storm still raged inside him, a tempest of doubt and self-recrimination. Could he truly forgive himself? Could he ever escape the shadow of his mistakes?

The chisel's rasp broke the silence, harsh and uneven. Caleb's grip faltered, and the blade slipped, scoring a thin, crooked line through Christ's robe. He sucked in a sharp breath, staring at the damage like it had opened something in him.

"No. No, no—" He pressed his fingers against the wood, as if willing the mistake to disappear. But it was there. Permanent. Just like everything else he'd failed to undo.

His shoulders hunched forward, the weight of memory pressing down like an avalanche. He wasn't seventeen anymore, full of fire and foolish hope. He was thirty-two. Old enough to know better. Old enough to have ruined lives and buried dreams.

"Why do I even try?" he muttered. His voice sounded foreign, distant, as if it belonged to the boy who'd walked out that night and never came back whole.

Footsteps crunched over the gravel outside. A shadow crossed the threshold, hesitated, then entered the workshop without a word.

Joshua Shepherd's presence filled the room without asking permission. He said nothing at first, just leaned against the doorframe and crossed his arms, his worn denim shirt dusted with sawdust, like he'd just come from the same kind of war Caleb was still fighting inside.

Caleb didn't turn around. "If you're here to watch me fail, you're right on time."

Joshua let out a soft grunt. "Wasn't here for the show. Was hoping for something more useful. Like a chair that doesn't lean like it's been drinking."

Caleb forced a dry laugh, but it cracked midway. "You want straight lines? Find someone with a straight past."

Joshua pushed off the wall and stepped forward. "We all lean, Caleb. Some of us just learn how to balance anyway."

Silence stretched between them like a frayed rope. Caleb stared at the carving—Christ's limp body, the mourners' etched anguish, the heavy stone barely begun. It was a scene of mourning, of silence, of waiting. It felt too close, like staring into his own tomb.

"I can't finish it," Caleb said quietly.

Joshua moved beside him, eyes scanning the carved scene. "Why not?"

Caleb hesitated. The words felt too raw, too dangerous. But they pressed forward anyway. "Because I'm not finished. Not really. I thought I was past it—past the shame, the guilt, the anger. But it's still here. All of it. Right here." He pressed his palm flat against his chest.

Joshua studied him, his gaze steady, like he saw through the façade Caleb wore around town. The good son. The quiet servant. The man who returned.

"You think carving Christ's descent is gonna fix it all?" Joshua asked gently, but without pity.

"No," Caleb whispered. "But maybe it can fix something. Or remind me that it's possible to be brought back from the dark."

Joshua nodded slowly. "That's what faith is, isn't it? Not certainty. Just… courage. Enough to keep moving, even when the road's covered in fog."

Caleb looked down at his hands—scarred, calloused, stained with both sap and sin. "What if I don't have that courage anymore?"

"Then lean on someone who does," Joshua replied, placing a steady hand on his shoulder. "That's what grace is for. When yours runs out, someone else holds it for you. Until you can believe again."

Caleb's throat tightened, the raw honesty in Joshua's words cutting deeper than the chisel ever could.

"I'm scared," Caleb confessed. "Not of failing. Of being forgiven. Because if I am… then what's left to hold on to?"

Joshua didn't flinch. "Then you hold onto purpose. And you carve your way forward. One stroke at a time."

The silence that followed wasn't empty. It was heavy. Sacred.

Caleb took a step back from the carving, heart pounding, hands shaking. "He's supposed to look… at peace," he said, gesturing to the lifeless figure of Christ. "But all I see is myself. Caught between death and whatever comes after."

Joshua nodded once. "Then maybe it's time you decide what comes next."

The workshop felt different now—still oppressive, still stifling—but something had shifted. A crack in the walls Caleb had built around himself.

He turned back to the cypress slab, lifted the chisel again. This time, his hand didn't tremble. Not as much.

With each stroke, memories returned—his father's laughter, his mother's soft hymns drifting through the evening air, the day he first carved a dove into a broken fence post and his father smiled like it meant something. But also, the night he left. The slamming door. The wreck. The hospital. The funeral he didn't attend. The God he stopped speaking to.

The wood welcomed the blade, each cut cleaner, deeper. The robe fell into folds. The tomb took shape. Christ's body, once rigid and abstract, softened into something vulnerable. Human.

Caleb worked in silence until his shoulders ached and the sun cast long, golden shadows across the floor.

Then, without warning, the blade caught a knot. The chisel jerked, gouging the edge of Mary's hand.

"No," Caleb whispered. His breath caught in his throat. "No, no—please."

He stood paralyzed. A single tear tracked down his cheek, unbidden. His voice cracked open. "I ruin everything. Even this."

Joshua moved to his side. "You didn't ruin it."

"You saw it. It's ruined."

Joshua shook his head. "No, Caleb. It's real. That's what makes it holy. You think Mary's grief was smooth? Think the tomb was clean? Perfection isn't what redeems us. It's the cracks. The wounds. The broken places where grace leaks through."

Caleb stared at the gouge. At the imperfection.

And he began to weep.

He hadn't cried like this in years. Not since the night he'd walked away from everything—faith, family, forgiveness. Not since he'd sworn, he didn't need anyone or anything but wood and silence.

The sobs came like waves. Ugly. Loud. Raw.

Joshua didn't speak. He just stood beside him, silent, present.

Eventually, Caleb's shoulders slumped, exhaustion overtaking him.

"I'm so tired, Josh."

"I know," Joshua said softly. "But you're not alone. You never were."

Caleb nodded slowly, blinking through the blur of tears. He turned back to the carving. The gouge remained. But now, it looked less like a flaw and more like a wound—an intentional one. A reminder that even holy hands bore scars.

He reached for the chisel once more, steadier now.

"I'll finish it," he said.

Joshua smiled. "Good. And when you do, we'll carry it up together."

Caleb didn't answer, but he didn't have to. The resolve in his movements spoke louder than words.

The final cut would come. Not perfect. Not unbroken. But whole.

And maybe—just maybe—that was enough.

Sweat beaded on Caleb's brow, the scent of cypress heavy in the air, a familiar comfort battling the rising tide of doubt. Each chisel stroke had been a prayer, a testament to the grace that had pulled him from the wreckage of his past. His father's hands, rough and strong, had guided his own, teaching him not just carpentry but faith. This wasn't just wood; it was a resurrection, his resurrection, carved in the heart of the cypress.

Joshua Shepherd stood behind him, a silent sentinel, his gaze steady, a weight of unspoken understanding hanging between them. Joshua knew the wood. He knew the weight of the world, its unforgiving grain, the stubborn resistance that mirrored the battles waged within. Caleb felt a kinship with the man, a brotherhood forged in shared sorrow and quiet strength. They were both men carved by life, shaped by loss.

With a final, decisive stroke, the last chip fell away. The finished carving stood before him, a breathtaking testament to suffering and grace. Tears welled in his eyes, blurring his vision. He'd done it. He'd finally done it.

But the relief was quickly replaced by a chilling emptiness. The creation was finished, but what about the creator? He was still broken. Still flawed. Still in need of forgiveness.

He looked at Joshua, a silent question hanging in the air between them.

"Now what?" he whispered, the words barely audible above the frantic hammering of his own heart.

Joshua didn't answer right away. His boots creaked against the wooden floorboards as he stepped closer, casting a long shadow across the carving. He studied the figure of Christ, eyes tracing the bowed head, the weight of the cross etched in the woodgrain. Then he looked at Caleb, and something flickered across his face—pride, maybe. Or pain.

"Now?" Joshua's voice was gravel soaked in reverence. "Now you let it breathe."

Caleb's mouth opened, but no sound came out. He turned back to the sculpture, heart pounding. Let it breathe? That implied it had life, that it needed space. But what about the raw, gaping ache in his chest? He had carved something that felt alive, yes—but could he say the same for himself?

"I thought finishing this would fix something in me," Caleb confessed, his voice tight. "I thought if I poured everything into it, the guilt would leave."

Joshua's expression didn't change, but his silence spoke more than a sermon.

"It's still here," Caleb went on, breath hitching. "The guilt. The anger. The shame. I still wake up with it lodged in my throat like a splinter."

"You carved your soul into this wood," Joshua said quietly. "But wood can't absolve you, Caleb. Only grace can."

Caleb laughed bitterly. "I don't think I know what grace is. Not really. It always feels just out of reach. Like… like my father's approval." His jaw clenched, the old wound splitting open like it had never healed. "He built everything in this workshop but never once said he was proud of me. Not once."

Joshua exhaled slowly. "Maybe he didn't know how. Maybe he thought the work would speak for him."

Caleb shook his head, frustrated. "And if it didn't? If all I heard was silence? Am I supposed to be okay with that?"

"No." Joshua stepped beside him, voice firm now. "You're not supposed to be okay with it. You're supposed to be honest with it. Mourn it. Lay it down like Christ did his life."

Caleb blinked. The figure before him blurred again, not from tears this time, but from the truth in Joshua's words crashing against the brittle walls he'd built inside. "I keep trying to prove something. That I'm worthy. That I'm enough. But it always feels like I'm just… pretending."

Joshua's brow furrowed. "Pretending to be what?"

Caleb's voice cracked. "Forgiven."

The silence that followed was deafening.

The last curve whispered into being under Caleb's chisel. His father's laugh, deep and booming, a phantom in the workshop's dustmotes. The salt spray of Port Angeles, the reckless freedom of those cliffside days—it all clawed at him, a ghost of a life lived. Then Saint Peter's, that quiet sanctuary by the sea, waiting for this. The melody of his life—joy and gut-wrenching sorrow intertwined—had led him here, to the final, agonizing stroke.

He stepped back, eyes tracing the Christ figure—burdened, resolute, fallen yet rising. His breath hitched. The brow's tenderness, the robe's fall, the sorrow and hope battling in the eyes… it wasn't just wood. It was the damn essence of everything. Christ's journey, yes, but his damn journey too.

This last Station wasn't just skill but the bloody testament to his climb out of the darkness, his desperate, silent plea for redemption. The silence in the workshop pressed down, thick and heavy, except for his ragged breathing. The impossibly alive figure seemed to breathe with him, sharing the ache in his bones.

It offered a glimpse of grace, a fragile thing he'd been clawing for.

This workshop, once a battlefield of frustration and self-loathing, felt holy. A refuge. His faith, delicate as a newborn bird, had taken root here, and forgiveness, slow and agonizing, was shaping him as indelibly as he'd shaped the wood. He ran a hand over the rough grain, a choked sob catching in his throat. He'd almost lost it all. Almost.

The final Station hummed under Caleb's touch, the polished oak warm against his fingertip, a pulse of life beneath the wood. Once thick with the stink of fear and regret, the air now carried the clean scent of sawdust and salt, a tangy reminder of how far he'd crawled from the wreckage. Here, in this sanctuary, he'd learned forgiveness wasn't a weapon but a fragile consolation, painstakingly applied to wounds that ran deeper than bone.

Joshua Shepherd filled the doorway, his silhouette framed by the fading light. Quiet pride, etched deep into his face, mirrored the calm settling over Caleb. Joshua wasn't just a mentor; he'd been a lifeline, a hand reaching through the blackest waters of Caleb's grief.

He hadn't offered solutions, just his presence, a steadfast silence that had spoken volumes when words failed.

"Your hands," Joshua said, his voice low, husky with years and understanding, "they've shaped more than wood, Caleb. They've carved a space for grace. In the oak… and in you."

The words hung in the air, heavy with unspoken things. Caleb couldn't speak. Gratitude choked him, a vast, unwieldy thing too big for words. Without Joshua, he knew, he'd still be drowning, a broken man tossed on the unforgiving waves of his guilt.

Joshua had been his anchor, not by fixing anything, but by teaching him the slow, agonizing process of healing—both the wood and the soul. A process Caleb almost hadn't survived.

The weight of that near-death experience pressed down on him, a sudden ache in his chest.

He swallowed; his throat tight.

"Thank you," he whispered, the words cracking with emotion, the raw gratitude tearing at his carefully constructed calm. "For... for being there when I couldn't be there for myself." His voice shook, a tremor of the old fear threatening to resurface.

He looked up at Joshua. "I almost... I almost didn't make it."

The confession hung between them, a stark reminder of how close he'd come to losing everything.

Joshua's smile, crinkled at the corners, felt kind and unsettling. "We all walk the Stations, Caleb. Even when it feels like we're alone, we're not truly carving this path by ourselves."

The words hung in the air, a consolation and a challenge.

Alone? Caleb wasn't sure. The weight of his father's legacy, the years of unspoken resentment, still pressed down on him, a ghost in the workshop. He turned back to the finished Station, the last of the fourteen. It stood, a towering testament not just to his perseverance but to a quiet strength he hadn't known he possessed—a strength born of surrender, of finally letting go and trusting the process, trusting the divine hand that had somehow, against all odds, shaped him.

The setting sun painted the workshop in hues of gold and amber. It wasn't just a workshop anymore; it was hallowed ground, a sanctuary for his soul, chipped and scarred but slowly becoming whole.

He was the carver and was the carved. The realization both thrilled and terrified him.

The thick, familiar sawdust smelled like home, forgiveness, and a slow, hard-won peace. He stood at the threshold, his father's workshop, a vessel containing tools and wood and the ghosts of their fractured relationship. A low hum vibrated in the air—the quiet strength of weathering the storm, the calm after the tempest.

Each breath was a prayer, anchoring him to where his journey of forgiveness began, a journey that had been more brutal than he'd ever imagined. His fingers traced the worn wood of the doorway, the ridges and smooth lines almost imprinted on his skin, echoing the rhythm of his own heart.

This wasn't just a doorway; it was the passage between past and future, between the man and the man he was becoming. Behind him stood the final Station, his father's legacy entwined with his own, not just art but a raw, unflinching mirror reflecting his soul: suffering, redemption, and the fragile grace he'd found in the process. Each carve, a step on his pilgrimage, each stain, a testament to his struggle. It was complete. The hammer and chisel were still witnesses to his doubt and discovery. Their absence in his hands was profound, yet there was no loss, only a quiet, deep sense of closure. The last stroke, the final note, played. The silence felt like a blessing, a gentle relief on his wounds. But a profound unease settled in his gut. Was this indeed the end? Or just the beginning of a new, terrifying chapter? The peace felt too fragile, too quickly shattered. He wasn't sure he was ready for whatever came next.

The door creaked open, sunlight blasting Caleb in the face, a physical slap after years spent in his workshop's dim, sawdust-choked air. He flinched, a reflex betraying the tremor in his hands. This wasn't just sunlight; it was freedom, a promise whispering on the wind, and a terrifying unknown expanse. The workshop, his sanctuary, his prison, shrunk behind him, swallowed by the blinding brightness. He hesitated, a knot tightening in his gut. Beautiful? Maybe. But beautiful things could also be fragile, easily broken. The gravel crunched under his boots, a grounding sound, but it couldn't steady the frantic beat of his heart.

Port Angeles – the raucous cries of gulls, the low murmur of the town, the relentless rhythm of the ocean – assaulted his senses. It was a cacophony, not a symphony, each sound a sharp reminder of the life he was leaving behind, a life of quiet desperation and self-imposed exile.

No dramatic explosion, no heavenly chorus. Just a slow, agonizing release. A weight lifted, yes, but it left a hollowness behind, a space echoing with the ghosts of his past. The memories, sharp splinters of grief and guilt, still pricked at him, even as he tried to shed them like old skin. Each one was a betrayal, a reminder of the man he'd been, the man he desperately wanted to leave behind. His gaze drifted to the horizon, the ocean a vast, indifferent expanse. An invitation? Or a threat?

The Stations of the Cross, those painstaking carvings – his confession, his penance – had brought him to this stark crossroads. Wood and hammer, his tools of atonement, had served their purpose. But now? The blank page terrified him more than it inspired. He wasn't sure he knew how to write a new story. "Be well, Joshua," he breathed, the words catching in his throat. The simple phrase held a lifetime of unspoken things: gratitude, regret, a plea for forgiveness. Joshua, his apprentice, his surrogate son, was the only link to a life he almost didn't want to abandon. It wasn't about elaborate goodbyes but about acknowledging the unspoken bond.

He glanced back at the workshop, the silence pressing down on him like a heavy weight. He turned, and a single tear tracked a path down his weathered cheek. The town of Port Angeles watched, impassive, as Caleb Martin, a man marked by time and toil, took his first step into the uncertain future. Each footfall was a gamble, a commitment to a life he wasn't entirely sure he deserved. The afternoon sun dipped, casting long shadows mirroring the darkness still lingering. The road ahead was long. And terrifyingly, beautifully open.

* * *

The wind bit at Caleb's exposed skin, a familiar chill that mirrored the harsh grasp of his past. Another autumn. The air carried the scent of pine and salt, but even nature's rhythm couldn't soothe the ache buried deep in his chest. This year, the changing leaves didn't just mark time—they bore silent witness to a man in flux. He tried to convince himself he was different now. He wanted to believe the pain had carved something holy into him. But truth lived in his bones, and it gnawed at him mercilessly.

"God, I've tried," he muttered. "But maybe I wasn't made for redemption."

His knuckles whitened around the handle of his walking stick, the gnarled oak slick with sweat. He planted it into the damp earth, grounding himself as the memory of his darkest day threatened to surface—the moment he'd stood before that wooden cross, not as a believer, but as a man drowning in shame.

That carving, that first Station, had nearly broken him. The weight of it still haunted his nights.

He didn't hear Sarah approach until her boots snapped a twig nearby. She'd always walked lightly, but today her presence was thunder.

"Caleb?" she called gently, as if afraid her voice might drive him deeper into his shell.

He turned slowly. She stood a few feet away, wrapped in her worn navy peacoat, her gray-streaked hair swept back in a loose braid. She looked older than he remembered—maybe grief aged everyone—but her eyes still held that quiet fire that once terrified and captivated him all at once.

"You look... troubled," she said. Her voice was soft but unwavering, like someone offering shelter during a storm.

His shoulders slumped, and for a moment, the stick held more than his weight—it held his will keep standing.

"I don't know what I'm doing anymore," he said. "I thought I did. I thought finishing the Stations would give me peace. But now... I feel more lost than ever."

Sarah stepped closer. She didn't touch him yet; she waited, sensing the tight coil inside him.

"Redemption isn't a finish line, Caleb. It's a direction."

He let out a bitter laugh. "I don't even know which way I'm facing."

A long silence passed between them, broken only by the wind rustling through the fir trees and the low drone of distant waves.

"Do you remember what you told me that day I brought you the first commission?" Sarah asked, her eyes fixed on his.

He looked up slowly.

"You said, 'I don't carve for money. I carve for ghosts.'"

He chuckled grimly. "I was being dramatic."

"No, you were being honest. You were working through something. That first carving wasn't just wood—it was your way of saying sorry without speaking. Every Station since has been a conversation between you and the One you thought stopped listening."

He blinked, taken aback.

Sarah pressed on, her voice gaining strength. "Do you think faith is about forgetting? About erasing what came before? That's not what Christ did. He bore the wounds. Even after the resurrection, they were still there. He didn't hide them. He showed them."

Caleb's throat constricted. "But what if my wounds make people turn away?"

Sarah didn't flinch. "Then they never deserved to witness your healing in the first place."

He looked away, ashamed.

"I lied to Joshua," he said, almost inaudibly. "I told him I was ready to leave, but I wasn't. I'm still scared."

"Of what?"

He hesitated, then breathed out the truth: "Of becoming someone again. Of having to live up to the man he thinks I am."

Sarah finally reached out, her hand resting gently on his arm. Her touch was warm, steady.

"Joshua doesn't need you to be perfect. He just needs you to keep showing up."

Caleb closed his eyes, feeling the truth of her words settle deep. He thought of the boy's hopeful eyes, the way he had looked at him like a father and mentor and flawed man all at once.

"I walked away from everything, Sarah. From the life I ruined. From the God I betrayed."

"You walked into a place of stillness to heal," she said. "That isn't the same as giving up. It's what Christ did in the garden—he withdrew, he wept, and then he stood again."

He opened his mouth to respond, but the words crumbled under the weight of emotion.

Sarah stepped in front of him now, forcing him to meet her gaze.

"I see the man you're becoming, Caleb. Not because of your carvings, or your silence, or even your repentance. But because you're still here. Still choosing to fight through the fear and walk forward. That's faith."

His lip quivered, and he bit it hard to keep from breaking. But a tear still fell, unbidden, carving its path through the dust on his cheek.

"I don't know if I believe the way you do," he said.

"You don't have to," she replied. "You only have to be honest. Belief grows best in soil tilled by honesty."

He nodded, slowly. The wind had quieted. A bird trilled in the distance. Somehow, the silence no longer pressed down on him. It held him.

"I want to try," he said, voice cracking. "I don't want to be alone in this anymore."

Sarah smiled, and the light that caught in her eyes reminded him of something long forgotten—hope, persistent and patient.

"You won't be," she said. "You never were."

They stood there together, two people stitched with loss and grace, their shadows long and converging. Caleb felt the hollowness inside shift—not vanish but soften. The road ahead no longer looked like a sentence. It looked like a calling.

He turned to walk, and this time, he didn't hesitate.

* * *

He glanced back at the workshop, the silence pressing down on him like a heavy weight. He turned, and a single tear tracked a path down his weathered cheek. The town of Port Angeles watched, impassive, as Caleb Martin, a man marked by time and toil, took his first step into the uncertain future. Each footfall was a gamble, a commitment to a life he wasn't entirely sure he deserved. The afternoon sun dipped, casting long shadows mirroring the darkness still lingering. The road ahead was long. And terrifyingly, beautifully open.

CHAPTER 18

Unveiling Redemption

THE SALT SPRAY stung Caleb's face as he hauled himself up the steps to Saint Peter's by the Sea. The church loomed, a gothic monolith against the bruised purple of the twilight sky. His breath hitched—a ragged, desperate gasp. This wasn't just some dusty old building; it was the crucible where he'd be judged, his life's work laid bare. The weight of it pressed down, a physical ache in his chest, mirroring the gnawing anxiety that clawed at his insides. He paused, the scent of brine and beeswax—the sea and the church—a familiar comfort. Yet, the memories clinging to him were anything but comforting. The sharp tang of sawdust, the ghost of his father's calloused hands, the rhythmic thud of the carpenter's mallet… all of it flooded back, a tidal wave of grief and unspoken words. His father's unfinished business and legacy were a burden he carried like a second skin. The workshop, their sanctuary, where his chisel had whispered prayers into the wood, now felt like a tomb.

"Damn it all," he muttered, shoving his hands deep into his pockets. This wasn't some ritual; it was a confession. A desperate gamble. He pushed through the heavy oak doors, the squeak a painful counterpoint to the hushed murmurs inside. The air hung thick with incense and anticipation. Above, the organ groaned, a mournful counterpoint to his trembling heart. He scanned the familiar faces—etched with their stories of struggle and faith. These weren't just parishioners; they were the jury of his life. They'd seen his failures, his stumbles, his quiet triumphs. Now, they watched as he walked the tightrope, his entire future hanging in the balance.

Father Mike stood at the altar; a figure of stoic strength bathed in flickering candlelight. Their eyes met. There was no judgment in Mike's gaze, only a quiet understanding, a shared burden borne of years of unspoken camaraderie. It was a flicker of hope in the gathering storm of Caleb's self-doubt. But even that tiny flame felt fragile, threatened by the winds of his fear. "I'm ready, Father," Caleb whispered, his voice barely audible above the swelling music, but the tremor in his voice betrayed his fear. The words were a prayer, a promise, and a desperate plea all rolled into one.

Sarah's strawberry blonde hair, catching the candlelight, framed a face both serene and fiercely determined. Her green eyes, usually sparkling with mischief, held a quiet intensity as they locked with Caleb's. The unspoken promise in that gaze—years of shared secrets, whispered hopes, and the unspoken weight of their family history—steadied him. He saw not just support but a reflection of his doubts, magnified and yet softened by her unwavering faith. He swallowed, the lump in his throat a tangible thing. "This is it," he thought, "everything hangs on this."

The weight of the community pressed down, a sea of expectant faces blurring at the edges of his vision. He could almost feel the wood of the Stations, the grain rough beneath his calloused fingers, the ghosts of his father's hands shaping the same wood decades ago. This wasn't just craftsmanship but a confession, a testament to a fractured and painstakingly rebuilt life. His father's legacy was redemption, a desperate prayer carved in oak. The fear gnawed. "What if they don't understand? What if it's not enough?"

Father Mike's voice, deep and resonant, cut through the suffocating silence. The words, familiar yet charged with meaning, resonated in the cavernous nave. But Caleb heard only the undercurrent, the unspoken weight of the priest's struggle, a shared burden of faith and doubt.

"Today," Father Mike's voice boomed, each syllable carrying the weight of decades spent bearing witness to the human heart, "we celebrate not just the artistry, but the journey… the 'sacrifice'… that brought these Stations to life."

The solace of Father Mike's words offered temporary solace, but a cold dread coiled beneath the surface. His dedication? It was more than just time spent carving. It was years spent wrestling with God, with his father's memory, with the crippling guilt that still clawed at him. A journey he'd never chosen, but one that had irrevocably shaped him.

"Each station," Father Mike continued, his voice a steady hand on Caleb's trembling soul, "reflects the trials we all endure, the grace we all seek. It's a mirror to our own lives—a testament to the struggle, to the possibility of redemption." He paused, his gaze sweeping across the congregation. "Remember this: In the darkness, we are never truly alone."

Sarah squeezed Caleb's hand, a silent reassurance that cut through his fear. He returned the pressure, a silent vow to face whatever came next. The unveiling was no longer just about the Stations but about facing his past, claiming his future, and daring to hope again.

Father Mike, a man whose own weathered face mirrored the ancient pews, stepped aside with a barely perceptible nod. The congregation shifted, a ripple of hushed anticipation—the rustle of starched cotton, the creak of wood groaning under decades of whispered prayers. Caleb's heart hammered a frantic tattoo against his ribs, each beat a deafening drumbeat in the sudden silence. He felt sweat prickling his skin beneath his worn shirt. This wasn't just wood and chisel work; it was his lifeblood, his father's legacy, laid bare.

His hands, calloused and trembling, hovered over the heavy cloth draped over the Stations of the Cross. He could almost taste the dust of his workshop, the scent of cedar, and the phantom ache in his muscles from countless hours spent hunched over the wood. Each carving held a piece of his soul, a prayer whispered in the solitude of the night, a desperate plea for understanding, for absolution from the guilt that gnawed at him. He'd poured his grief, rage, and desperate hope into these figures; could they bear the weight of his confession?

A silent prayer escaped his lips, a ragged breath choked with fear and faith. "Let them see," he breathed, the words catching in his throat. "God, let them understand." The words weren't just a plea but a demand, a desperate assertion of his worthiness. He needed them to see the skill and the soul behind it, the man behind the masterpiece. His grip tightened on the cloth, a lifeline in the churning sea of his anxiety.

With a sharp intake of breath, he pulled. The fabric fell away with a soft sigh, revealing the intricate Stations.

The raw emotion of the carvings punched the air, a visual testament to his struggle. Each panel was a silent scream, a whisper of forgiveness, a desperate yearning for redemption. This wasn't just about showcasing his talent; it was about his survival.

A collective gasp rippled through the congregation. The light, fractured through the stained glass, cast shifting hues over the worn pews and solemn faces, illuminating the raw agony on Jesus' face in the first station, the weariness of Simon carrying the cross, the quiet grief of the women who wept. But this wasn't just a depiction of suffering; it was a mirror, reflecting the pain carved into Caleb's own heart.

He could feel the weight of the eyes upon him. Pity in some. Awe in others. But mostly… understanding. And with it, a sharp pang of fear. Was this understanding enough? Could it erase the dark stain of his past, the failures that still gnawed at the edges of his soul? Or would it simply expose them further, deepening the shadow of his secret?

The unveiling was over, but his reckoning had only begun.

The twelfth station hit like a gut punch—the Crucifixion. The church, usually filled with whispered prayers and the rustling of robes, now held its breath. Christ on the cross wasn't just carved wood, but a manifestation of anguish itself, raw and visceral, etched into every splintered line. The weight of suffering clung to the grain, a paradox of torment and grace interwoven like an open wound laid bare.

Caleb's eyes flickered to Sarah, seated near the front. Her hands were clasped tightly in her lap, knuckles white. Next to her, Thomas Martin—his father. His face was carved from the same wood as the stations, each line a testament to a life of hardship and quiet suffering. He shifted, as if something in the air had changed, as if some old wound buried deep within him had begun to ache in time with the scene before them.

Then came the final station—the tomb.

The room seemed to contract, the air dense with a presence that lingered somewhere between reverence and grief. The dark wood walls pulsed with an almost unbearable intimacy, as if they held whispered memories in their grain. It wasn't merely the image of burial—it was the breathless pause after goodbye, a still, aching vibration of sorrow and waiting. Caleb felt it press against his chest, heavy and unrelenting. The aroma of incense mingled with the deep, earthen notes of aged timber, a fusion so potent it wrapped around him like mourning itself—familiar, inescapable, and years deep.

A wave of nausea rolled through him. He had spent decades hardening himself, brick by bloody brick, building walls against the relentless tide of loss and regret. But looking at his own work, at the truth etched into the wood with his own hands, the walls began to fracture. His defenses—the ones that had kept him from feeling too much, from hoping too much—buckled beneath the weight of what he had created. The fog that had choked him for so long began to lift, not into sunshine, but into something colder, sharper—clarity.

Thomas let out a whisper of breath, a sound barely more than a ghost of words. His fingers twitched before reaching forward, stopping just shy of the carving. His hand hovered above the figure of Christ, trembling, as if afraid that touching it would undo something fragile within him. His breath hitched; a jagged sound swallowed by the sacred hush of the church.

"Damn..." The word slipped from his lips, unguarded, raw.

It wasn't profanity. It wasn't anger. It was something closer to revelation. His fingers curled into his palm, the tremor refusing to subside. Each meticulously carved wound, each delicate fold of fabric, spoke not just of Christ's suffering, but of his own. Each stroke of Caleb's chisel had unearthed something buried deep within him, something he had fought to forget.

Caleb stood frozen, watching his father—a man who had spent years trapped in his own silence—confront something neither of them had ever put into words.

The congregation was still, their murmurs a distant hum. Caleb's pulse pounded, drowning out everything but the sound of his own heartbeat. He saw it—pity in some faces, reverence in others. But in the faces of the men and women who had known loss, who had known what it was to break under the weight of life and still stand, there was something more. A kinship. A shared sorrow. A silent acknowledgment of a battle waged in the quiet corners of the soul.

A tear, slow and deliberate, carved a path down Thomas's weathered cheek. Not of despair. Not of weakness. But of something else entirely.

Acceptance.

A frail, unsteady hope took root in Caleb's chest, fragile as a newborn bird testing its wings.

He swallowed hard, blinking against the sting behind his own eyes. For the first time in years, the silence between him and his father wasn't a void but something else. Something softer. Something full.

Caleb took a step forward, then another. It felt like walking across broken glass, every movement laced with the weight of old wounds, old disappointments. His father had been a fortress of quiet neglect for so long that the idea of bridging that chasm made his breath come faster, shallower. Fear clawed at his ribs, cold and familiar. What if this moment shattered the second, he reached for it? What if they both retreated back into their respective silences, letting this fragile thing crumble before it even had a chance?

But something deeper pulled him forward. Not just longing. Not just regret. A reckless, desperate hope.

The past stretched behind them, a landscape of things unsaid, of resentment left to fester. But ahead of them—stained glass shimmered, casting halos of light against the walls. A promise of mercy. A beacon in the storm.

The voices of the congregation faded as Caleb stopped in front of his father. Their eyes met, and for the first time in years, they weren't separated by the weight of silence but bound by something greater.

The weight of the past was still there—tangible, inescapable. But it was no longer an impassable wall. It was something they could step over. Something they could choose to lay down.

For the first time, Caleb allowed himself to believe in the possibility of peace.

His strides lengthened, closing the distance. The years of silence, the nights of regret, stretched out between them, thin as smoke. His hands—the same hands that had carved these stations, that had shaped his father's pain into something tangible—ached to grasp onto something real.

And then he was there. Face to face with Thomas, the air between them charged with everything left unsaid.

The neglect. The resentment. The ache of things never spoken.

But beneath it all, something else shimmered, delicate but unyielding.

Redemption.

Caleb took a breath, his voice raw, unsteady. "Dad…?"

Thomas exhaled, his gaze never leaving the carvings. And then—slow, hesitant—he turned, his eyes locking onto his son's. The same tremor that had lived in his hands now flickered in his voice.

"You carved this?" It wasn't just a question. It was an opening.

Caleb nodded; his throat too tight to speak.

And then, after a lifetime of distance, after years of silence and regret—Thomas Martin placed a hand on his son's shoulder, his grip firm, steady.

A bridge finally built.

Their eyes locked—two shades of ocean blue, stormy seas finally settling into a tranquil bay. In that gaze, Caleb saw everything: the regrets, the misunderstandings, the ghost of what could have been. Unspoken apologies hung thick and heavy in the air as golden specks floated through the slanting light, like memory fragments suspended in time. Words felt clumsy, inadequate. The years melted away in that silent connection, the weight of their estrangement palpable in the tension between them. This wasn't just about forgiveness; it was about facing the truth, however brutal, together.

Thomas's eyes, usually clouded by a lifetime of regret, snapped into sharp focus. The storm inside him, a tempest of unspoken things, finally showed a crack of light. Caleb saw it—more than the battle-worn lines etched deep into his father's face, more than the ghosts of overseas conflicts and the silent wars waged at home. He saw a man starved for peace; a heart bruised raw by years of swallowed pain. Those damn letters, gathering dust in the corners of their lives, whispered of a father torn between duty and the love he should have given. A love Caleb had craved like air.

Caleb's eyes—the keen, precise gaze of an artist, yet softened by a lifetime of yearning—mirrored that hope. A fragile hope clung to the belief that even the most shattered pieces could be made whole again. He knew it. He'd spent years coaxing life into broken wood, patching the cracks, revealing the beauty beneath the damage. He had to believe he could do the same with his fractured relationship with his father. His own hands trembled slightly. He didn't wait. He moved, the church's silence amplifying the urgency in his heart. He wrapped his arms around his father, a hug that felt desperate and fragile.

Time dissolved. They were just father and son, soldier and artist, man and boy, caught in a desperate act of mutual repair. Caleb felt the weight of his father's arms, once iron-hard, now softened by a surprising tenderness. The calloused hands that held weapons and shaped wood now held him, a love finally bursting free from years beneath the armor of pride and pain.

"Dad…"

Caleb's voice, thick with emotion, barely rose above the gentle hush of the church. Thomas didn't speak, but the subtle tightening of his grip spoke volumes—a quiet acknowledgment of the years that had slipped away, the bridges left smoldering in silence. The warm trace of beeswax and incense lingered in the air, weaving through the tension between them like a memory refusing to fade. The Stations of the Cross, solemn and still, bore silent witness to their unspoken pain and the fragile hope of redemption. In each shared breath, a fragment of bitterness dissolved. With every heartbeat, the invisible walls between them began to crumble, one unspoken truth at a time.

The unspoken words hung in the air, heavier than the incense, raw with regret and hope. This was it. This was their chance. And Caleb wasn't going to let it slip away.

The hug lasted an eternity, a damn oasis in the desert of their lives. Caleb felt the years melt away, the lead weight of regret lifting. He finally let go, not of Thomas, but of the past's suffocating grip. The past was a broken chair, splintered and unusable, but the future? The future was raw lumber, waiting to be shaped. He'd shaped wood all his life; now it was time to shape their lives. Stepping back, Caleb's heart didn't thud like a trapped bird anymore. It settled, finding calm in the harbor of forgiveness. Thomas wasn't some distant, judgmental ghost. He was a fellow craftsman, a brother who'd toiled alongside him in the trenches of sorrow, a man who'd worked his ass off to mend what was broken.

The church held its breath—a collective gasp of relief. From the pews, eyes glistened, mirroring the stained glass, the whole damn place vibrating with unspoken emotion. This wasn't just "their" moment; it was for anyone who clawed for healing, redemption, and a second chance. Father Mike stood to the side, hands clasped, a ghost of a smile playing on his lips. His eyes, soft with quiet satisfaction, witnessed their quiet triumph. This wasn't just some feel-good story for Caleb and Thomas; it was a damn testament to the grace that ran through their community, a grace that healed their cracks, that restored their faith. He'd seen the worst of them, the deepest wounds, and to see this... was something.

Sarah watched, silent. Her strawberry blonde hair, a halo in the church's golden light, framed a single tear that traced down her cheek—a tear of pure, unadulterated relief. Her eyes, bright with a newfound hope, never left them. Caleb's journey had shown her a path, a damn lifeline. The road had been brutal, a lonely hell, but she saw her healing in this sanctuary. The past was a ghost, but this sacred moment whispered a new beginning—a chance to tend wounds and rewrite her story. She'd been lost, adrift, but now... now she saw the shore.

Caleb and Thomas finally broke apart, eyes burning, not with anger, but with a raw, exhausted love. A love forged in the white-hot crucible of forgiveness. Sarah saw the crack in the dam of years, the flood of mercy breaking through. She'd almost choked on the bitterness of it all, but now, something bigger filled her. It was a fragile thing, this peace, but holy. The hug hadn't been a quick, perfunctory thing. It had been a damn earthquake, a silent conversation spanning decades. Years of icy resentment, of swallowed words and choked-back tears, melted away in the heat of that embrace. Each man finally gave what the other desperately craved, a silent plea answered across the chasm of their estrangement. Understanding. Forgiveness. A promise, unspoken but keenly felt, to build something from the wreckage.

The air in Saint Peter's held the weight of something unseen yet palpable, thick with tension and the lingering echoes of old wounds. The hush wasn't empty—it pulsed, alive with the unspoken emotions of a town teetering on the edge of reconciliation. A congregation that had once been divided now stood frozen in collective anticipation. They had come expecting a sermon, maybe some small measure of peace. Instead, they had witnessed something far greater—a father and son, once broken, finding their way back to each other.

It wasn't just Caleb and Thomas standing in the chasm between past and present. It was all of them. Strangers. Neighbors. Old friends who had forgotten how to look each other in the eye. The shift was imperceptible at first, a ripple of recognition, an understanding that spread through the pews. Someone let out a shaky breath. Another wiped away a tear, embarrassed but unable to stop. Forgiveness had taken root, not just between the two men at the center of it all, but within the very foundation of the church itself. The walls that had held so much grief and resentment now absorbed something softer, something sacred.

Thomas exhaled a breath he hadn't realized he was holding. "It's... it's over," he whispered, the words trembling like fragile glass.

Caleb stood beside him; hands unsteady at his sides. He wanted to believe it. Wanted to let go of the years spent in the shadows of his father's disapproval, of his own failures. But absolution wasn't a switch that could be flipped. It was a slow unraveling, a step forward that still left scars behind.

He swallowed hard. "Yeah," he rasped. "It's over."

And yet, in the quiet that followed, he wasn't sure if he meant it.

Sarah stood a few steps away, her breath catching in her throat as she watched the moment unfold. She had been with Caleb through his darkest nights, had seen the weight he carried even when he pretended it was gone. He had rebuilt his life with calloused hands, chipping away at his pain the way he carved wood, with precision and an unrelenting need to shape something whole from the fragments. She knew better than anyone that this wasn't the end of the battle. It was merely another beginning.

Father Mike wiped a hand across his damp brow, his usual composure cracking under the sheer weight of what had transpired. He had pushed for this, prayed for it, but faith alone wasn't always enough to mend broken things. This town, this congregation, had long been a place where old grudges festered like wounds left unattended. And now, here it was—proof that even the deepest fractures could be healed.

But the question remained: would it last?

Caleb felt the weight of every eye on him as he turned toward the towering Stations of the Cross lining the walls. His father's masterpieces, carved with hands far steadier than his own, loomed over him like silent witnesses to his own failings. He had spent so long trying to escape the shadow of those carvings, of the man who had created them. And now, he couldn't look away.

Sarah's fingers brushed against his, grounding him. "He's really doing this," she murmured, as if speaking the words aloud might make them real.

Caleb barely heard her. His pulse roared in his ears, a chaotic drumbeat against the silence. The fear clawed at him, the doubt creeping in. What if this peace was temporary? What if the past came clawing back the moment, they left this place? He clenched his jaw, forcing himself to meet his father's gaze one more time.

Thomas nodded, a flicker of something unreadable passing between them. Not everything could be spoken. Not everything needed to be.

Caleb's throat tightened. "Thank you," he managed, barely above a whisper.

It wasn't just gratitude—it was a plea. A promise. A fragile hope that this wouldn't break apart the moment they stepped outside.

He turned toward the doors, his steps slow, deliberate. Every movement felt weighted, as if he carried something invisible on his shoulders. The cold stone of the church floor grounded him, a stark contrast to the uncertainty swirling inside. He knew better than to believe in instant absolution. Forgiveness wasn't a single act—it was a daily choice, a battle waged in the quiet moments when no one else was watching.

He hesitated as he reached the doorway, his gaze flickering once more to the Stations of the Cross. The final carving—the resurrected Christ, light radiating from every chiseled detail—felt almost mocking in its perfection. He was not whole. He was not new. He was still piecing himself together, still searching for the man he wanted to be.

A bitter chuckle escaped him. "A tribute to my father," he muttered under his breath. But it was more than that. It was a confession, carved in wood and regret. Every chisel stroke had been a plea, every imperfection a reflection of his own fractured soul. The town had forgiven. His father had forgiven. But could he?

The question lingered as he stepped into the cold light of the evening, the doors creaking shut behind him. The past would always be there, etched into the wood, into the stones of the church, into the very bones of this town. But for the first time, Caleb Martin wasn't running from it.

He was walking forward, one step at a time.

CHAPTER 19

New Paths, New Beginnings

CALEB'S BOOTS CRUNCHED on the damp sand, each step a deliberate counterpoint to the frantic rhythm of his heart. Beside him, Sarah walked with a controlled grace that belied the tremor in her hand, a hand he'd seen tremble only once before—the day her mother died. The salty air stung his eyes, mirroring the sting of guilt that clawed at him. This wasn't just a stroll down memory lane; it was a desperate attempt to outrun the truth, a truth that threatened to drown them both.

"Remember building those sandcastles?" Sarah's voice, brittle with unshed tears, barely carried over the crashing waves. The carefree memory now felt like a cruel joke, a stark contrast to the storm brewing inside him. Caleb's gaze was fixed on the horizon, the setting sun a fiery omen. He swallowed the lump in his throat thick with unspoken words. "Castles meant to defy the tide," he finally managed, his voice rough. The half-smile felt like a mask, a pathetic attempt to hide the turmoil within. He needed to tell her. He *had* to. But the words wouldn't come. The silence stretched, heavy and suffocating.

He stooped, picking up a smooth, grey stone—a perfect circle, mockingly flawless against the backdrop of his fractured life. The weight of it felt less like grounding and more like the weight of his secret, pressing down on him. With a sharp, almost violent flick of his wrist, he sent the stone skipping across the water. Each bounce was a fleeting moment of hope, quickly swallowed by the vast, indifferent ocean. He watched, transfixed, the stone's journey a microcosm of his own.

"Life's like that, isn't it?" he rasped, the words escaping in a breathless whisper. "We fight, we strive, but the tide always wins." The confession hung between them, unspoken but heavy in the air. The tide wasn't just the ocean but the relentless current of consequences pulling them under. Sarah watched the ripples spread, her eyes searching his.

"But it's the ripples, Caleb," she said softly, her voice gaining strength. "The impact, the way they touch everything… like your father's carvings. They touched so many lives, even after…" Her voice trailed off, her gaze lingering on the unfinished *Stations of the Cross*, half-hidden in his father's workshop—a masterpiece that had brought healing and solace to their small town. A masterpiece that Caleb had abandoned, a secret betrayal weighing on him heavier than any stone.

The wind struck Caleb's face with stinging force, his hair snapping across his vision like threads of memory he couldn't untangle. The tang of saltwater clung to his skin, raw and biting, like unspoken truths wedged beneath his ribs. All his life, he had poured fragments of his soul into wood, trying to carve permanence from something as breakable as breath. But legacy wasn't just etched in timber or timeworn hands—it lived in the quiet spaces left in the hearts of those who believed in you, in the moments you showed up, and the ones you didn't.

And he had betrayed that trust.

His father's faith in him, Sarah's belief—he had let them slip through his fingers, had convinced himself that silence would be kinder. That by holding it all inside, he could spare her the weight of knowing. But the truth was a living thing, clawing at his insides, suffocating him.

He swallowed against the dryness in his throat. The words teetered on the edge, fragile as the foamy waves curling around the rocks. His mouth opened, the confession forming—raw, desperate—

"Sarah, I—"

"Maybe you're right," she murmured, cutting him off without realizing it. She wasn't looking at him, not really. Her gaze was fixed on the water, on the way the setting sun melted into the waves, streaking them with fire and gold. The wind tugged at her hair; her face illuminated by the last dregs of daylight. She looked so much like the girl he'd known—before everything cracked apart—that it hurt to breathe.

For a moment, he thought she might turn to him, might see him the way she used to. But instead, she reached down, tracing a finger through the damp sand. The ripples smoothed beneath her touch, only to return with the next pulse of the tide.

"These ripples… they're all that's left, aren't they?" Her voice was quiet, almost lost in the hush of the waves. "Like the carvings. Lasting longer than we ever will."

The words struck something deep, hollowing him out. He clenched his jaw.

"They don't last forever," he admitted. "Not really."

She finally turned then, her eyes catching his. "Then what does?"

He had no answer.

Because the things that should have lasted—the faith between them, the trust—he had broken those with his silence. And now, all he had left were the remnants. Fragments of something that once felt whole.

The horizon bled into twilight, lavender and rose washing across the sky, their beauty stark against the growing darkness. But even as the world softened, his chest remained tight, the confession still caught in his throat.

Would she even forgive him if he said it now? If he laid it all bare? Or was it too late—his silence already an echo of something lost to the tide?

They walked, the damp sand cool beneath their feet, the silence heavy with the weight of unspoken things. It wasn't an uncomfortable silence, but one thick with a shared history and burden. Time stretched and warped around them, a distorted mirror reflecting the years that had pulled them apart yet somehow kept them tethered.

Then, Sarah's laughter shattered the fragile peace. A playful nudge, a light touch, the sound as sharp and unexpected as a gunshot. "Race you to that driftwood!" she cried, her voice a youthful echo of their past, a past Caleb desperately wanted to reclaim, to hold onto, before it vanished altogether.

A ghost of a smile touched Caleb's lips, a flicker of warmth against the icy grip of his grief. His heart, a hardened fist, loosened just a fraction at the sound of her unrestrained joy. He couldn't help himself; he ran, his limbs remembering a speed he hadn't felt in years, the years that stretched between them like a chasm.

"Slow down, Sarah!" he yelled, his voice raspy, roughened by years of battling silent demons, of carrying a weight too heavy for one man to bear. She glanced back, her green eyes sparkling like emeralds in the fading light.

"Catch me if you can!" she teased, her laughter ringing out, clear and bright, a defiant counterpoint to the unspoken despair that clung to them both. She reached the driftwood first, collapsing onto it with a breathless grin. Caleb followed, his pace slowing as he reached her side. Her laughter—that familiar, vibrant sound—melted some of the tension that had coiled tightly within him. He hadn't even realized how tightly it had been wound.

They sat together, the endless ocean stretching before them, a vast and unforgiving expanse mirroring the vast and unforgiving emptiness he felt inside. Caleb traced the surface of the weathered driftwood. Its rough texture mirrored his soul, shaped and battered by time and loss. They were both carved by life, changed irrevocably, yet strangely unchanged.

"Remember how we used to pretend this was a ship?" Caleb's voice was barely a whisper, soft as the waves lapping at the shore, each word pregnant with unspoken longing, with a desperate need to reconnect, to rebuild what they'd lost. The unspoken question hung in the air: Could they, do it? Could they salvage their fractured relationship, or was the damage too significant? His gaze locked onto Sarah's, searching for an answer he wasn't sure she could give.

The last sliver of sun caught in Sarah's hair, turning it into a fiery halo. "We were pirates, explorers… anything we damn well wanted to be," she breathed, a ghost of a smile playing on her lips, a stark contrast to the tremor in her voice. The memory, once a source of wild exhilaration, now tasted like ash in her mouth.

The wind whipped around them, a salty kiss brushing their skin, and the crisp aroma of pine needles pierced through the briny breath of the sea. For a fleeting heartbeat, they were children again—wild, weightless, untouched by time. Laughter echoed in the back of their minds, like a ghost clinging to the edge of memory. But the illusion fractured as quickly as it had formed, swept away by the gusts of truth. In its place settled the chill of remembrance—the weight of everything they'd lost, and everything they'd never dared to say.

Dusk bled across the sky, a bruised purple giving way to angry crimson. Caleb and Sarah remained perched on the driftwood; two figures etched against the dying light. They'd survived storms that would've broken lesser souls, but the peace in Quiet Town felt fragile, a thin veneer over the cracks in their hearts. Redemption felt like a distant star, its light barely piercing the darkness.

The silence wasn't peaceful; it crackled with unspoken fears. Caleb shifted, the rough wood groaning under his weight. He glanced at Sarah, her profile sharp in the fading light, the worry etched into her face mirroring his own. Roughened by years of hard living, Sarah's hands tightened around the driftwood.

"I've been thinking," she began, her voice catching, a vulnerability that laid bare the turmoil within. "About the future. About… planting roots. But the ground feels… shaky." Her gaze drifted to the restless ocean, a mirror to her unsettled soul. "Can it really hold me?"

A choked laugh escaped Caleb. "Shaky ground? You, Sarah? After everything we've been through. The woman who sailed through hurricanes and laughed in the face of death?" He chuckled humorlessly, his eyes filled with admiration and worry. "You think a little unsteady earth is gonna stop you now?"

Sarah's eyes burned with unshed tears. "It's not just the earth, Caleb. It's… us. Can we build something lasting? Something strong enough to withstand… everything?" Her voice cracked; her unspoken fears heavy in the air.

Caleb met her gaze, his own filled with a fierce intensity that belied his calm exterior. The ocean's rhythm mirrored the relentless beat of his heart. He saw the doubt in her eyes; the fear mirrored his own. He'd spent years running, avoiding the ghosts of his past, but Sarah... Sarah was different. She was the anchor he never knew he needed, the still point in the storm of his life. And the thought of losing her, of failing her, was a terror that clawed at his gut.

He reached out, his calloused hand covering hers on the driftwood. "We'll build it together, Sarah," he said, his voice low and confident. "Together. We'll make the ground firm beneath our feet." The unspoken promise hung between them, fragile yet powerful, a testament to their shared resilience and their desperate hope for a future built on forgiveness, trust, and the unwavering strength of their love. The stars began to appear, their light a beacon in the growing darkness, a silent promise of hope against the looming uncertainties.

Sarah," Caleb said, his voice rough around the edges, a low rumble that spoke of years spent wrestling with ghosts. The setting sun painted his face in bruised purple and orange shades, highlighting the lines etched deep around his eyes—lines earned, not given. "Life's been a sonofabitch, hasn't it? Shattered me more times than I can count. Every piece a damn scar." His blue eyes, usually bright, held a weary intensity, the past a raging storm reflected in their depths. "Dad's letters... they were a damn mess, mostly. Pain. Searching. For something he couldn't even name. That's what haunted him, Sarah. And haunts me." He looked at his hands, calloused and scarred, each a testament to a hard life. "Those Stations... they taught me how to *try* to forgive. One damn step at a time."

He turned to her, the fading light warming them both like a dying ember. "I can't promise you a smooth ride, Sarah. Shit's gonna hit the fan, I know it. Earthquakes, tidal waves—the whole damn shebang. But I've learned something. We build our own damn sanctuary. With faith, and whatever scraps of love we can find. A place where we stand, no matter the storm." The silence stretched, thick and heavy with unspoken fears and shared burdens. The weight of their dreams pressed between them, a tangible thing, held together by the fragile threads of their shared history. They sat, two survivors carved by life's relentless knife, finding strength not in escaping the past but in forging something new from its wreckage.

Caleb picked up a piece of driftwood, smooth under his thumb, the grain mirroring the lines on his palm. The wood felt familiar, a ghost of his father's workshop, of simpler times before the world fell apart. A ghost that still threatened to pull him under. He glanced at Sarah, her strawberry-blonde hair catching the amber light. He saw the girl she once was, vibrant and full of life, but also the woman she was now—weathered, yes, but with a resilience that mirrored his own. The question hung between them, unspoken but heavy. Could they rebuild what was lost?

"Remember that driftwood fort we built?" he asked, a hesitant smile on his lips. The memory was a lifeline, a fragile thing in the face of the harsh reality. Sarah laughed, a low, throaty sound, the music of memories against the rhythmic crash of waves. "How could I forget?" she said, her eyes sparkling with the shared memory. "Our damn castle. Untouchable." But a shadow flickered in her eyes, a doubt that echoed Caleb's fears. Was it genuinely untouchable? Or was the storm just waiting to break?

"Feels like a lifetime," Caleb rasped, the words catching in his throat. Nostalgia warred with a raw, unsettling awe. He'd thought they'd crumble under the weight of it all. The sheer number of storms they'd weathered felt almost unbelievable. Sarah's smile, a slow, radiant bloom, chased away the shadows clinging to him. "And yet, here we are," she said, her voice a quiet strength. "Still standing." The words, simple as they were, struck him deep. He loved her fiercely, but a cold dread, a familiar serpent, coiled in his gut. He hadn't told her about the letter. The one that could tear everything apart. Their history wasn't just a tapestry; it was a battlefield littered with the casualties of their fights. Each scar a testament to their resilience and a constant, nagging reminder of their fragility. He'd pushed her away, time and again. He'd nearly lost her. The thought clawed at him, a relentless, icy grip on his heart.

The sun bled into the ocean, a fiery farewell. He reached for her hand, the gesture involuntary, primal. Their fingers laced; a silent conversation older than their words. "Your hand," he whispered, his voice thick with unshed tears, "it fits mine. Like it was made for me."

He squeezed her hand tightly, a desperate plea for reassurance. This wasn't just about their love. It was about his survival, his desperate need for her forgiveness.

"Like two pieces of the same broken wood," Sarah corrected, her voice barely audible, but the pressure of her hand spoke volumes. She knew him too well. She felt his fear. The promise they renewed wasn't just about the future; it was about facing the past, the ghosts that haunted them both. The legacy they built wouldn't just stand on forgiveness; it would be forged in it. Would she forgive him? Would *he* forgive himself? The question hung heavy in the air, a silent undercurrent to their quiet moment. They sat on the driftwood, the crimson and gold sky a brutal backdrop to their fragile peace. The rhythmic sigh of the waves was a cruel counterpoint to the storm brewing within him. The breeze carried the scent of salt and fear.

The storm wasn't entirely quelled. It simmered beneath the surface, a dangerous calm. The scars remained, etched deep, both visible and hidden. The unanswered questions weren't gone, merely suppressed, waiting for the opportune moment to erupt. He had to tell her. Soon. He had to risk it all. Fragile and precious hope flickered amidst the wreckage, a tiny spark against the overwhelming darkness of his guilt. But hope, he knew, could be extinguished just as quickly as it ignited. He only hoped he wouldn't snuff it out himself.

The sun bled orange onto the horizon, painting Sarah's face in hues of fading light. Her green eyes, usually bright with mischief, held a gravity that made Caleb's gut clench. He knew this wasn't just some casual conversation. This was a reckoning. "Caleb," she began, her voice a low hum against the crashing waves, "what's your future look like? Honestly." The question hung between them, raw and exposed, as sharp as a shard of sea glass. He glanced at the restless ocean, a mirror to the turmoil inside him. Sarah's unwavering gaze pinned him, forcing him to confront the ghost of his past—the mistakes, the regrets, the man he'd almost become.

He'd built walls around his heart, brick by painstaking brick, but Sarah's quiet strength chipped away at the mortar. A bitter laugh caught in his throat. "A future? I used to think I knew. Thought it was all carved in stone, a path paved with... well, let's just say regrets." His voice was rough, the words tasting of ashes. Sarah squeezed his hand, her touch surprisingly strong. "Then tell me about the path you *want*." The weight of her belief settled on him, a heavy cloak of hope.

He closed his eyes, the image of his workshop flashing before him—the scent of sawdust and varnish, the feel of the smooth, yielding wood. It was a sanctuary where he could lose himself in the rhythm of creation. But the ghosts still haunted him. The shadows of the choices he'd made, the ones that almost swallowed him whole. "I... I don't know," he finally admitted, his voice cracking. "But wherever it is, it has to be real. Real to me. Real to the work I do. To the people who..." He swallowed, the words catching in his throat. "To the people who need what I can give, even if I don't feel worthy."

A single tear escaped Sarah's eye. She understood the burden he carried, the doubt that gnawed at him. She'd seen him battle his demons, and she'd seen the flicker of the incredible man beneath. "Caleb," she whispered, her voice thick with emotion, "your worth isn't defined by your past mistakes. It's written in the strength of your hands, the honesty in your eyes, in the way you pour your soul into every piece you create." She traced the line of his jaw. "That's what shines. That's what matters."

Her words were a lifeline. He felt the tightness in his chest ease, the weightlifting, though the ghosts still lingered at the edges of his vision. The future remained uncertain, but for the first time in a long time, he wasn't paralyzed by fear. He had her, and that was a foundation he could build on. The path was still uncertain, but he wasn't walking it alone.

The last sliver of sun bled into the churning Pacific, painting the sky in bruised purples and angry oranges. Caleb and Sarah stood on the beach, the retreating tide whispering secrets only the ocean understood. Their footprints, quickly erased, mirrored the fleeting nature of their lives up until now. But this... this felt different. Caleb's gaze was a hawk's, fixed on the horizon. The vastness of the sea mirrored the vastness of the decision gnawing at him. He'd always lived in his father's shadow, the scent of sawdust and ambition clinging to him like a second skin. He clenched his jaw, the weight of expectation pressing down.

Sarah," he began, his voice rough, the words catching in his throat. "I've spent my whole life in Dad's workshop. His legacy... it's a beautiful thing, but it's also a cage."

His gaze locked onto hers, searching, hoping she could see past the words to the raw truth beneath them. He needed her to understand. He needed her more than he could ever admit.

Sarah's hand rested on his arm, a silent affirmation. She knew. She had seen the weight of it, the silent burden passed down like an heirloom neither asked for nor could refuse. But worry flickered in her eyes, undeniable.

"What are you saying, Caleb?"

He inhaled deeply, the salty air filling his lungs, grounding him. "I'm saying I need to break free. To build something... "mine.""

The words tasted like freedom and fear. Fear of failure. Fear of disappointing his father. Fear of disappointing *her*.

"Joshua..." Caleb's voice strengthened, finding steadiness in the storm inside him. "He taught me more than just carpentry. He showed me that beauty exists in imperfection, in the knots and the grain. Our lives are like that wood, Sarah. We carry our scars, our stories, but they don't define us. They shape us. They make us *who we are*."

His eyes burned with a newfound conviction. "I want to use that wisdom. Build something real here... in Port Angeles. Something... healing."

Sarah's smile was hesitant at first, but then it bloomed into something radiant. "A place where people can find themselves?" she whispered, her voice thick with emotion.

"Exactly," Caleb breathed. "A workshop, yes, but more than that. A community. Like the forest, intertwined and strong. A place where people can heal, find peace... find *themselves*."

His voice cracked, the weight of his dreams and anxieties pressing against him. He turned to her, his eyes pleading. The urgency, the unspoken question, hung heavy between them.

"And us, Sarah? Could this be... *our* place? Could we plant our roots here, grow old together, listening to the whispers of the sea and the pines?"

The words were a prayer, a desperate hope he couldn't bear to voice as anything less.

Sarah's eyes welled up. This wasn't just about a workshop. It was about their future, their life together. The risk was enormous. She reached for his hand, her fingers lacing through his.

"Yes, Caleb," she breathed, her voice trembling but resolute. "Yes, let's build it together."

The fear was still there, a shadow lurking at the edges, but overshadowed by the thrilling promise of a future born from their shared dream.

The ocean roared its approval.

The unspoken question lingered, a promise and a threat all at once. Caleb felt it, a knot tightening in his gut—not the comfortable weight of expectation, but the terrifying heft of a leap of faith. He pictured a future, Sarah beside him, a life built from scratch, a monument to their love, their resilience, their sheer stubborn refusal to be broken. But the image flickered, edged with doubt. Could he really do this? Could *they* do this?

"Building a life here... with *you*..." Caleb's voice hitched, the words tasting like ash and hope. "It's terrifying, Sarah. Absolutely terrifying. But... God, it's also the only thing that feels real."

His hand clenched into a fist, the raw vulnerability stark against the bravado he usually projected.

Sarah didn't answer immediately. Instead, she leaned against him, the silent affirmation fragile, easily shattered. He felt the tremor in her shoulders, the unspoken fear mirroring his own. They were two figures etched against a bruised twilight sky, the world a hushed witness to their internal battle.

The silence wasn't peaceful; it throbbed with unspoken anxieties. With its echoes of the past and whispers of the future, Port Angeles felt less like a sanctuary and more like a battlefield. Ready? He wasn't sure he was ready, but the alternative was unthinkable.

The tide, relentless and indifferent, gnawed at the shore. Its cold fingers seemed to pull at them, urging them forward or dragging them under. Rising, they faced the ocean, the distance shrinking with every step, each footfall a testament to their shared journey, a fragile bridge built across a chasm of uncertainty.

"Another chapter," Caleb murmured, his voice barely a breath against the roar of the waves.

The rhythmic crash echoed the relentless cycle of life—loss and gain, hope and despair. Would they survive the next wave?

Sarah's smile was brittle, a mask barely concealing the fear in her green eyes.

"Yeah," she whispered, her voice catching.

The setting sun painted the sky in fiery hues, a deceptive beauty mirroring the precariousness of their situation.

The vast and unforgiving ocean reflected their uncertain future—a mirror to everything that had passed and the terrifying unknown that lay ahead. Each footprint in the wet sand marked their commitment, a step further into a future they couldn't fully grasp, a future built on shaky ground.

As the sun dipped below the horizon, the town of Port Angeles loomed before them, its familiar buildings silent judges of their audacious dream.

The weight of their decision pressed down, heavy and inescapable.

They had chosen.

Now, they would face the consequences—together.

"Uncertain, ain't it?" Caleb muttered, the words catching in the salty air as much as in his throat. He wasn't warning Sarah; he was confessing his unease; a gnawing doubt that shadowed the peace he pretended to find. The journey, he'd learned wasn't a smooth river, but a damn rapid. "But hell, I'm trusting the current more than some promised shoreline."

Sarah's breath hitched. "Redemption," she whispered, the word a raw, wounded thing. "That's what we're clinging to, isn't it? Along the way." Her voice, usually so steady, trembled. The weight of unspoken things hung heavy between them – the ghosts of their past mistakes, the choices that had scarred them both. Caleb saw the fight in her eyes, the same flickering defiance he saw in his reflection. Her hand brushed his, a fleeting touch that spoke volumes. Their shared history – a tapestry woven with heartache and bitter separations – had somehow forged a bond stronger than anything he'd ever known. The broken pieces, jagged and raw, had been painstakingly reassembled into a mosaic of resilience.

"Redemption," he echoed, the word rough on his tongue, tasting of ash and hope. It wasn't merely a word—it was memory incarnate. It was the air in his father's workshop, heavy with cedar and pine, a mix of resin and timeworn earth. It was the trace of sawdust suspended in morning light, the lingering presence of calloused hands guiding his own across raw timber. His father, a man shaped by the very hardwood he shaped, had passed down more than skill—he'd offered a way of seeing the world, where broken things could be made beautiful again. Caleb understood then: Redemption wasn't a place you arrived at. It was a process—a relentless chiseling away of doubt, shame, and fear until something true emerged from the grain.

As twilight bled into night, the stars flared into existence above the Whispering Cliffs, their pale glow etched against the bruised sky. The cool hush of evening wrapped around him, stark and clean, but the warmth of Sarah at his side grounded him more than anything. Every step forward felt like a wager—on trust, on healing, on a future they were brave enough to imagine. His boots pressed into the boundary where sand met grass, the earth firm and chill beneath him. He drew in a deep breath. The air carried the tang of sea brine and the earthy sharpness of pine needles, conjuring images of wood shavings curled on a workbench, sunlight catching on worn tools, and the silent strength of a father who'd taught him how to shape meaning from splinters.

Sarah's voice, soft as the ocean breeze, cut through his memories. "Beautiful, huh?" Caleb doesn't answer immediately. He needed a moment to let the fragile, hard-won peace settle in his bones. The waves crashed against the shore, a rhythmic pulse against the silence in his heart. "More than ever," he finally said, his voice a low rumble. This town, this sea, this quiet solitude was where he'd learned to carve not just wood but a new life from the wreckage of the old. He'd learned the art of faith, not in some divine being, but in the unwavering strength of his hands and Sarah's hand in his. The rhythm of the waves was the rhythm of his soul, a constant reminder that even in the darkest moments, the tide always turns.

Twilight painted the sky in bruised purples and angry oranges. Caleb burned the image into his mind – the raw, gritty texture of the sand, the ocean's endless expanse promising both oblivion and escape. The chill wind bit, but it felt cleansing, a brutal scrub against the grime of his past. He sucked in a lungful of the salty air, tasting regret, hoping for redemption.

"Ready?" Tight with a suppressed fear he knew mirrored his own, Sarah's voice sliced through the silence. The simple word hung heavy; a loaded gun pointed at the fragile peace between them. He met her gaze – the sunset's fiery reflection in her eyes, a brave defiance against the gathering darkness. But beneath the surface, he saw the flicker of doubt, the same icy dread that gnawed at him. He'd promised her a new life, a fresh start. Could he deliver? A grim determination settled in his gut.

"Yes," he said, the word a hard-won victory over the tremor in his voice. "Time to walk into… our tomorrow." The words felt hollow; a lie whispered in the face of his uncertainty. Their footsteps crunched on the sand, each a deliberate erasure of the past, a refusal to look back. But the vast, unforgiving beach felt less like a farewell and more like a silent judge. With Sarah beside him, the weight of loneliness was lessened but not lifted. The fear was still there, a cold knot in his stomach. He was a man running from a ghost, and that ghost walked hand-in-hand with the woman he loved.

Port Angeles loomed, its familiar streets hushed and expectant, bearing witness to their return, surrender, and possible failure. He allowed himself one last look – the relentless rhythm of the waves, a cruel parody of the steady beat of his own racing heart. But with Sarah's hand clasped tight in his, he felt a fleeting moment of something akin to strength. The past, a festering wound, started to bleed less. He turned, his gaze fixed on the uncertain future, their intertwined hands a fragile promise.

CHAPTER 20

The Master's Hands

SWEAT BEADED ON Caleb's forehead, and the afternoon sun reflected a relentless glare on the polished wood of his workbench. The chisel, worn smooth in his calloused hand, felt like an extension of himself, a familiar weight grounding him in this solitary sanctuary. He glanced at the half-finished figure – a rough-hewn hawk, its wings still unfurled – a silent testament to his struggle. The wood was stubborn, mirroring the resistance he felt inside.

"Damn it," he muttered, the sound swallowed by the rhythmic tap-tap-tap of the chisel. His breath hitched, and a raw sob caught in his throat. This wasn't just about carving wood but cutting away the ghosts that haunted him. The hawk was supposed to represent freedom, escape – a mocking reminder of what he'd lost. A sudden crash from the house jolted him. His heart hammered against his ribs, a frantic drumbeat against his work's slow, deliberate rhythm. Fear, cold and sharp, pierced the tranquility. He knew that sound. It was Sarah.

The chisel slipped from his fingers, striking the wooden floor with a sharp, metallic clang that echoed the turmoil inside him. Caleb barely noticed. His breath hitched, his heart hammering against his ribs like a prisoner pounding on the walls of his own cell.

"Sarah?" he called, his voice raw with something between fear and urgency.

Silence.

A silence so thick it curled around him, pressing into the spaces between his ribs, tightening like a noose. The workshop, once his sanctuary, felt suffocating. Dust hung in the slanted afternoon light; slow-moving particles suspended in time. His promise—*I'll protect you.*

Always. —felt as fragile as the wood shavings at his feet. He clenched his jaw.

Not again.

He tore off his apron, boots scraping against the worn planks as he lunged toward the door. He didn't think. His body moved on instinct, heart jackhammering, lungs straining. Each step toward the house felt like wading through thick mud, through *memory*.

The sharp tang of pine and sawdust lingered on his clothes, an earthy presence that clashed with the bitter, metallic taste of fear crawling up the back of his throat. He shoved the door open with trembling hands, his pulse a thunderous drumbeat in his ears, each beat louder than the last.

Sarah was there.

Alive.

Not hurt.

But something was *wrong*.

She stood rigid by the window, her back stiff, fingers twisted around a crumpled letter. Her face—usually bright with laughter, with exasperation, with *something*—was drained of color. Her hands trembled. A hollow space where her breath should be.

Caleb swallowed hard, taking an unsteady step closer. His voice, when it came, was rough, frayed at the edges. *"What is it, Sarah?"*

Nothing.

Her eyes flickered to him but didn't focus, as though she wasn't really seeing him, as though she were standing at the edge of something vast and terrible, teetering.

He moved closer, his fingers brushing against her wrist, grounding her. "Sarah. Talk to me."

Her breath caught, then shuddered out. Her voice was barely a whisper, yet it carried the weight of something that could shatter them both.

"It's… it's about your father."

A cold hand clenched around his spine.

Sarah blinked rapidly, gripping the paper tighter, knuckles whitening. "They found him…"

The words hung in the air, unfinished, fractured. But he didn't need her to finish. He already knew.

His knees nearly buckled. The room tilted. The walls pressed inward, squeezing the air from his lungs. A phantom ache curled around his chest—grief sharpened by regret. His father's voice, buried deep in his mind, clawed its way out: *You'll understand one day, Caleb. A man carries the weight of his own choices.*

A strangled sound—half laugh, half breath—escaped his throat. The hawk on the workbench, wings half-carved, seemed to watch him, its unfinished form a cruel mirror of himself. The chisel on the floor might as well have been miles away.

His father.

Gone.

And Caleb wasn't sure if the grief or the guilt would swallow him first.

* * *

A floorboard groaned, slicing through the heavy silence in Caleb's workshop. He didn't look up; he didn't need to. Joshua Shepherd's presence was a familiar weight settling beside him, grounding him in a way nothing else could. Their eyes met, and for a moment, words felt unnecessary. Joshua didn't just see him—he saw through him, saw the cracks Caleb worked so hard to keep hidden.

"Damn, Caleb," Joshua finally said, his voice low, a rumble thick with understanding. "You're a machine."

Caleb grunted, his grip tightening around the chisel as he set it against the wood. "Just getting it done." The words came out clipped, a shield against the emotions clawing beneath his ribs. He felt Joshua's gaze, steady, unyielding. It was a silent challenge: *You're not fooling me.*

Joshua hadn't needed words before, but now, Caleb felt an unbearable urge to push him away, to shove down everything threatening to break loose. The workshop, once a sanctuary, now felt too small, the air too thick. He dug the chisel into the wood, harder than necessary, feeling the resistance, the satisfying snap as a sliver curled away.

Joshua sighed; the kind of exhale that said *I've been here before*. He leaned against the bench, watching. "You're not just carving wood, Caleb."

Caleb's jaw tightened. "Yeah? Then what am I doing?"

Joshua hesitated, then nodded toward the hawk's unfinished form. "Trying to carve yourself out of the wreckage."

The words landed like a punch to the gut. Caleb inhaled sharply, his fingers trembling where they rested against the wood. His father's hands had once held his, guiding his strokes, teaching him patience. Now, the absence felt unbearable, a chasm he couldn't bridge. He forced out a bitter laugh. "That obvious, huh?"

Joshua didn't smile. "Only to me."

Silence stretched between them, weighted and thick. Caleb hated it. He hated how Joshua could read him so easily, how his presence chipped away at the walls Caleb had spent years building. The grief, the anger, the self-loathing—it all sat heavy in his chest, pressing against his ribs until he could barely breathe.

"It's beautiful, Caleb," Joshua said softly. There was something raw in his voice, something deeper than admiration. Understanding. Recognition. He knew the battle Caleb fought because he'd fought his own.

Caleb finally looked up, his eyes burning. "Beautiful?" He let out a short, humorless laugh. "It's just wood, Josh. Nothing more."

Joshua stepped closer, his hand resting lightly on Caleb's shoulder. "No, Caleb. It's more than wood. It's you. And you're more than what happened to you."

The words hit Caleb like a wrecking ball. His breath hitched, and for a terrifying second, he thought he might break apart right there. The anger, the pain—it was a flood that threatened to drown him. He swallowed hard, fighting to keep his voice steady. "I don't know if I'll ever be…more." The confession barely made it past his lips, a whisper swallowed by the workshop's dim light.

Joshua didn't let go. "You already are. You just don't see it yet."

Caleb closed his eyes, his grip slackening on the chisel. He wanted to believe him. He really did. But the weight of his past, of his father's absence, pressed down on him like an iron brand, whispering that some wounds never healed.

And maybe, just maybe, he wasn't strong enough to carve his way out.

Joshua squeezed his shoulder gently. "You are more, Caleb. You're stronger than you think. You're fighting. And that's everything." His gaze held a fierce determination, a silent promise.

Caleb looked back at the wood, the rough form slowly taking shape, a tangible representation of his relentless struggle. In the silence, he found a flicker of hope, a sliver of possibility amidst the shadows of his past. The chisel felt lighter in his hand, and the work, though still grueling, no longer felt like a burden. It was his fight, his life reborn, and he knew he could face the future in this shared space with his friend beside him. He was carving a new beginning, one agonizing, beautiful stroke at a time.

Caleb's arm ached, the chisel trembling in his sweat-slicked grip. The oak fought back, stubborn and dense, mirroring the knot of anxiety in his gut. He wasn't just carving a family; he was carving a prayer, a desperate plea for forgiveness he couldn't voice. The swirling grain, the stubborn resistance of the wood, it felt like his own life – chaotic, beautiful, and achingly vulnerable. He saw his parents' faces in the emerging curves, their intertwined hands a silent testament to a love shattered by the tragedy he couldn't fully comprehend.

His breath hitched. Could he genuinely capture that love? Could he even begin to atone? This wasn't just art; it was an expiation, a brutal, honest confession carved in oak. Each precise cut was a whispered apology, a frantic attempt to mend the gaping hole his recklessness had torn in his life. The Stations of the Cross at Saint Peter's – his father's favorite – were suddenly heavy. He was meant to be better than this, like his father who had carved those sacred scenes with grace and devotion.

He paused, wiping his brow with the edge of his sleeve, the sharp aroma of sawdust and pine clinging to the air, barely concealing the cold, iron-laced taste of fear rising in his throat. The chisel in his hand had grown unbearably heavy, its weight no longer just steel but the embodiment of regret. He stared at the half-carved figures before him—the once-tender embrace now softened into an indistinct blur, like a memory fading under the strain of sorrow. Was there still time to atone? Could his hands, so skilled at shaping wood, also mend the splintered fragments of a soul worn thin by remorse?

The rhythmic chop of the chisel resumed each swing a small victory against the crushing weight of his past. With every shaving that curled and fell, he felt a sliver of the burden lift, a tiny crack in the wall of self-recrimination. But it wasn't enough. He needed something more. Something…forgiving.

His sanctuary, the workshop, usually a haven, now felt suffocatingly tight. The relentless thundering of the ocean waves crashing against the shore mocked his struggle, each wave a reminder of life's unforgiving nature. The pungent aroma of pine, once soothing and familiar, now seemed overpowering, almost as if it were closing in around him. He was drowning in regret, the rhythm of the ocean a twisted soundtrack to his despair. He wasn't simply carving a path to redemption; he was carving a frantic escape from the torment of his own making.

"Caleb?" The voice, low and steady, cut through the suffocating silence. Joshua. His presence was a calming comfort on his frayed nerves. Relief flooded him, followed immediately by a wave of shame. He hadn't even heard him enter.

Joshua stood behind him, silent for a long moment, his gaze fixed on the carving. Caleb couldn't bear the weight of his judgment. "It's… it's not finished," Caleb mumbled, his voice tight with frustration and self-loathing.

Joshua's hand settled gently on his shoulder. "I see it, Caleb," he said softly, his voice a warm counterpoint to Caleb's turmoil. "I see the struggle, and the love." The words hung in the air, a lifeline in the storm of his self-doubt. A genuine understanding could save him from the relentless tide of his guilt.

Your father would be proud," Joshua murmured, his voice a low rumble that cut through the quiet workshop. It wasn't just praise; it felt like a lifeline. The weight of Joshua's words landed on Caleb's shoulders, not as a burden, but as a damn affirmation, a damn validation he'd craved for years. Joshua's hand, calloused and strong, rested on Caleb's shoulder. The simple touch spoke volumes – a silent acknowledgment of the shared struggle, the unspoken understanding between two men forged in the fires of their hells. Caleb's journey, the brutal scars etched onto his soul, were now carved into the wood itself – a testament to his resilience. Joshua saw it, not just the sculpture, but the raw, bleeding heart behind it.

Caleb closed his eyes, the scent of pine and oak filling his lungs, a familiar comfort. He inhaled deeply, not just the wood, but the hope clinging to it like morning dew. Renewal. The knowledge that each swing of the chisel and agonizing choice was building a future he could finally face. When he exhaled, it was like releasing years of pent-up ghosts – regrets, doubts, the gnawing fear that had haunted him for so long. They vanished on the breath, carried away on the currents of air. What remained was a fragile peace, the calm he'd been chasing, a hard-won certainty of redemption. But a flicker of doubt still burned – was this redemption? Or just a fleeting illusion? He opened his eyes, meeting Joshua's gaze. In those deep pools, he saw a reflection of his own brutal, unfinished journey. A journey forged in the crucible of faith, forgiveness, and a love that had nearly been lost.

Right here, surrounded by the tools of his trade, he knew this workshop wasn't just a workshop anymore. It was sanctuary, not because of the walls but because of the transformation it witnessed. "It's almost done," Caleb breathed, his voice thick with emotion. The years of torment and the weight of his past mistakes were all fading now, replaced by a profound sense of purpose. He stepped back, a deep breath catching in his throat. The nearly finished carving stood tall, a raw, powerful testament to his struggle. Every curve and every line spoke of love endured, of survival against impossible odds. A smile – a rare, breathtaking thing – cracked his face. It wasn't just accomplishment but peace he thought he'd lost forever.

But even as he smiled, the old fear snaked its way back. What if this was just a reprieve? What if the storm returned, harsher than before? He ran a hand over the smooth, cool wood, a silent prayer etching itself into the grain. He wasn't finished yet. Not by a long shot. But today, he felt like he was finally on the right path.

Sweat beaded on Caleb's brow, mingling with the fine grit suspended in the amber light slanting through the open window. Hunched in the shadows, Joshua felt a familiar pang of pride—sharp and sudden—followed closely by a gnawing unease. Caleb's progress was undeniable, the transformation nearly sacred in its unfolding. But the weight of what lay ahead pressed down on him, heavy and real, like storm clouds gathering over still water. This wasn't just a carving; it was Caleb's testament, his bloody-knuckled climb out of the abyss. And though quiet joy swelled in Joshua's chest, dread curled cold and silent beneath it. He'd seen this before—this edge of hope, this trembling hush before the fall.

The room, bathed in the last gasp of sunlight, felt intimate and vast. Caleb laid down his tools – each a chipped and scarred veteran, resting now with a weary dignity – with the slow, deliberate care of a soldier preparing for a final stand. His hand lingered on the chisel, tracing its dulled edge, a ghost of past battles etched into the steel. He wasn't just looking at the tool; he was looking at the years it had consumed, the blood, sweat, and tears that had shaped it, and, by extension, himself.

Caleb finally looked up, meeting Joshua across the worn workbench. His eyes, usually bright and mischievous, were clouded with a profound gratitude, a vulnerability that clenched Joshua's gut. "Josh," Caleb's voice was rough, with a low rumble and the words a physical strain. "Thank you," he breathed, the simple phrase hanging heavy with the weight of untold sacrifices.

Joshua's smile was tight, a thin line against the fear rising in his throat. He couldn't speak; the years of shared silence, of unspoken understanding, rose between them, thicker than any wall. He knew what Caleb hadn't said, what hung unspoken between them like the stench of impending doom. This carving represented a new beginning, but it felt like a final reckoning for Joshua. He reached out, his hand trembling slightly as it hovered over the unfinished work. The wood felt rough beneath his fingers, cool and unforgiving.

Caleb mirrored his movement, his touch hesitant, almost fearful. The unfinished carving, a landscape of potential, felt less like a promise and more like an open wound, exposing the raw vulnerability of the man it represented. Each curve, each unfinished line, was a decision yet to be made, a battle yet to be fought. The silence stretched, taut and agonizing, the unspoken questions hanging heavier than the scent of sawdust. It wasn't just a carving; it was a gamble. And Joshua feared they were about to roll the dice.

"Still a way to go," Joshua murmured, the words soft but laced with a steel-hard certainty that sent a shiver down Caleb's spine. It wasn't just the miles left to travel, Caleb knew; it was the weight of expectation, the crushing pressure of legacy. He saw it in Joshua's eyes, the same haunted look he'd glimpsed in his reflection countless times. The road was long, the journey far from over, and doubt gnawed at him. Could he genuinely carry this burden?

Caleb swallowed, and the lump in his throat physically manifested his fear. He met Joshua's gaze, a silent acknowledgment passing between them. Uncertainty was a suffocating beast, but hope was a flickering candle in the howling wind. He'd learned to trust the process, he told himself. To trust Joshua. To trust…the memory of his father, a ghost that haunted and spurred him onward.

"There's a hell of a lot left to do," Caleb finally said, his voice rough around the edges but firm with resolve. "But I'm ready…I think." The uncertainty in his last words hung in the air, unspoken but palpable.

The setting sun cast long, skeletal shadows across the workshop, transforming familiar tools into ominous silhouettes. The sanctuary, once a place of comfort, now felt more like a prison, the silence pressing down like an invisible force. The earthy aroma of sawdust and aged timber—the very essence of his father's presence—clung to the air, thick and suffocating, a constant reminder of the insurmountable challenge ahead. He had to finish this, not just to honor his father's legacy, but to prove something to himself. To show that he wasn't a failure, to demonstrate that he was deserving.

The creak of the old timbers was the only sound, the ticking clock of an impending deadline. Caleb felt the weight of his father's legacy, a suffocating blanket woven from expectation and the ghosts of unspoken words. Joshua was a constant, a rock in the storm. But even his unwavering support couldn't completely silence the whispers of self-doubt. Could he truly live up to it all?

He thought of his father's hands, gnarled and strong, shaping wood with a grace Caleb could only dream of. This wasn't just about craftsmanship; it was about proving himself worthy of the man he was, the man he wanted to be. Joshua, understanding his silent turmoil, simply nodded.

In that shared silence, a fragile peace settled over them in the unspoken understanding. "Tomorrow, then," Caleb said, the words a hard-won victory over the fear clawing at him. The resolve he felt wasn't a steady flame but a fragile spark he had to protect fiercely. Joshua's response was a low hum of agreement, a quiet benediction in the fading light.

Tomorrow promised a new beginning and the stark, terrifying reality of unfinished business. And Caleb, weary but resolute, would face it.

Caleb's gut clenched. He couldn't tear himself away. The half-finished carving – a snarling wolf, claws outstretched, its eyes burning with a fierce, almost sorrowful intelligence – pulsed with a life of its own. It wasn't just wood; it was their shared struggle, their damned, beautiful redemption, carved into the very grain. Each chipped detail mirrored a scar on his soul.

"Damn thing's got more heart than most men I know," Joshua rumbled, his voice rough as bark, a hand resting on the rough-hewn wood. He didn't need to say it, but Caleb heard the unspoken question: "Are you ready, Caleb?" Caleb swallowed, the lump in his throat as thick as the resin they'd used to seal the cracks. "Ready as I'll ever be," he lied. Doubt gnawed at him. The carving was finished, but the healing… was that indeed done? Could he walk away from the years of blood and sweat, the ghost of his father's rage still whispering in his ears? He wasn't sure. But the alternative – staying here, trapped in the shadow of the past – was unbearable.

Joshua squeezed his shoulder, a silent affirmation. The weight of unspoken things pressed heavily between them, years of loyalty and shared grief etched into their bond. It was a brotherhood forged in the crucible of hardship, and the quiet understanding passing between them now was more potent than any words. Caleb inhaled deeply, the earthy aroma of sawdust and pine wrapping around him like a familiar embrace, offering a strange sense of solace. He didn't look back as they stepped out of the workshop, the soft thud of the closing door echoing the finality of what he'd left behind.

The sun bled across the sky, painting Port Angeles in fiery shades, starkly contrasting the chill creeping into his bones. The town, beautiful as ever, felt alien. He was a different man, forged anew, but the fear, that cold, familiar serpent, coiled in his belly.

"It's not over, Caleb," Joshua said, his voice cutting through Caleb's thoughts. "This… this is just the beginning." Caleb nodded, the words a weight on his chest. A new path lay ahead. A path strewn with unknowns. But he wasn't alone. He had Joshua. And that, for now, was enough to face the uncertainty. He just hoped it would be enough.

The sun dipped, a final, almost reverent bow to the day's work. Caleb felt it – a shift, profound in his bones, not just in the seasoned wood of the newly finished sculpture. He'd poured his soul into it, a raw, aching confession carved in oak. But the relief wasn't just about the completed project; it was the quiet acknowledgment of something larger, a change echoing far beyond his workshop walls.

An immense and exhilarating weight settled on his shoulders – a mantle of responsibility. He was ready.

"Damn, Caleb," Joshua breathed, the salt-laced evening air ruffling his dark hair. His voice, usually a low rumble, held a hint of awe. "It's… breathtaking."

Caleb managed a shaky smile. "It's done. But I feel like I've barely scratched the surface." A tremor ran through him, a mixture of exhaustion and a nervous anticipation that gnawed at the edges of his satisfaction. This piece, more than any other, carried a burden – a desperate hope for a future he wasn't sure he could deliver.

The familiar fragrance of pine and saltwater filled the air, wrapping around him like a comforting cloak that softened the gnawing unease in his gut. Above them, a gull cried, its lonely call cutting through the stillness between them. Joshua's hand, warm and steady, settled on his back – a wordless gesture of reassurance. Yet this time, the touch failed to completely quell the tremor deep within Caleb's soul, as if something larger, darker, still lingered on the horizon.

Doubt, a cold serpent, coiled in his stomach. "What if they don't understand?" he muttered, the words escaping before he could stop them. The weight of expectation pressed down, heavy as the sea itself.

Joshua's hand tightened for a moment before releasing. "They will, Caleb. You've poured your heart into this. They'll feel it." His voice had a firmness, a quiet certainty that did little to calm Caleb's racing heart. He knew Joshua believed in him, but the doubt felt stubbornly entrenched.

The first stars pricked the darkening sky, cold pinpricks of light. They looked like the chisel marks on Caleb's hands – a brutal map of his struggles, each scar a testament to the years he'd spent shaping wood and forging himself anew. These stars and marks weren't just memories; they were promises. But promises, Caleb knew, could break.

They reached the Whispering Cliffs. The ocean stretched before them, vast and indifferent. The rhythmic crash of waves felt like the frantic pulse of his fear. He stood at the precipice, staring into the boundless expanse, its immensity mirroring the enormity of the task ahead. This wasn't just about the art; it was about proving he could be the man he'd strived to become. It was about redemption.

Joshua stood beside him, silent but unwavering, a lighthouse against the gathering storm within Caleb. He'd guided Caleb, not through commands, but through the quiet strength of his being – a steady hand in a chaotic world. But even Joshua's steadfast presence couldn't entirely erase the terrifying question that haunted Caleb: What if he failed? What if this wasn't enough?

The sun bled out, painting the sky in bruised purples and angry oranges before surrendering to the encroaching night. But Caleb felt no fear, only a bone-deep quietude. This darkness wasn't an enemy; it was the counterpoint to the light, the shadow that gave the light its definition. He finally understood. The valleys and the darkness weren't absences but essential parts of the whole.

"It's like carving, isn't it?" Caleb murmured; the words heavy with a thousand unspoken thoughts. "We chip away the excess, revealing what's already there, hidden beneath the surface." A tremor ran through his voice, a subtle confession of the turmoil he'd carried for so long. This newfound peace felt almost fragile.

Joshua's chuckle was low, a warm rumble against the backdrop of the fading light. "Aye, Caleb. But the beauty isn't just in the finished piece. It's in the spaces, the struggle, the very act of creation itself. The mess, the doubt... it all becomes part of it." He looked at Caleb, a knowing glint in his eye. He saw the fight in Caleb, the uncertainty.

Caleb swallowed, the lump in his throat thick with unshed tears. He nodded, the truth of Joshua's words sinking into his weary soul, a salve to his long-festering doubts. He'd almost given up, nearly let the darkness consume him entirely. This small victory felt immense.

They stood at the cliff's edge, the ceaseless whisper of the ocean a constant rhythm against the rocks. Each wave was a relentless reminder of the inevitable march of time, a mirror of their unwavering commitment. A promise, stark and uncompromising, of tomorrow's work, their continued struggle.

Joshua turned, his gaze catching the first hesitant pinpricks of stars. "Tomorrow," he said, the word hanging in the air, a shared weight, a mutual pledge.

Caleb's voice was barely a breath. "Tomorrow." The word was both a relief and a challenge. The peace was still tentative. Would the doubts return? Could he face another day, another carving, another story? He glanced back at the workshop, its darkened silhouette a promise and a threat. It represented the refuge and the challenge, the solace and the endless battle against the inherent imperfection of his craft, and perhaps, of himself.

But now, with Joshua by his side, the looming task wasn't as terrifying. Tomorrow, they would face it together. For now, the darkness held a different kind of promise, the promise of rest, of a brief respite before the dawn broke again.

END